THE GODS WHO HARVESTED MEN

Book Two of the Panagea Tales

McKenzie Austin

The Gods Who Harvested Men by McKenzie Austin. Published by KDP.

www.treethatgrewthroughiron.com

Edited by Andrea Raymaker

Cover by Consuelo Parra of C.P Book Covers

Model: Mjranum-stock.deviantart

Paperback ISBN: 978-0-692-18211-6

Map by exoniensis of Fiverr

To everyone who has ever messaged me with a voice of gratitude.

To everyone who said "this moment spoke to me".

To everyone who shared my love for these characters.

To everyone who, inadvertently or otherwise, inspired me to continue writing.

Thank you.

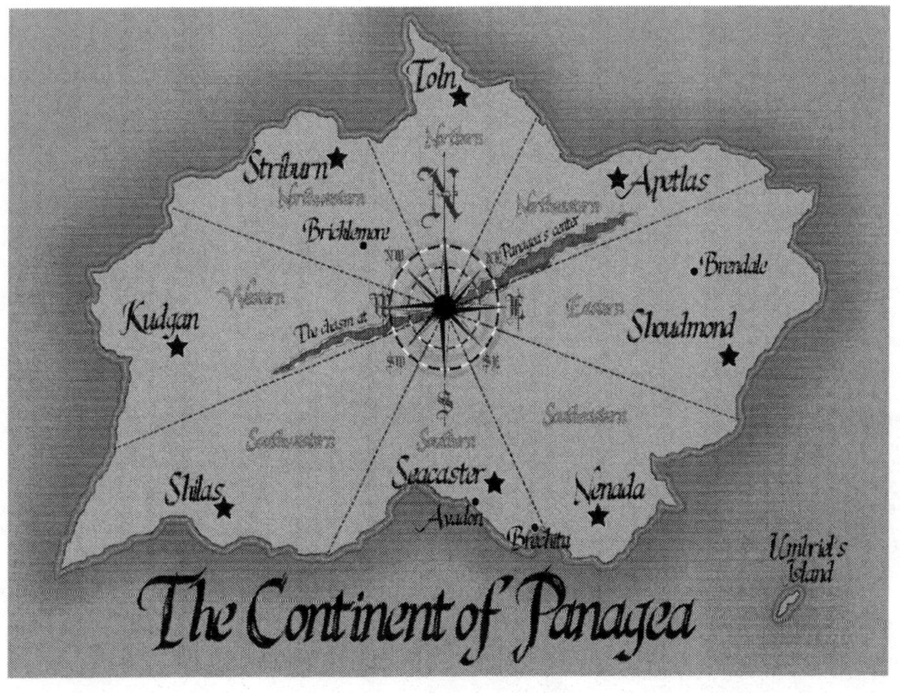
Toln
Striburn
Apetlas
Bricklemore
Brendale
Kudgan
Shoudmond
The chasm at
Panagea's center
N
Seacaster
Shilas
Nenada
Avadon
Brichita
Unilrid's Island
The Continent of Panagea

CHAPTER ONE

He clutched the bag in his hands. His tight grip reflected every accumulated ounce of anxiety that weaved through his veins over the last year.

"This will work," Jodathyn announced, feeling only a mild sting of foolishness for declaring his hopes out loud to himself, and nobody else. The lack of strength in his words betrayed his doubt. But it needed to work.

His life depended on it. The lives of his family members depended on it.

Humans lacked patience. The virtue flew through their skins and straight out the other side, unabsorbed. Machines built that ideology, manufacturing goods at an unprecedented rate. It birthed expectations that crushed mankind's tolerance for waiting. The flaw infected every person, some more than others. Jodathyn was no different.

The man stared at the parcel of land dedicated to his gardening efforts. The crisp chill of morning surrounded him. He wore his frustration on his face. Only small sprouts poked their heads through the dark soil. They mocked him with their slow growth.

He should have celebrated the moment. A year ago, no exposed earth existed. Growing food was unheard of. Panagea's citizens relied on industry to produce their nourishment for them. The efforts of Nicholai, Umbriel, Kazuaki, and their crew changed many things in all the continent's divisions. Others did not share Jodathyn's irritation in the leisure their plants took to flourish because most of them did not know any better.

But Jodathyn witnessed Umbriel's abilities in Avadon's slums. He saw her raise seeds to inches in seconds. With Nicholai's help, the plants reached maturity and fruited in less than a minute. It took six months and several attempts for him to get as far as the Earth Mother and Southeastern Time Father did. He lost many weeks in Southern's restoration efforts, but still, he thought he'd be further along by now.

Weeks ago he sent a letter to Nicholai and Umbriel in their home town of Nenada. He begged for them to make a short trip to Avadon. Jodathyn knew Nicholai could not leave Southeastern for more than twenty-four hours without the risk of rendering his division's time still, but with the emerging popularity of flying machines spreading through more divisions than just Northern, he hoped the Time Father might make an appearance.

The letter remained unanswered.

Jodathyn's grip tightened on the bag he held. With a deep breath, he opened it, removing the object inside.

The old leather cover of the book yielded under the pressure of his fingers. He wouldn't fail at this. A new wave of interest in fresh, organic crops flooded the marketplaces of Southern. Home-grown food fetched a high price. The lust for currency fueled him. After all of the time his family spent in the slums, he had a lot to make up for. They deserved to taste a small sliver of luxury for the shit storm they endured last year.

The man tipped the book open into his hands, and he skimmed the pages again as he walked. An identifiable limp in his leg remained: a gift from Bermuda when she shredded his calf with her blade. It existed as a constant reminder of when he needed to steal for food. If the pages in this book proved to be his salvation, those days were long behind him.

Bartholomew Gray opened up many doors for the Southern division's people. He led with an honest sincerity the citizens were unaccustomed to. The Southern Time Father shared his open penchant for science, but he did not condemn those who still prayed to Darjal Wessex.

The late Southern Time Father conditioned many to believe omnipotent blood flowed through his veins. He ruled for almost forty years. Though some rejoiced at the oppressor's death, it wasn't easy convincing everyone that their entire lives were built on a lie.

After Bartholomew drudged all the old books sealed in the catacombs of churches throughout Southern, he put them in the public library. The construction was a grand undertaking, housing an impressive collection of the written word dating as far back as language itself. It was there Jodathyn found his potential salvation. A last-ditch effort to ensure his family's future.

Jodathyn was accustomed to prayer. He spent his entire life in Southern, where every man, woman, and child was forced to attend a daily service honoring Darjal Wessex. Despite Darjal's constant efforts to convince everyone he was a god, a large part of Jodathyn's mind never took him for one. But constant exposure to an idea made it easier for the potential to creep into a man's subconscious. For this reason, he did not find it strange to appeal to gods and goddesses.

The ancient books in Southern's library detailed the lives of many. There had to be *some* truth to their existence. Whether or not it was accurate, Jodathyn lived in anxiety for quick results. He was willing to try just about anything.

The father's eyes flicked down to the fragile pages. He shielded them with his hand, fearful a strong wind might blow them straight from the decaying spine. The chapter about Havidite, Goddess of Harvest, stared back at him. Her favor was promised for a small sacrifice, with a preference for blood.

It did not come across as macabre to Jodathyn. The text illuminated the goddess's predilection for an equal exchange. Not unlike food, blood was a life-giving substance. The offering of one equated to the other.

He bent at his knees and, with gentle hands, placed the book on the dirt surrounding his feet. He then removed the blade from his boot.

Now was the time. The bite of pre-dawn fell over his shoulders from the sky. While his wife and children slumbered, safe from witnessing the ridiculous scene of a desperate man, Jodathyn placed the cool steel against his palm. He survived a deep puncture wound to his calf. He could survive this.

"Havidite, hear my prayer," he whispered to the wind, too insecure to speak his words at full volume. "I offer thee an exchange. Life for life. Please, take watch over this harvest and lend your grace to it."

The dagger's edge split his skin and a red river grew in his palm. Jodathyn tightened his fingers together to summon more blood forth before he reached out and gave it to the earth. It seeped into the black soil. Its new home. Then, he waited.

Eager eyes scanned his seedlings. Their sudden movement excited him, but after a moment, he realized it was caused by nothing more than a breeze. He studied them, scrutinized their every appearance, down to the beads of dew that rested on their tiny leaves.

Minutes passed.

He knelt in the soil until the pins and needles of stagnancy stabbed at his ankles. Nothing changed.

It was either too good to be true, or it needed time. The higher the sun rose into the morning sky, the more doubtful he grew. The more paranoid he felt that his family would find him pleading for help from fairytales.

Jodathyn rose to his feet and attempted to return blood flow to his sleeping legs. His gaze fell to the deep cut in his hand. A scar lived in his future. A reminder of his ridiculous efforts to summon a goddess.

He turned to head back to his homestead. His children would wake soon. He did not need them to see their father standing like a fool in a small field, begging for plants to grow.

Another gust of wind blew his hair. He stopped. A strange feeling cemented his legs from moving farther, joined by an abnormal surge in his stomach. Compelled by an unseen force, Jodathyn spun on his heels to face the garden again.

A woman stood barefoot in the soil. Dark hair flowed around her in waves, cascading down between her shoulder blades. His heart jumped. He wasn't sure why, but he dropped to his knees again, and bent over in submission. "Goddess Havidite." His body trembled as he breathed her name. "You're here."

"I am." She stepped toward him, leaving no footprints in the soft ground as she crossed the distance. She showed care not to step on the small seedlings, and once she stood before Jodathyn, she placed gentle hands on his shoulders and raised him back to stand. "It's been a long, long time since a man has uttered my name. Longer still since one has gifted me his blood."

"Y-yes," Jodathyn stuttered, swept up by the surreal condition of his environment. "Havidite, I require your gifts. My harvest, I wish it to grow stronger, fuller. Panagea's soil remains depleted from hundreds of years' worth of neglect. My plants are slow to grow. Please, take pity on my garden. I offer life for life."

The ethereal woman tilted her head, slow in her movements as she studied his face. Her lips split into a smile and she reached out to caress his cheek. "Jodathyn, your sacrifice is most appreciated. I will help you."

Relief exploded from inside him. Jodathyn exhaled and nodded. "Thank you, thank you," he repeated, bringing his palms together in gratitude. "You have no idea what this means to me, to my family."

Havidite beamed. "It is my pleasure to help those who know my name." She turned, graceful as she held out her hand. Jodathyn's seedlings rose an inch in height before she dropped her arm and returned her attention to the man. "May the gods be with you always."

Jodathyn watched, slack-jawed, as she started to walk away. "Wait!" he shouted, taking several daring steps toward her. His shoulders squared and he gripped his still-bleeding palm. "I ... I am grateful, goddess, but I had hoped ... I had hoped, perhaps, you would help them develop more."

Havidite stopped and glanced over her shoulder, her expression curious. "Oh, Jodathyn, I would *gladly* assist you in this endeavor." She turned, resting her chin in her hand. "But you see, a goddess can only give as much as she gets. Your offering, while appreciated, was very small."

She mesmerized him. Her words spilled out of her mouth like a smooth cream. Jodathyn recalled Umbriel possessing a similar effect, but Havidite ... she held it on a grand scale. The goddess's presence summoned such a large amount of calm, he did not even find alarm in her unfortunate message. "You require more?"

The goddess only smiled.

"I see." His eyes fell to the ground. Jodathyn studied his seedlings. The need to bring in more money screamed louder. Those memories of his family in the slums seemed accentuated in his mind. He recalled every injustice they had suffered in that place.

They deserved better.

"How much more?" he asked.

Havidite purred. Her hand swept up her cheek and into her perfect, silken hair. She combed her fingers through the strands and said, "How much is your family's security worth?"

He couldn't take his eyes off her. The goddess'ss words held an irrefutable ocean of sense. It went without saying that they would; she was a supernatural creature filled with the knowledge of a thousand lifetimes. Jodathyn swallowed. "It's ... worth everything to me."

"You're a loving man, Jodathyn," Havidite glowed as she praised him. "I suspected it might be."

Jodathyn's eyes found hers. The goddess's irises were stunning. Opalescent and spiked with countless shades of vintage color. They possessed a comforting softness and confidence he couldn't deny. She would save his family. He knew it. He felt it in his bones. In the molecules of his organs. All it required was a bigger sacrifice.

Jodathyn loved his family. He'd do anything for them. The logic was undeniable.

"Jodathyn. You know what you have to do."

The way she spoke his name ignited him. A velvet attraction lingered in her voice. She wanted what was best for him. For his wife and children. It lured him to her. Mankind praised gods and goddesses for their efforts for countless years. It all made sense to him now. They only wished to give the best of themselves to their admirers.

"Are you scared?" she whispered as he walked toward her, stopping inches from her body.

Jodathyn gripped his dagger in his hand. He didn't even feel the sting from the slit he made in his skin earlier. He kept his eyes on hers, the all-encompassing orbs of poise and comfort. The tip of the blade touched the soft skin under his jaw as he smiled. "No," he replied, his words absent of any distress. "I have never been more certain of anything in my life."

Havidite's lips curled into a smile. She watched the measured trickle of red appear below his chin, to which she gave an approving nod. "Good man."

* * *

Jodathyn's eldest daughter was the first to rise. Idie's small feet flew from the warmth of her blankets and she rushed to the door. She loved checking the mail. More than that, she loved the attention that delivering good news brought. Idie wanted to be the first one to deliver any good news, should the Southeastern Time Father have written a reply. She lived for the thrill of seeing joy on Jodathyn's face.

Eager fingers rifled through the post. When she spotted an envelope bearing the wax seal of the Southeastern division's insignia, her heart soared. Excitement propelled her to tear the letter open and her young eyes scanned the contents with expedience.

The elegance of the writing told Idie it was penned by the Earth Mother, herself. Idie squealed, delighted. The contents dictated that she and Nicholai would be honored to take a day and visit Jodathyn's small garden to help however they could.

Idie ran to find her mother in the kitchen. She was preparing breakfast; her actions showed familiarity as she heated the manufactured foods they bought from the market earlier. Though their taste buds craved the deliciousness of the whole foods that spiked in popularity, the cost remained too high for them to enjoy it regularly.

"Momma! The Earth Mother and Southeastern Time Father finally replied!" She waved the letter in her mother's face. "Where's Daddy? I want to tell him!"

Tabitha's eyes widened as she reached over to skim the letter. She felt relief in her heart. "He'll be very pleased to hear that," she said with a smile. "He's been worrying himself sick over the harvest for months."

"Do you know where he is?" Idie bounced up and down on her toes, too impatient to wait any longer to deliver the good news.

"I suspect he's in the same place he always is." Tabitha smirked, and she nodded her head toward the back door. "Probably out in the garden again. Why don't you go check? I'm sure it'll be a huge weight off his shoulders once you give him that letter."

Idie screeched with joy and rushed outside. The door slammed open and closed with the force of her excitement. Though her legs were little, they carried her forward at a speed unmatched by many other children.

She came to a sudden halt when she saw the garden.

Seedlings that once existed in a small state were now huge. Squash sprawled forth from countless vines, luscious and plump as they rested in the soil. Fat, red tomatoes reached for the sky, so large that it seemed a miracle the stalk held them up at all. The garden prospered overnight in a way Idie never witnessed.

The child spied her father's clothing hidden in the mountain of thriving vegetables. He laid in the earth, unmoving.

"Daddy!" Her innocent brain deemed him asleep as she smiled and walked closer. Her father existed as a hard worker, obsessed with his plants. He must have overworked himself to grow them like this. Obviously, his exhaustion made him lower his body, and rest in the company of his beloved harvest. "The Earth Mother and Southeastern Time Father wrote you back, daddy!"

He did not move. Idie made a face. She'd have to shake him awake. The little girl edged closer and knelt. She shook his arm before she caught sight of the crimson liquid spilling from his throat. It stained his skin as it slithered down his body and into the dirt. Idie stepped back. Her eyes fell on the dagger, still coated with her father's blood.

The color drained from the small child's face. A low-hanging tomato crushed under the weight of her foot as she stumbled back. The letter fell to the ground, landing in the wetness of the flattened fruit.

Wind howled through the stalks of Jodathyn's garden. It was joined by an ear-piercing shriek from Idie as she called for her mother.

CHAPTER TWO

Visiting Lilac's grave left Nicholai with more of a yearning than peace. Each time his eyes fell on the flower-covered stone slab that bore her name, he felt hollow. A man with more common sense would stop putting himself in situations that did more harm than good. But Nicholai was content to trade his common sense away for a false feeling of being near her. Even if it left him worse for the wear.

Lilac called to him. From the other world, she sang like a siren that offered promises of serenity. But the promises were always empty. Still, he returned, each day hoping the destitute feeling might be replaced with acceptance.

The Southeastern Time Father emerged from the forest that contained Lilac's final resting place, heading back to the home he shared with Umbriel. The Earth Mother was a refreshing companion to have around. Her supernatural aura eased his tension. Though whispers filtered through Southeastern about the unnatural relationship the two shared, they fell on deaf ears.

Vicious rumors aside, a pang of guilt came with being the guardian of Southeastern. It held much of its structure, the only division in all of Panagea that did not wear the scars of the past disasters on its surface. As Nicholai wove through his untouched town, he couldn't help but think of the other divisions that failed to hold their forms.

Nobody would have known it to look at him. Nicholai did not project the failure he knew in his life. He did not wish to pass it on to his people. Each day, he displayed nothing but his standard, unassailable humanity. He wore it in his eyes and his movements. He wanted the citizens to see him as someone they could trust. Especially after his previous actions betrayed them so terribly.

"Morning, Mr. Addihein."

Nicholai lifted his eyes from the ground and spied one of Nenada's residents: Rhirvin Kelum, the machinist who had perfected his mechanical forearm. He issued a smile and a formal tip of his hat. "And a good morning to you as well, Mr. Kelum."

Rhirvin grinned, a picture-perfect gentleman, though covered in grease. "How's the arm holding up?"

Nicholai lifted his hand and flexed the fingers, each steel digit bending with ease. He rotated the wrist for good measure to showcase he still held a full range of motion. "Never better, Rhirvin. Thank you. Your mastery knows no bounds."

"Ah, stop," Rhirvin waved a hand, "I couldn't have done it without your prototype. Stellar idea for prosthetics, Mr. Addihein. It's both fortunate and unfortunate that business has been so well if you know what I mean."

Nicholai nodded. He knew what he meant. The natural disasters of Panagea's past, coupled with the small-scale uprisings that occurred throughout the divisions, and all the footmen who suffered in the one-day war at Panagea's center, birthed a high demand for prosthetic limbs. Talented machinists answered the call, fashioning arms and legs from various metals.

For now, they were mostly aesthetic. Elowyn of Eastern propelled medical sciences further than they'd ever been before, but the Earth Mother's supernatural abilities were still the only way to connect a person's nervous system with the faux-limbs.

Some traveled to see her. If Umbriel was present, she provided the service at no cost. But reforestation efforts made her a fluid creature; she did not dwell in one place for very long. The best time for citizens to catch her was when political obligations kept Nicholai from their nature developments.

The woman possessed a boundless heart that Nicholai admired. His own bleeding heart had been tempered after Lilac's passing.

He hoped to believe in mankind's goodness again one day, as strongly as Umbriel did.

"How is your new project coming along?" Nicholai asked, content to make small talk.

Rhirvin winced. "It's ... progressing. It's like nothing I tried to build before so," he laughed, "there are some issues I need to work out. But it'll get there."

"Good to hear it." The Southeastern Time Father mustered a smile. "Well ... keep up the good work, my friend."

Rhirvin nodded, a grin on his face. "Most assuredly, Mr. Addihein. You have yourself a good day."

Nicholai swept through Nenada, his hands in his pockets. The familiar rattling of industry flourishing around him quieted the demons in his brain. They didn't bother him often. Mostly after he left Lilac's grave. They whispered of mankind's foulness into his mind's ear, reminding him how men like Rodgie existed to steal women's lives for personal gain. That there were plenty of other men like him out there.

The demons never won. Nicholai starved them of success. They lingered dangerously close to the line of victory some days. The Time Father had to ward off assassination attempts and received death threats from Panagea's society of elites for his efforts to redirect the world. But no matter how hard they fought, their battles always fell a little short of his humanity.

His house came into view, as it had countless times before when he returned from the forest. This time was different. Nicholai stopped. He stared at Umbriel from across the distance, sitting on the bench outside their home with an unidentified figure. His pulse quickened. For a moment, the scene took him back to Lilac sitting on that same bench with Rodgie. It made his feet move faster.

"What's going on?" Nicholai narrowed his eyes and met Umbriel with a sense of urgency. When his eyes fell to the young teenager who sat beside her, a wave of embarrassment washed over him. A girl, or a woman, but barely—she looked harmless as she stared up at him from behind her freckled face.

"Nicholai," Umbriel stood, tilting her head to the side. His aura of anxiousness accosted her, but a quick touch from the woman brought him a sense of peace. "This is Avigail."

The Southeastern Time Father rubbed the back of his neck, letting his sheepish feelings vacate his body. "Many apologies for any standoffishness I may have projected, Miss Avigail," he reached out a hand and smiled, "though the day has barely begun, it's been a long one, I'm afraid."

Avigail jumped to her feet. She looked star-struck. The woman stared at Nicholai's hand as if it were made of diamonds.

The Time Father blinked. He looked down at the mechanical hand, oftentimes forgetting it could be an off-putting image to those unaccustomed to seeing metal where skin should be. He grinned and tucked it behind his back, offering her the other. "It seems I must ask for your forgiveness twice. First impressions and I, we don't get along so well."

Avigail released an awkward laughed and shook her head. "No, it's, please—um ..." She grabbed his hand and shook it, blushing, "it's just ... you're, I've never met a Time Father before, and you're ... different than I was expecting, I guess."

Nicholai straightened his posture and a small laugh escaped him after they shook. "Dare I ask what you were expecting?"

Avigail hitched a shoulder, her cheeks still blossomed in redness. "An old person."

Umbriel and Nicholai exchanged glances with one another. The Earth Mother raised a hand to her lips in an attempt to stifle her giggles. Nicholai smirked, nervous, and tried to brush it off. "What can I help you with today, Miss Avigail?"

"Nicholai," Umbriel interrupted, placing a soft hand on his arm, "it seems the focus of Avigail's quest here isn't you, but rather someone you know. Can I ask, do you know where Kazuaki has gone off to?"

Nicholai arched a brow. "He said he was taking the airship out for a voyage. They're chasing after some legend they read about in one of their books. An enchanted sword, or a dagger, or ... something," he trailed off. "I'm sorry, Umbriel, whenever

Kazuaki gets on a tangent about weaponry, I tend to tune him out. I told him we wouldn't need any extra protection since we're headed to Southern to assist Jodathyn with his crops."

"Oh." Her face fell. "Do you know when he's set to return?"

Nicholai shrugged. "I told him to expect us to be absent for at least a week. I thought we'd coast through Southeastern for a few days and reforest more plots before we arrived at Southern's edge. It'll take less than a day to help Jodathyn; we'll be back in Southeastern's borders by nightfall, then another couple days back." The man grew skeptical. "Why?"

Umbriel looked to Avigail once and returned her gaze to Nicholai. Before she opened her mouth to speak, Avigail interrupted.

"I'm looking for Revi Houton. My father."

Nicholai whipped his head toward her. His stomach twisted at her confession. That one of Revi's children sought him out after a decade of abandonment caught him off guard. "I'll be damned," he whispered as he shifted his eyes to the young woman, trying to recover from his shock. "I have no doubt he'll be ecstatic to see you, Avigail—" Nicholai hoped. Her presence would no doubt stir up many emotions in the man. "I'm afraid it's going to be about a week before he returns, but—"

"I waited ten years," she admitted, apathetic. "Another seven days won't kill me."

"Right." Nicholai moved his eyes to Umbriel. Uncertainty rested inside the cobalt spheres. "We're set to leave tomorrow morning. I suppose Malcolm could watch her?"

Avigail laughed with fragments of pride. "I'm eighteen years old. I don't need a babysitter."

Nicholai crossed his arms over his chest as he thought. "I didn't mean to imply that, but ... let's just say our efforts in rerouting Panagea have earned us some enemies. It would be better if you had a set of eyes on you while you wait for your father to return."

A slow smile bloomed on Avigail's face. She tucked a strand of hair behind her ear. "I could go with you to Southern," she offered, as her foot twisted in the dirt beneath her. "What better set of eyes to watch over me than the hero of Panagea?"

Nicholai arched a brow as an uncomfortable expression claimed his face. "I ... don't ..."

Umbriel giggled once more into her hand, unable to quiet her amusement. When she composed herself, she found Nicholai's attention. "She really should accompany us, Nicholai. If anything were to happen to her while we were gone, Revi would be devastated."

The Southeastern Time Father felt his shoulders tense. "I could hire some footmen to stay with her here— "

"Nicholai," Umbriel tilted her head and tried to issue a confident smile, "Revi is our friend."

The man stared into her persistent eyes for a long time until he drew in a relenting breath. "Okay. You're right. She should come with us."

Avigail grinned and jumped up, excited. "Just tell me when. I'm already set. You won't regret this, Nicholai. Can I call you Nicholai? Do you prefer Mr. Addihein? I— "

"Nicholai is fine," he offered with a forced smile. He extended his arm toward his dwelling. "Well, Avigail ... make yourself at home. We'll head out tomorrow at dawn."

The young woman scarcely contained her enthusiasm. She dashed into the house after a quick 'thank you', thrilled to explore the home of a Time Father.

"You're doing right by Revi," Umbriel said, staring into the open door Avigail entered. "He'll appreciate knowing she's in good hands until he returns."

"Yes," Nicholai sighed, his gaze also fixed on the door. "I suppose if we survived the wrath of footmen and natural disasters, we can survive a hormonal teenager."

Umbriel pinched her lips together to hold in more laughter. She turned to face Nicholai, planted her hands on his shoulders, and said, "Gods-speed." She patted his arm twice and turned around, following Avigail into the house.

Nicholai cleared his throat and adjusted his hat. One week. That wasn't so long. He *did* want to keep Avigail safe. For Revi. "Gods-speed, indeed," he repeated, shaking his head before he entered his homestead.

CHAPTER THREE

Insects never used to be a concern. The irritating creatures landed on Jernal's ears, flitting their disgusting wings against the tender cartilage. A small, but incessant noise buzzed from the bugs, and though the pests were insignificant in size, the sound that emanated from them was hard to ignore.

Jernal swatted at them as he trudged through yet another island Nordjan suspected to be Mimir's home. The behavior became instinctual. This was the third island that he and his team had scoured since leaving the Northern division in a flying machine fit to carry them all.

The Northern Time Father employed many individuals thought to possess the knowledge that would expose the secrets of Mimir's hiding place. Nordjan wanted Kazuaki Hidataka out of the picture. With the cutthroat immortal gone, Nicholai Addihein would be a raw nerve, easy to pluck from Panagea's infected jaw. Mimir was the key to the captain's fate. The lesser god had dibs on Kazuaki's soul. Nordjan wanted that debt to be paid. And Nordjan was the one who paid Jernal.

The soldier started to think it wasn't enough for the nightmares he endured.

Every suggestion ended the same as it began: empty of anything resembling worth. Despite Nordjan's ramblings that old world gods and goddesses would resurface in droves due to Nicholai's negligence at Panagea's center, Mimir was difficult to find.

The endeavor wouldn't have been as suffocating if Jernal had been able to handpick his crew. As a man of the Southern division, he had served dutifully under the late Darjal Wessex for his entire adult life. He bonded with the men in its military. He guided them. Led them. He clawed his way to the top of the military hierarchy. But when Bartholomew Gray laid claim over the Chronometer and initiated a new rule over Southern, Nordjan made Jernal an offer he couldn't refuse; he begrudgingly abandoned the division he knew. Dipping his toe in the Northern military's pool of soldiers became something he regretted more and more each day.

The men were lawless. The chain of command meant little to them. Regardless of Jernal's superior rank, he did not hold the respect of most Northern soldiers. They had their own ideas of what made a man worthy, what made him someone they would follow into the mouth of the Underworld.

Jernal did not fit the bill.

Darjal had grown Southern into a religious-driven division. He painted himself as a god, resurrected churches that backed his egotistical system, and force-fed his ideologies so consistently to his constituents, that they genuinely came to believe he was a god in his forty-year rule. Mothers and fathers passed those beliefs down to their children, who in turn passed them down to theirs. Despite the man's death, enough people remained in Southern to carry on his legacy.

Northern was *not* a religious-driven division. On the contrary, Northern thrived on hard work and sacrifice. It believed in results birthed from the hands of the men and women who dwelled in the wintery world rather than Time Fathers who painted themselves to be gods. They relied on themselves. Anyone who failed to do so fell under the judgmental stares of those who fueled themselves on Northern pride.

Jernal's falchion cut down another branch that hindered him. The metal had become dull from weeks of shredding anything that stood in his way. He wanted to finish this task. He wanted to be free of these irksome men under his command. With Nordjan's lust for correcting Nicholai's egregious error satisfied, Jernal could return to his wife and kids and put this nauseating mess behind him.

"Jernal," a footman behind him snickered as he ducked to avoid a low branch, "you know what might help us out? If you pray to Darjal Wessex to guide us."

A second footman snorted. His boots crunched the dead leaves beneath his feet. "Braser's right. Your god solves everything for you, doesn't he?"

Jernal scowled from his position in front. "The only thing I'm praying for right now is silence."

"Is it working?" Braser smirked. With a heap of sarcasm, he added, "I heard it's an incredibly effective tactic to getting what you want."

Jernal stopped. He turned around to eye the two men behind him. The greatest shame of his nightmarish situation was that these two were his preferred options. The men left behind to guard the airship showcased even more obstinate behavior than Braser and Yaurel. "I know of only one tactic more effective," he murmured, his grip on his falchion's handle tightening. "It's a pity my honor prevents me from executing it."

"Oh," Yaurel grinned, holding up his hands in feigned fear. "I believe our commander is threatening us, Braser."

"Most unbecoming," Braser mused, mimicking Yaurel as he, too, held up his hands. "I thought you Southern boys were more hospitable than all that."

Jernal closed his eyes and drew in a tired breath. He exhaled after repeating a calming mantra in his mind. It was a wonder how Northern won the short battle with Northeastern. These men weren't soldiers; they were jokes. Poor excuses for organized combatants.

After summoning additional control over his growing rage, Jernal turned on his heels and continued. What they lacked in duty he made up for tenfold. His mission remained: find Mimir and free him from the well. Having lived as a soldier his entire life,

Jernal had endured worse things than the insubordination of Yaurel and Braser.

The quiet only soothed him for a moment before the two started up again. "Dear Darjal Wessex, great god of Southern," Braser placed his hands together in mock prayer, "please hear my plea. Bless Commander Jernal with the foresight to find Mimir, and also the knowledge that he lacks the basic skills necessary to be an adequate man in charge."

"—and," Yaurel continued, "send us some gods-damned food. We're feckin' hungry. Glory to the all-powerful god."

Jernal's blood boiled. Months of unsuccessful hunts ravaged every last shred of restraint he harbored. He spun on his heels and swung his arm out, the pointed tip of his metal blade stopping inches from Braser's throat. "Listen here, you cock-eyed sons of bitches—"

The soldiers' expressions shifted. Faces that once portrayed conceited arrogance twisted to unimaginable shock. Jernal sneered. His blade remained unmoving. The men said nothing, only stared beyond him, brought to wordlessness through what Jernal imagined was his surprising show of aggression. "Tread lightly." He slowly lowered his falchion. "Next time, I may not be able to calculate the distance at which you stand. Your throat may not be so lucky a second time."

Braser and Yaurel looked as though they were trying to speak. Their jaws moved, but the only things that escaped their mouths were tightened squeaks of words unspoken. Satisfied, Jernal turned, ready to begin the mission again with fresh authority. He staggered back when his eyes fell on the unexpected figure before him.

It couldn't be. Impossibility confronted him. Jernal's tongue dried inside his mouth as he stared at the man who appeared out of thin air. Down to every last wrinkle, he knew that face. Necessity urged him to speak. He needed to know if he'd gone mad. "D ... Darjal?" he uttered. "Is that you?"

The grandiose figure narrowed his eyes. "I prefer Lord Wessex, Jernal. I should have thought you, of all people, would remember that."

His voice boomed with a paranormal force. Jernal felt his heart thundering inside him. He knew the man's face, he served him long enough to never forget it. And the voice ... Darjal's unmistakable voice. "How is this possible?" he asked, feeling the uncertainty of Yaurel and Braser emanating from behind him.

Darjal scowled. "Southern prayer has birthed me anew. Nicholai Addihein has no idea what he invited back into Panagea." He looked to Yaurel and Braser, those who summoned him with their mock prayer. His eyes shined when he witnessed the terror that gripped them.

Darjal returned his focus to the commander. "The lesser gods rise, Jernal. And as I understand it from this senseless man's prayer, you are currently seeking one. Should you lend me *your* prayer," he started, a maniacal grin spreading across his face, "I do believe I could help you with that."

* * *

Kazuaki never suspected that any form of air travel would replace the thrill of the sea. He was right. The ocean still gripped his heart. Saltwater coursed through his veins like a renewable resource, embedding into his organs. He remembered each wave that rocked his lost ship like it was yesterday.

But air travel ... air travel was a different breed of excitement.

Each cloud he gutted gave way to a new lust for commanding the skies. He gripped the wheel of the airship, similar enough under his calloused hands to remind him of his sunken vessel. His hair tossed in the strong winds, and whipped behind him, exposing the half-mask he still wore over his face. A gaping hole where an eye should have been was an unsightly thing. Kazuaki was not a vain man, but since it served as a horrid reminder of his encounter with Mimir, he preferred the company of the patch.

Panagea sprawled with its man-made structures from the tip of Eastern's coast, all the way to Western's edge. From the top of Northern's land and down to the Southern division, there was no mass untouched by industrial or residential influences. More earth gave way to forests as Nicholai's and Umbriel's efforts grew, but Panagea as a whole remained claimed by people. Claimed, at least, in all the habitable areas.

As the airship climbed higher into the sky, the oxygen thinned. It was a familiar feeling. The once treeless Panagea often gripped the starved lungs of its inhabitants and squeezed. Thinning air remained a concern, but the slow growth of the forests steadied the deprivation. It was mankind's familiarity with oxygen-depleted environments that gave the captain and his crew all the equipment they needed.

Brack appeared behind the captain, an oxygen mask pulled down over his face. He spread his arms out at his sides as he laughed through the screaming winds. Though the mask muffled his words, his exuberance carried them through. "Oi, Cappy! We almost there? It's been too long, my palms are burnin' for some exploits!"

Kazuaki guessed that wasn't the only burning body part the Rabbit possessed. He bit his tongue, as their exploits with Nicholai earned Rabbit a legendary tale to share with any maiden who would listen. "Nearly there, Rabbit. Alert the others."

"Right-o!" Brack grinned. Though his facemask shielded his jubilant expression, Kazuaki saw it in his eyes. He departed, leaving the captain at the airship's wheel.

Kazuaki turned back to the sea of mist stretched out before him. The mountain's peak came into view. Their destination. A piece of land that lingered so high in the atmosphere that it lived in purity, untouched by mankind's hands. The piece of land that contained Brufesphe, the sword forged by a mortal blacksmith long dead, and blessed by the lesser god Olnos, to whom the blacksmith prayed.

Brufesphe. The focal point of their expedition.

The captain ripped the legend from one of the many books which had surfaced from Darjal's underground libraries. A sword with the power to cut through anything in one swing. It was unheard of for a common man to forge anything worth discussion, but Olnos, the God of Metal, took to the blacksmith's craftsmanship. In exchange for his praise, he blessed the sword with its unmatched ability.

Or so the myth went. Kazuaki knew a margin of error existed in all tales passed down from the mouths of men.

Rough hands guided the airship downward. A jaggedness infected the mountainside; finding a suitable landing spot proved difficult. Kazuaki felt the burn of oxygen withdrawal claim his lungs, but the immortal was too stubborn to attach his breathing apparatus. The lack of oxygen was uncomfortable, but it wasn't as if it could kill him.

"Easy does it, Captain," Bermuda's voice sounded from behind him, distant beneath her mask. She smirked from behind it, shifting her eyes from the approaching terrain up to Kazuaki. "One-eyed men can't exactly boast about their immaculate depth perception."

Kazuaki matched her devilish grin, but he said nothing as he jerked the airship's wheel. The quartermaster stumbled on her feet from the sudden action and gripped the captain's arm to steady herself. "What I lack in depth perception, I make up for in sure-footedness," Kazuaki retorted.

Bermuda scowled, though a playfulness lingered in her faux irritation. The woman mastered planting her feet firm to the boards of Kazuaki's old sea vessel, but she had not yet adapted to the airship's unpredictable ebbs and flows. "Hardy har-har," she muttered, her fingers still clutched to his forearm.

The longer the pressure of her touch lived on his arm, the more he questioned his spirited decision to buck her feet. Despite his best efforts, her proximity still lit him on fire in the most inebriating way. Kazuaki drank in the feeling of her hand on him. Savored it. Then distanced himself from it before he surrendered his sanity.

"There's a clearing," he announced, focusing on the whirring of the propellers as he brought the ship down.

Bermuda followed his gaze to the opening. It looked questionable, but it was their best shot on the vertical peak. She was slow to ease her grip on the captain's arm. It reminded her of what it felt like when they shared a dance in Aggi Normandy's residence. The memory made her stomach tighten. It was a hazardous feeling, but one she found herself chasing more often than she should.

The airship thudded as it struck the uneven ground. Kazuaki heard the contents of the vessel shift in protest, but despite the rocky landing, it came to a safe stop. He looked over his shoulder when he heard the familiar *click, click, click* of the beast's claws on the airship's deck.

Granite's dog launched itself off the vessel and onto the rock-strewn terrain. White and gray hairs had formed around the creature's muzzle, but its age did not stop it from enjoying its patented excitement at touching the earth again. It stopped to itch its ear, bending awkwardly as it attempted to scratch. But even with the prosthetic, the three-legged mongrel failed to succeed.

Granite exited the airship's cabin, an air mask on his face. He hurled a pack of supplies over his shoulder and leaped from the deck with a grunt. Several swift steps had him over to the beast, and he eased the animal's itch by scratching it for him.

Revi, Brack, and Penn trekked out to the main deck. They all looked to Kazuaki with inquiring eyes. "Who's staying with the ship, Captain?" Revi asked, waiting to see if he needed to gather his own supplies.

"Just Penn." Kazuaki eased himself out of Bermuda's grip as he walked toward them, though it pained him to do so.

Penn arched a brow. "Really? Me alone?"

Kazuaki hitched a shoulder as he grabbed a pack of medical supplies. "Not a soul alive is going to be on this mountain. The ship's in no danger. But even if it was," he leaped from the deck and landed on the pointed surface below, "You've proven your ability to man a vessel solo."

Penn straightened his posture and tried to hide his proud grin. Manning Kazuaki's old ship from the Southern division's waters to Brechita last year was the biggest challenge he had faced in his adult life. While it felt good to know the captain appreciated his efforts, he said nothing. Penn Elmbroke was not a sentimental man.

"All right." Revi bent down and scooped up the last two packs before he shoved one into Brack's hands. "If he's not doing any heavy lifting, then I expect a four-course dinner when we get back."

Penn spat as he leaned back against the exterior walls of the airship's cabins and crossed his arms over his chest. "You'll eat whatever I make."

"Too right, that," Brack laughed and gave Revi a shove. "Come on now, quit flirting and get on with it. I want to see this sword."

Revi scoffed and exited the ship to follow after Kazuaki and Granite. "That's it, then? We just find the sword and head home? I have a hard time believing that's as easy as this is going to be."

"Arriving at the mountaintop is the first obstacle," Kazuaki muttered as he walked, careful to test the durability of the rocks beneath his feet before he applied the entirety of his body weight to them. "It's said the sword is guarded by the lesser god who blessed it. The God of Metal."

"Right." Revi waited for Bermuda and Brack to catch up before he continued to follow the captain. "That makes sense. I'm sure you haven't tired of dealing with lesser gods after how well it went last time."

Kazuaki paused long enough to throw a heated stare Revi's way. "Belay that."

"You got anything that could kill a lesser god?" Brack wondered out loud. "Been a long time since I read a thing about the buggers, but I know they're not easy to kill."

"As far as I know," Kazuaki murmured, leaping over a chasm in the narrow mountain trail, "they're impossible to kill."

Bermuda cocked her head to the side as her face twisted. She jumped the gulf with grace and came up beside the captain. "Pray tell, Captain, how exactly do we plan to get this sword then?"

"The same way we got everything else," he quipped. "By taking it."

A brow rose on Revi's face. "That clears the battle strategy right up, then."

"Come on, mates!" Brack came up behind Bermuda and Revi, placing his arms over both of their shoulders, as he sandwiched himself in the middle. "Ye of little faith! You forget our beloved captain shares a common thread with those lesser gods, he does. Immortality ain't reserved for the omnipotent, aye, Cap?"

Kazuaki drew in a deep breath, though it left him wanting more. His lungs griped about their emptiness, but he remained too stubborn to reach for his oxygen mask. "Rabbit's right. Once we find the God of Metal's hiding spot, just try not to die."

"Excellent," Brack beamed, releasing Revi and the quartermaster from his grasp. "I'm quite good at not dying."

"Much to everyone's joy," Revi muttered with sarcasm. He stopped behind the captain as the beast ran circles around Granite's legs, impressive in his movements for an otherwise clumsy animal.

The trek fell silent for some time. The crew chose to conserve their oxygen. Small patches of snow graced the peaks in the distance. Some rested in patches near their feet. The wind matched their surroundings in its temperature, threatening to chill anyone who chose not to wear appropriate attire.

Kazuaki stopped when he recognized an unnatural structure jutting out of the mountainside. Though a light dusting of flakes covered it, a well-timed breeze blew the coating away.

"This is the place." Kazuaki knew it from the texts he had obsessed over for the last several weeks. Staring at the crew from the place it was first crafted, intricate stairs greeted them, carved into the rock and rubble.

They were perfection, each step encased in a thin layer of brass that had no business being on an untouched mountain, far from mankind's reach. The alloy shimmered in brilliance, despite a lack of sunshine. It looked otherworldly, an ethereal structure of impeccable angles surrounded by the jaggedness of natural imperfection.

"I'll say it is." Brack placed one foot on the first step and tested it. "Looks godly to me."

The beast cared little about waiting for the others. Gripped by an eagerness that never faded with age, the mutt hobbled up the stairs and disappeared into a fine mist collecting at the top.

Granite frowned and pushed passed the others, following after the creature in the event he found himself in a dangerous situation. With no hesitation, Kazuaki and the others followed. Rushing into perilous situations was a skill that remained alive in them all, sewn and grown from one situation to the next. This time was no different.

A haze surrounded them the farther they ascended. The crew tried to keep their eyesight keen to their environment, but it gave little away. As the thickness became more apparent, the most they could do was trust each footstep would meet another stair.

Brack panted through his breathing mask, but the endeavor only filled him with more excitement to match his physical fatigue. "Beasty!" he called out, his voice echoing in the highland air. "What do you see up there, boy?"

The dog's bark sounded far away, joining Brack's voice as it bounced off the mountains. Kazuaki felt the familiar touch of Bermuda's hand slip onto his arm as she came up beside him. "I can't see a foot in front of my face," she admitted, trying to downplay the offense. "If I fall, I'm taking you with me."

Kazuaki tempered his hunger, but he leaned into her body despite his mental chastising. Ignoring his natural urge to be near her grew more difficult by the day. Harder still, that she seemed to disregard caution as well. "For the best," he said as they climbed, "then you can break my fall."

A smirk crept onto the quartermaster's face. It was not long after that when she felt her boots meet the final step. The mists thinned out, but it remained a struggle to see everything with clear eyes.

Granite spied a whipping tail poking above the mist. He scooped down and picked up his dog, cradling it in his massive arms. The behemoth did not want to risk losing the mutt to a misplaced step at this height.

"Tread lightly," the captain ordered as he placed his palm atop the hand Bermuda weaved into his arm. The cover of the mist filled him with boldness, as it helped to shield his actions from the eyes of his crew. He gave her hand a reassuring squeeze before he took several steps away, testing the earth around them before his comrades had to take the risk for themselves.

"So, I know the plan is to take the sword," Brack started, trailing after the outline he saw of Kazuaki in the mist, "but how do we take something from someone who can't be killed? Not as if he'll just hand it over, Cap."

Before Kazuaki opened his mouth to reply, a strong gust cut through their bones. The wind brought an iciness with it that penetrated the crew, but each person held fast to the serrated ground where they stood.

Kazuaki narrowed his eye. He peered through his strands of black hair, as a long table fashioned entirely from steel, appeared after the curtain of mist was carried off with the flurries. He held his arms out from his sides to prevent any of his crew from advancing.

Atop the pristine silver table laid a body. A man. White hair cascaded around his frail frame. Sunken eyes lived inside his skull, cheekbones protruded from the thin skin of his face. Unblemished robes that matched the color of his hair adorned his body. In his hands, bony fingers wrapped around the hilt of a magnificent, polished sword.

"Feckin' hell." Brack stared at the body on the table, unceremonious in his actions. "If that's him, he don't look all that immortal to me."

Olnos gasped for air as he slowly lifted his head. His neck creaked as he gazed upon those who invaded his space. His arms shook and his grip on the sword tightened. "Who ... goes ... there?" he asked, his tongue dulled from centuries of immobility.

Revi, Brack, Bermuda, and Granite braced themselves. Bermuda squared her shoulders. Revi's hands lingered near his sides, where he knew his guns and blades hid, though his brain reminded him he could do no damage to a god. Granite tucked the beast under one arm in the event he needed his other.

Kazuaki stepped forward. He loomed over the bedridden figure, inches away. His eye scrutinized every detail of the pathetic creature splayed on the flattened surface. He did not look to be a god. But no mortal could have endured a lengthy existence in this place.

"History has painted you to be much more than you appear," the captain said, ignoring the lesser god's question.

Olnos huffed. His chest looked as though it might collapse in on itself. "History ... is all-knowing ... but the present ... is forgetful."

Kazuaki flicked his eyes to the sword. "Is that Brufesphe you clutch so tightly, old man?"

Olnos glowered, though his withered face already looked to house a permanent scowl. "I am no man."

"I know what you are," Kazuaki murmured. He reached out to grab the sword.

Skeletal fingers released the hilt and tangled around Kazuaki's wrist. The captain looked unimpressed. He stared down at the lesser god, who trembled as he spoke. "Speak my name, young man."

Kazuaki's expression flattened further. Olnos' grip felt cold on his skin. "I do not submit to orders."

The lesser god struggled to inhale. His grip on Kazuaki's wrist increased. "Speak my name. I beg you. Utter a small prayer unto me, and I shall give you Brufesphe."

Brack stepped forward, unable to keep silent for longer than a few moments. "What's it to you? You forget your own name?"

Olnos tried to raise his head, but it fell back against the unforgiving steel bed. "What I would give … to hear a human speak my name … to pray to me … one more time."

The crew stared at him. The picture that the words in the ancient book painted held no comparison to what laid before them. Shriveled and pathetic, a small part of them pitied Olnos' current state. His fate on the cradle of steel was uncomfortable to look at. Doomed to live in weakness on a flat, metal plank, with nothing but the mountain wind for company, unable to even enjoy a peaceful death.

Kazuaki knew the perils of what Olnos suffered. He knew them well. But it did not earn the lesser god the immortal's pity.

The captain leaned forward and lowered the hand Olnos gripped. He took up Brufesphe in his palm and with a forceful jerk, he ripped the sword from the lesser god's grasp.

"Please," Olnos pleaded a final time, trying to stretch his hand out to reach Kazuaki. He could not move from his metal prison. "Even once will be enough to restore me to dignity …"

Kazuaki tightened his jaw. He stared at Olnos for a long time. After what felt like hours to the crew, the captain slid the sword into an empty sheath at his side, turned around, and started for the staircase.

The crew exchanged glances with one another, clinging to their pity until they ripped themselves away from Olnos' presence. Their feet carried them after Kazuaki, careful as they descended the staircase.

"He seemed … like he needed an assist," Revi admitted as they trailed in a line down the steps.

"He's a lesser god," Kazuaki interjected. "He needs nothing from us."

They walked in silence until they met the bottom of the stairs. Kazuaki continued toward the airship without looking back. When they arrived at the walkway to board the vessel, Brack placed a hand on the captain's shoulder.

"Oi, Cappy—"

Kazuaki turned to face him.

"Look, mate, I'm not sayin' I know what's best, but," he paused, looking over his shoulder in the direction Olnos was left, "that bugger did look a bit of a mess. Should we say a small prayer for him, do you think? I know gods is immortal and all that, but he looked in a great deal of pain to me."

Kazuaki narrowed his gaze. He established his relationship with lesser gods when Mimir severed Bermuda's hand and ripped his eye from his socket. The creatures were nothing but trouble. Beings that once served to honor humanity's wishes fell away from Panagea for a reason. Any pity Brack harbored for Olnos was lost on the captain. "No," he said, his voice firm. "I'm not a religious man."

CHAPTER FOUR

Prior promises carried Umbriel, Nicholai, and Avigail outside the Addihein house as soon as morning's light pierced the windows. After a brief chat with Malcolm to ensure he'd keep watch over the homestead, they gathered everything they thought they'd need and pressed onward toward the Southern border.

Smoothed stones, worn down by years of wear, graced a majority of their journey. When coupled with the accommodating citizens that lived in the cities through which they weaved, the adventure was an easy one.

Day gave way to night without event. After slumbering in nearby inns along the way, the trio continued with only the sun and each other for company. The closer they came to the Southern border, the more the manmade structures gave way to the raw wilderness.

Nicholai's division remained the one most covered in thick patches of trees, given his inability to reside outside his borders for longer than a day. He held on to the hope that one day he would have more time to re-forest outside of the Southeastern division, but he hadn't yet discovered how to achieve the feat without risk. The Time Father never wished to put himself in a situation where he'd jeopardize the lives of his constituents again. He already felt he owed his people a debt for his past behavior.

Southern's border rested beyond the small forest they found themselves in. Avigail walked closer to Nicholai than he would have preferred, as she had the entire journey, but his kindness allowed it without verbal protest.

As shadows from the treetops above blocked the sun's light in waves, the young woman glanced around, enamored by her unusual surroundings.

The chirping of insects was a strange contrast to the whirs and clicks of machines. Singing birds, though small in numbers, still sounded odd when compared to the rattling bodies of passing steam cars. Avigail glanced over her shoulders and all around, absorbing the sights her new environment provided.

The towering trees were peculiar things. They commanded a lot of space, but she did not feel suffocated by their presence. On the contrary, she experienced irrevocable captivation.

Vibrant green mosses grew over shimmering remnants of metal. As Southeastern held no land untouched by structures, Nicholai had to make some decisions on where to invite forest growth. Buying citizens out of less populated, less successful small towns was the only fair option he arrived at. Rather than waste additional funds destroying the buildings that made up the smaller villages, the Time Father and Earth Mother let nature take over.

It was not hindered by homes or cobblestone streets. The perseverance of nature coexisted with its metal environment for several months before it dominated it entirely, enveloping abandoned steam cars, residential districts, factories, and city streets in earthen shades of greens, golds, and browns.

"You created all this?" Avigail asked, reaching her arm out to touch the rough bark of a tree trunk as they walked passed.

Nicholai stole a glimpse of her from the corner of his eye, too apprehensive of sending mixed signals to grant her his full attention. He fought off Avigail's shameless advances since they had left the homestead days ago. "Umbriel and I both, yes. Nature and time ... it's a bit of a team effort."

Umbriel walked behind the pair, her eyes closed as she traipsed forward. She carried her boots in her hands, letting her bare feet grace the soft earth beneath her. The soles blocked the connectedness she shared with the terrain. She abandoned them at every opportunity. Though the Earth Mother pressed on with closed lids, she seemed to know each step with an intimacy lost on the two who used their eyes to walk.

"It's stunning." Avigail grabbed a branch and rubbed a leaf between her finger and thumb. It felt unlike anything she'd ever touched before. Soft. Textured. Alive. Each small vein running through the emerald foliage caressed her fingertips. She smiled. "It's so different. From everything."

"Funny," Nicholai offered her half of a smile, "I'm sure Panagea felt the same way when men introduced industry."

"I applaud the change," she said, trying to sound older than she was. "Panagea needed something different. It was so ... lifeless. Before you fixed it, I mean."

Nicholai ducked to avoid a low-hanging branch. His boots crunched through dried leaves that blew across covered chunks of cobblestone. "Before *we* fixed it," he corrected. "Your father was a big help, you know. Everyone in Kazuaki's crew was."

"Was he?" She rose her brows in mild suspicion. "When I first heard he was a part of the revolution, I have to admit, I had a hard time picturing the role he played." She frowned. "After I recovered from the initial shock that he was alive, I mean."

"He craved the change you applaud so much," Nicholai said, pulling forth his memories of the events. "He never confirmed it out loud, but I know his drive to give you and your siblings a better world to live in was the only thing that fueled him most days."

Avigail fell silent, but the moment did not last long. "I don't remember much of him. I was only eight when he left."

The trees thinned out. Clusters of plants thinned across the earth as they reached the edge of the small forest. Nicholai spied the next town over: Springden. Jodathyn's new home town after he left the barren land of Avadon following the revolution. The town remained several hundred feet away. Plenty of room to expand the forest. Nicholai stopped, glancing over his shoulder at Umbriel.

As if she knew why he paused, she opened her eyes and greeted him with a smile. “Would you care to plant a little more before we carry on?” she asked.

The Southeastern Time Father returned her smile and nodded. As Umbriel summoned seeds from within herself and laid them down, Nicholai glanced again at Avigail. They hadn’t discussed Revi much since their departure. Or her abandonment. The topics carried an awkwardness with them. But given that he kept himself at arm’s distance from Avigail the entire trip, he did not want her to mistake his detachment for callousness. “That must have been hard. Eight is already a difficult age without throwing a missing parent on top of it.”

Nicholai shared her age when his mother passed. He tried not to think about it often, but whenever the topic surfaced organically, he remembered everything as if it happened yesterday.

Her expression fell, but she recovered. “It was no big deal. Mom was strong.”

Concern claimed Nicholai’s face. He tilted his head to the side. “Was?”

“Yeah,” Avigail cleared her throat and stood up straighter. “I mean ... she was until the city’s welfare personnel took the younger ones away. Dad’s leaving tore her up, but it didn’t destroy her. Losing Natty, Garin, and Yolsa did though.”

Though she hid them well behind the wall she built, Nicholai saw enough of her emotions to know that she had endured more than she spoke of. He almost reached a comforting hand out to place on her shoulder, but thought better of it and crossed his arms over his chest instead. “I’m sorry, Avigail.”

The young woman forced a smile. “It’s fine. I mean ... I wish I knew where they were. Or if they were still alive. I heard they were adopted ...” She shook her head. “It’s fine.”

Umbriel looked up from the seedlings she grew. They hovered near her ankles in height. “You had to grow up quite fast, didn’t you, Avigail?”

Nicholai stepped away and reached his hands out to the seeds. Avigail watched him, though she directed her words to Umbriel. "Best gift my dad ever gave me was forcing me to grow up. Panagea is a rough place."

Nicholai relinquished his years to the plants. They rose, unhindered by the traditional rules of time. When the plants reached maturity, Nicholai dropped his hand back to his side. Avigail watched on, smitten.

"Nicholai," she blushed when she said his name, as if the single word twisted her insides in a wonderful way, "that's really amazing."

The Southeastern Time Father winced when she said his name. She packed a lot of desire into that single word. He disguised his discomfort behind a compulsory smile. "Thank you, Avigail. Umbriel's talent knows no bounds."

The Earth Mother closed the short distance between herself and Nicholai and gently touched his shoulder to restore the years he gave to the plants.

Avigail flicked her eyes from Nicholai to Umbriel. Umbriel responded with a soft look. "All the world is a rough place, Avigail. You are fortunate to be so well adjusted. I know with my whole heart your father will find Panagea a little less rough when he's blessed with the opportunity to see you again."

Avigail blinked. She dropped her eyes to the ground once more. "Yes," she replied, adjusting the pack she held over her shoulder. "I'd be lying if I said I wasn't anxious to see him again, too."

"Well then," Nicholai stole a final glimpse of the plants to assess how well they established themselves in their environment, "let's hurry up to Southern and help Jodathyn. The sooner we get there, the sooner we can get you back to your father."

Avigail watched as Nicholai and Umbriel continued onward. It took her a moment, but an eventual push urged her feet to follow. "Yes," she said again, though her agreement held anxiety inside it. "Can't wait ..."

It took several long strides to close the distance, but the Time Father walked up to the edge of the Southeastern border. He stared into the city of Springden. It looked the part of an active municipality.

Men and women hurried around the cobblestone streets by foot, by bicycle, by steam car. Footmen directed traffic away from streets that still suffered from corrosion. Each division stretched its finances thin to repair everything affected by the disasters. Though citizens pitched in when and where they could, a lot of work remained.

Nicholai frowned. Guilt lived in his chest whenever he laid eyes on the devastating aftermath of Panagea's past. It was with some luck he didn't see much of it in Southeastern.

Then again, it was good to have a reminder every once in a while.

The Time Father sighed and pulled his Chronometer from inside his attire. He glanced down at the device, studying the time as he wound the top. Twenty four hours to find Jodathyn, grow his crops, and return to Southeastern's border. He placed the object back into the safety of his shirt and took the first step into Springden.

"Nicholai," Umbriel gestured to the side, "we have company."

The man followed Umbriel's hand to the objects that caught her attention. Three footmen approached from their right, slowly, until they recognized who emerged from Southeastern land, and broke out into a run.

Nicholai's muscles tensed. A series of flashbacks triggered. The man took a deep breath and exhaled, trying to remember that the days of running from aggressive footmen were long behind him.

"Nicholai Addihein," a footman called out, stopping to issue him a formal salute when he stood close enough, "Bartholomew Gray received word of your arrival. He has instructed us to escort you to Jodathyn Breed's homestead."

Avigail's eyes brightened. She flicked her gaze to Nicholai, unable to temper her wide grin. "This is incredible. Do people always treat you like this?"

Nicholai removed his hat and bowed to the three footmen when they settled in front of him. He had no idea how Bartholomew learned of his arrival, but it did not surprise him. The scholar was full of insight. "Unnecessary, but appreciated, gentlemen." He followed them as they turned, looking down at Avigail. "It's a mixed bag, I'm afraid. Praises or death threats and little in between. Luckily, Bartholomew is a friend."

Avigail followed with unbridled enthusiasm, besotted to taste a world beyond scrounging for scraps of food and a safe place to sleep. Umbriel sauntered behind, serene as she summoned and sprinkled wildflower seeds from her open palm.

The footmen stopped at a steam car. One crawled into the driver's seat. A second offered a hand to Umbriel and Avigail to assist them into the vehicle. The third offered the remaining front seat to Nicholai, but he held up a hand.

"It's fine, really," he said as he climbed on the back. His metal hand clanked when it gripped the vehicle's frame. The first-class treatment felt strange to the Southeastern Time Father. Part of him missed the rough conditions Kazuaki forced him to adjust to. He felt more like himself then.

The footman shrugged and climbed into the passenger's seat himself. The third joined Nicholai, hanging on the back. Without delay, the steam car carried them through the rugged streets of Springden.

Though nobody said much, the trip was far from quiet. Laborers shouted orders to one another as they ripped up decrepit chunks of road and laid new stone down. Steel beams raised with the help of machines, repairing the damaged buildings that didn't survive the quakes. Patrons in the marketplace bustled through the collection of businesses, exchanging their hard-earned money for various goods.

Umbriel spied a horde of citizens clamoring around booths of fresh produce and herbs. She inhaled the scent of rosemary on the wind. It brought a smile to her face. "I see the people are enjoying the fruits of their labor," she said to the driver.

The footman made a face as he weaved his way around a group of people. "A little too much at times. It's hard for the farmers to keep up with the demand."

Umbriel sat back in her seat and rested her hands in her lap. "Hopefully we can help a little with that while we're here."

"I hope so." The driver turned, heading down a long road leading to Jodathyn's homestead. The small structure was farther than others from Springden's city center. "Jodathyn invested in all this land shortly after he left Avadon," he explained, jostling up and down on the bumpy road. "He's been struggling to find his fortune. Things aren't as fertile out here as he thought, I wager."

"It'll take a while for the land to recover. Much poison remains in the soil, I'm afraid." Umbriel looked over her shoulder at Nicholai as the sunlight struck her blowing, silver hair. She smiled. "But it's nothing a little time can't cure."

Avigail spied the smile the Earth Mother issued to Nicholai and subconsciously pressed her lips together. Undeniable affection subsisted in that smile. It made her stomach do an unwelcome flip. Determined to squash her unflattering feelings, she turned her attention back to the front of the steam car, catching sight of Jodathyn's house. It was not all she saw. Avigail squinted at the frantic movement ahead. "Who's that?" she asked, staring at the figure running toward them.

The driver frowned and slowed the vehicle to a crawl on the edge of Jodathyn's driveway. Tabitha sprinted forward, a dark stain of red soiling her white dress.

The footman stood from his spot in the driver's seat and shouted toward her, "Mrs. Breed? Are you all right?"

"Jodathyn!" she screamed as she hurled herself onto the hood of the steam car. Blood smeared across the vehicle's cover, transferred from her soiled hands. "It's Jodathyn! Thank the gods you're here!"

Tabitha was difficult to understand through her hysteria. Nicholai and the footmen exited the car and approached her while Umbriel and Avigail leaned forward in their seats. Everyone looked on, alarmed.

"Mrs. Breed, please, calm down." The driver placed his hands on her shoulders as he tried to soothe her. He forced himself to keep his attention on her and not the obvious crimson stains covering her clothing. "What happened to Jodathyn?"

"He's dead!" she squealed, swollen red eyes leaking countless tears. "He's dead, he's dead, in the garden!"

The driver motioned to the other two footmen to investigate. They nodded, unsheathing their falchions as they broke out into a run toward Jodathyn's homestead.

"Now, deep breaths, Mrs. Breed, we're going to take care of you." The driver rubbed her upper arms for comfort as he attempted to find her eyes. "We're going to take care of this, okay, love?"

Tabitha gasped for breath. While it was difficult for her to control her emotions, she forced herself to nod. Nicholai stole a glimpse of Umbriel, his face concerned. "We should check it out, too," he announced. He turned back to Tabitha, pulling forth the memory of Jodathyn's youngsters when he last saw them in Avadon's slums. "Mrs. Breed, where are the children?"

The frenzied woman sobbed as she looked back toward her house. "They're inside—Idie was so excited to tell him you were coming, Mr. Addihein—" Her voice cracked. She fell apart. Her knees buckled, and the driver caught her in his arms. "Idie found him, Mr. Addihein—she found him like that—"

Nicholai lowered a sympathetic stare to her. He gazed out to the garden, his eyes falling on the tall, flourishing crops. They did not look like crops that needed any assistance from the Time Father and Earth Mother, but he did not wish to upset Tabitha further with questions. "We'll help you gather the children and get you all a safe place to sleep tonight."

"Of course," Umbriel agreed as she slid herself out of the steam car. She approached Tabitha, still held up by the footman. The Earth Mother leaned over, trying to find the wild woman's eye level before she rested gentle hands on her tear-stained cheeks. "It's going to be all right, Tabitha." She brushed a new tear away with her thumb. "Everything is going to be all right."

Tabitha's eyes darted back and forth over Umbriel's tranquil face. The Earth Mother's otherworldly aura softened her and she eased into the footman's arms. "I don't know how this happened," she whispered.

Satisfied she was able to calm her, even to a minor degree, Umbriel straightened her posture. "We'll figure it out," she reassured her. "I promise."

The footman exchanged concerned glances with Nicholai before he helped Tabitha into the car beside Avigail. Nicholai motioned Umbriel to follow as they trekked the rest of the way to Jodathyn's homestead on foot, the steam car trailing slowly beside them.

By the time they arrived, the other two footmen had gathered Jodathyn's children out front. They all looked dismayed, which paled in comparison to the horror that lived in Idie's face. Her eyes looked as though they relived the moment she found him, over and over.

Nicholai remembered the look. It was the same one Rennington had for weeks following Iani's death.

Avigail exited the vehicle and helped, trying to sooth the kids with kind words. They reminded her of her siblings, prior to all of them being taken away. Similar ages. They were easy to talk to. Avigail was accustomed to speaking with scared children. That's all she and her siblings ever were after Revi left.

Nicholai pulled the driver aside as the other footmen loaded the children into the car. "Take them to a good bed and breakfast," Nicholai whispered, handing the footman a satchel of coins. Though the currency belonged to the Southeastern division, the exchange rate would still insure them several weeks in a comfortable room. "Alert Bartholomew that my presence will be shorter than anticipated. He may also wish to send word to Emont of Southwestern. I know he and Jodathyn were friends ..."

The footman nodded. "Right away, Mr. Addihein. We'll send the steam car back to retrieve you as soon as we find them suitable accommodations. Are you going to be okay here until we return?"

"Yes, yes, we'll be fine," Nicholai waved his concern away with his mechanical wrist. "We'll take a look around the property in the meantime. See if we can't figure out what happened. But don't worry about returning. We'll find our way back."

The footman did not look convinced. "Are you sure, Mr. Addihein?"

"It's fine, really," Nicholai patted the man on the shoulder. "It'll take time for you to locate proper housing and even more time to make Bartholomew aware of the goings-on. I'll need to return to Southeastern before then. We'll head back after we're through here."

The footman stiffened. Nicholai knew he mulled around in his mind whether Bartholomew would be upset at their abandonment of the Southeastern Time Father, but he was right. It would take a while to get Mrs. Breed and the children settled, and even longer to secure a meeting with the Southern Time Father. "Fair enough. My apologies for the inconvenience, Mr. Addihein." The footman bowed and jumped into the steam car, turning it around to guide it back toward Springden's center.

Nicholai watched until it faded from his vision. He sighed, removing his hat to run his fingers through his hair and collect his thoughts.

Avigail watched, unsure of herself. She took several cautious steps toward him. "I ... I'm really sorry," she started. "Was he a good friend of yours?"

Nicholai held fast to his hat. His memories of Jodathyn were fleeting. He remembered their first encounter, when the man tried to rob them of their money in Avadon's abandoned factory. The first one they brought plant life into. But that memory was not who Jodathyn was. They spent a lot of time together building up the people of Avadon's slums. Jodathyn took over for Emont when he followed the crew to Southwestern. He did what needed to be done, whether or not he had the skills to do so. Nicholai returned his hat to his head and tilted his neck back to look up at the sky. "Good enough that the world will suffer from the loss of him," he said. "Jodathyn made some mistakes. But he was a decent man."

Umbriel took quiet steps away from Nicholai and Avigail. She walked backward until the height of Jodathyn's crops brushed up against her spine. The Earth Mother turned, disappearing into the thriving harvest. Her bare feet crept across the soil, silent as the dirt squeezed through her toes.

It didn't take her long to find him. Umbriel gazed at Jodathyn's fallen body and felt remorse that his young child discovered him like this. She crept toward him and knelt, extending a hand to touch his skin. Cold. He fell victim to death in the early morning hours.

Umbriel inhaled and closed her eyes, whispering a quiet prayer for his soul. When she opened them again, a burst of redness fell into her vision. She took it for a tomato at first, but upon further inspection, she discovered it was not. Her eyes narrowed. She reached forward and placed her fingers around the flower's stem before she plucked it from the earth.

Umbriel held it in her fingers for several minutes. With her free hand, she grasped Jodathyn's shoulder, and with respect for the dead, she gently moved him aside.

Beneath him, growing in all the places where his blood stained the earth, more sprouts of scarlet anemone flowers emerged. She stood, slow in her movements, her stare affixed to the red petals. Her fingers curled tighter around the anemone flower until it pressed into her palm. The Earth Mother's face fell. She knew then what initiated the end of Jodathyn Breed's life.

"Havidite ..."

CHAPTER FIVE

"I hope the weakness of your soldiers is not a reflection of your leadership, Jernal."

The commander straightened after Darjal's criticism and glanced over his shoulder. Yaurel and Braser were long gone. They ran, abandoning him to the lesser god who appeared out of nothing but mock prayer.

Jernal grimaced. He understood their apprehension. The Northern division did not familiarize themselves with gods. Nordjan took whatever measures he needed to be sure they fell from the peoples' memories during his decades as their ruler. Jernal was more comfortable with the concept; as a man of Southern, his entire life was fixated around the idea Darjal was a god.

But even Jernal had a difficult time absorbing the sight before him.

"You must forgive me, my Lord," Jernal shifted, unable to remove his cautious eyes from Darjal. "It's ... unsettling ... to see a man come back to life."

Darjal scoffed. He turned, motioning for Jernal to follow him. "Men don't come back from the dead, Jernal. I was a god to Southern then, and I remain a god now."

Jernal followed though he wasn't sure why. An ethereal aura from Darjal pulled him forward. A part of him was certain he wanted to follow, but a larger portion remained apprehensive.

Though Jernal was a religious man, he never considered Darjal's claims to godliness to be truthful. He honored the late Southern Time Father as a god during his reign, the tale was tough to swallow in its entirety. There was something about omnipotence that mortal men seemed too insignificant to touch, regardless of how many years they pounded such claims into one's mind. "What … what have you been doing, then? It's approaching a year since your death."

Darjal continued walking, directing his words to Jernal without turning his head. "I've been fueling on the prayers of Southern citizens. The more they whisper my name, the stronger I grow." A smug grin claimed his face. "I am the most present in peoples' memories. These archaic gods that dwell in the shadows … they are nothing more than garbage. Weak from years of absence. It pains me to even share a label with them."

Jernal studied Darjal as he walked behind him, still uncertain whether he hallucinated his presence or had gone mad. "You're saying there are others? Beyond you and Mimir?"

"Countless," Darjal huffed. "Every lesser god or goddess who has ever gained enough energy through prayer. It takes many voices … but soon the whispers become words and the words become roars. After enough time passes, all gods ever hear are the voices of the people out there, begging for their assistance."

The soldier tried to wrap his brain around it, but he only shook his head. "It sounds maddening."

"It is."

"Do you answer their prayers, then?" Jernal asked, curious as to whether death changed Darjal's attitude toward humanitarianism.

The lesser god balked at the inquiry. "I'm far too busy with my own concerns to pay heed to theirs."

While the encounter with Darjal came as a huge surprise, his admission to negligence did not. It seemed even in death, the late Southern Time Father remained the same. "What concerns are those?" Jernal asked, too uncomfortable with silence to allow any to linger.

Darjal stopped. His eyes turned to slits as he swung back to face Jernal. "Nicholai Addihein."

The commander bristled under Darjal's intense stare. Not much existed that Jernal shied away from, but he found himself taking a step back. "Still?" he dared to ask. Jernal knew of Darjal's hatred for the Southeastern Time Father. He followed that hatred across the ocean in an ironclad.

"Still, indeed," Darjal seethed, his shoulders ruffling at the rage that crawled through his body. "The man is a sinner. He betrayed his division by stopping his time, and he betrayed Southern by smothering their god. The mighty shall smite the wicked if the world is to make any sense at all."

Jernal cleared his throat. "I haven't been on Panagea's soil for months now, my Lord, but I do not think your death is something he brags about. To be honest, I thought it was Kazuaki Hidataka who ended your life."

"Your thoughts are irrelevant, Jernal." Darjal turned away from him, returning to his quest of leading him through the terrain. "Kazuaki Hidataka is venom, but Nicholai Addihein is the snake."

The two men continued to cut through their surroundings. Jernal kept an even pace behind. He studied the back of Darjal's head, trying to figure him out. "With all due respect, Lord Wessex ... if you've achieved as much power as you claim to have gained through the Southern peoples' prayer, what stops you from killing Nicholai Addihein? I thought lesser gods were—"

"Lesser gods cannot alter mankind's free will," Darjal interrupted with poison in his tone. "It's a foolish law. A law I found I am unable to alter, despite my best efforts. I am no sooner able to issue him physical harm, as he is able to issue physical harm unto me."

It took an effort to process everything Darjal told him. Jernal swatted more bugs away as he traipsed farther toward the destination the lesser god led him to. The experience remained surreal, but duty compelled Jernal to suspend his disbelief. If Darjal led him to Mimir's well, it would satisfy Nordjan. Perhaps, then, he could return to his family with the wealth the Northern Time Father promised him, retire, and forget this lunacy.

Though instinct instructed him to keep his mouth shut, Jernal could not fully abandon his inquisitiveness. It helped to know Darjal was incapable of issuing him bodily harm. Without the risk of injury to stop him, he couldn't help but pry further. "If you cannot hurt him, how do you intend to end him?"

"All in due time, Jernal. Soon, everything will become clear."

It was a disturbing reply. "Forgive me for asking, my Lord. The whole situation ... it's just ... I'm trying to understand it all—"

"The minds of mortals are limited. If you knew everything the lesser gods did, you would collapse under the weight of your intellect." Darjal peered up at the sky. "But those limited, weak minds are easy to mold. Easy to exploit." He stopped again and turned to face Jernal. "Do you know how many terrible thoughts creep through the dim corners of human brains?"

Jernal halted. A murky feeling in his stomach boiled from Darjal's stare. "I have an idea," he admitted, having seen mankind's darkness on the battlefield before.

Darjal's expression warped into a distasteful glare. There were not enough of those thoughts in the Southeastern Time Father. Darjal tried to whisper countless times across the expanse into Nicholai's mind, tried to breed discontent in him. Tried to emphasize any dark thought he might possess. His efforts to manufacture malevolence were unsuccessful, and they would continue to be until Darjal could locate his physical body. Until then, the connection remained too weak for victory.

The commander stared, unable to rip his gaze away from Darjal's maniacal eyes. "Well, if it's any consolation," he muttered, "there's no shortage of people who'd like to see the Southeastern Time Father's head on a pike. Panagea's society of elites is pretty pissed he severed a lot of their industrial ties with all the businesses that fell."

Darjal sneered. "Then it will be easier than I thought. As soon as Kazuaki Hidataka is out of the way, he will fall."

It made sense now. Darjal only helped Jernal to satisfy his own agenda. With Mimir freed from the well, he could settle his debt with Kazuaki Hidataka. And with the captain gone ...

"Now," Darjal spat and turned away, "enough mindless chatter. Mimir's well is on the other side of the island. If you intend to make it there by nightfall, you'll have to pick up the pace."

Jernal frowned as he followed Darjal again. "Even if we find him in good time, it'll take me all night to return to the ship. I'm not even sure Yaurel and Braser won't have left without me by then."

An eerie smirk spread across Darjal's lips. "Leave the soldiers to me."

Something about the way he said it made the hair on Jernal's arms rise. But the lesser god's confidence assured him he'd have a way back to Panagea, so he chose not to question it. With an incredible tolerance, and a desire to absorb everything he'd fallen into, Jernal convinced his legs to keep moving. One step closer to freedom. One step closer to a worry-free life for his family.

The rest of the journey was long and quiet. Though they suffered limited setbacks, it still took what felt like countless hours to reach their destination. Darjal's guidance was merciless. He labored across the island without breaks, seeming to take no qualms in the rigorous expedition.

Jernal, however, agonized from the arduous trip. His mortal limbs screamed in protest with each new stride. His muscles begged him to stop. To rest. But he feared if he did not keep up with the pace Darjal set, the lesser god might infect his mental integrity. It wasn't a risk he was willing to take.

Though Jernal grew to favor the silence over Darjal's heavy conversation, he delighted in the next sentence uttered by the lesser god.

"We've arrived."

The soldier narrowed his eyes, trying to will his vision to work better in the darkness that surrounded them. A barren land greeted him, with only raw, gnarled shapes poking up from the dry ground. The well appeared only as a shadow in his night blindness, but the shape was unmistakable.

"What do we do now?" Jernal asked.

Darjal stepped aside and motioned an arm forward. "Destroy the well. Terminate his prison."

Jernal felt a breathlessness claim him. A cool wind swept over his face as he stepped forward to approach the well. It looked as though it already suffered several travesties, held together only by luck and old mortar. He laid a hand on the nearest brick, giving it a firm tug. It resisted, but after digging his heels into the ground and pouring more effort into his action, the brick gave way and fell into his palm.

"One down," Darjal jeered, unimpressed. "Only several hundred more to go."

Jernal bit his tongue. It was fortunate he gained much practice soothing his ego in the moments spent with Yaurel and Braser. With more force this time, he kicked at the bricks with his boot. Chunks fell into the chasm and disappeared into the blackness.

Darjal folded his hands into the large openings of his sleeves. Though time held no effect over him anymore, he appeared ravaged by impatience.

Beating the well started to feel cathartic to Jernal. Much frustration had grown in the soldier over the past year. It sank into every tissue and subsisted there. Every demeaning comment Darjal uttered in his life. Rennington and Iani's escape from his capture. The embarrassment he suffered under Nicholai's engagements. Failing to subdue Kazuaki Hidataka. The mixed emotions that surfaced with each new revelation he made about the situation he found himself in. The confusion as to whether he was doing the right thing. He gave it all to the well in a series of blows.

When his feet felt the aches of his aggression, Jernal removed his sword. It didn't feel as comfortable in his hands as an old-fashioned Southern division falchion, but he did not wish to further dull his beloved blade.

The man adapted and swung with all his fury. Shrapnel from bricks chipped away, flying off into the shadows. Jernal lifted his steel to unleash another forceful swing but stopped himself when he caught movement from the mouth of the well.

From the abyss, the creature emerged. One wraithlike arm stretched from the black hole, followed by the other, and soon Mimir poked his head up from the blanket of darkness that made up his prison.

A weak ray of moonlight highlighted the lesser god's face as he arched an unimpressed brow. Glowing eyes scanned the broken condition of the well and his gaze flew to Jernal. "Rude," Mimir muttered, flicking a small lump of broken brick away with his finger.

Jernal caught himself as he took a sudden step back. Though Darjal's presence introduced the soldier to the reality of lesser gods, Mimir's appearance still shook him as something that shouldn't be a reality. He did not look human. "So, the demon exists," he breathed, gripping his sword.

Mimir perched on the crumbling edge of his well, trying to find a solid place to rest his feet. "Why does everyone refer to me as a demon?" he wondered out loud. "I am as much of a lesser god as he is." Mimir thumbed toward Darjal, who kept his place at a distance.

Darjal scowled. "Perhaps it is because you look more monster than man."

Mimir squinted his shining eyes as he lifted his arms and assessed himself. A gelatinous, onyx-colored combination of sludge and shadows comprised his form, but his overall shape reflected that of a human being. "Many apologies," he muttered with cynicism, "I am sorry I do not adhere to your preconceived notions of what a lesser god should look like."

Darjal waved his wrist to dismiss Mimir's words. Jernal looked back and forth between the two before he settled his eyes on the creature who crawled from the well. "I've come to free you from your cell," he started, "so that you might stake your claim over Kazuaki Hidataka."

Mimir's head shot toward Jernal. He grinned. It split his face in half, inhuman in how far it stretched across his cheeks. "My friend, the captain ... how I've missed him. Has he cleansed his soul?"

Confusion showed in Jernal's expression. "I don't know," he confessed with a small shrug. "I only know I've been ordered by Nordjan of the Northern division to find your well and free you."

"I see." Mimir sat back and stroked his chin. "I have heard my name whisper in Nordjan's thoughts over the months. I would be happy to leave this place, young man, but I am afraid, like our dear acquaintance, the captain, I am bound to a situation I do not prefer."

Jernal tilted his head, crestfallen by Mimir's admission that his task would not be as easy as he had hoped. "I don't understand. Can I not just destroy the well that holds you?"

Mimir snickered but startled when a brick fell beneath his foot and collapsed to the ground. After he corrected his position on the well, he said, "The Unnamed has doomed me to this place. It turns out It takes the Law of Freewill quite seriously."

"The Unnamed?" Jernal glanced over his shoulder to find Darjal, a questioning look on his face.

Darjal snorted and crossed his arms over his chest. "The Unnamed. The top link in the hierarchy." He used his hands to explain, holding them at different levels. "Men." He raised his hand. "Lesser gods." He raised it again, apathetic, and as if the very two words ignited a jealous rage in him, he murmured, "The Unnamed."

"Yes, yes. It chained me to this well after I sought a *tiny* bit of revenge on those who forgot me," Mimir chuckled. "It was only a little. I don't know why It got so angry."

Jernal felt a queasiness when the two spoke of The Unnamed. He just discovered the existence of lesser gods; to throw a more powerful omnipotence on top of that knowledge nearly crushed his mental wherewithal. He shook it off, focusing on the task at hand. "Is there nothing I can do to free you?"

"Well," Mimir grinned, reaching out to poke Jernal in the side to gain some insight from the touch, "we could make a bargain. I am very good at those."

The soldier stared, skeptical. His hand placed his sword back into its sheathe. "That wasn't part of the deal," he muttered.

Mimir sank his neck into his shoulders. "It seems foolhardy to throw away your chance at financial independence simply because you're too afraid to make a bargain, Jernal."

The creature's knowledge gripped him. Jernal knew he had not given Mimir his name, nor the details of his circumstances. Still, a truthfulness hid in the demon's words. Jernal wanted his freedom. He wanted a life for his family, absent of any burdens. The commander straightened his posture. "What do you want?" he whispered.

"You want my freedom," Mimir reiterated. "I will grant your wish ... in exchange for a favor. I will need assistance when I am released from this place. I will call upon you in a time of great need. You must perform my request. And if you do not, you belong to me."

Jernal withdrew, insulted. "I cannot agree to that."

Darjal sighed. "We're wasting precious time."

Mimir tilted his head so far it looked as if it might detach from his neck. "Tick tock, Commander. I have nothing I need at the moment, but much I will need later. That is my final offer."

"You cannot expect me to agree to those terms when I have no indication of what it is you'll ask of me—"

"I can assure you, Commander, I will not ask you to do anything you haven't already done before." Mimir leaned closer to him without lifting his hands or feet from the well. "All I want is the captain. I do not know what role you will play yet, but what I do know is what I ask of you will directly correlate to his fate. Not yours."

The commander allowed Mimir's confession to settle over him. Kazuaki Hidataka. Though Jernal lived in relief the captain had not killed him on the ironclad that fateful day, he continued to harbor resentment for the man. It was at Nicholai Addihein's insistence that he lived, despite the immortal's wrath.

He was so close to freedom from the military, he could taste it. The feeling of easiness nestled into his tongue. Jernal clenched his hands into fists as he lifted his head and met Mimir's gaze. So long as it affected Kazuaki Hidataka and not himself. He extended an uneasy hand. "You have a deal."

The lesser god beamed. "Perfect," he purred, lifting a bucket from his well that appeared out of nowhere. He dipped his viscous fingers into the vessel and flicked several droplets onto Jernal's skin.

The commander swallowed as he felt the water soak in. It seemed final. In desperation to rid himself of his small feeling of regret, Jernal turned. "It's done. We should return to the ship. I'll take you back to Panagea and you can find the captain."

Darjal and Jernal started back in the direction they came. When Jernal realized Mimir did not follow, he halted, turning to look over his shoulder.

"Are you coming?" Darjal bellowed, already irritated he had to slow himself to a mortal's pace.

Mimir stared at the ground. The once jubilant creature stretched an uncertain arm forward. It hovered an inch above the earth. Jernal almost thought he detected a fearfulness, but soon Mimir placed his hand on the rocks below. He loitered there for a moment, as if the act of touching the land outside his well was something he needed to savor. Or adjust to.

"I'm coming," he whispered, still staring at his hand. His second arm followed. Then one foot. And the other. When all four of his limbs rested below his body, detached from the well, he slowly uncurled his hunched posture.

No punishment. No retaliation from The Unnamed for abandoning his cell. It worked. Mimir tore his gaze away from his hands and grinned at his two acquaintances. "Let's go find the captain."

CHAPTER SIX

"That's it? We're just leaving?"

Avigail walked alongside Nicholai and Umbriel as the sun crept closer to the horizon. They stayed on Jodathyn's property for hours, but Nicholai found no clues as to what caused the man's death. When time ran out, he proposed they return to Southeastern's border.

Umbriel remained quiet as she sauntered beside the two. Nicholai noticed her look of uneasiness when he stole occasional glimpses of her, but he chalked it up to Jodathyn's death. "Unfortunately, there's nothing we can do right now," Nicholai explained as they traveled through Springden. "I need to return to Southeastern. I'm sure Bartholomew will put his best men on this."

The news seemed disheartening to Avigail. She pushed a strand of hair from her eyes as she walked. "Your friend died, Nicholai. It just seems like we're abandoning his family."

A frown crossed the Southeastern Time Father's face. It was natural for Avigail to relate the situation to her own. He didn't expect her to understand. "I would have loved to secure his family's safety with my own hands," he admitted, "but I have duties to Southeastern. I cannot abandon the needs of the many for the needs of the few."

Avigail did not appear to accept his answer, but she held her disagreement inside. The three carried on, passing the small houses that sheltered Springden's people. They passed the lamplighters as they climbed their ladders to ignite the candles that lived in their posts on the streets. Soon the forest's edge came into view.

Nicholai sighed, relieved. Every time he stepped foot outside of Southeastern, a fearfulness existed that he would be unable to return in time. It was a concern that he couldn't outgrow, after everything that happened last year.

As each stride brought them closer to the boundary, Nicholai continued to sneak momentary glances of Umbriel. A cloud hung over her. It was a worry he never witnessed on the otherwise serene woman's face in all the time he knew her.

"Umbriel?" he finally asked, his voice low. "Are you all right?"

The Earth Mother lifted her head, unaware she had been staring at the ground as she walked. "I ..." She did not wish to tell him. Though Umbriel dreaded little, she feared Nicholai's reaction. Particularly if she illuminated the entire truth. But as she stared into the genuine empathy of his eyes, she knew she couldn't lie to him. "Nicholai ... about Jodathyn— "

A body hurled itself into Nicholai with an unexpected force. The Time Father fell to the ground with a grunt, but dug his metal palm into the earth, utilizing the power of the mechanical arm to thrust himself up. The figure clung to his back, a knife in his hand. He struggled to find Nicholai's skin with the blade.

Umbriel gasped, cross with herself that she was too lost in her mental dilemma to sense the impending arrival of an attacker. She moved to help, but a second assailant caught her attention from behind. He approached her, dagger drawn. A vacantness in his eyes as he glared at her.

Avigail took several steps back and bumped into a third aggressor. He wrapped his arms around her and snarled. "Bear witness, Darjal!" He cried out as if his actions would earn him a reward. "See that I follow and know you have my faith!"

Nicholai scowled and whipped his head back. His hard skull collided with his attacker's nose. The dagger fell. Hands flew to bleeding nostrils, as the aggressor staggered back, cursing.

"Darjal is gone," Nicholai muttered, unsure what the man meant by his statement, as he found Avigail's captor. "Let the girl go."

As Umbriel's quick feet avoided her frenzied attacker's swings, Avigail writhed under her enemy's grasp. He winced as she stomped his feet, but held tight to her frame with both arms. "You cannot kill a god," the man breathed, increasing his hold on the young woman.

Nicholai opened his mouth to speak but spun on his heels when he heard a hammer draw back on a pistol. Though his nose leaked blood like a river, Nicholai's former assailant abandoned his dagger and brandished the gun instead. "His greatness lives on in us." He squeezed the trigger.

The Southeastern Time Father raised his iron arm. Sheets of metal ejected from the sides and locked in place, forming a shield he used to protect his head and torso. Nicholai's expression hardened when he noticed the bullets dented his protection, but he did not have time to dwell on it.

When the gun emptied, Nicholai ran full force, slamming into the man with his shield. He fell to the ground. Where his body landed, the Time Father spied a creeping ivy vine, an invasive weed that crept from the woodlands in Southeastern. Without delay, he extended his hand.

The vine aged years, sprawling forth in length. The fallen man's proximity served as a frame for the plant. It weaved around his legs, up to his stomach, tightening as it coiled around his arms and neck. He struggled against its constriction, but the stubborn plant held strong.

Umbriel watched, wide-eyed. She darted away and scooped up a long vine of her own. Looking back at her attacker, she wrapped the vine around her hands and stretched it out, prepared to use it as a binding. "Keep your distance," she cautioned, calm but firm, "or you will end up like your companion."

With one man restrained, Nicholai directed his attention back to Avigail's captor. "I'll ask again," he said, his voice low, "let the girl go."

The man snorted as he tugged the flailing woman tighter into his chest. "You will suffer for your sins, Nicholai Addihein."

The Time Father's eyes narrowed. He familiarized himself with assassination attempts before, but those were more artfully orchestrated. This display was nothing more than untrained laborers recklessly swinging sharpened blades and pistols. Something was off. "Release the young woman and I will accompany you willingly."

Avigail snarled as she dug her fingertips into the man's skin. He cursed and shook her, but refused to let go. "You destroyed all that was good in Southern," he seethed, "how am I to trust the words of a demon?"

Nicholai's expression remained unchanged. "You sound just like your god," he muttered, nonchalant as he retracted the metal plates of his shield back into his mechanical arm. "I'll give you one more chance to release her."

As Umbriel's attacker charged her, she spun, catching his wrist with her vine. Fluid stems wrapped around it and pulled, causing the blade to fall from his grasp. As the man spun from the force of the Earth Mother tugging him in the opposite direction, she brought him to his knees and bound his wrists behind his back.

Though both of his comrades fell, Avigail's captor showed no distress. He glowered at the Time Father. "I don't submit to sinners," he spat.

Nicholai sighed. He took no pride in injuring his fellow man, but months of warding off murderous efforts had hardened him to the reality that, at the very least, he needed to render his assailants immobile. "Very well." He lifted his arm. His thumb extended at a strange angle. Nicholai pulled back on it with his flesh and blood fingers. Another compartment opened at the wrist, as the metal hand bent back.

The man didn't even feel the dart when it first sank into his forehead. It was so small. But soon the tranquilizer radiated through his wrinkled skin. He tried to shout his disapproval, but paralysis claimed the muscles in his mouth and jaw. The feeling of immobility slithered down his neck and into his arms.

Avigail shoved herself out of his weakened grasp and ran to Nicholai. The Time Father watched as the non-lethal poison spread to the man's knees. He buckled under his weight and joined his comrades on the ground.

"What did you do to him?" Avigail breathed as she clutched Nicholai's arm.

"It's just a tranquilizer," he informed. "In several hours, he'll be fine."

Umbriel stood from the spot where she had restrained her aggressor. "Is everyone all right?" she asked, looking from Avigail to Nicholai.

"I'm fine," Avigail replied, though adrenaline still coursed through her veins. She looked down, realizing her hands lingered on Nicholai's arm. The young woman did not care to move them.

Nicholai took notice. He cleared his throat and slowly eased his arm out of her grip. "No injuries," he informed Umbriel. "Though Rhirvin will be sorry to hear he has some dents to buff out of my shield."

"You handled yourself quite well," Umbriel complimented as she smoothed her hair back. "Sparring alongside Kazuaki has paid off, it seems."

"Yes," Nicholai flexed his artificial wrist and elbow to be sure they still operated after the abuse. "I'm sure he rests a little easier at night knowing I'm at least somewhat capable of defending myself."

Umbriel nodded, then shifted her attention to the immobile men. "What will we do with them?"

The man that Umbriel subdued growled from his place on the ground. "You cannot run forever, Time Father. We are Darjal's legion, and we will right your injustice so that our lord might shine his favor upon us."

Nicholai blinked. Memories of Darjal's demise surfaced in his thoughts. The guilt. He lived with it daily. But the longer he stared at the man, the more his guilt turned into anger. Frustration. What would it take to finally be free of Darjal Wessex' influence?

He shook his head. It couldn't have been the late Southern Time Father that threw these men in his path.

Darjal Wessex was dead.

Nicholai took several strides over to the man and knelt, resting his hands on his bent knees. "Who *really* sent you?" he asked, growing suspicious that angered laborers of Southern had crafted a resistance toward him that he did not know about.

The man grinned as he struggled against the vines. "I was chosen by my Lord. The great Darjal Wessex."

"I see." Nicholai's brows furrowed together and he stood to his feet. Rather than speak of Darjal Wessex for another second, he looked to Umbriel. "Leave them," he said as he turned and started toward the Southeastern forest.

Surprise infected her expression. "Excuse me?" she asked, staring after him as he traipsed away.

Nicholai stopped, though he did not turn to look at her. "Someone will come looking for them. They might go a bit hungry and thirsty until they're found ... but someone will find them."

Concern spread across Umbriel's face as Nicholai walked away. Avigail glanced at her once, then scurried after the Time Father. It was unlike Nicholai not to extend a compassionate hand, even to his enemies. His conduct worried her. Though she knew he was right that these men would be found within the day at the longest, something about the way Nicholai Addihein discarded them to their fate ate at her.

The Time Father may not have believed the confessions that slipped from the mouths of their attackers, but Umbriel had her doubts. The men's actions seemed disjointed. Unexpected. Applied by blind faith. It was a condition she'd seen before, a long, long time ago. A condition she knew Jodathyn fell to.

Their thoughts were manipulated by omnipotent forces.

The Earth Mother convinced her feet to follow, though it unsettled her. This wasn't how things were supposed to be. The return of the lesser gods was intended to be a positive thing. But with Jodathyn's death and the new attack on Nicholai's life,

Umbriel found herself questioning the entire outcome of her efforts.

* * *

Firelight brought a sense of warmth and comfort to the shadows of the woodlands. Though the tall trees blocking the moon's light seemed suffocating to some, Umbriel thrived in the environment. It was a great shame she was too burdened by worries to fully enjoy it.

Nicholai sat on the ground, the orange glow molding around the surface of his face, as he assessed the liveliness of the flames. Avigail fell victim to sleep several feet away, a blanket from her pack wrapped tightly around her body.

The scent of the blistered tomatoes and fire-roasted nuts they ate prior still clung to the air around them. It put Nicholai in mind of the time he spent with Penn aboard Kazuaki's ship. The fleeting memory was a welcome distraction from the thoughts he carried with him after leaving Southern.

Umbriel absorbed his dismal sensations. She felt them grow the farther they crept from Springden. The Earth Mother glanced at Avigail to be sure she found rest before she slid closer to her companion. "What happened back there, Nicholai?" She wanted to ask him for hours, but her own distractions diseased her courage. Seeing him now, like this, a victim to something she couldn't pinpoint ... his distress overshadowed her own.

The Time Father stared at the flames. Though the intensity of the fire burned his corneas, his deep contemplations dulled the irritating sensation. "I'm not sure. More hires from the blue bloods, perhaps. They've been after my head since their businesses—"

"That's not what I meant," she interrupted, tilting her head to the side. "Nicholai, in all the time I've known you, to leave someone like that ... in that situation ... it's unlike you."

He managed to rip his concentration from the fire but still couldn't face her. His eyes closed, but he still saw the flickering flames burned into his lids. "I'm sorry, Umbriel. I know. I ... I can't explain it."

She placed a soft hand on his leg. "Try."

Nicholai opened his eyes and stared down at her fingers. The Earth Mother's classic calm radiated from her palm. He felt the tensed muscles in his shoulders ease. "It's ... a bit humiliating," he confessed.

She smiled. "I harbor no judgment, Nicholai. I only wish to help if I can."

He swallowed. In his discomfort, a dim chuckle escaped his lips. "I've ... had dark thoughts, as of late. Voices that whisper unflattering things. I thought, perhaps, they would fade when I had more time to adjust to Lilac's passing, but ..." He shrugged. "They only seem to speak louder. Sounds ridiculous, doesn't it?"

Umbriel's expression transcended into concern. "Not at all."

"When they spoke of Darjal," Nicholai slid his hands through his hair, stopping at his ears, as if he tried to block out a voice he didn't want to listen to, "it triggered something in me. Guilt, I guess. I don't know. I still can't forgive myself for killing him, Umbriel."

She watched as he writhed in contempt. It pained her. Though she couldn't know for certain, she feared she knew the source of his voices. Not unlike the men who attacked them, Nicholai's mental anguish had the markings of a lesser god's work. Whispering words into the minds of men was a skill possessed by many.

She didn't want him to find out about the lesser gods like this. The lesser gods *she* invited back. She wanted to tell him after moments of prosperity. After the omnipotent beings showed kindness and fortune to the people they used to adore.

But to witness the man she loved die on the inside ... she couldn't do it. Though she feared the repercussions, Umbriel inhaled and uttered, "I know how Jodathyn died."

As if it took a moment to absorb her declaration, Nicholai craned his neck toward her. "What did you say?"

"I thought—" She paused, her fingers unconsciously curling into her palms, "I thought the return of the lesser gods would be a positive thing, Nicholai. I still think it can be. They used to love humans. But ..." She closed her eyes. "Jodathyn died by his own hand. But it was Havidite who compelled him to do it."

Havidite. The name did not ring any bells. Nicholai's eyes narrowed as he glanced over his shoulder to be sure Avigail still slept. He turned back to the Earth Mother and lowered his voice. "What are you saying, Umbriel? Did Jodathyn die by suicide or not?"

"Yes and no." She sat, enduring his judgmental stare as punishment for her actions. "I found red anemone flowers under and around Jodathyn's body. The flower grows where blood is spilled in exchange for Havidite's favor. As the Goddess of Harvest, I have no doubt he summoned her to escalate the success of his crops. I'm sorry, Nicholai. I should have told you sooner."

The Time Father turned away, his pupils darting around the darkness as he tried to comprehend her admission. He knew of lesser gods. Mimir, at least. Conversations with the members of Kazuaki's crew illuminated minimal knowledge on the subject, but he never fully bought into the fairytale. The world persisted without gods since his childhood and long before. A godless world was the only reality he knew. "Why would Jodathyn—why would she kill him?" he asked, attempting to piece the puzzle together before Umbriel responded.

The Earth Mother sighed and withdrew her hand from his leg. "The lesser gods cannot harm mortals. But they do have the ability to enhance thoughts men and women harbor within themselves. Even if a small shred of Jodathyn was willing to lay down his life for his family's benefit, Havidite has the power to make that thought dominate his brain. I can only speculate, but ... I'm fairly certain that's what happened. In his mind, he gave his life for his wife and children's prosperity."

"Feckin' hell, Umbr—" Nicholai raised his voice but stopped himself when he remembered Avigail slumbered only several feet away. He rubbed his face with his hands and dropped his tone. "Why didn't you tell me when we were there?"

Her shoulders tensed. "I did not want you to think that the lesser gods returning would be a bad thing."

"Well, it doesn't seem to be going in a very progressive direction so far," he whispered, frustrated more with the knowledge that she hid something from him, rather than the reemergence of old deities.

"Nicholai, please forgive me for not telling you sooner. I didn't want to believe it, myself." She studied him, contemplating how far she should go with her confession. But she couldn't leave him in the dark. "Your voices ... the ones that haunt your mind ... I suspect they arise from a lesser god, as well."

Nicholai pinched his lips together. He nodded, contemptuous. "Of course they are. It's not enough to have Panagea's elites and a handful of commoners commissioning assassination attempts. Might as well throw an omnipotent being or two in there."

The woman frowned in the face of his sarcasm. "This is nothing to joke about, Nicholai. The lesser gods may not be able to issue physical harm, but they are powerful creatures."

"Oh?" He picked up a small twig from the ground, inspected it, and threw it into the fire, unable to look at her. "Then why did you think their return would be a positive thing?"

She noticed he held to his anger but did not blame him for his frustration. "Their presence used to bring greatness. I had hoped it would again."

Nicholai found her eyes in the darkness. "A man is dead, Umbriel. Where is the greatness in that?"

The Earth Mother maintained his gaze. She tightened her jaw. "I need them, Nicholai."

"For what?"

"To restore what was taken from Panagea hundreds of years ago," she admitted, sliding her hands into her lap. "To restore what was taken from *me* hundreds of years ago."

Something in her tone softened his resentment. Nicholai searched her face, finding nothing but determined resolve. He cleared his throat, feeling remorseful at the attitude he had just taken with her. "Could you please elaborate?" he asked, calmer.

Umbriel sighed. "I did not want to come across as selfish, but ..." She rubbed her arms as a cool breeze chilled her. "Time Fathers and Earth Mothers share an intimate history with the lesser gods. It has since faded from the memories of most, but, your Chronometers ... they were hand-forged by the lesser gods. An indestructible gift to mankind. After men birthed the deities, they prayed to them for everything. Food. Shelter. Health. Prosperity. The deities rejoiced. They lived in harmony. The Chronometers were a grand gesture ... to let men know the gods trusted them with one of the most important components of living: time, itself."

Nicholai arched a brow. He learned more about the Time Fathers from Umbriel than he ever had from history books or his father. Though he struggled to believe her in the past, he accepted her revelations without hesitation now. She lived through that time. She knew. "Indestructible, huh?" He wrinkled his nose. "I guess all those classes I took on Chronometer maintenance were for naught ..."

Though she knew he joked in response to situations that unnerved him, Umbriel found no humor in the scenario. "Time Fathers will always exist. You will continue to pass the Chronometer down from one man to the next. But Earth Mothers ... our bond with the deities is not rooted in an object. We are not indestructible."

She looked gutted. It hurt Nicholai to look at her. Umbriel always maintained a picture of self-assurance, but she appeared to wither into herself the more she spoke. He slid his hand across the forest floor until he touched her finger. "I know you're the last one. That must be a lot of pressure, especially given the condition Panagea is in."

"Yes." She took a deep breath into her lungs, finding small comfort in his touch. "And I will be the last until the end of my life. Unless the lesser gods return. Time Fathers are born of their

Chronometer. But Earth Mothers are only born when lesser gods join bodies with mortals. We are their blood."

Nicholai's eyes widened. "You—you're saying ... your parents are—"

"A mortal man ... and a goddess."

The Time Father shifted his position. It was no wonder Umbriel remained the last of her kind. Without lesser gods to fill the wombs of mortals, or vice-versa, no new Earth Mothers could be birthed. It struck him now, why their return held such importance to her. He closed his eyes, feeling like even more of an ass for berating her before. "I'm sorry, Umbriel. I didn't know."

"It's okay," she whispered, sliding her hand closer to his. "I should have told you sooner."

Though he now knew the circumstances of Umbriel's past and what she hoped to accomplish in her future, it seemed her plans went astray. Nicholai stole a glimpse of her from the corners of his eyes. "I know your intentions were good," he admitted, "but so far, Umbriel, I must say, they do not seem to look favorably on humanity."

"I did not think it would go this way," she admitted as she lifted her chin to the stars. "They used to love humans so much. I did not think they would cling to their grudge so tightly."

Nicholai returned his attention to the fire. He watched the flames in silence. The lesser gods were, perhaps, allowed to feel slighted, if men truly did discard them when they ran their course of usefulness. It was not a flattering thing to be forgotten, particularly when they gave much of themselves for nothing more than words. But whether their sentiments were rational or not, Nicholai feared for Panagea's people. Even if the lesser gods were incapable of slaughtering men physically, they seemed to have no issues accomplishing their goal of punishment. "How far will they take this?" he dared to ask, shifting to face Umbriel.

The Earth Mother stared ahead, her eyes vacant. "I don't know."

An uncomforting response. Nicholai took a chance by asking a second question. "Is there anything we can do?"

Umbriel locked into his stare. She wanted to project confidence. Powerful calm. Like always. But all she did when she looked into his questioning eyes was admit the truth. “I don’t know.”

CHAPTER SEVEN

It took effort to exude calm while the trio made their way back to Nenada. Umbriel and Nicholai did not speak again of deities. Avigail occasionally voiced her concerns about leaving Jodathyn's family. Swift and thoughtful responses from Nicholai eased her worries, but not her questions.

How often did men attack him, like those in Southern?

How many times did he leave Southeastern?

Was it always for business or pleasure?

How hard was it to run an entire division?

Nicholai tried to find Avigail's behavior complimentary, but questions that began as nothing more than curious inquiries evolved, bringing more uncomfortable undertones.

Was there anybody he missed while he was away from his home?

She knew it was rare for a Time Father to take on a lover due to their political responsibilities claiming most of their time. Her limited knowledge of Panagea's history told her most ruling division leaders preferred the simplicity of celibacy. They were married to their responsibilities and nothing else. Did Nicholai support the controversial theory that a man of power could have the best of both worlds?

Did he see himself in a relationship at any point soon?

He deflected most of her questions with obscure responses. The Southeastern Time Father sighed with relief when they approached the end of their journey. He spotted Kazuaki's airship across the distance, sitting in its designated spot near Nicholai's home. His legs were tired, but not as tired as his mouth and mind from answering Avigail's endless series of interrogations.

"Home." Umbriel exhaled, setting the primary concerns at the forefront of her mind aside as she walked past Nicholai and Avigail to find Revi. She headed straight for the building constructed near Nicholai's home where the crew dwelled during their interims in Southeastern. They were never far from Nicholai's reach in the event he needed them to ward off any assassination attempts.

Avigail watched her go, extending a hand out to grab Nicholai's arm before he followed. "Nicholai," the Houton girl cleared her throat and summoned courage. A final question lived inside her, one she waited to ask the entire trip, but feared the answer. "Are ... are you and Umbriel—um ..."

The Southeastern Time Father grew rigid under her touch. His perceptiveness broadened with his age. He knew what she tried to ask, but it did not make it any less embarrassing. It seemed however he replied, he doomed himself one way or another. "No, Avigail," he said, favoring the truth despite his apprehension she might misinterpret it as an open invitation. "Umbriel is a dear companion, nothing more."

The news made her smile. Nicholai forced a similar expression and carefully pulled his arm away to follow the Earth Mother. A quick assessment let him know Nenada seemed no worse for the wear since their departure a week ago. Life carried on as usual.

Nicholai wished to issue a letter to Bartholomew to be sure someone found the three men they left on the Southern/Southeastern border. But Umbriel's reemergence caused him to put that on hold. She dragged Revi behind her, holding his sleeve as he trailed after, confused and irritated.

"That was quick," Nicholai uttered, watching as Kazuaki, Bermuda, Granite, Brack, Penn, and the dog emerged from the homestead where the crew housed themselves. They appeared as perplexed as Revi Houton, who rested in the comfort of a chair until Umbriel had burst in, and pulled him from his peaceful place.

"All right, what the feck is this all about?" Revi pulled his arm from Umbriel's grasp when he grew tired of following. He stared at her, bewildered. "We've only been back from the mountains for an hour, is it too much to ask that I get— "

Umbriel placed a well-timed finger on his lips. It silenced him. Her expression took on an empathetic softness and she looked over her shoulder to guide his eyes. When she gestured with her hand to Avigail, his gaze followed.

Nicholai remembered what it felt like when time stopped around him. To describe the stillness was impossible. But when he stared at Revi Houton, he knew in some way, he felt the same gripping paralysis. The moment he looked at his daughter for the first time in ten years, time around him ceased to exist.

The young woman watched him from behind her freckled face. Like a terrified, wild animal, she did not move.

Revi recognized her immediately. He sensed every milliliter of blood his heart pumped. Each passing second fed it with more force. He wanted to take a step forward but could not feel his knees.

The moment his brain caught up with his eyes and the shock of the moment eased, the guilt came. Like a typhoon that made all of Panagea's past natural disasters look like soft rain, his culpability devoured him. It was his shame that weakened his voice the most.

"Avi ..."

The crew observed but maintained their distance upon the realization of the event's importance. Umbriel stepped out of Revi's path and fell back in line next to the others. Nicholai soon found himself to be the only one near the estranged father and daughter. His discomfort called him to slither away from the pair and find a place near the crew.

Avigail pinched her lips together and swallowed. Her fingers curled into the cloth at her hips as if holding the material would steady her shaking hands. "I didn't think you'd recognize me," she admitted.

His mouth dried. His throat tightened. Revi parted his lips to speak but nothing exited. When he finally convinced his legs to take several uneasy steps toward her, he pulled himself together enough to say, "How could I forget? I see you every time I close my eyes."

Avigail said nothing. Her pupils scurried over his face, taking in the sight of him. He had aged, ravaged by physical and emotional turmoil over the years, but he was unmistakably her father.

Revi reached out his hand to touch her face but stopped himself. He did not know how far he was allowed to tread the line of her comfort level. His eyes drank in the sight of her. A once small, enthusiastic 8-year-old blossomed into a youthful woman in his absence. His mind had vied with his heart. His stomach shriveled into itself. Sweat coated his palms. More than every battle he had entered, Avigail's presence made the contents of his body's interior catch fire. "How did you find me?" he asked.

She stared at him, unmoving. He stood within her grasp for the first time in a decade. When his anxious eyes found hers again, Avigail felt the sting of tears. Before she fell victim to vulnerability, she summoned all her strength, drew back her fist and punched Revi straight in the jaw. When he collapsed back onto the ground, she loomed over him and scowled. "I *looked*!"

Each member of the crew cringed as he fell. Nobody moved. Even Revi laid on the ground, immobilized. He stared at the sky for some time before he pushed himself into a sitting position, rubbing his pulsing jaw. "Guess you didn't need your old man to teach you how to throw a punch," he murmured, opening and closing his mouth to be sure it still worked.

Avigail glared. "I didn't need you for a lot of things. I *couldn't* need you, because you weren't feckin' there!"

Revi closed his eyes. This was it. The confrontation he feared since the day he left. The very one he tried to escape for ten long years. He finally ran out of road. There was nowhere left to run.

He pushed himself to his feet and stared back at the freckled face Avigail inherited from her mother. The man wrote a thousand and one monologues in his head about what he'd say, how he'd explain his actions, why he'd never returned. But everything he ever practiced in his imagination melted into oblivion. Only one thing stood out at the forefront of his thoughts. "I'm sorry."

"You're *sorry*?" She laughed, though the noise marinated in sarcasm. "That's it? Ten years summed up in two words? Well, I have two words for you too, Revi." She stepped forward and thrust her hand in front of his face, ticking the words off with her fingers as she said them. "Feck. You."

The man watched as she spun on her heels and stormed off. He looked over his shoulder at the crew. They all stared at him, wide-eyed until they realized his stare sought their advice. Penn and Granite averted their gazes. Brack shrugged. Kazuaki and Bermuda stared, slack-jawed. Nicholai looked sympathetic. Only Umbriel showered him with any useful assistance, motioning him to follow with her hands, hoping he bought the encouragement.

It worked.

Revi chased after Avigail, running in front of her and holding out his hands. "Avi-girl, please, stop—"

"Do *not,*" she started, her eyes narrowed, "call me that."

"Look kiddo, here's the thing," Revi sighed, "I made a mistake. A colossal one. I can't undo it. I can't. You're pissed, I get it, but you're here—I'm here. Ten years, it's a long time," he said, exasperated, the words flowing out of him with the speed of his rattled nerves, "but I got at least ten more in me. And if you let me, you can have them all, and whatever's left. I'll spend every minute of my life making it up to you."

Avigail eyed him. Suspicion subsisted in her. "I only came here to prove to you how easy it is to find someone if you look hard enough."

Revi nodded. "And to give me a well-deserved punch in the face, yes."

His words did not amuse her. She looked behind her, taking in the sight of the crew that lingered in the distance before she returned her attention to Revi. "Are you and Nicholai good friends?"

Revi's face twisted at her strange query. "What?"

"Nicholai," she repeated, crossing her arms over her chest. "Are you friends? Do you guys spend a lot of time together?"

The man's brows furrowed together. "I ..." He did not enjoy the term 'friend'. It made him feel soft. Weak, somehow. He would put his life on the line for Nicholai. He respected him. The Southeastern Time Father had grown on each member of Kazuaki's crew over time. " ... suppose," he finished, still confused by her question.

Avigail inclined her chin. She studied her father's face. It reflected desperation. Remorse. A microscopic shred of her pitied him, but she squashed it as soon as it surfaced. "I'll stay for a little while," she said, easing the agony he writhed in. "But I want you to know I can leave whenever I want."

Revi's shoulders dropped. He released the large breath he held. "I'll take whatever time I can get."

"Great," she muttered, turning away from him before she fell victim to his relief. A small falter made it seem as though she wanted to say something else, but she started back toward the others instead.

Revi watched her go. He felt the weight of the world crumble away after her agreement to stay, but the reprieve did not last long. Revi Houton endured many things: stabbings, gunshot wounds, near drowning, physical and mental turmoil beyond most men's comprehension. Experience guided him through each of those moments. He knew how to sterilize and stitch a wound. He knew the capacity of his lungs and what his body and mind could withstand.

But he had no idea how to handle an aggrieved, teenage daughter. *Have mercy*, he thought to himself as he followed after her, hoping with every inch of his soul he did not mess up this opportunity.

Brack was the first to spot Avigail approach. He swatted Granite and Penn, muttering, "Don't look, don't look, don't look," as he pretended to direct his eyes elsewhere.

Everyone bristled at her reemergence. Nobody expected her to knock her father in the jaw, much less with enough force to throw the ground out from beneath him. It was a feat for grown men to knock Revi Houton off balance. To observe an angry young woman accomplish what most failed to do was uncomfortable.

Revi caught up with her quickly. He rubbed his hands together as if he didn't know what to do with them. Everyone stared, having never witnessed the otherwise stoic Revi in such an uneasy state. "Avigail has agreed to stay with us for a while," he announced.

Brack blinked and stole a glimpse of Revi's daughter. "Oi, I beg of you to keep your fightin' fists off my mug then, love. This here's my money-maker."

A brow rose on Avigail's face. She looked unconvinced. "Is it?" she asked, unable to reign in her disbelief.

The Rabbit stared at her, his expression falling flat. The look only lived on his face for a second before he grinned and busted a gut. "I like her! A real judgmental Judy, just like you, Rev!"

"Don't," Revi admonished. He needed to surround Avigail in a relaxing environment if he had any hopes of her staying.

Nicholai coughed into his hand, turning to segue into a conversation with the captain now that the moment settled itself. "If I could discuss something with you for a moment, Kazuaki ..."

The captain nodded. "Anything to get away from ... this," he said, ushering Nicholai away from the others.

The Southeastern Time Father peered out to be sure the others were out of earshot before he lowered his voice. "Something's happened in Southern. Jodathyn's dead."

If Kazuaki felt surprised at Nicholai's revelation, he concealed it well. "I know you wouldn't bring this to my attention if he died of natural causes."

"Right." Nicholai straightened his posture and shoved his hands into his pockets. He knew it sounded ridiculous before he finished his sentence, but he laid it out on the table. "Technically, he died by his own hand. But his hand was ... influenced ... if you will ... by a goddess."

"A goddess?"

"A goddess."

"A goddess," Kazuaki repeated, causing Nicholai to question the sanity of his admission. "And how did you come to that conclusion?"

Nicholai hitched a shoulder. "Umbriel said she spotted some flowers near his body. Red anemones, I believe. She said they bloomed wherever blood for her was spilled."

Kazuaki lifted his eye to the sky, calling forth his memories of all the legends he poured into his mind over the years. "The Goddess of Harvest."

"Yes," Nicholai proclaimed, surprised Kazuaki knew of whom he spoke. "That's what Umbriel said. I believe her name was Havidi—"

"Do not give power to their names, Nico," Kazuaki interrupted. "The less they have, the better."

Nicholai's eyes took on a sheen of understanding. "Then you know what they're capable of."

The wind blew the captain's hair around his face as he stood. "Their departure from the tangible world was still fresh when I was a boy. I heard occasional whispers, but anyone who spoke of them did not linger in the city's presence long. I did not live through their golden years. But I know enough."

"Then you'll know what we should do?" Nicholai asked, hopeful. "If she's out for the blood of innocent people, we can't let her continue to roam about Panagea."

Kazuaki appeared lost in thought. He crushed Nicholai's hope for a practical solution when he said, "You cannot kill a deity, Nico."

The Southeastern Time Father groaned. "I didn't mean to imply we *kill* her. I meant ... send her away, somehow. It's achievable if we've done it before, is it not?" He frowned. "How is it that murder remains your go-to solution after everything we've been through?"

The captain glanced down at the sword he had stolen from Olnos on the mountain: Brufesphe. The blade rested beside the guns he wore at his hip before he looked to Nicholai again. "Because it's effective."

"As you so aptly put," Nicholai said, "I have a feeling, in this case, it won't be. What do you do when you can't shoot or stab your problems away, Kazuaki?"

The two men locked into an intense staring contest, waiting for the other to relent. It was with fortune, or misfortune, that their concentration broke with the rapid approach of Lilac's father.

Malcolm panted as he rushed over, holding various papers in his arms. "Nicholai, I'm glad you've returned," he breathed, his chest rising and falling with each summoned gasp for air. "These came for you, from the other divisions. They seemed quite urgent."

Nicholai continued to stare at Kazuaki, who challenged him to be the first to look away. Having no other choice, the Southeastern Time Father ripped his gaze from the captain and took up the parchments Malcolm handed to him. "Thank you, Malcolm," he said as he looked at them all. There were six in total, all bearing the wax seals of their division's insignia. "These are from the other Time Fathers," he announced, a frown finding its way to his face.

"And Time Mother," Malcolm corrected. "Elowyn of Eastern has sent one, as well."

Nicholai opened the first parchment. Edvard Addihein of Western detailed concerns of skyrocketing suicide rates. Men and women with no previous criminal records suddenly derailed into hideous, violent acts. When arrested, they raved of nonsensical things, of gods, goddesses, righteousness, injustice, and more. He inquired as to whether Nicholai's division suffered a similar epidemic. Before he finished the letter, Nicholai tucked it under his arm and opened another from Emont of Southwestern. It read similar to Edvard's.

"I don't understand," he muttered, tearing open a third letter from Elowyn of Eastern. Her people endured a comparable crisis.

Aggi Normandy. Bartholomew Gray. They all said the same thing.

The last letter he opened was from Nordjan of the Northern division. Expecting to see contents that mirrored the others, Nicholai unfolded it, gripping the sides. Only five words lived on the cream-colored page, but they made his blood run cold.

"I tried to stop you."

He creased the parchment back over and held it in his hands. "They're everywhere," he breathed, forgetting for a moment Malcolm stood beside him. Had they been to Southeastern? What did he miss in his absence?

"Almost," Kazuaki interjected, looking to Lilac's father. "Did nothing arrive from Vadim Canmore?"

Malcolm shook his head. "Nothing that I know of. It's possible it got lost in all the other letters, but these were hand-delivered by the diplomats of each division. They stressed their urgency." His muscles hardened as anxiety took hold over him. "What do they say, Nicholai?"

The Time Father tightened his jaw and closed his eyes. Without looking, he slid the letters into his vest, locking them away from prying eyes. "I need to go away for a little while, Malcolm."

"Again?" His forehead wrinkled in surprise. "But you only just returned."

"I'm afraid so." Nicholai placed both hands on the man's shoulders. "Please, look after the homestead for me again. I'll hire additional envoys to help maintain any pressing political matters."

Malcolm nodded without fail. "You know I'll do my best, Nicholai."

The Time Father smiled. He trusted Malcolm with his whole heart. "Good man," he said, patting him once before he slipped passed and headed to his home. He needed to issue letters to the other division leaders.

Though he could've waited for the rest of his natural-born life to step foot at Panagea's center again, it seemed he'd need to face the climatic location of his past sooner than he thought. Nicholai had hoped he wouldn't have to look at the gaping symbol of his failure for another ten years. But they had no choice. It was the only place all of the division leaders could speak together without risk to their land. And the last thing they needed, particularly now, was an additional risk to anything.

CHAPTER EIGHT

Jernal found fortune in the large dose of shock his body supplied to him. Were it not for his brain's ability to create a healthy level of disassociation, the knowledge that lesser gods accompanied him back to the airship would have broken him. He lived in a comfortable denial for most of the trip. But Mimir's incessant chattering made it harder to ignore the elephant in the room.

"A bird!" The sludgy lesser god pointed a dark, dripping finger to the dull sky. "Sweet, serenading avian, spread your wings and fly. Nothing stops you from touching the clouds, does it? Not man, nor god, you bow to nothing and call no creature master."

Darjal rolled his eyes and rubbed his temples. He had adopted a familial understanding of all the lesser gods at his resurrection. Mimir was a wild card, waffling on the uneven ground of genius and insanity. He couldn't have cared less about the once well-bound god. Darjal couldn't care less about any of them. Though they shared the title of lesser god, they were not his allies. He was superior. They were nothing to him, only fragmented ideas that faded from memory long ago. He had put in a lot of effort never to be near another, finding them a disgusting objection to the religion he built during his reign in Southern.

He had to live in the presence of one now.

It was ... unpleasant.

"Many centuries have come and gone since I last saw a bird." Mimir dragged himself across the barren earth, enamored. "Commander, when is the last time you laid eyes on a bird?"

The brows on the commander's face rose. "Are ... are you serious? Just now. You pointed right at it."

Mimir stared at Jernal for several seconds, as if the words he uttered stemmed from a foreign language. A gradual, cheeky grin soon crawled onto his face. "So I did. You're an observant man, Commander. The captain is an observant man, as well. When I find him, we will spy many birds together."

Jernal shuddered at the thought. Though he did not save any space in his heart for pity toward the immortal captain, the thought of spending an eternity with Mimir seemed like a nightmare. Even with denial numbing him, the last handful of hours spent with the lesser god were trying.

Jernal experienced a great relief when the airship came into view, but as they drew closer, his respite felt short-lived.

Slumped over the airship's railing, he spotted a body. It sat too far away to absorb any details, but Jernal did not need to stand near it to know the man died. Lifeless, devoid of any movement, he thought it looked like Yaurel. The man squinted to try and see better, but Darjal confirmed his fears first.

"Insubordinate creature," he huffed. "Death was too good for him, but I found it was quicker than other solutions."

Jernal felt his intestines compress. "What did you do?" he uttered, surprised he managed to issue any words at all. "You were with me the entire time, how did you ...?"

"My body was with you," Darjal confirmed. "But a god is both a thing and an idea, Jernal. And ideas do not bow to the rules of travel. They are powerful and limitless."

"Lesser god," Mimir corrected.

Darjal turned to scowl at the creature. "Excuse me?"

Mimir did not shy away from the late Southern Time Father's vehemence. "Lesser god. You are a *lesser god*. You are lesser than godly gods, than elementals, than the Unnamed. You. Are. Less."

"Bite your tongue, heathen." Darjal's fists clenched at his sides. "Do not forget, as man can slaughter man, gods can still slay other gods."

"Lesser gods," Mimir repeated.

Darjal jolted toward Mimir, but Jernal held out his hand. "Please, Lord Wessex," he sighed, running his hands through his hair, feeling the grief and guilt set in at losing soldiers under his command, "tell me, how many of my men are dead?"

After drawing his wrathful eyes away from Mimir, Darjal begrudgingly returned to a calmed position. "Only five. You'll be proud to know the others put them down before they did much damage."

"But ..." Jernal refused to remove his gaze from the body, though he saw many corpses in his service, "why?"

A disgruntled sound rumbled through Darjal's lips. "Their fear at the sight of me made them weak. Weak men run. You did not want them to whisk away with your airship and abandon you here, did you?"

Jernal's eyes closed. The integrity of his legs felt feeble. But he did not intend to showcase faintness in front of Darjal. Not when the lesser god capitalized on it. "I suppose not."

"Wibble-wobble, wibble-wobble," Mimir chirped as he slithered toward the airship. Jernal did not know why the creature muttered such nonsense, but he suspected it was meant to be a tactful indication that he smelled the commander's fear. His knees neared a shaky state, but he held himself together as he followed.

"Commander?"

An uneasy voice from the airship sounded as Jernal's body came into view. The commander straightened, spying one of his men holding a gun as he peered out from an open cabin door. "Yes," Jernal raised his hands, "hold your fire, soldier."

It took a moment for the soldier to believe him. He eyed Darjal and Mimir, hesitant at the appearance of the unnatural figure and a second man. But when he convinced himself the approaching person was, indeed, Jernal, he withdrew his weapon. "We've lost some men, sir. I ... I know it sounds ludicrous, but they went mad," he announced, the freshness of the memory still alive in his eyes, "just shooting at themselves and others. We've no idea why."

He spoke with a detachment that Jernal recognized from all Northern soldiers, but he saw a hidden panic the soldier couldn't camouflage. "I see," Jernal replied, glancing at the body that remained on the rails. "Gather those who survived and ready the airship. We have Mimir. We're to return to the Northern division immediately, and deliver him to Nordjan."

The soldier spied the unruly Mimir, his face a concoction of skepticism and disbelief. He thought Nordjan had lost his intellect when he ordered them to find the demon. In the minds of Northern men and women, gods did not exist. But there Mimir stood, tangible and undeniable.

His attention shifted to Darjal. He possessed no knowledge of the mysterious companion Jernal had pulled from the depths of the island, but he did not question it, compelled to adhere to his orders better than he had previously. "Yes, sir," he said, cautious as he slinked away to prepare the others.

The three neared the airship and ascended the ramp to board. Darjal disappeared into the cabins without a word. Jernal experienced relief when the lesser god vanished from his sight.

Mimir stopped to poke the corpse several times before he shoved it onto the unforgiving earth below. He cringed when it hit the rocks with a thump.

Jernal wondered where the other four bodies had fallen. He wondered what thought Darjal capitalized on to get them to destroy themselves. Or what he did to get them to attempt to destroy each other. The commander was certain Darjal would have ended the entire crew if he had the skillset. Perhaps the others were too strong-willed to allow his dark thoughts into their heads.

It felt like hours, but it didn't take long for the soldier to return. "Everything is set, Commander. We can go airborne with your signal."

Jernal had hoped the Northern men would come to respect him organically. Though it was music to his ears to see them receptive and compliant, he couldn't help but feel he hadn't earned it. Their obedience was birthed out of fear. Uncertainty. Whatever Braser and Yaurel told them when they ran back from the middle of the island, it made these men see Jernal in a new light. It was all he ever wanted.

Why, then, did it still feel wrong?

At Jernal's orders, the airship rose into the sky. The commander peered over the ledge, watching the island below grow smaller and smaller. Any relief he felt at completing his mission soon filled with dread. Jernal did not know what he was bringing back to Panagea. His orders were to return Mimir, but what were the consequences of such an action? Was there a reason the creature was trapped in that well?

It was easier not to think about it.

As the man approached the cabins, hoping to turn in for the night and find what little sleep his racing mind allowed him, Mimir's voice made his ears pulse. He turned, watching as the creature curled his toes and feet around the airship's railing, balancing himself with purposeful skill. Jernal's eyes narrowed. Though the wind obscured his words, it almost sounded as though he sang.

"Mimir, Mimir, the time is near,
for thou to blesseth me,
Mimir, Mimir, come forth, appear,
for I'm your devotee."

Jernal edged closer, compelled. He tried to approach the lesser god without drawing attention to himself.

"Mimir, Mimir, I give unto thee
whatever it is you may ask of me.
Mimir, Mimir, a bargain's been made,
an even trade, a debt repaid."

When a lingering silence followed, Jernal felt strange having crept up on the creature. He didn't know what possessed him to do it. With his fresh curiosity dissipated, the man attempted to slink back into the confines of the airship's cabin, but Mimir's voice stopped him.

"They used to sing that all the time," he said, his voice distant. "It was ... intoxicating."

Jernal leveled himself, unsure how the lesser god knew of his presence. He had been so quiet. Rather than linger in ambiguity, the commander coughed to ease his tension. Something about the way Mimir acted roused the man. The being showcased many personalities since freed from the well. He hadn't met this one before. It was almost sad. Forlorn. He didn't know why he asked; he didn't think he cared, but Jernal found himself uttering, "Are you all right?"

Mimir seemed more human than he remembered him looking before. The lesser god maintained his unnerving appearance, but it shifted. The changes were microscopic, yet Jernal noticed.

Mimir tilted his head as he watched the mists pass by. "I am ... happy. I think. I do not remember what happiness feels like." He laid a hand over his chest. "What does it feel like, Commander? Describe it to me."

The soldier's rigidity eased at Mimir's confession. He walked closer to the creature and leaned his arms on the railing, following the lesser god's glowing eyes into the abyss of the sky. A long time passed since Jernal felt happiness. He held it once, briefly, when the revolution at Panagea's center ended. When Darjal's relentless hunt for Nicholai Addihein closed. When he got to spend time with his wife, his kids.

Before that, he gripped happiness when he thought he captured Rennington and Iani, the deserters of the Southern army. It felt good then, to feel as though he brought justice to his unit and his division.

Things like that seemed less important as time passed.

The soldier inhaled as the breeze caressed his face. Though Darjal was out of his field of vision, he still sensed his presence on board the airship. It felt suffocating. He stole a glimpse of Mimir from the corners of his eyes and shrugged. "I wish I could. I'm starting to forget, myself."

* * *

The twilight hours bred fear. Darkness earned a bad reputation for housing men and women of ill-repute. Those who crept through the cover of shadows lived and breathed for the night, igniting terror in anyone who dared to step into their territory. Concerns like those were lost on Umbriel. She did not dread the night. She found it peaceful.

Her bare feet slid in silence across the cobblestones of Nenada. The smoothed rocks felt warm under her feet, still warm from the sun that set hours ago. The city candle lighters had done their job and slumbered, leaving the street lanterns to guide the few who traipsed through the city in the after hours.

But it was not the candle lights that guided Umbriel. She followed the ethereal glow of the moon.

It led her past the manmade structures of Nenada, into the forest she and Nicholai spent a majority of their time raising in the beginning months following the events at Panagea's center. Somewhere, hidden in the comforting arms of the trees, Lilac's grave rested. Umbriel didn't need to travel that far into the woodlands. She needed only a minimal amount of cover, in the rare event a wandering pair of eyes treaded the outskirts of town this late at night.

When she found a suitable place, where several towering trees enclosed her, she knelt. Her knees nestled into the soft earth as she tucked her feet beneath her and sat. Her eyelids lowered to a close. She drew her shoulders back. Then she prayed.

"Naphine, Goddess of Love, please, hear my prayer," she whispered to the wind. "It's been a long time. For that, I am sorry. But I know your power must grow with the others. I beg you to surface. We have much to discuss."

Umbriel knew before she opened her eyes that her mother had appeared. She blinked several times to adjust her vision. Though darkness surrounded them, Naphine's presence exuded an otherworldly glow.

"Hello, darling," Naphine inclined her chin, further emphasizing her grandiose posture.

Umbriel rose to a stand and tucked several pieces of hair behind her ear. "Hello, mother."

"You're looking well," Naphine said. "I see you've discovered a way to return to Panagea."

"Yes," Umbriel straightened her arms at her sides. No matter how many times she encountered her mother, she still ignited a nervousness in her daughter. "I see you have, as well. And the others."

"Some," Naphine corrected, placing a finger on her chin. "The knowledge of the gods' existence has only resurfaced a short time. Only those men who have needs have returned the lesser gods' strength to them. But it won't be long before the rest find their way. Is that what this is about?"

Umbriel retained her serious expression. "I think you already know the answer to that."

Naphine laughed. Her voice sounded sweet, like honey, coated in silk. She extended her arms. "Come, Umbriel. Tell mother what troubles you, darling."

Her gaze fell to her mother's inviting arms, but Umbriel held her ground. "Please, tell me I am wrong. Tell me the others who have risen are not out for mankind's blood."

"Oh, sweetheart," Naphine dropped her arms and tilted her head with excessive pity, "you know lesser gods can't hurt mortals."

It only lasted for a moment. Umbriel found herself clenching her jaw. Her second of frustration faded into the ocean of tranquility she commanded. "You know what I mean."

"Umbriel, love, I do not blame you for being foolish." Naphine wrapped a finger around her flawless golden locks and curled it. "It's only natural you would develop a fondness for humanity when you share their bloodline, but, darling," she paused, "do not forget, you also share mine. Men have besmirched the gods' favor. There are consequences for immoral actions."

"Those who allowed you to fall to the dust have long since died," Umbriel said a little too passionately. "Surely you must know that countless generations separate the men and women who walk Panagea now from those who forgot you."

Naphine made a noise. It was one of mock pity. "Do not frown like that, love. It makes your face look unbecoming."

Umbriel sighed, clinging to the small thread that attached her patience to her brain. "Mother ... I urge you to reconsider. There is no revenge to be had. Tell the others to back down. I know they'll listen to you. You are by far the eldest— "

"Shush, please," Naphine smoothed out the cream-colored gown that adorned her perfect body, "a woman never reveals her age."

The Earth Mother made no progress. She suspected as much. Still, she tried to break through to the Goddess of Love. "Mother," Umbriel's voice grew firm, "I harbor a particular concern about one of your newest affiliates. What do you know of Darjal Wessex?"

Naphine laughed again, her ruby lips sparkling in the moonlight. "That old badger? I'd hardly call him a lesser god. He's so fresh. So green. He's never done a godly thing in his life, let alone his afterlife."

"I suspect he never intends to," Umbriel said, taking a step toward Naphine. "I believe he's been whispering dark things into the Southeastern Time Father's mind. Nicholai Addihein. He's trying to break him, mother. I don't know how much longer he can hold to his empathy. I've already seen a change. He's also utilized his followers in Southern in attempts to take Nicholai's life. I need you to stop Darjal. I would if I could, but regardless of how fresh he is, I know only a lesser god stands a chance at— "

"Oh, my dear," Naphine's lips danced across her face as she smiled, "you love him. It's all over your face."

Umbriel flinched. She knew she couldn't hide such things from the Goddess of Love, but still, she did not expect her to announce it. "I just want to be sure he is safe," she said.

"Umbriel, I am far too busy with my own important goings-on to stop Darjal from his pointless side-project," she explained, putting a hand on her hip. "But, oh, I could always make him fall for you. Even if just a tiny shred of him has *some* feelings for you, I could embellish them. Then, at least you could enjoy him for as long as he's alive. Would that help?"

"No!" Umbriel blurted, her fingers balling into fists. "Mother, *please*, I'm asking as your daughter to—"

"My word, you have a thing for Time Fathers, don't you?" Naphine giggled into her delicate hand. "Come now, I helped you enjoy A'ronn while you had him, did I not? It's a shame his fellow division leaders killed him. Yet another symbol of the ugliness of man. Why you adore them so, I'm sure I'll never know."

Umbriel's eyes narrowed. "You did not help do anything with A'ronn," she said with confidence. "A'ronn loved me."

"Of course, of course," Naphine waved her hand to dismiss Umbriel's rising aggression. "I mean, at least a small part of him must have."

The Earth Mother released her grip on her fortitude. A rare streak of anger bested her. She glowered at Naphine and took a defiant step toward her. "Leave. You are no longer welcome here. I relinquish my prayer, mother. Begone!"

"Darling," Naphine smirked, her head falling to the side as she gazed upon her daughter with shining eyes, "you can never get rid of me. I'm half of what makes you. Don't you worry, love. Soon you'll see the wisdom of your mother."

"Go!" Umbriel barked, her order echoing off the trees.

"The face, sweetheart," Naphine pointed at her scowling expression one final time. "Remember. Unbecoming."

Before Umbriel had a chance to say anything more, Naphine whipped the train of her elegant dress around her and vanished from sight. She stared at the place where her mother had disappeared, digging her toes into the earth in an attempt to regain her lost composure. After several deep breaths and a calming mantra, Umbriel's fists loosened. Her muscles eased. She turned to return to the homestead, nearly jumping when she saw a silhouette in the distance.

How did she miss this person's approach? The Earth Mother issued immediate blame to her uncontrolled emotions. Naphine remained the only soul she'd ever met who undid her otherwise tightly woven serenity. She did not know how much the figure had seen. Umbriel stared, waiting for the witness to speak first.

"Family reunion?" the shadow asked.

She recognized the voice immediately. "How much did you hear?"

Kazuaki stepped into an opening in the forest, where the moonlight illuminated his frame. "Enough."

Her expression remained unchanged, though the captain sensed it took a great deal of willpower to achieve. "Are you going to tell Nicholai?"

Kazuaki arched a brow. "I think that's the least of our troubles, Umbriel."

"We have to get to Southern," she announced, seeing no point in feeding illusions. The captain was a perceptive man. Any attempt to convince him that what he had seen wasn't real was not only an insult to his intelligence, but it was a waste of time as well. "We need to tell Bartholomew to destroy any churches that still pray to Darjal. If he has no prayer to sustain him, he will have no power."

Kazuaki's harsh countenance tempered. He knew the pain she writhed in. The uncertainty. Love remained the only thing that rendered an otherwise sane person irrational. But unbridled emotion was no excuse for sloppy executions. "That's a temporary solution, Umbriel. You know that."

"We have to start somewhere. Darjal is a fresh god. We can still weaken him if his prayers taper off. But the old gods," she paused, sliding her hands up her arms as if she felt a chill, "they've been around as long as humanity. They may not be able to swing the sword, but they are powerful, Kazuaki. Once the few gods that men have returned strength to slip into the minds of other men, they will give people cause to pray to the other gods. Their return will spread like wildfire. If they come, we cannot fight them."

Kazuaki's eye fell to his hip. Her statement put him in mind of his previous escapade. "I acquired a sword while you and Nicholai were gone. Brufesphe. I pulled it straight from the God of Metal's hands."

Umbriel flashed him a startled look but pulled in her surprise. "You went looking for a god?"

"I went looking for the sword," Kazuaki corrected. "In any case, I should hardly think you've earned the right to condemn me when you deliberately summoned one not five minutes ago."

The Earth Mother closed her eyes and nodded. "Forgive me, Kazuaki. Naphine ... she brings out the worst in me. The hundreds of years I spent achieving a balanced state vanish in her presence. When she's around, I only feel like a child, unstable and admittedly a little terrified. Just as I felt when I was a girl. I suppose I never outgrew it."

The captain remained stoic. His arms crossed over his chest. "Brufesphe was forged by a blacksmith and blessed by the god I took it from. It's said to cut through anything."

"I know you're used to cutting through your problems, Kazuaki," Umbriel said with a sigh. Though her words seemed harsh, her tone held defeated pliability. "But a sword made by a man, regardless of whether it was blessed by a god, cannot cut through one. Only objects made by the lesser gods themselves stand any chance at all of holding them back."

"I see." Kazuaki lifted his chin to look at the foggy evening sky. "And where would I acquire a weapon built by the gods?"

"You wouldn't," Umbriel informed him. "They need to be gifted to you by a god. I sincerely doubt any of them would look so favorably on men now, after having been abandoned for centuries."

Kazuaki nodded. He suspected as much. Encountering legendary man-made weapons remained an improbable feat. He imagined chancing upon a weapon forged by omnipotent hands would be downright impossible.

His eye rested on the Earth Mother, vulnerable in the darkness. Never did he suspect he'd bear witness to susceptibility in the woman. From the day he met her, she was a fortress of self-assurance. She knew who she was and reflected it in every word she spoke. Excess time had a way of shaping a person into a statue of certainty. Years bred critical moments that evolved with experience, in turn solidifying the individual. Kazuaki knew the fact better than most.

He also knew that even immortals, or beings with the ability to extend their lifespans beyond natural limitations, were susceptible to the flaws shared by common men and women.

"Okay," he murmured, his rough voice holding a softened edge. "Nico is planning a gathering of the Time Fathers at Panagea's center. We'll talk with Bartholomew. We'll tell him about Darjal. He can decide the churches once he has all the information."

A sudden relief exuded from the woman. Though it was far from a permanent solution to the greater concern of the gods' return, knowing it might help Nicholai eased her. They would figure out the rest. "Kazuaki," she started, trailing off moments later.

"I won't tell Nico."

Umbriel smiled. She laid a hand on his arm. "Thank you. I fear it would only complicate things."

Kazuaki huffed. He turned back to look in the sleepy town's direction. People rested in their beds, unaware of what horrors awaited those who were vulnerable enough to fall victim to the lesser gods' whispers. "I think it's a little late for that."

CHAPTER NINE

The table felt like ice against the bare skin of Nicholai's back. He stared at the ceiling without ceremony, listening to the clanks and whirs of Rhirvin making adjustments on his arm. Every once in awhile the taste of iron crept onto his tongue and gave cause for him to frown. He swallowed the metallic flavor into his throat each time.

Rhirvin loosened the bolts holding the sliding shield plates in place and set the damaged pieces on the table beside him. Nicholai heard him make small, disgruntled noises with each one he separated from the arm's base.

"Apologies, Rhirvin." Nicholai tried to lighten the machinist's frustration with a smirk. "I know you take pride in your work. I assure you, I did not set out to damage it intentionally."

Rhirvin's eyebrows rose on his face. He failed to notice that he uttered his sounds of dissatisfaction out loud. The man chuckled, lightening his sour expression. "It's fine, Mr. Addihein. It did what it was supposed to do. At least these dents are in this metal and not your chest."

"Yes," Nicholai rested the muscles in his neck, easing the tension he held the entire time Rhirvin worked on him. "My body appreciates the sacrifice made by your hard work."

Rhirvin grinned and wiped his hands with a dirty shop towel. "It'll take too long to buff out the damage. I had the foresight to keep some precut sheets in back that match the dimensions you need. Something told me you'd need them eventually."

"Yeah?" Nicholai laughed, though the sound reflected only dim humor. "What gave it away?"

"Probably the third or fourth assassination attempt," Rhirvin replied, nonchalant as he disappeared into a back room. "I can't remember which one exactly," he called out from the space he vanished into.

Nicholai closed his eyes and swept his organic hand over his face, rubbing away the fatigue from a night of poor sleep. "Thank you for squeezing me in on such short notice. I'm in a bit of a time crunch."

The sound of various metals tapping against one another emanated from the room where Rhirvin resided. He searched for the pieces he had stashed away for Nicholai, sifting through assorted fragments of scrap until he pulled them from a dusty corner. "Anything for Southeastern's Time Father," he replied before pulling the sheets out and cleaning off the filth with his hands.

Nicholai laid in silence until Rhirvin returned. He went to work without delay, installing the new pieces where the damaged ones had been removed. The machinist stole occasional glimpses of the Time Father as he mounted the parts. He lived in a stillness that differed from the norm. Rhirvin had become well acquainted with the silence that claimed Nicholai each time he returned from visiting his late lover's grave, but the aura that came from him now was a new breed altogether.

This knowledge, coupled with the Time Father's urgent request that his arm be repaired as quickly as possible, ignited a small wonder in the metalsmith that he couldn't ignore.

"You know, Mr. Addihein, I haven't known you long," he started, his wrist twisting as he tightened a bolt, "but I have a sneaking suspicion you're having a particularly bad day, and my gut's telling me it's not just the dents."

A smirk crossed Nicholai's face, but it was absent of genuine amusement. More a subconscious reaction than anything else. Nicholai liked Rhirvin. The man proved himself to be a hard worker and an honest civilian. He was someone the Southeastern

Time Father trusted, which became rarer by the day. But politics often overshadowed personal feelings. "I won't insult your intelligence by denying my concerns, Rhirvin," Nicholai said as he laid unmoving on the table, "but know that I cannot divulge much else." Not until he had more answers. Nicholai did not want to escalate any emotions the lesser gods could use as a weapon.

"That bad, huh?" Rhirvin slid the metal components of Nicholai's shield out to be sure they worked. Dissatisfied, he reached for some lubricant to increase the efficiency in which the plates spread. "Does it have anything to do with that sword Mr. Hidataka came back with?"

Nicholai blinked, lost for a moment about what Rhirvin referred to. He remembered moments later that Kazuaki had left to hunt a weapon of sorts. The captain must have found it. Nicholai had been busy upon his return from Southern, not only with the goings-on there but with Avigail. He failed to notice Kazuaki's trip was successful. "No," he replied. After some thought, he added, "At least, I don't think so." The captain had a way of stirring the pot. Nicholai couldn't deny a possibility existed that there was a link, though he doubted it.

"Just a guess," Rhirvin said as he slid the plates back into place and closed the opening to the internal components of Nicholai's arm. "It caught my eyes immediately. Fine craftsmanship, that sword. My family's been in the metal-working trade since man first manipulated it to his liking. You could say iron runs in my veins." He tapped Nicholai's arm and grinned. "You're all set to go, Mr. Addihein."

Nicholai sat up from the table and flexed his mechanical fingertips. Satisfied, he slid his legs over the edge and returned to the floor. "Thank you, Rhirvin." He nodded as he reached for his clothing and slid his shirt on over his head. "I'll be sure the treasurer gets you your pay."

"Ah," Rhirvin waved his wrist, unconcerned. "I know you're good for it. If you ever need anything else, just let me know."

Nicholai tipped his hat as soon as he returned it to his head. "Your craftsmanship truly knows no bounds. I trust everything is going well with your new project?"

Rhirvin could not hide his proud grin. "Indeed, it is. I know you're in a bit of a hurry, but come." He motioned Nicholai to a back room with his hand, approaching a large object, concealed by a tarp. With a brightness in his eyes, he drew the sheet away, revealing the piece hidden beneath. "It's almost near perfection," he beamed, circling the cycle with satisfaction.

Nicholai leaned down, inspecting every polished piece of metal and the bolts that held them in place. The mechanics were beyond their years, each part integrating into the other to give the cycle not only an unmatched aesthetic but a function beyond modern ability. The engine, the cylinders, the valves, each promised a connection to one another that boasted of an untouched superiority to the conveniences of the now. Nicholai grinned. "It's very impressive, Rhirvin."

"A few more months and I think I'll have everything worked out." Rhirvin gazed upon it, his achievement reflecting in his eyes. "It'll open new doors when it comes to traveling, that's for sure. The fastest mode of land transport to date, second in efficiency only to air travel."

Nicholai grinned, nodding. "And to know its inventor crafted it in my division is an honor the likes of which I cannot even begin to describe."

Rhirvin snorted, flashing Nicholai a look of playful sarcasm. "Soon as I patent this baby and make my fortune, maybe I'll buy my own division."

"You'd be a great leader," Nicholai grinned, pointing his finger at the machinist. Unable to delay much longer, the Time Father started for the door.

Something stopped him before he exited, and Nicholai lingered in the doorway. With Kazuaki and the crew accompanying him to Panagea's center, there weren't many men left in Nenada he trusted more than Rhirvin Kelum. He had paid recruits on standby and seconds-in-command for any necessary political issues that required immediate attention, but those men were on payroll, motivated by money and not much else. Rhirvin was a good man. An unpretentious, reliable man. Nicholai turned around.

"Can I ask a favor in my absence, Rhirvin?"

Rhirvin looked up, wiping beads of sweat from his forehead with his sleeve. "Of course, Mr. Addihein. Anything."

"Could you keep a keen eye on Malcolm Finn for me while I'm gone?" he asked. "He's too stubborn to accept the presence of any hired guards, which I must admit I admire. However," Nicholai forced a smile, "I'd feel much better knowing he had someone looking out for him."

A broad grin claimed Rhirvin's face. "I like Malcolm too, Mr. Addihein. You can count on me."

"Much appreciated," Nicholai replied with obvious relief. "And please, Rhirvin, you can call me Nicholai. Or Nico, if you prefer. All my other friends do."

Rhirvin nodded, his smile still a constant. "Go on then, Nico. No frets. I'll keep watch over Malcolm."

* * *

Touching solid ground affected Jernal in a way he didn't expect. The soldier laid claim to a constant proficiency he carried since he first became a soldier to the Southern military many years ago. Even in his early career, he did not balk at any duty asked of him, regardless of how much he questioned it. Jernal performed with a solid, unadulterated evenness. Every report with his name in it dictated as much.

But landing the airship on Northern ground left him queasy. Unbalanced. He teetered on the edge of this mission's completion. The thought left his brain with a hazy feeling, as if he'd been drugged. He was minutes away from putting this nightmare behind him. He only needed to find Nordjan, prove he acquired Mimir's freedom, receive the benefits that would ensure his family's wealth and security for the remainder of their days and be done with it.

The return ride to Northern strangled him. The men under his command kept their distance. They performed as instructed, surfacing only for meals, orders, and little else. Jernal felt their restlessness with a force unmatched by anything he'd experienced before. He thought he'd appreciate the absence of their mockery, but it only fueled his edginess and pointed a glaring finger at the obvious: something wasn't right.

A darkness lived aboard the airship the entire flight home. It infected every being who lived in its proximity. A darkness, he feared, he invited back with him. A darkness he used to serve.

Jernal tried to keep the thoughts out of his head. He didn't know if they were safe there. The limits of Darjal's abilities were unknown to him. As if the late Southern Time Father wasn't a large enough obstacle for his sanity, Mimir was no pleasure to be near through the trip either. The lesser god lived in a state of wavering emotion. From serious to delirious, the creature flew from one end of the rationality spectrum to the other with no indication as to when he'd shift.

Jernal bristled when Mimir walked passed him, exiting the airship's ramp, and walking onto Northern ground. The soldier noticed a change in the lesser god's physical appearance. The hunch in his back had straightened over time. The gelatinous fingers and arms took on a more defined shape, showcasing various muscle groupings. With each passing hour that Mimir breathed Panagea's limited oxygen, he seemed more like a man, and less of a beast.

"Returned at last to where mortal feet grace the terrain," Mimir purred, tilting his chin to the gray sky. Delicate snowflakes filtered from the lifeless expanse above until they fell to their death on the ice-covered earth. The darkness that made up Mimir's body was a blunt disparity to the bleached flakes that accumulated in piles around him.

Jernal made a face. Mimir returned to his cryptic self. The soldier did not know which he preferred more: this version or the more erratic form. One ignited an irritation in him, while the other sent tremors through his nervous system.

Footmen from Nordjan's residence poured out to meet the airship. The well-dressed men of the Northern military saluted Jernal while keeping sharp eyes on the unnatural creature in his company. They knew he had been sent to collect something of importance. Nordjan did not highlight exactly what it was, knowing full well the Northern soldiers would not buy into talk of lesser gods.

They only knew Jernal was to return with what Nordjan referred to as 'an undesirable thing'. By the looks of Mimir, they guessed he was it.

Darjal descended the ramp and came to stand beside Jernal. The hair on the back of the commander's neck stood on end. Without turning to look at the lesser god, Jernal asked, "Will you be taking your leave now? To find Nicholai?"

"No," Darjal replied, his tone blunt. "Why do you think I followed you both here? Mimir will lead me to the captain. The captain will lead me to the physical body of Nicholai Addihein."

Jernal's expression adopted a look of confusion. "I thought you already knew where he was," he admitted. "You claimed to tap into his mind already. To darken his thoughts."

"Pathetic mortal," Darjal straightened, irritated. "His physical location is being shrouded by a supernatural force. Even if it were not, the presence of peoples' minds in the astral world is like ripples in the ocean. It's easy to see the swells—they spread outward, limitless. It's much harder finding the rock that made them. Only his prayer is a beacon in the darkness," he continued to explain, "but I sincerely doubt he will take to a knee and summon me of his own free will."

"Right." Jernal absorbed the information with forced calm. Darjal followed them only to use Mimir as a pawn. He needed to remind himself the late Southern Time Father had no interest in what Jernal did. Only Mimir.

When he rid himself of one, the other would fall to the wayside. He was in the home stretch.

The soldiers on the airship were slow to emerge from their cabins. They did not approach the ramp until Darjal walked out of their sight, trailing after Jernal as he entered Nordjan's home. The three walked in silence, footsteps echoing off the corridors as they approached the Northern Time Father's primary room. Jernal knew the route well. In the short time he spent in Nordjan's employ, he memorized the layout of his dwelling. Recalling every nook and cranny was the only thing keeping his mind occupied enough to draw focus away from his discomfort at remaining in Darjal and Mimir's company.

At the door to Nordjan's chamber, Jernal kicked off the snow that still clung to his boots. The soldier found it strange that no footman waited outside the Time Father's entrance, but dismissed it. He lifted his hand, knocked, and waited.

Nothing.

Jernal frowned. Growing desperate to rid himself of his company, he knocked again.

Silence.

Trying to contain his panic, he grabbed the handle of the door to push it open. Locked.

Mimir looked at Jernal, his eyes aglow. "It seems the source of your liberation has vacated the premises, Commander."

"No," Jernal rattled the handle harder before he cleared his throat and regained his composure. "No, I'm sure he's just ... elsewhere. A Time Father never wanders far."

Darjal huffed, impatient.

Jernal turned on his heel, preparing to find another footman who could explain Nordjan's location. Before he walked down the hall, he spied a man peering out from around the corner of the corridor, watching the three with keen suspicion.

"You there," Jernal addressed, taking several long strides toward the footman, "where is Nordjan?"

The soldier became rigid when he found himself under the scrutiny of the trio's stares. "H-he's gone, Commander. There was a last-minute meeting that called him away to Panagea's center. He did not go into detail."

Jernal's face fell. It did not take an intelligent man to know meetings at Panagea's center only occurred when all division leaders needed to be present. Whatever called Nordjan there had to be serious. He had hunted Mimir for many months, absent from Panagea. Something must have gone awry in that time frame.

"Did he say how long he'd be gone?" Jernal asked, knowing the traditional time constraints did not affect Nordjan as long as his feet remained inside the Northern border.

The soldier ripped his eyes away from Mimir and turned to Jernal once more. "He did not, Commander."

Despite his best efforts, a small groan escaped Jernal's lips. He forced himself to turn to the lesser gods in his company. "We should wait for him to return," he muttered, summoning the necessary resolve to remain in their presence longer than he wanted. "He shouldn't be gone long."

Mimir shot out an arm and gripped Jernal's wrist. "Nonsense," he whispered, wrapping his fingers around the commander's skin as a slow grin divided his face. "The Time Fathers and Time Mother gather at Panagea's heart. And where there is Nicholai Addihein, Kazuaki Hidataka will not be far behind."

Alarmed eyes fell on Mimir. Jernal lifted his hand to rest it on his temple. How did Mimir know the existing division leaders would gather there? How did he know there was now a Time Mother? Did he pry it from his thoughts? Had he been able to comb through his internal dialogue this entire time with just a touch? Perhaps more disturbing, did Darjal share the same ability? He shifted an apprehensive gaze over to the late Southern Time Father.

Darjal met Jernal's eyes with disdain and nothing else.

The soldier did not know if Darjal's malice stemmed from anything other than his usual disgust. Either way, his stomach churned at the sight. "I disagree," he uttered, at last able to summon words from his throat. "It'll be more efficient if we wait. We could miss him en route if he's already on his way back."

"You forget, Commander," Mimir craned a disproportionate neck to his traveling companion, "you did not free me to wait for Nordjan. You freed me to lay claim over our friend, the captain."

Jernal held his ground, though Mimir's intense stare and inhuman voice urged him to withdraw. He knew now which version of the lesser god he preferred. The erratic form was much less chilling.

"It pains me to say, but I agree with the creature," Darjal muttered. He needed Nicholai. Thoughts of his suffering plagued him, consumed him. Darjal needed the egregious error to be corrected. The immoral must agonize for their sins. Punishing Nicholai Addihein was his destiny, and he ached to fulfill it. "Come, Mimir," Darjal walked, carrying himself toward the exit. "I know exactly where the Time Fathers meet."

Mimir slithered after him without fail. He knew Jernal would follow. He had to. Until he fulfilled his debt, the commander belonged to him.

Jernal observed them go, watching as his only chance at proving Mimir had been returned to Panagea slipped through his fingers. He needed to present him to Nordjan. He had to prove he had completed his mission. Nordjan did not seem the type to settle for words alone.

He took one step toward the duo when the other soldier's hand flew up to stop him. "What are you doing, Commander? Let them go."

Jernal looked down at the hand on his chest. He felt a small relief. That hand was an excuse, a perfect thing he could latch on to and breathe in the logic it tried to shove into his body. But Jernal knew the relief would be short-lived. Regret would soon replace it. No loose ends. He couldn't retire with a job half done.

"This is my last mission, soldier," Jernal pushed the man's hand aside, staring after his traveling companions. "I have to see this through."

CHAPTER TEN

The airship ride to Panagea's center struck Nicholai harder than he thought it would. It brought with it many memories of the past. Though clouds replaced the waves that lapped against the ship's edge, it put him in mind of the countless days spent on the captain's now-sunken vessel.

They had not begun as easy days, but he found himself missing them.

The feeling of trepidation that stemmed from crawling closer to Panagea's heart, however, was a feeling he did not miss. The ravaged lands lived as a constant reminder of every awful thing the last year birthed. He clutched a breathing mask to his face as his eyes struggled to see passed the surrounding mist.

Things looked small down there. But the devastation was monumental. The efforts put into restoration had been great in all divisions, but what took months to damage would take years to rebuild. As the airship trailed through the Southeastern border, Nicholai felt the familiar guilt rise in his chest and throat. It was never far from his thoughts.

Though the feelings that rose from staring at the ruin mocked him, he preferred it to the painful awkwardness of eavesdropping on Revi and Avigail. He drew in a deep breath of oxygen. The wind against his ears blocked some of their discussion from him, but he wished it blocked more. Despite his effort to tune them out, occasional pieces of their conversation broke through the powerful gusts.

"So ... did you ... finish your schooling, then?" Revi asked as he sat on a crate.

Avigail rested across from him, one of her legs crossed over the other. She arched a brow, unimpressed with his attempt at making small talk. "The volunteers in the home didn't have much time to educate us. There were sixty children for every one volunteer."

"You were sent to a home?" Revi took on a look of dejected failure. "Did you at least get to board with your brothers and sisters?"

"No." Her words were blunt and they cut like a knife. "Natty, Garin, and Yolsa were taken away. I heard they were adopted by some rich broad who couldn't have her own children." She leaned back on the crate and blew a strand of hair out of her eyes. "The rest of us were too old, I guess. Jacob and Amadeu went to Yiddleton's Home for Wayward Boys, and I went to Edephat's Home for Girls."

Her confession created more discomfort in her father, but he tried to disguise his remorse. Though her words pained him, Revi delighted in the fact that she talked to him at all. Getting Avigail to open up proved to be a difficult task.

"No shame in growing up in a home," Penn chimed in as he set a box of supplies onto a nearby barrel.

Avigail adopted a look of mild irritation. "What do you know of it?"

Penn's gaze flat-lined into classic annoyance. He abandoned his chore and approached her, bending over to rest his palms on his knees. He met her eyes and leaned in, lingering a foot away from her face. "I know the sounds," he started. "I know the cries of hungry children echoing off paper-thin walls at night. But they don't cry for food. Their bellies are hungry, sure, but they're starved more for attention than meals. They get their three squares a day. Mostly spoiled shit donated by those who want to feel good about themselves, so they send it to the home instead of the trash so they can pat themselves on the back.

"I know the taste. I remember every bite of boiled garbage I ate, risen to temperature to kill any bacteria, slapped onto a dirty plate and thrust into the shaking hands of terrified children with no appetite.

"I remember the smell. The blankets smeared with feces because the elder kids gotta share them with the babies who are too young to piss and shit in the latrines. No money for diapers and only scratchy paper to wipe their asses with. No rest, on account of you're afraid to roll over on the little ones and accidentally suffocate them in their sleep.

"And the touch. The cold iron bed frames and pointy feckin' mattress springs that gutted you if you rolled over on them wrong, because the cloth they laid over it was so damn thin you felt every coil. And that was if you were lucky enough to even get a bed that night.

"Then there were the sights. But you know the sights can't be described with human words, don't you, kid?"

Avigail stared at Penn, wide-eyed. She only nodded once.

Penn huffed and straightened his posture, looming over her. "A lot of it is shit. It burns into your memory and doesn't let go. But you know what I remember best?"

Avigail shook her head, unable to detach her gaze from the man.

"Camaraderie. Sacrifices. Brotherhood. I remember living for each other because that was all you had. The home doesn't give you much ... but it gives you all the tools you need to be a stronger person." He bent over and retrieved his box of supplies. "You just gotta be smart enough to use them." Penn stole one glance at Revi before he walked off to finish his task

Revi blinked several times to clear away the horrid image of squalor that Penn had painted in his head. To think Avigail lived through anything resembling Penn's experiences eviscerated him. He looked at his daughter and tried to gauge her reaction.

She sat on the crate, her eyes on the ship's floorboards, as if she still tried to digest what Penn had said to her.

Revi cleared his throat and attempted to reengage her. A hasty subject change lived on the tip of his tongue, but he needed to know. "Your mother ... what did she name the baby?"

Any progress that Revi made halted at that moment. Avigail dismissed any internal thought she possessed regarding Penn's speech. Her eyes turned to blades and carved into his heart. "I don't know," she choked out. Her cheeks reddened with rage and her words developed a tightness. "She threw herself into the ocean before she had it. Left a note. Said she wanted at least one child they couldn't take away from her."

The blood in Revi's veins iced over. His legs felt numb, seized by a paralysis he became all too familiar with since Avigail surfaced. Time stopped again.

He wasn't able to process her departure when his daughter rose to her feet and walked away, leaving him to his damnation. When he realized she was gone, he wanted to follow, but could not convince his body to move.

Brack observed Revi as he leaned against the exterior of the airship's cabin. His eyes switched to Avigail as she stormed off. Though he enjoyed the view of the young woman's departure, he pitied Revi's situation. Brack hoisted himself off the wall and traipsed over to Nicholai, pounding his palm down onto his back.

"Oi, you sure it was a good idea to bring the Houton girl? She's guttin' Revi up something fierce," he said, thumbing toward his miserable crewmate.

Nicholai startled at the Rabbit's sudden appearance. He turned to glimpse Revi and frowned, lowering his voice. "I hear you, Brack. I fear it would have destroyed him further to leave her behind. They only just reunited."

"Yeah, yeah," Brack leaned his back against the airship's railing and crossed his arms over his chest. "And you're sure it's got nothing to do with her giving you the googly eyes, then?"

The Time Father's bones stiffened at Brack's accusation. "Excuse me?"

"Come on, a blind man could see it!" He laughed. "She's got it bad, mate. Probably undressed you with her mind ten times over by now."

"That's—gods, Brack, I—" Nicholai lifted uneasy hands over his ears. "Please, do not put images like that in my head. It's bad enough avoiding Avigail, without being reminded of why I'm doing so."

"Girl's got a craving," he said, nonchalant in his admission. "The younger women are the hardest ones to fight off. Eager little things."

Nicholai grimaced. "Do bite your tongue, Brack. Please." His expression flattened. He had a difficult time believing Brack ever fought off a woman's advances in his life. "I'm just trying to get through this with as little tension as possible."

Brack laughed. The sound competed with the violent winds and won. "Good luck with that one, mate! As of late, tension follows us everywhere."

The Time Father swept his hands through his hair and sighed. "So it does."

Bermuda stared down at Brack and Nicholai from her position with the captain above. The airship presented a similar design to the old sea boat with its varying decks. She turned her attention back to Kazuaki as he guided the vessel through the skies, a hand on her hip. "I was excited the last time a lesser god was on our agenda," she admitted. "I have to say, I'm less enthusiastic this time around."

"I thought the events with the God of Metal went well," Kazuaki said, his hands gripped on the airship's wheel.

Bermuda reached up to tie her hair back, taming the wild strands from attacking her vision. "I was referring to Mimir," she proclaimed.

Kazuaki did not react.

"I'm getting a sour taste in my mouth regarding lesser gods, Kazuaki." Bermuda stepped up beside him and stared ahead, unaffected by his lack of acknowledgment. "I'd hate for more to return."

The captain issued an eventual nod. "As would I."

"Do you think about him much? Mimir?" Bermuda glanced at Kazuaki.

"Not if I can help it."

The quartermaster smirked. Standard Kazuaki. She turned her attention back to the air, her smile fading. "I worry sometimes," she started, "that he still has rights to your soul."

Her words were sentimental, but she said them with a roughness. It remained Bermuda's usual tactic of driving home a point without wavering on the edge of displayed vulnerability. It made Kazuaki's blood quicken. "Wouldn't matter if he did," he reassured her. "I don't have any way to 'lighten my soul' anymore, as he so aptly put it."

"Right." Bermuda felt a heat rise in her cheeks. Recollections of the night she ripped out his cursed eye spilled into her thoughts. The night they shared a dance in Aggi Normandy's chambers. She recalled with vivid detail the way her body felt when it pressed up against the captain. It was similar to how her body felt in his proximity now. She remembered the scent of the whiskey on his breath, the melodious tune melting out of the phonograph. She remembered everything. "Sorry about that," she uttered, gesturing to his missing eye.

Half of a smirk formed on the captain's face. He, too, often lived in that memory. It returned to him every night he closed his eye. He looked over at her. His grin broadened, despite his determination to smother it. "It's all right. It wasn't all bad."

His tone invited the electricity of lightning in her chest. It pulsed through her with such force, that she prided her ability to remain steadfast. Bermuda tried in vain to dismiss her flourishing lust for the captain since that auspicious night last year. She was not accustomed to failure. But with each passing day, he destroyed her fortitude more and more.

His eye danced over her face. Kazuaki's focus bounced from the curves of her cheekbones to the way her expression stilled when she forgot to breathe. Her lips were his final resting place until he pulled his gaze away. "Here we are," he muttered, both relieved and dismayed that they arrived when they did.

Bermuda followed his focus to Panagea's center, quieting her covetousness and burying it back where it belonged. "It seems the others beat us here," she said, spying the small forms of the division leaders as they stood in their respective places.

The captain watched the bodies that stood in each division where Panagea's center split, assessing their closeness before he turned over his shoulder. "Prepare to land!" Kazuaki's voice slaughtered the skies and met everyone's ears.

All hands organized for the airship's descent. Revi joined Penn, Granite, and Brack, while the beast scampered about the deck. Umbriel appeared from out of the cabins to watch and help if she was needed. Deep thought secluded her for the majority of the trip.

As the ship descended closer to the ground for mooring, the team cranked the levers that brought out the wheels. Avigail re-emerged from the cabin, having heard the captain's shout. She glanced over at her father as he primed the aircraft with the others, but the environment soon caught her attention instead. She spied the large chasm slicing through the earth, with jagged rocks still rising from the broken ground.

The young woman approached the railing and wrapped her fingers around the iron. The split was massive. The terrain was corroded in a way she'd never witnessed before. Though the world Avigail grew accustomed to was broken in ways that weren't tangible, this was a much different form of deterioration.

Many efforts were made by all divisions to remove the bodies of fallen soldiers that had died at Panagea's center last year. Months of rain washed away the blood. Volunteers and hired hands hauled away the skeletons they could reach. Regardless of their efforts, nothing scrubbed away the feeling of dismal energy that lived in the air. It caused Avigail to shudder.

"Easy does it," Kazuaki murmured, touching the ground with as much grace as he mustered. The ship lurched forward when it hit the earth, sending crates and supplies sliding across the floorboards. Avigail found fortune that she gripped the railings as tight as she did. It was the only thing that kept her from tumbling to the deck.

"Landings get better and better every time, Captain," Bermuda eyed him with a sarcastic grin. She started down the stairs, preparing to disembark.

Kazuaki watched her go and shrugged. "I didn't think that one was too bad," he said, securing the wheel and following after her.

Granite lowered the ramp. As everyone approached and started to walk down, Avigail reached out to tap Revi's arm. Startled, the man spun to face her.

"You were here?" she asked, gesturing to the cataclysmic damage suffered by the neighboring earth.

Revi, still trying to recover from Avigail's earlier confession, straightened his posture. "Yeah. I was."

The young woman rubbed her arm, absorbing the destruction. "Were you scared?"

Revi looked out at the abyss. Like every other dissatisfying moment of his life, he tried to forget that day. But much like those dissatisfying moments, he couldn't. "Not of dying," he admitted.

His daughter fixed her gaze on him until he forced a small smile. "You can stay on the airship if you'd like," Revi offered. "They're going to be discussing some daunting things, Avi. I ... I don't want you to worry unnecessarily, but ... if you want to hear it," he paused, shrugging, "I know you can handle it."

Avigail flicked her eyes down to the other Time Fathers and Time Mother. They seemed like statues standing there. She returned her eyes to Revi, lowering her defensive status. "Okay."

He stared at her for a moment longer before he, too, followed his comrades down the ramp.

Nicholai found Edvard in the small crowd and approached. He stood before his father, the picture of political professionalism. "Dad," he said with a small smile, holding out his hand, "it's been a while."

Edvard returned his smile, though the gesture looked strange on the stoic man's face. "I've enjoyed our letters," he replied, shaking Nicholai's hand.

"Bart! Elowyn!" Brack shoved passed everyone and tackled Elowyn with an aggressive hug. He scooped her feet from the ground and jostled her back and forth in his arms before he set her back down. "Great to lay eyes on you, love! How's tricks?"

Elowyn coughed at the Rabbit's physical display of affection. She cleared her throat when her feet found solid ground again, and though her eyes held dark circles beneath them, she smiled. "Hello, Rabbit," she said, issuing a tired laugh, "I've been well."

"Gods, you don't look it," he stated, grabbing her face with his hand and turning it from left to right. "Politics got you sleepless most nights, aye? Gotta be hard work running a division."

She swatted his hand away and smoothed out her attire. "Yes," Elowyn sighed through a smile. "Many are still resistant to the idea of a woman in a position of leadership, but I'm making headway."

"I knew you would, love." He grinned and gave her shoulder a playful punch. "You always had greatness runnin' through those tiny bones." Brack spun on his heels and laid eyes on Bartholomew. He and Kazuaki were in the midst of shaking hands, but that didn't stop him from barreling over with outstretched arms. "Bart! Give ol' Rabbit a hug!"

Bartholomew's eyes widened, unable to protect himself before Brack swallowed him into an embrace. "Good to see you as well, old friend," the scholar choked out as he attempted to pat him on the back.

"Hold up," Brack uttered, staring past Bartholomew's shoulders at the two men the Southern Time Father brought with him. "I recognize that handsome face!" He grinned at Rennington, who stood proud in his Southern military regalia. "But I don't know this other gent."

Bartholomew pried himself out of Brack's arms and released an exasperated chuckle. "Yes, I brought my finest Southern soldier, Rennington, of course. And Southern's finest ambassador has also agreed to accompany me. This is Kal Rovanas."

"Kal Rovanas, aye?" Brack neared the well-dressed man, who stood as tall as he could under the Rabbit's scrutiny. He presented himself well, not a wrinkle detected on his clothing. His dark hair laid smooth atop his head, held in place with a product of sorts. Brack leaned in and gave him an unceremonious sniff. "Gods-be-damned, mate, you smell as nice as you look."

Kal blinked and his dark eyes bounced over to Bartholomew, seeking his advice on how to react. Brack followed his gaze, watching as the scholar's traditional resigned expression implemented an undeniable, yet microscopic grin.

Kal returned his attention to Brack and smiled, holding out a hand to shake. "You must be the Rabbit," he said. "I've heard a great deal about you."

Brack gripped his hand and pulled him in, refusing to let go. He leaned in close to Kal's face, his lips blossoming into a devilish smirk. "I suspect if I hung out with Bart more often I'd hear a great deal about you too, mate."

Kal bristled but held fast to his lighthearted demeanor. "What do you mean?"

"What do I mean? What do I *mean*?" Brack laughed uproariously as he looked to Bartholomew. "You thought you could hide this strapping young lad from us, aye, Bart? Come on now, no shame in playing games, ol' Rabbit's got a keen eye for lust, you know that!"

Bartholomew's muscles tensed. He looked mortified beyond belief, surrounded by his fellow division leaders. "That's enough, Brack."

"Shush up, Bart. You know no judgments lived on board the ship, just because she's sank doesn't mean that ol' adage died with her. I adore young love in all its forms," he said, still gripping Kal's hand. He laughed as he shook it, turning to the ambassador with a wink. "You and Bart look good together, mate."

"Brack Joney," Bartholomew urged, his voice growing deeper, "please unhand my ambassador."

"Ah," Brack released Kal and turned to Bartholomew with a grin, "he puts the 'ass' in ambassador, don't he, Bart? Ah, come here, mate, I'm happy for you!" He opened his arms to hug Bartholomew once more, but Bermuda pulled him away.

"Sit," she ordered, forcing him away from the humiliated scholar. As she commanded Brack, Granite's dog sat, wagging its tail.

Granite looked down at the beast. "Good boy."

Aggi offered nods to everyone to draw attention away from the embarrassed Bartholomew. "It's been too long," he said, stepping outside his boundaries for only a moment to grab Umbriel's hand. He smiled at her, bowing before he turned to the others. "I just wish our reunion was on better terms."

"Yes," Emont stepped forward, bringing himself closer to the others who gathered. "I echo Aggi in that it's good to see you all again," he said, "and in good health."

"Good to see you as well, my friend." Nicholai issued a formal nod. "And my countless apologies about Jodathyn. I know you two were friends."

"Yes." Emont lowered his head. "He was a good man."

Nordjan lingered in the background. Nicholai met his gaze after the thrill of the reunion calmed down. He saw the Northern Time Father's focus fall to his mechanical arm, but instead of drawing attention to it, he only said, "You're late, as usual."

Nicholai ignored his hostility and placed his hand behind his back. It almost felt as if Nordjan's eyes made his arm burn from the memory of the man severing it from his elbow. "Not as late as Vadim," he observed, staring at the vacant spot where the Northwestern Time Father should have been. "Has anyone heard from him?"

Each division leader shook his or her head in turn. "Not for months," Edvard admitted. "To be fair, I have not sought his attention."

"Nor I," Aggi admitted. "We've only maintained icy neutrality since last year's events."

"Perhaps he'll catch up later." Nicholai glanced at the others. "We really can't wait for him. This issue needs immediate attention. What are the details of your divisions?"

"The same as yours, I imagine," Elowyn said as she stepped forward. "An unprecedented rise in deaths, most of which appear self-inflicted. By the time they arrive in Eastern's hospitals, there's little my medical teams can do for them. Those they managed to save appear disillusioned, suffering from some sort of mental hallucinations."

"It's not just the suicides," Aggi interjected. "Town representatives from all over Northeastern have alerted me to rising acts of violence as well. Rational men and women have gone mad, killing strangers, neighbors, even their own family members in some of the more horrific cases."

Bartholomew dropped his head. "Forgive me for prying open old wounds, Nicholai, but," he lifted his gaze, feeling obligated to look the Southeastern Time Father in the eyes, "many of the men and women in Southern who have showcased an escalation in violence are continually trying to cross the border into Southeastern, and I fear they share a common thread."

Nicholai narrowed his eyes. "Which is?"

Bartholomew frowned. "They all claim to act in the name of Darjal Wessex."

"They're insane," Emont stated, shaking his head. "The victims who survived in Southwestern talk of gods and goddesses. It's lunacy. Do you think it could be viral?"

Elowyn turned to Emont for a brief moment before she threw a cautious gaze at Bartholomew. "The residents we admitted to the mental health wards claim ties to various deities as well," she disclosed. "I was hesitant to believe the claims my doctors made, but ... we all had our experience with one."

Mimir. The lesser god at the forefront of the crew's thoughts. Nicholai tried to gauge everyone's reactions and noticed Edvard and Nordjan both stood in silence, undaunted by the revelations. He suspected Nordjan would showcase no surprise. The letter he received from the Northern Time Father indicated as much. But Edvard's lack of astonishment plagued him somehow. "Did you know?" he asked, skeptical.

Edvard met his son's eyes. Before he answered, Emont interrupted. "Know what?" he questioned with a shade of rattled nerves in his tone.

Umbriel, who stood in the back of the crowd to distance herself from her inevitable admission, at last convinced her body to take several steps forward. "I know what's happening to Panagea's people," she said, voice soft.

"The lessers have returned," Nordjan interjected, casting vile eyes to the Southeastern Time Father. "I *knew* that as soon as man's interests devolved toward archaic habits they would resurface. Darjal Wessex banned those texts containing word of them for reasons beyond his own absurd objectives. Why else do you think we tolerated his ridiculous claims of superiority? Humanity no longer needed the gods' help, Nicholai. Do you know how much work it was to ensure they forgot they ever needed them at all?" He hissed, turning then toward Bartholomew. "Your depraved desire to build your historical library has doomed us all. *You* unearthed those outlawed texts. You handed them our damnation bound in leather."

"Knowledge isn't meant to be buried," Bartholomew responded. His calm demeanor angered Nordjan more, but he continued. "Erasing history only serves to threaten the present, should preceding problems reappear."

"Our forefathers eliminated the threat," Nordjan scowled. "You all brought it back."

"They were never a threat." Umbriel inclined her chin, her words anchored in strength. "Humanity did not forget them because they were a danger, Nordjan. The lesser gods and men worked together harmoniously until peoples' egos grew beyond repair. They forced the lessers out. Starved them of prayer. The gods, they're just angry. They're hurt."

"They're vengeful," Nordjan finished with a glare. "The details are irrelevant, Earth Mother. They're back, and Panagea's people are suffering greatly for it." He turned to Nicholai and thrust a finger toward him. "Never let it slip your mind that I tried to stop you. These deaths are on your hands." The Northern Father snapped an angry glance at Edvard. "And *you* helped him. You of all people should've known better," he said in a heated whisper.

A distrustful frown crossed Nicholai's face. He exchanged looks with Edvard and Nordjan, trying to dissect their conversation. He did not get far before Umbriel spoke up.

"What's done is done. We need only to convince them we are remorseful. They loved us once, they will forgive us." She seemed convinced, but her look of determination slipped when she threw a glimpse Bartholomew's way. She took several steps toward him, her palms together as her arms outstretched. "There is only one who I do not feel we can convince to yield with words ..."

Bartholomew narrowed his eyes. "Who?"

The Earth Mother claimed a stillness. "Darjal Wessex."

"Darjal Wessex is dead," Bartholomew replied, paying no mind to the collective feeling of surprise that surfaced after Umbriel's admission.

"Yes," the woman agreed with a nod, "but he is no longer a man. The power of worship has rebirthed him as a god. Countless thousands still pray to him throughout the Southern division, Bartholomew. It was people who manifested the original lesser gods out of need," she said, "and they have done it again. I'm afraid Darjal Wessex's years of influence in Southern have earned him immortality in the form of godliness."

Nicholai's interest in the subtleties that laid under Nordjan and Edvard's hushed whispers faded when he heard Umbriel's deduction. "Darjal has returned?" he asked, flashing back to the time he had spent with Umbriel and Avigail in the woods. Around the campfire, he recalled it vividly. She tried to tell him then. Darjal was the lesser god she referred to. The one she believed responsible for inoculating Nicholai's mind with foul thoughts. "Why didn't you tell me sooner?" he asked, taking a step toward her.

"I needed to be sure," Umbriel replied with a sigh. The confirmation she received from her mother was weak, but all the proof she needed. "But we can still eliminate the threat." She turned to Bartholomew, her eyes shining with a plea. "Destroy the churches that still revere him in Southern. Please. He will not die, but without their prayers to energize him, he will be far too weak to have any influence over—"

"Umbriel, I cannot do that," Bartholomew said, causing everyone to grant him their attention.

Bermuda's eyebrows rose in speculation. "Why? It seems solid. You're not exactly a religious man, Bartholomew. Those churches are a smear on the Southern division anyway."

"They are," he admitted, his forehead creasing as he frowned. "I don't deny that. But my icy relationship with the church has nothing to do with any of this. They're still critical to some of my citizens. Knowledge was my religion before Vadim destroyed all the learning institutions in Northwestern when I lived there," Bartholomew explained. "I don't agree with their worship, but I will not force them to relinquish it. I won't do to them what Vadim did to me."

Revi scoffed and shook his head. "Bart, that's the most ridiculous thing I've ever heard. You're going to choose what's best for god-fearing men? The same religious fanatics who condemn a whole part of who you are?"

"I'm choosing logic over emotion," Bartholomew replied without sentiment. "I can see the frustration in it, but the Southern division is no dictatorship, Revi. Not anymore. In time, the people will see the faults in Darjal Wessex' religion of their own accord. If I force them into submission, they will only feel oppressed."

"Umbriel makes a solid point though, Bartholomew." Aggi cradled his jaw in his hand as he contemplated. "If Darjal is fresh, perhaps he can still be eliminated."

The Southern Time Father stared, unrelenting. "And what is one fresh lesser god in a sea of ancient ones?"

"One lesser god who is trying to bring about Nicholai's destruction," Umbriel protested.

The Southeastern Time Father winced. Bartholomew shook his head. "You are thinking with your heart, Umbriel. Nico is a dear friend to all of us, but he is one man in a continent of people." The scholar looked to Nicholai, his jaw tight but his eyes compassionate. "I'm sorry, Nico. But as a division leader, you of all people should know, especially after everything you've been through, the collective comes first."

"It does," Nicholai agreed. He stole a glimpse of Umbriel, taking in her worried face. "It's okay, Umbriel. I can keep Darjal at bay."

She did not appear convinced. Nicholai's mental fortitude harbored an unmatched strength, but Umbriel knew all it took was an infinitesimal shred of doubt. If Nicholai's empathy wavered for even a moment, Darjal could use it to his advantage. "Nicholai—"

"It's okay," he repeated. "Bartholomew is right. We can't ask him to destroy his churches. Now, what *can* we do to stop the ancient gods from continuing to wreak havoc?"

"Panagea got rid of them once before," Aggi said. "We should be able to do it again."

"We don't need to get rid of them," Umbriel urged. "We need to apologize. We need to bargain with them, show them today's generation can live with them in coherence again."

"Umbriel," Kazuaki glared, his tone clashing with his expression, "bargaining with lesser gods did not work well for us last time."

Before the Earth Mother injected another comment, the sound of propellers summoned the attention of everyone's ears.

"Vadim?" Emont wondered out loud. "It's about time."

"No," Nordjan's eyes drew to slits. "The Northwestern Father does not command an airship."

The group watched as the sunlight above silhouetted the approaching craft. Kazuaki's hand edged toward Brufesphe's hilt at his side. Bermuda's fingers slid to the handles of her dual daggers. Granite's dog barked as Revi, Rennington, Brack, and Penn dug their feet into the earth to brace themselves. Even Kal, who appeared more of a diplomat than a soldier, stepped in front of Bartholomew and withdrew a blade none knew he possessed.

The airship landed on the uneven rocks, appearing unstable as it settled. Without delay, and to everyone's surprise, Jernal made his exit. He unleashed a direct stare at Nordjan, lifting a finger to point at him as he ignored all the others. "I delivered him," he muttered, his voice hoarse. "Send my pay to my home address. I'm done, Nordjan. Consider this my formal retirement."

Nordjan's look said many things, the forefront of which was his unhinged nerves at Jernal's sudden appearance.

"Found who?" Brack asked, staring at the small aircraft Jernal rode in on.

From the open door, a dark foot emerged, crawling on the ground. A second followed it, and in moments, the nightmarish head, held up by a shadowed neck, peered out from around the corner. Mimir's gaze cut through everyone as though they were glass. He honed in on his target and grinned. "Hello, Captain," he said, a maniacal look dominating his face. "It has been far too long."

CHAPTER ELEVEN

"What does he mean he 'delivered' him?" Kazuaki's untapped aggression flowed into his eye as he threw his focus to Nordjan.

The Northern Father shuddered under the intensity of his rage, but only for a second. He said nothing.

Jernal felt the weight of a thousand bricks fall from his arms. He had completed his mission. No dishonor would live in his name. He had no interest in loitering here any longer than he needed to. The commander turned, ready to instruct Darjal to abandon the airship, too.

But the lesser god was gone.

Jernal flinched, his concentration on the empty craft. His adopted air of confusion lived and died quickly, as Bermuda shoved him aside to clear a path to Nordjan, daggers drawn.

"You'd better start talking," she seethed, her fingertips white from their forceful grip. Nicholai, Bartholomew, and Emont rushed to stop her, two gripping her arms while a third stood before her.

"We can't, Bermuda," Bartholomew urged, his body language pleading her to ease up. "There are treaties in place that are fragile enough as is; we can't risk hunting down a replacement."

"What happened to you, Bartholomew?" The quartermaster's look pierced him. Malevolence exuded from her, tinged by betrayal. "You took up that watch for only a year. You've spilled blood with us for nearly a decade—where do your loyalties lie?"

"In the greater good," he said, calm and unaffected by her vehemence. "You must trust that I know what's best."

"I'd love to stay and chat," Jernal muttered, shoving thoughts of the missing Darjal from his mind. It was no longer his problem. He started for the airship. "But I've a family to return to."

"Now, now, now," Mimir chirped, wagging a finger back and forth at Jernal. "You may have severed your ties with the Northern military, Commander, but like Mr. Hidataka here, you still owe me a debt."

The soldier froze. He tasted bile as it rose from his stomach and touched his tongue. "What?" he uttered, unable to summon additional words.

"Do not play coy with me, Commander. You remember." Mimir beamed, slithering over to Kazuaki with a toothy smirk. "And you, Captain—" He leaned in, giving him several quick whiffs. A look of displeasure swept his previous joy away. "You reek of emotional baggage. Of heaviness. Darkness. Still haven't cleansed that soul, I see. No matter. I will travel at your side until you do."

Kazuaki glared at Mimir with unbridled malice. "I would sooner lower myself straight into the mouth of the Underworld."

"Oh, I know you would," Mimir said, patting the captain's cheek with his hand. "That is why you are in this whole predicament, isn't it?"

With the fluidity everyone came to expect from Captain Kazuaki Hidataka, he pulled Brufesphe from its sheathe. The enchanted weapon's blade sliced Mimir's arm clean off his body. The second swing occurred quicker than the first, detaching Mimir's head at the shoulders.

Mimir's body stood, apathetic. It lurched over to the severed arm and picked it up, then used the disconnected arm to retrieve the head. "Temper, temper," Mimir's head uttered, though it remained separated from the torso. He placed his head back in its traditional spot, where viscous elements of skin and sludge melded it back to the body. "Your sacred weapon might seem impressive in human hands, Captain, but you know as well as I that against a lesser god, it's just a piece of polished steel sprinkled with pixie dust."

Kazuaki felt blood pulse in his eardrums. Careful hands eased the blade back into its sheath as he focused on the serrated earth, trying to assemble his thoughts.

The fur on the beast's back rose, his lips peeling back to snarl at Mimir.

The lesser god clapped his hands together and lowered himself to the mutt's level. "I remember you," he whispered, looking to the animal's leg. "It seems you've been playing the same dangerous games our quartermaster and the Southeastern Time Father have. Lost limbs aren't in short supply around you lot."

Granite stepped in front of his dog and glared down at Mimir. "Recede."

With a look that was both cynical and empathetic, Mimir gazed up at Granite. "Enjoy your feelings for this creature while you can, my friend. How soon you lose their affection." He examined the graying hairs around the mongrel's eyes and muzzle. Mimir tilted his head. "He won't deny you love as men have denied me. Not on his own accord. He worships you far too much. But whether by choice or by death, it still stings when the adoration falls silent."

Granite's muscles twitched. He was no fool. He knew the beast showed his age more with each passing month. But even intelligent men preferred the comfort of denial. "I said recede," he repeated, more aggressive the second time.

Mimir chuckled. Though there was nothing Granite could do to issue him harm, he withdrew and returned his focus to the others. "But lost adoration is no longer a threat to me. Imagine how happy we'll all be," he said. "The captain, the commander, and the lesser god they venerate." He closed his glowing eyes and basked in the reverie. He would live forever, far from the prison that was his well. Though only Jernal was duty-bound to him at the moment, he would secure the captain soon enough. No more falling out of mankind's memories. The souls of Kazuaki and Jernal would keep him company forever, now and in the afterlife.

The lesser god opened his eyes in time to spy Avigail as she stood on the airship's edge. She gasped and became frozen under his examination. He inhaled, sucking on the anxiety that emanated from her body. "Fresh," Mimir purred, chuckling as he looked to Revi. "She looks just like you."

Revi stepped in front of Mimir to block the creature from spying his daughter. "Keep your distance, demon."

Mimir frowned and tapped the side of his jaw with his index finger. "Such tension. You respond to me as if I harbor the plague. I assure you all, lesser gods do not carry diseases that endanger mortals."

"This is ridiculous," Nordjan snapped, cutting the air with his arm to invite silence. "We're getting nowhere with this incessant interruption."

"*You're* the one who invited him," Bermuda glared, pulling her arm free from Bartholomew's grasp. "You condemn Nico for paving the way for the lessers to return and here you are, feckin' hiring someone to unleash one directly!"

Nordjan scoffed, his strain rising. He took a long stride over to Bermuda, his face inches from hers. "Do not flap that serpent's tongue at me, wench. My title commands respect."

Kazuaki shoved passed Nicholai and Bartholomew and seized Nordjan's clothing, balling it into his fist as he pulled the Northern Time Father close. "Yours is the tongue that should bite itself," he whispered, "or it'll be flapping on the ground when I rip it from your skull."

Bartholomew grimaced. "Captain—"

"He is no longer your captain," Nordjan barked, a microscopic tint of fear tightening his voice. "Release me!"

Jernal held his head in his hands, his concentration on his feet. "This can't be happening," he chanted to himself. He did not consider a lifetime tied to Mimir's hip when he made that bargain. Only a single, potential moment of hardship.

Kal stole a glimpse of Bartholomew. Sensing his measured unease, he waltzed into the confrontation amassing in the center. "Mr. Hidataka, I request that you put the Northern Father down."

"Oi! We're losing sight of what we're here for!" Brack shouted.

Granite's dog barked, wild and unhindered.

Jernal looked to Mimir, his voice uncharacteristically desperate as he said, "I know I agreed to this, but I released you from your well, is that not gift enough?"

Avigail's anxious tone rose from the airship as Revi approached the accruing source of antagonism shared between the collective. "Dad—"

"You are the start of all this," Nordjan shouted at Edvard, still hovering an inch above the earth in Kazuaki's unforgiving grip. "You of all people should have known!"

Edvard whipped his head from Nordjan to Nicholai, as if inspecting his reaction to see if he heard. Nicholai identified an apprehension from his father, but he didn't understand it.

Rennington advanced, arms outstretched. "Let's all just—"

He couldn't finish his thought before heated voices competed with one another. Penn stepped back and held up his hands, unwilling to enter the fray. Emont tried to get a word in edgewise, but his efforts fell against the wrath of the others.

Nicholai stepped back. He looked to Umbriel, the foundation for his calmness, but her consideration was given to the quarrel. She looked frazzled. She looked fearful. It was one of the few times since he met her she looked unequivocally human.

The vehement voices of the group swirled around him. Men and women devolved into chaos. Treachery, disagreements, fears, and disparities became convoluted, melding into a sphere of debauched energy before him. They were animals. For the briefest of moments, Nicholai's compassion fell away. For a millisecond, he hated them for what they were.

A millisecond was all it took.

He didn't feel the rise in his blood pressure. Or his heart rate. Even the increase in arterial tension bypassed his senses. A floodgate of testosterone spilled into his veins and simultaneously melted every shred of compassion that Nicholai Addihein had. A man possessed, he threw his hands out toward the crowd, burning with an unidentified madness never witnessed before in the Southeastern Time Father.

"Silence!"

His single word brought disorder with it. From him, a pulse emerged, spreading outward like a spiral of invisible napalm. Every person halted when they felt the throb in their lungs. For a moment, each held a paralysis in their bodies. It took several seconds for their hearts to catch up to the sensation. The organs quickened to make up for the moments of blood that went unfiltered.

Every set of eyes stared at Nicholai, quiet. Though he did no more than lift an arm, their ribs felt bruised by the pulsation. The ripple in time.

Mimir grinned. "So," he whispered to himself, "that's where our dear Mr. Wessex went."

Umbriel put a hand to her chest. A rage flowed from Nicholai's eyes, raw and anarchic. He looked like a stranger to her, panting like a beast from the unnatural discharge he released. While everyone else lived in temporary paralysis, she stepped toward him, unafraid, and placed both hands on the sides of his face.

"Nicholai ..." She tried to capture his focus, but he pierced right through her. "Nicholai, look at me."

His mechanical arm shot up and gripped her wrist. Gears clicked as it compressed her. She did not react.

"Nicholai, talk to me ..." Her identifiable inflection. The soothing resonance. It struggled in the beginning to penetrate the thick level of animosity that hemorrhaged from him. Though the reaction speed was slow, she felt the tightness in his bones ease. His muscle's rigidity reduced. His eyes, bloodshot from burst vessels, took on their usual sense of benevolence. He stared at her, mouth open, unsure of what to say.

"Nicholai," her soft lips repeated his name a final time, the warmth from her palms flowing down his neck and into his chest, "are you okay?"

"I ..." He gazed at her long enough to absorb her tranquility. Upon finding his composure again, he looked past her, to the others. Their questionable glances left him with an uncomfortable feeling. "I don't know what came over me," he admitted. "I'm sorry."

"It's all right," Umbriel said, sliding her hands off his cheeks.

"No. It's not." Nicholai shook his head and removed his hat, feeling attacked by a sudden, challenging heat. "I apologize. It won't happen again."

The Earth Mother did not appear convinced. She stood beside Nicholai, too troubled to move. The Southeastern Time Father faltered in the stress of the environment. She knew he put too much pressure on himself to ensure the security of others. Umbriel needed to decrease the tension. With a firmness, she turned to the group. "Ignore Mimir for now. He cannot hurt Kazuaki, nor does he possess the ability to take his soul as it stands. We need to devise a plan regarding the other lesser gods before more damage can spread amongst the people."

Mimir made a face. He hated being ignored.

Bartholomew nodded. "Umbriel speaks a lot of sense," he said, trying to spread her calm over the lot. "We'll focus on the most critical task at hand."

Aggi, Emont, and Elowyn joined Bartholomew in his approval. "Yes," the Eastern Time Mother said, "Our people are far more vulnerable." She glanced at Kazuaki. "With all due respect, Captain, they need our leadership and encouragement right now."

Kazuaki appeared irritated, but his aggression did not belong to Elowyn. "Focus where you must. I can handle him," he said, thumbing toward Mimir.

The lesser god grinned, pleased to have Kazuaki's attention, if only for a moment.

With an additional nod, Aggi turned to Umbriel. "You are the most experienced out of any of us regarding the lesser gods," he said, ignoring Mimir as instructed. "Do you have any ideas?"

"The lesser gods feed on vulnerability," Umbriel explained. She was unable to stop her concentration from drifting to Nicholai. "Even the briefest thought, if felt with conviction in your head and your heart, becomes a weakness they can exploit. They're powerless against stable people."

Emont shook his head. "The world is full of unstable people, especially after the events last year brought."

Umbriel bit her bottom lip. "Yes. If we can't prevent them from manipulating people, we have to appeal to their sense of decency."

Nordjan scoffed. "Lesser gods have no sense of decency."

Mimir's posture deflated as he sat, offended. "Most ungentlemanly."

"Should we tell the people?" Aggi asked, disregarding Mimir as he sulked. "If they're aware, they can better protect themselves."

"If we tell them," Nordjan interjected with force, "we risk making it worse."

Elowyn narrowed her eyes. "How so?"

"After everything they've suffered," Nordjan explained, "if men learn gods will grant their desires with little wait, chaos will spread. Awareness will ignite prayer, which will only serve to give them more power."

"I fear it's true." Emont buried half his face into his hand, exasperated. "If Jodathyn fell victim to impatience, then anybody could."

"No." Nicholai stood firm, injecting extra rationale into his tone. "Keeping people in the dark did not work out well for us last time. It caused further confusion, riots, and uprisings across all divisions."

"Divided they stand," Mimir chirped, "united they fall."

Bermuda shot daggers at the lesser god. "You're not helping."

"But he's right," Aggi stated, crossing his arms over his chest. "We can't be divided again. It tore Panagea apart in more ways than one."

Nordjan prickled under his comrades' ignorance. "I refuse to give them an opportunity to grow again."

"People *need* to know." Nicholai locked onto Nordjan's simmering eyes with fortitude. "We can't keep lying to them. We need to trust the public's ability to do the right thing."

"Like *you* did the right thing, Nicholai?" Nordjan hissed. "What do you think of your ideology now?" He threw his vehemence toward Umbriel. "It seems the grass isn't always greener, is it?"

Umbriel brushed Nordjan's rage off with effortlessness. "Your anger only stems from fear. Remember, lesser gods and men once cohabitated well."

The Northern Time Father lurched away from Umbriel's brazen righteousness. "If we cannot come to an agreement, perhaps the divisions should go their separate ways on the matter."

"You'd like that," Aggi muttered. "Classic Nordjan. If they don't bend to your belief system, you'll just damn the gentlemen's agreement and do your own thing."

Nordjan jeered and reviled Aggi's behavior. "Still sour because of how events unfolded at the border war, Mr. Normandy?"

Mimir's head whipped back and forth between the arguing men, his mouth open to soak in the entertainment.

"Gentlemen, we need a solution." Elowyn slapped a clenched fist into her open palm to punctuate her urgency. "I will not return to Eastern without an answer for my people."

"I still think we should try to salvage as many relationships as we can with them," Umbriel urged. "We can mend those broken connections. The lesser gods were made by men in their image, it's only natural they adopted some of humanity's ego. We can fix this."

Mimir tapped his chin, growing bored once the heated energy between Aggi and Nordjan drew to a close. He looked over at Kazuaki and Jernal, his pets. He adored them, he decided. Wishing to spend more time with his companions and less time waiting for emotional humans to come to a decision, he uttered, "Tick tock, Time Fathers and Mother. I'd hurry up and decide on something if I were you."

Nicholai knew they agreed to ignore Mimir until an agreement was made. But something in the lesser god's tone of voice irked him. He knew something he wasn't saying. Against his better judgment, his focus fell on the creature. "What do you mean?" he asked.

"Well," Mimir said, inattentive as he picked invisible pieces of debris off his body and tossed them to the floor, "it just seems you are running on borrowed time. The lesser gods already claimed a great deal of Northwestern."

The collective bridled at his confession. Rennington separated himself from the crowd and found Mimir's eyes. With caution, he murmured, "What are you talking about, demon?"

Mimir plucked the last piece of imperceptible dust from his skin and looked up at Rennington. A colossal grin tore his face asunder. "Oh, dear, simple human. Why else do you think Vadim Canmore hasn't shown?"

CHAPTER TWELVE

No wasted moment ticked by. Though they couldn't agree on a solution, Mimir's confession birthed an urgency shared by all of the division leaders and their companions. Someone needed to evaluate the state of Northwestern and its people. Kazuaki did not need an exchange of words to know who the burden belonged to. With the Time Fathers and Mother bound to their divisions, he and his crew were the only ones capable of the job requirements.

Mimir could not contain his jubilance. He watched, fascinated, as everyone tied up as many loose ends as they were able. His eyes shimmered with delight. He cherished the freedom of watching the people. They amused him.

Nicholai approached Kazuaki as he stood at the ramp to his airship. The Southeastern Time Father removed his hat and tucked it under his arm, posturing as he scratched at an imagined itch on his scalp. "Kazuaki," he sighed, "thank you for taking up this challenge. I know there's no man more capable. I only wish I could go with you."

The captain inclined his chin, inexpressive. "It's just as well. You obviously have your own problems you need to iron out."

Nicholai flinched. He knew of what Kazuaki spoke, but he feigned innocence and uttered, "What do you mean?"

"You know what I mean," the captain replied, checking to be sure his weapons were secure at his sides. "Your little 'outburst' earlier."

The Time Father found himself clenching his jaw. An unpleasant feeling of embarrassment gripped him. He said nothing.

Kazuaki studied his face. He recognized the humiliation. No man enjoyed owning up to failure. The captain looked around to be sure no others paid attention before he crossed his arms over his chest. "Listen, Nico. Not to the whispers in your head, no matter how loud they grow." He tapped him on the chest with his index finger, hard. "*This* is all you need to pay attention to. Hold fast to yourself." His voice lowered. "And no matter what happens ... don't let go."

Nicholai stared at the captain, trying to absorb the impact of his words. Before he could utter a reply, Aggi strode over and laid a hand on Kazuaki's shoulder. "Captain Hidataka, I appreciate your swiftness in addressing this situation. Should you need any recruits from the Northeastern military, do not hesitate to ask."

"Or Eastern," Elowyn echoed Aggi's offer, closing the gap between her and Kazuaki. "We're admittedly short-handed, what with the need for the footmen to detain the more violent citizens, but my offer stands. If you need anything, Captain ..."

"I don't," Kazuaki replied dispassionately. "Not until I know what we're up against. I'm not sure I trust anything that spills from that vile mouth," he muttered, motioning toward Mimir with his head.

Mimir sat up straighter and grinned, bathing in the captain's attention, regardless of its negativity.

Emont joined the others, rubbing at the back of his neck with his hand. Anxiousness radiated from his body with an unmatched thickness. He recalled the side effects of keeping citizens in the dark from last year, but Nordjan made some sense. "I'm still not sure telling the people is the right thing," he admitted. "But I stand with the others in terms of back up. I gathered recruits for you nearly a year ago, and I wouldn't hesitate to do it again."

"Good." Kazuaki nodded his approval and looked to Granite, Penn, Revi, Brack, and Bermuda. "Ready?"

The crew nodded.

Bartholomew watched from the sidelines, a frown on his face. He turned to Rennington, who stood beside him. "You should go. I admire the captain greatly, but I know he suffers from delusions of grandeur. Though he won't ask, I'm sure he could use the extra help."

Rennington tugged at the collar of his uniform, suddenly feeling hot beneath its weight. "Bart ... you know I'd do anything for the captain ... but leaving Southern ... it's hard now. You know ..." He trailed off, pausing for a moment before he shook his head. "Apologies, sir. If that's an order—"

"I'll go," Kal interjected, cutting Rennington off. "It seems the captain has enough soldiers. He excels with a sword, from what you tell me. He needs an ambassador, should things require a more diplomatic approach."

The scholar became rigid, though he tried to disguise it with a quick readjustment of his stance. "With all due respect, Kal, I've spent much of my adult life with the captain. His thirst for peril is unmatched. Hazards tend to follow him around without restraint."

One side of Kal's mouth tugged into a smile. "You're adorable when you're worried, Bartholomew."

"Then I must look an absolute vision," he replied, sarcastic as well as concerned. "I would prefer you not do this, Kal."

The ambassador glanced at his boots to hide his quiet laugh. When he returned his eyes to Bartholomew, they shined with amusement. "I know you would."

Rennington eased away from the two, sensing a tender moment in his near future that he did not want to encroach upon. Bartholomew pinched his lips together, mulling the circumstances over before he released his apprehension in a weighted breath. "I can't think of any logical reason to ask you not to go."

"Anxiety is rarely based in logic," Kal said, suave in his approach as he weaved his fingers into Bartholomew's hand.

Despite his deep concern, the scholar smirked. Kal had a way of coaxing smiles out of the otherwise consistent man. "Kindly return in one piece."

"Impossible," Kal whispered, leaning his forehead against Bartholomew's. "As I'll be leaving a piece of me here with you."

"Get a room, mates!" Brack shouted from the ramp of the airship, a classic grin spread over his face.

Kal and Bartholomew cleared their throats and backed away from one another. The scholar gave the ambassador's hand a gentle squeeze before he placed his arms back at his sides.

"I'll be all right," Kal reassured him with a smile. "You've never seen me with a weapon before. You never know, I might be quite good."

Bartholomew pressed his fingers into his temples with a grim laugh. Kal Rovanas was the picture of administrative perfection. He had a hard time imagining him wielding any weapon more dangerous than a book. "Stay safe, Kal."

With a heartening nod, Kal slipped away from the Southern Time Father and crossed over to Kazuaki, issuing him a formal salute. "With your acquiescence, Captain Hidataka, I present myself as available to represent the Southern division in your quest to Northwestern."

Kazuaki arched a brow. He could not remember the last time anyone had saluted him in his long life. "Right," he muttered, apathetic to Kal's courageous show of interest. He glanced over the ambassador's shoulder and spied Bartholomew before he returned his attention to Kal. "Any … *friend* of Bartholomew's is a welcomed addition. Climb on board."

Kal's chest swelled with admitted pride as he ascended the airship's ramp and took a stand beside Brack and the others. He glimpsed the Rabbit from the corners of his eyes, a smile on his face. "So, how long have you all known Bartholomew?"

Brack flourished under Kal's attention and laughed as he put his arm around him. "Mate, have I got stories for you."

Rennington could not help but stare at the look on Bartholomew's face. His division leader tried and failed to mask his apprehension under a dutiful appearance, but years of familiarity allowed Rennington to see through it. The risk of losing a loved one was a terrible thing. Bartholomew Gray remained a logical man, but even Rennington knew emotion weaved through his veins now and again.

It had taken a long time for the scholar to feel comfortable enough to take a chance on a relationship with Kal when he discovered him on the Southern division's staff. Not wanting to mix business and sentiments, Rennington had watched the two pussyfoot around for months before they took the plunge and acknowledged their feelings for one another. Bartholomew shared no romances in the time Rennington knew him. Even in the time before he knew him, the soldier recognized Bartholomew's opportunities for happiness came with great limitations. It tugged at his heart. The unknown of Kal's well-being would haunt the Southern Time Father both day and night.

Rennington couldn't allow that to happen.

"Bart," he said, his hands behind his back as he stood, "I'll go."

The scholar nearly broke his neck turning to look at his comrade. "You will?"

"Yeah, mate," Rennington smirked, nudging Bartholomew with his elbow. "I'll keep a watch. So long as you return the favor."

The rate at which the apprehension melted from Bartholomew's face made Rennington feel better for his offer. "Of course," Bartholomew replied, nodding. "I'll hold down the fort in Southern."

"You haven't disappointed me so far." Rennington stretched his arms over his head as he started toward the captain. "See you in a few, Mr. Gray."

Bartholomew watched him go, issuing a farewell wave to Kazuaki and the crew, as well. Though Rennington was a mortal man, he felt a sense of peace knowing the soldier would keep a watchful eye on Southern's ambassador.

Nicholai approached Edvard as he returned his hat to the top of his head. "Well, Ed ... dad," he corrected himself, still struggling with paternal titles with the man who both betrayed him and saved his life, "it was good to see you. I ..." He paused, skepticism in his expression as he recalled Nordjan's cryptic statements earlier, "I hope everything has been well."

Edvard unbent his aging spine. He looked every bit the part of the formal politician from Nicholai's childhood, despite wearing the decades that weathered his body. "All is well," he reassured his son, identifying the incredulity in his face. "I hope for the same regarding your situation, Nicholai."

Nicholai chuckled, though the sound harbored insincerity. "I'll be all right. Haven't died yet."

"Yes," Edvard said. "Let's keep it that way."

The Southeastern Time Father started to turn but stopped himself. If he didn't ask while he had the opportunity to gauge Edvard's reaction with his own eyes, he would regret it later. "Dad," Nicholai said, studying him, "what did Nordjan mean when he said you of all people should've known better?"

A microscopic fleck of fear flashed through Edvard's face. With swiftness, he blinked it away. "Nothing, son," the Western Time Father said. "Just the incoherent babbling of an angry man."

Nicholai calculated Edvard's response. For a moment, he said nothing. He wanted to believe him. It was one less thing to worry about. After his deliberation was satisfied, Nicholai nodded. "Right. Of course. Take care, dad."

Edvard nodded, unyielding as he stood. "Take care, my son."

Umbriel slipped over to the captain, one hand on her opposite arm, as she held it at her side. "Will you be needing my assistance on this trip, Kazuaki?"

The immortal cast his eye upon her, mulling the offer over. The ethereal abilities of the Earth Mother proved useful in the past. There was no doubt in his mind that she'd make a valuable accompaniment. Her abilities, coupled with her knowledge of the lesser gods, made her presence beneficial. "No," he said. "It's best if you stay with Nico."

She knew the sacrifice he made. He knew it, too, in the way she stared at him. "I'll try my best to keep him ... himself," she finished.

"Good." Kazuaki turned away, evaluating the airship for readiness. With Umbriel watching over Nico, he had one less thing to worry about.

Revi sat on a crate aboard the airship, his hands in his lap. He eyed his daughter from the corner of his peripheral vision. "What do you want to do, Avi?"

The young woman tilted her head, sitting across from him. "What are *you* going to do?"

Revi knew where his duties rested. The father sat up, finding his child's eyes. "Knowing Kazuaki, probably something dangerous. I don't want to tell you to stay with Nico in Southeastern, but ..."

"You think I should," she finished for him.

"Yes. But only for your protection."

Avigail frowned. She seemed hesitant to relent to his suggestion. "Who protects you?"

"They all do." Revi thumbed toward his comrades. "We protect each other. We always have."

"When will you come back?"

The man stopped breathing for a moment. It must have been a misplaced memory, as he stole away in the middle of the night when his children slept those ten years ago, but she uttered words she very well could have said as a child. "I don't know. It depends on what's happening there. On how badly people need us."

His answer did not seem to satisfy her. "Will you be all right?" she asked, voice harsh as she tried to disguise her fear with anger.

Revi attempted a smile. "I've always been before."

Avigail sighed. Her fingernails scraped against the manufactured material that made up the crate beneath her. After some time contemplating, she nodded. "Fine. I'm staying with Nicholai, then?"

"And Umbriel," Revi added, adopting a cynical look. He did not enjoy his daughter's eagerness to reside with the Southeastern Time Father. "I'll be back as soon as I can."

"All right." She sat in silence before she stood to depart. Revi thought that was the end of their conversation, but as she neared the airship's ramp and placed a gentle hand on the railing, she turned and added, "Stay safe."

She disappeared before he could say anything. It didn't matter. He didn't know what to say. But as Revi Houton rose to his feet, his false smile shifted from a forced one to a more genuine one.

With Avigail off, all the crew, save for Bermuda, had their feet on the airship's deck. Mimir grabbed Jernal's hand and pulled him toward the ramp. The soldier felt like a dead weight against the lesser god's forceful tugs but relented upon the realization that he was stuck in his bargain until further notice.

Kazuaki swept a hand out in front of Mimir before his first foot touched the ramp. "No stowaways on my ship," he glowered.

"Oh, Captain," Mimir radiated with beguilement, "you have no choice."

His arm remained unmoving. He knew Mimir was right; there was nothing he could do to prevent the lesser god from climbing aboard. If he could not end his problems with his unscheduled decapitation earlier, there were not many other solutions he knew of to rid himself of the annoyance. A heated eye flicked to Jernal, still clad in his Northern military battledress. "I don't have to take *him*," he muttered.

Jernal drew his shoulders back as he stood under the fire of Kazuaki's stare. "It's not as if I want to come," he shot back.

"You two," Mimir chuckled. "Bickering like children, yet you have so much in common. Come, Commander, you never know when you'll need to satisfy your debt."

Jernal watched as Mimir pushed passed Kazuaki's arm, and ventured onto the airship's deck. He sighed, admittedly beside himself as he followed the lesser god's footsteps. Before he ascended, the captain seized his bicep.

"It's a dangerous thing making bargains with lesser gods," he growled.

Jernal looked down at Kazuaki's scarred hand before he lifted his eyes. "You're one to talk, *Captain*." It embittered him to address the immortal with any sense of formality, but if he intended to live long enough to see his bargain with Mimir end, he needed to appease the man capable of destroying his life.

Kazuaki's expression flattened. He leaned in, inches from Jernal's face. "Know that whatever hell you'll face with Mimir," he said, tightening his grip on the soldier's arm, "will pale in comparison to the hell you'll endure on my ship if you raise any trouble."

Jernal caught himself as Kazuaki thrust him forward. He stumbled several steps on the ramp before regaining his footing and joined up the others at the top. The commander closed his eyes. He wondered if it was worth it. If he shouldn't have forgone Nordjan's offer.

Thinking of the stable future it promised to buy his family, he decided it was. With swallowed pride and a bruised ego, Jernal stood beside the others on deck.

Bermuda spied the crew on board, ready for departure. Spiteful pupils zeroed in on Nordjan, who stood with a detestable amount of self-importance. With Bartholomew's attention on Kal and Emont exchanging words with Elowyn, she slipped over to the Northern Father and lowered her voice. "Don't think for a moment I'll forget your hand in Mimir's reemergence," she hissed. "The Time Fathers may fear Northern coming to a standstill at your death, but I assure you, I do not share their concerns."

Nordjan did not give her the satisfaction of a response. He only stared, his expression unchanging.

When Nicholai noticed the stand-off, he took several hurried steps over toward them, opening his mouth to speak. Bermuda turned away and strode toward the airship before he got anything out.

With a frown, Nicholai redirected his focus to Nordjan. He put their history aside, forgoing the emotional aftermath of Nordjan severing his arm for the sake of diplomacy. "I know I can't force you to do anything. You're an intelligent man capable of making your own decisions. But I want you to know I'm going to tell my people. As I know it, Bartholomew, Elowyn, Aggi, and Edvard are doing the same. Emont remains unsure, but know that word will spread. You can either be viewed as a truthful leader or a reticent one, Nordjan. You decide. I just know from experience that secrets lead to angry citizens. You should, too."

Not unlike his exchange with Bermuda, Nordjan said nothing. When Nicholai realized he wasn't going to receive a response, he sighed. "Gods-speed, Nordjan." He turned, joining Umbriel and Avigail where they stood near Kazuaki.

Nordjan glared at the Southeastern Time Father before he snapped his eyes toward Jernal. The commander loitered on the airship's edge, gripping the rails. His eyes pleaded with him to send help. To allow the Northern cavalry to free him from his prison sentence with Mimir. Nordjan saw every atom of hope in Jernal's stare.

He turned his back, disregarding them all, as he headed toward his flying machine and climbed in.

Nicholai watched as Elowyn, Emont, and Edvard said their adieus and parted ways. For a final time, before his comrade made his exit, he looked to Kazuaki. "Please alert me as soon as you are able. I'd like to know what's going on up there. Umbriel and I will work on appeasing whatever lesser gods we can summon in Southeastern."

Kazuaki nodded. He knew Umbriel would keep the Time Father grounded, but he still scrutinized Nicholai with classic precision. "Tread lightly, Nico. Lesser gods are devilish things." He felt Mimir's focus burning into the back of his brain just then. The captain ground his teeth. "Trust me. I know all too well. Do you need a ride back?"

"No," Nicholai shook his head. "Make haste. We'll head to the nearest Southeastern town and borrow a steam car to bridge the gap."

"Sounds like you have it all figured out." Kazuaki exchanged glances with the Time Father and Earth Mother as they stood beside Avigail. That was as close to a goodbye as they'd receive from the immortal. He turned his back and joined the others. "Raise the ramp!" he barked. "Onward, to Northwestern!"

* * *

Crawling along the Northwestern border proved uneventful at first. The airship soared high above the sprawling cities and villages. Revi kept a watchful eye on the land through a handheld spyglass. Nothing seemed out of the ordinary. Nothing, until they edged closer to Vadim's home town of Striburn.

Granite observed Mimir like a hawk. The lesser god killed time by playing fetch with the behemoth's dog. While it took several minutes for the beast to warm up to Mimir's grotesque aura, the mongrel harbored no resentments when the lesser god engaged him in play. It abandoned all former hostilities, chasing after the piece of rope thrown by Mimir time and time again.

Rennington and Brack swapped stories. The Southern soldier caught Brack up on his latest missions and endeavors. Brack caught Rennington up on how many women he had plowed since the revolution ended. Though he felt apprehensive at first, Rennington fell back into old times. Nostalgia resurfaced in the crew's presence. It reminded him of better days.

Jernal sulked in a corner, his back against the exterior cabin walls of the airship. He was never far from Mimir, hoping with each passing second, the demon would address whatever stipulation promised to free him from his debt.

Black boots took one stair at a time, as Bermuda wandered toward the captain. She looked over her shoulder, ensuring herself of the fact that Mimir remained occupied with Granite's dog. The quartermaster came up behind Kazuaki and stood. She knew he was aware of her presence, but he kept his hands firm on the wheel.

"Kazuaki," she finally spoke against the wind, "are you all right?"

Her words were flat, but the sentiment behind them burned with worry. Kazuaki's chest expanded as he tried to inhale the thin oxygen living at their elevation. Not unlike his current state of mind, his lungs remained unsatisfied. "I'll survive."

Mimir's return roused many mental burdens in the quartermaster. Bermuda followed Kazuaki's gaze outward, though clouds obscured their vision. "He can't take you," she reiterated, mostly to reassure herself, "if you can't lighten your soul."

"Precisely." Kazuaki's grip on the wheel increased. "We only need to tolerate him in the meantime, until we figure out how to get rid of him."

"I have half a mind to kill Nordjan," Bermuda muttered, sliding her hands over her arms to protect her exposed skin from the cutting winds. "How is it that feckin' bastard can damn Panagea, try to slaughter us all, sever Nico's arm, try to rid you of your soul, and still live to see another day?"

"Treaties and diplomatic nonsense. Panagea needs him," Kazuaki grumbled, guiding the airship dutifully forward. "For now."

Bermuda fell silent. She allowed the momentary quiet of travel to dissuade her murderous thoughts. A scuffle behind her caused her to turn and view Kal, who tried to recover from a playful slug from Brack. She found herself smirking. "I can't believe Bartholomew found a lover."

"Yes." Kazuaki reflected on the many nights spent with the scholar in the past. He was always tight-lipped about why he never shared the company of a woman, but the captain did not need a degree in human psychology to understand the nature of one of his most favored crewmen. "It just goes to show anybody can find happiness. Even in this shithole."

The woman laughed. Though steeped in misanthropy, Kazuaki's words reflected the truth. If the fastidious Bartholomew could damn society's expectations and find his own path to bliss in a sea of opposition, anyone could. The thought made her stomach swirl. She found herself turning toward the captain again. "He must have thought it was worth the risk," she said. "That happiness is worth ... breaking the rules."

Kazuaki paused. Her tone. It spoke to him on more than just an auditory level. He turned, slow to face her. "Sometimes it is," the captain responded, measured in his reply. He recognized a spark in her. A chance.

Perhaps logic existed in Bartholomew's method. The scholar was the most intelligent man Kazuaki knew. He approached each situation with a tactile sense of what generated the best result. For Bartholomew to not only damn the political pressure his title put on him to avoid taking a lover, but to condemn the ramifications of living his truest self in the eyes of a judgmental world ... Kazuaki applauded it.

It would be easy to cast cemented ideologies aside. Easier now, when he looked at her willing face. Kazuaki knew all along that mortals and immortals had no business with one another in a romantic setting. But the way she looked at him poked countless holes in the integrity of his decision. He couldn't deny the growth of their lust for one another. He suspected she couldn't deny it either. To linger on the edge of desire was painful some nights, knowing opportunity slumbered a few cabin doors away.

But things were much more complicated now that Mimir returned. Whether Kazuaki admitted it or not, a part of him wondered if the lesser god might find a way to complete the bargain he made years ago. To put Bermuda in that situation, where she risked losing someone she loved again ... he couldn't do it. Not after witnessing what happened last time.

"And other times," the captain forced himself to say, "the risk outweighs the reward."

Bermuda tilted her head. "Maybe for some."

She wrecked him. This woman who once bathed in vulnerability where matters of the heart were concerned. Time transformed her into something less fearful of emotional carnage. Temptation taunted his primal urges, beckoning him to abandon his sense of right and wrong. "Danger waits for men and women who risk too much. Have you no fear left in you, Bermuda?" he found himself asking, despite his conscience pulling hard on the reins.

The quartermaster slid her feet toward him, inching closer to his body. "Only the fear of living a life without risks," she said.

He looked down at her, the wind whipping her hair. The man tried once more to hold on to reason. "We throw ourselves in perilous situations daily."

Her shoulder rose into a tiny shrug. "Then what's one more?"

She had him. He was an immortal, but he was still a human being. The familiar feeling of covetousness lit up in his veins when she slid close enough that her arm brushed up against his. Her eyes strayed from the clouded horizon when she turned into him.

Time did more to heal her wounded heart than Kazuaki thought possible. The morphine of passing months eased her trauma, taking pieces of apprehension with it to the grave with each dying week. Her healing heart grew bold. What were once fleeting moments of eye contact, became covetous moments. But her rehabilitated state was fresh and their destinies were sealed, far too varying to converge on a happy ending.

Those thoughts fell to the wayside as he looked down at her, his pounding heart threatening to tear his ribcage apart. In a crippling moment of weakness, he lifted his hand, intent to slide it up the side of her neck and pull her face toward his, but Revi's bellowing voice massacred any transitory opportunity for forbidden romance.

"Captain! Smoke on the horizon!"

Bermuda closed her eyes, silently cursing as she and the captain turned away from one another and took in the sight. Through the mist of the clouds, they strained to see, but wafting up from the city below was a gray, burning haze. Seconds later, the scent of fire dove into their nostrils.

"Town's aglow!" Brack shouted, leaning over the airship's railing with little regard to how high they were. "Feckin' shit, it looks like the gods-damned mouth of the Underworld opened up down there!"

"Right," Kazuaki whispered to himself, trying to shake his carnal feelings away and replace them with more purposeful ones. "Bermuda ..." He paused. He didn't want to say it. Didn't want to send her waiting body away from his. But the fates had other plans. Plans set in sensibleness he should have obeyed from the start. "Prepare the airship for landing," he forced himself to say.

Bermuda glanced at the smoldering wreckage below them. Numerous buildings were engulfed in flames. The carnage spread from one blazing piece of architecture to another. She'd be lying to herself if she said it wasn't a pressing matter. "Yes, Captain." She slipped away, sliding down the banisters of the stairs leading to the main deck. "Revi! Scout a safe spot to land! Granite, you're on propellers! Brack and Penn, ready the wheels!"

Jernal observed as the crew choreographed a swift landing, working in synchronicity that would solicit jealousy from any mechanized device. Kal came up beside him, his hands in his pockets. "Are you all right, soldier?" he asked, recognizing the uniform as belonging to Northern.

"Yes," Jernal snapped, unable to remove his eyes from the fluid movements of each crew member. "Or if I'm not, I will be."

Mimir joined the two men, having deserted his game of play with Granite's dog. Jernal expected to hear some sort of condemning remark spill out of the lesser god's mouth, but Mimir adopted a quieter demeanor.

"Come on, quartermaster, don't count me out!" Rennington's voice rose above the chaos as he strode over to Bermuda. "It's been a while, love, but I'm still handy around a ship, you know."

Bermuda spun to face him, holding her hair out of her face with her metal hand. "You could help Revi with the landing. Man the steering fin if you must, just be sure we're far from any chance at catching fire when we land."

Rennington nodded and dashed off to assist. Locating safe territory was no easy feat. Much of the ground burned, blackening the sky the closer they soared. Kazuaki decreased the vessel's altitude, but no opportunities for landing presented themselves. Gliding through the town over a sea of flames, the destruction stretched as far as the eye could see.

An additional twenty minutes passed before they were able to spy an opening. When the wheels retracted from the ship's belly and touched the ground, a cataclysmic collection of ash leaped from the earth. The vessel lurched forward, coming to a rough halt in front of a dilapidated factory. Only bones were left of the building's original design, the rest cremated by flames long burnt out.

Bermuda did not wait for the ramp to be lowered. She hoisted her body over the airship's edge, landing in a crouched position below. The quartermaster frowned as she rose to stand, looking down at the thick layer of soot covering the palm of her hand. Something soft lived beneath her touch. She glanced down. They were tainted with debris, but she spied flowers. Thousands of them.

A sea of once red anemone flowers stretched out as far as she could see. The orange glow of embers still collected in parts of the gravel, but the fire that devoured this section of the city had crawled onward long ago. Nothing remained for it to feed on.

The crew was quick to join the woman's side, once the ramp dropped into place. One by one, they filed into the ravaged streets of Vadim's home town of Striburn. Granite's dog sniffed at what was once a human body. The canine sneezed, blowing particles of debris into the air.

"This is insane," Jernal muttered, his lungs writhing under the smell of burned flesh and melted metal. In every direction, more destruction waited to be viewed. Nothing but crisp darkness and absence of life. The only signs of movement were on the route they came from, and they only stemmed from the wild, towering flames. The picture before all of them was painted by the hands of a fire that had burned for days. "How could this have happened?" he asked, turning to Mimir. "How could no one have known?"

The lesser god stared ahead, stoic, and said nothing.

While the crew had been conditioned over time to remain nonreactive to such sights, Kal had a harder time reigning in his revulsion. "We need to alert the others," he stated, clearing his throat to erase his fear, "have them send as many reinforcements as they can to search for survivors."

Kazuaki glanced at the ambassador. "We'll send word. But not before we find Vadim. This is his home town, correct? Striburn?"

The name seemed ironic now, given the town's burnt state. "If he's dead, we'll need to find his Chronometer before time stops and we're all stuck here."

Kal's eyes narrowed. He hadn't considered the possibility. He surveyed the area, trying to recall the political knowledge he possessed regarding the existing division leaders. He knew much of the cities where they all made their homes, but the fire damaged a plentiful portion of the geography he had familiarized himself with. After several moments, his voice grew dim. "Of course. The only issue now, Captain, is the location of Vadim's property."

A scoff fell from Kazuaki's lips as he stole a glimpse of Granite and Revi to be sure they brought the supply bags with them. "Do elaborate, Mr. Rovanas."

"The issue, Captain," Kal started, lifting his finger to point to a tall, blackened building in the distance. Absent of windows, with exposed beams jutting out the sides of crumbling walls, it seemed a miracle the structure still stood, " ... is *that* is Vadim's property."

CHAPTER THIRTEEN

Impatient hands twisted the metal door handle and threw it open. Nicholai stared down at the glaringly empty space on his stoop. The look on his face gave away his dissatisfaction that no news arrived yet from his companions in Northwestern. He pushed his back against the open door's edge and closed his eyes, leaning his head back until it, too, rested against the frame.

Umbriel poked her head out from around the kitchen wall. She studied Nicholai, searching her mind for comforting words. The Earth Mother stepped out from behind the partition, holding a dish in her hand that she had been cleaning. "It's only been a few days, Nicholai. Even if Kazuaki mailed a letter immediately upon reaching Northwestern, there's no way a courier could have delivered it so quickly."

Nicholai's eyes shot open, unaware of Umbriel's proximity. He placed a hand over his chest to steady his startled heart and forced a smile to appear. "Umbriel ... I didn't see you there," he laughed, the sound absent of any authentic humor. "Yes. I suppose you're right. I'm sure he'll send word soon enough."

The Earth Mother's expression faded into worry. Though she still located the minuscule shine of Nicholai's unhindered compassion, his eyes were tainted by patches of darkness from sleepless nights. He tried to maintain his standard political appearance, but his clothing remained wrinkled; his goggles went without cleaning for days, accruing a thick layer of coal dust; and his boots went unpolished. The Time Father had even forgone the act of shaving, building up a fine coating of stubble across his constantly tensed jaw.

Nicholai saw the apprehension inside her. Guilt spilled over, knowing he was the cause of it. With a more sincere grin, he stepped back inside the building and closed the door behind him. "I'm sorry, Umbriel. I hope my attitude as of late hasn't inconvenienced you. I'm just ... I need to know if they're all right. It was a lot easier last year, you know, being in their presence rather than bound to my division."

"Easier is a funny word for it," Umbriel replied with a soft smile. "As I recall, when you were with Kazuaki, you chastised yourself for not being in Southeastern. Now, here you are, chastising yourself for not being with Kazuaki. It seems there's no winning for you, Nicholai."

He returned her smile. It held all of him in it this time, rather than manufactured contentment. "I know what you're trying to say," he said. "I'll be a bit more forgiving to myself in the future."

She didn't believe him. Not for a moment. Nicholai cared too much about what was best for everyone else and thought he could be the one to bring them the happiness they chased. Despite the pitfalls of the past, he still failed to see that such a utopia was an impossibility. But it was his supreme idealism that Umbriel admired most, despite how impractical it was. "Just try to relax if you can," she suggested. "Perhaps you can distract yourself by tying up any loose administrative ends before we summon the lesser gods tonight."

Nicholai nodded, clasping his hands behind his back as he paced the room. The quarters were tight; he did not feel the need to dwell inside embellished residences, as his fellow Time Fathers did. Several strides brought him up against another wall, where he turned and paced in the opposite direction. "I suppose I could answer some of the funding requests," he decided, after mulling over the list of things he needed to do in his head.

"That's the spirit." Umbriel gestured to the desk where Nicholai often sat to conduct his business. "If you need anything, just let me know."

Avigail entered the room with a yawn, her arms stretched up over her head. Her wild hair, having skipped a good brushing for several months, flared out at the sides of her head as she glanced from Nicholai to Umbriel with a grateful smile. "Good morning," she said to the pair, a self-conscious hand over her mouth to disguise her morning breath.

Umbriel smiled. "A good morning to you as well, Avigail."

Nicholai grabbed the brim of his hat and issued her a small nod and smile as he pulled his chair out and slid onto the base.

Though he applied minimal effort and said nothing, his half-grin alone made her blush. Avigail placed a hand on her stomach to steady her rising nerves. "Are ... are you working on something important?" she asked, peering over his shoulder as he gripped a pen and dipped it in ink.

Nicholai reached over to grab some stationery from his desk, staring down at the formal request for funding from one of Southeastern's cities near the coast. He re-read the same sentence several times and still couldn't remember the reason behind their application. "I think so," he replied, laughing despite himself. "Important, but rather boring, I must confess."

Avigail laughed a little too loudly at his statement. She tucked unkempt strands of hair behind her ear, reveling in Nicholai's nearness. "If there's anything I can do—"

"I'm all right, Avigail, thank you," Nicholai replied, tapping the edge of his pen on the paper as if that helped his brain retain what he'd just read. All it served to do was create a blot of collected ink. Though he seemed distracted, he asked, "I trust you slept well?"

"Yes, thank you," Avigail drew her shoulders back and stood up straighter, to improve her posture. "I like this place. It's comfortable. First time in a while since I slept in a real bed. I mean, since last time I slept with you—I mean, not *with* you, I mean here, with you, and Umbriel, in your house—before we went to Southern—"

"I understand," Nicholai said, forgoing the effort of lifting his eyes from the paper to avoid seeing the crimson sweep of embarrassment that invaded her cheeks. "I'm glad you slept well."

"Yes," Avigail uttered, her heart threatening to explode in her chest, "I ... I'm glad, too, thank you, again."

"Avigail," Umbriel called from the kitchen, "would you mind giving me a hand?"

The Houton daughter cleared her throat, looking at Nicholai. "I ... um, I'm gonna ... I'll be back." She stepped away, digging her fingers into her scalp as she internally berated herself for her mortifying behavior.

Umbriel looked up from the stove, the sound of sizzling food rising from a heated cast iron pan. She offered the girl a sympathetic smile, her head tilting as if she knew the depth of her humiliation. "Would you care to help me with breakfast preparations?" she asked, her voice light.

Avigail reined her embarrassment in and joined Umbriel at her side, peering down into the contents of the pan. "I'll try my best," she started, "but I've never cooked anything like that before. Is it from a can or a package?"

Umbriel poked the diced sweet potatoes with a fork, to test their doneness before she handed the utensil to Avigail. "Neither. We grew them in Malcolm Finn's greenhouse."

"Oh." Avigail stared at the fork, confused as to what she should do with it. "How do you know when they're done? Everything I've eaten before just needed to be heated up."

"Actually," Umbriel stood on the tips of her toes to reach a plate from a cupboard high above, "they're already done. But if you want to take them to Nicholai," she grabbed the pan's handle and tilted it, sliding the contents onto the plate and handing them to Avigail, "he should probably eat something."

Avigail held the plate, watching the steam of the hot potatoes waft upward and disappear into the air. She glanced at Umbriel with a perplexed look. "You called me in here just to bring him a plate of food?" she asked.

Umbriel smiled. "You looked like you needed an escape from that conversation."

Avigail blinked. Were her feelings that transparent? She remained skeptical, but Umbriel's unbridled sense of security helped her to feel less outlandish. Even still, she couldn't abandon the notion that the Earth Mother existed as some sort of competition for Nicholai's affection. "Thank you," she uttered with confused discomfort, turning on her heels to bring the food back into the main room.

Nicholai sat in the same position she left him, hunched over and staring diligently at the paper before him. His hands slid up under the brim of his hat and into his hair, bloodshot eyes continuing to re-read the same sentence to try and absorb it. Too consumed by his focus, he didn't even move when Avigail set the plate beside him.

"Nicholai?" Avigail tapped his shoulder when he failed to acknowledge the meal. "Are you hungry?"

The man looked up, staring as if he didn't recognize her, but only for the briefest of moments. He rubbed his face and shook his head, granting her a small smile. "Many thanks, Avigail. I'll get to it in a moment."

She took a step back and waited, but it seemed Nicholai had no intention of eating. At a loss for what to do, Avigail looked around the room, her arms folded in front of her. "Is this what you do when you're not initiating uprisings?" she asked, trying to joke.

Nicholai did not respond. He continued to loom over the document on his desk.

The silence only bred additional awkwardness in the young woman. She glanced at the plate, then back to the Time Father. She was certain she hadn't seen him eat much since they returned from Panagea's center. Avigail thought, for sure, he would be hungry. "Nicholai?"

Moments passed. When the memory of her words finally reached his sleep-deprived brain, Nicholai turned to face her. "I'm sorry—did you say something?"

He looked horrible. Avigail wanted nothing more than to help him. To be whatever he needed to get through the difficult time she supposed he was going through. But as she stared into his absent, fatigued eyes, she found herself at a loss for words.

"Avigail," Umbriel's voice sounded again, a beacon in the storm that was Nicholai's ravaged gaze, "care to join me outside?"

The young woman hesitated, looking over her shoulder at the Earth Mother. "Um ..." By the time she returned her focus to Nicholai, he was back to staring at his parchment. "Sure."

Umbriel waited for Avigail to exit first, closing the door behind her. The two ventured beyond the house at a slow pace, sauntering closer to the heart of the town. The liveliness of other citizens greeted them as they strolled. Umbriel issued a polite 'hello' to anyone who extended their attention to her. The residents of Nenada knew her well and came to look favorably upon the kind-hearted woman.

Avigail appeared less at ease than Umbriel. She kept a sharp eye out for anyone who seemed distrustful and held close to her limited belongings. Though Nenada did not boast a high crime rate, Umbriel suspected her actions were ingrained from living in less desirable places.

"I understand you have some feelings for Nicholai," Umbriel said, her words coming on rather sporadically. "They're perfectly natural for a woman of your age. I just wanted you to know that he's in a difficult emotional state right now. While it's great to show him kindness, I must ask that you do not apply any additional pressure on him in any form. He would never admit it, but his mind is fragile, and if he cannot maintain his resolve, it will put him in a dangerous position."

Avigail stopped walking. Umbriel's words shook her to the core. She did not know what to feel more—surprise that she knew, disbelief at her candor, embarrassment, or anger. With a ball of mixed emotions flooding her, Avigail settled on lashing out, as it was one of the only reactions she experienced in her life of solitude. "You just want me to back off," she accused, "I *knew* you two had something going on."

In the face of Avigail's anger, Umbriel stood calm and collected. "We do not," she admitted, stopping to gaze out at the hustle and bustle of Nenada's people. "I hate to be the one to tell you this, Avigail, but Nicholai's heart already belongs to another woman. A ghost long dead, I'm afraid. Miss Lilac Finn."

Avigail bristled. Her adrenaline told her to react violently again, but despite her upbringing, she was not an uncompassionate person. Still, the fists she clenched at her sides were slow to unfurl. "He had a lover? How ... how long has she been ...?"

"About a year now," Umbriel informed.

Avigail's eyes fell to the cobblestone streets beneath her. "I see."

"My intent is not to crush your feelings," Umbriel added, waiting until the noise of a passing steam car faded before she finished, "I only wanted to let you know that it's very unlikely he'll return your feelings." The Earth Mother failed to mention the glaring age difference or the fact that Avigail was a daughter to one of Nicholai's comrades. She did not need to destroy the young woman's hopes any further. She only wished to ease Nicholai from the burden of Avigail's constant advances.

It took time to absorb the news. Avigail shoved her mortification to the back of her mind, repressing it, as she'd learned to do with many things. "Did she die during the revolution?" she asked softly.

"No." Umbriel inhaled and let out a placid sigh. "A desperate man thought he could bend Nicholai's will and save his daughter with force. I suppose he did save her life, in the long run, but ... it cost Lilac hers."

"Oh." Avigail pinched her lips together, allowing a short-lived feeling of pity to consume her. It was quickly replaced by a concerned curiosity. "Did ... anybody you know die in the revolution? I mean ... I know a lot of people did, but ... anybody in Captain Hidataka's crew?"

Umbriel scanned Avigail's face. She knew her question stemmed more from a buried worry for her father's well-being. Revi had only just reunited with the fiery young woman, and though she harbored obvious signs of resentment, the Earth Mother detected a shred of love for the man who abandoned her. "Yes," she confessed, apprehensive to deliver the message, but unable to deny Avigail the truth. "Iani Platts. He was a dear friend and a brave man."

Avigail winced at the news. "I'm ... sorry to hear that."

Though the woman fell quiet, Umbriel detected that she held another uncomfortable question inside her. She waited, not wanting to force Avigail to sort through her feelings any quicker than necessary.

"Umbriel ..." Avigail lifted her eyes to find the Earth Mother's. "Did Revi ever ... get hurt? Doing what he does?"

Her anguish was present, though she tried to cover it with a veil of disregard. Umbriel saw through her. "Revi is a very capable fighter. I'm sure he'll return from Northwestern just as he has returned from every other hazardous occurrence he's participated in."

Avigail nodded. It was all she could do.

"Your father made some mistakes, Avigail." Umbriel's silver hair wafted around her as she stood. "You have every right to feel as you do. But good people make mistakes all the time. I have no doubt he'd be as good a father as he is a fighter if you gave him a second chance."

A small thread of hurt sliced through her and Avigail frowned. Discussing it opened the wounds and made them feel fresh again. "You have to say that," she muttered, "because he's your friend."

"No," Umbriel corrected her, smiling. "It's because he's my friend, that I know it's the truth."

Avigail hitched a shoulder and turned away. She wondered what he was doing at this exact moment. Umbriel followed her pondering gaze outward into the crowd.

The poor, unknowing people. Nicholai had yet to make the formal announcement to Southeastern about the lesser gods returning. He wanted to wait until after tonight, to see if he'd have good news to follow the initial terror his statement would likely bring. Umbriel shook her head. To distract herself from thoughts of lesser gods, she said, "Revi reminds me a lot of my father, you know."

Avigail arched a brow and peered at Umbriel from the corners of her eyes. "Yeah? How so?"

The Earth Mother smiled at the memories. "He was also a good man who made mistakes." The primary of which was taking Naphine for a lover. "But he showed me many things. What sticks with me most is how he taught me of the beauty that existed in living a perfectly imperfect life."

"Your life seems pretty perfect to me," Avigail murmured. Though disdain existed in her tone at the beginning of her sentence, it fell away shortly after. Umbriel was not her favorite person, but she felt undeniably at ease in the Earth Mother's presence. It was a rare feeling. "That's nice though. I wish my dad had taught me more things."

Umbriel's initial reaction was to reach over and lend a comforting hand, but she sensed Avigail's standoffishness and chose to respect it. With her hands moving behind her back, she looked up to the sky, watching the steam swirl with the colored smoke produced from burning coal. "I have no doubts he'll try, Avigail. No doubts at all."

* * *

Revi launched the heel of his boot into the torched remnants of the furniture that blocked him. The fragile material gave way under the force and crumbled. He gripped the smaller pieces, and hurling them out of his way, he crawled over the rubbish and ash to peer inside the incinerated room. His movements were quick and purposeful; though he felt he owed a debt to Kazuaki for everything he'd done, he wished to return to Avigail without delay.

"If Vadim's here somewhere," Revi muttered, gazing around the black floor, "there isn't much left of him."

"Keep looking." Kazuaki lifted a fallen beam to sift through the soot beneath it. "I couldn't care less if we find the body. We just need the Chronometer."

"Beg my plain speakin', Captain," Brack said as he blew a collection of dust into a black cloud and coughed. The man continued his fit, struggling to regain his breath. For a moment, his hands lingered near his pockets as he debated seizing his oxygen syringe, but after a few deep breaths, he found air again. With a squeeze on his voice, he finished, "if the fire was hot enough to melt his body, wouldn't his pocket watch be gone to shit as well?"

Kal, unafraid to get his fingers dirty despite his diplomatic appearance, looked up from a pile of burnt remnants he sorted through on the floor. "I suspect if it was already broken, time in Northwestern would be frozen."

"Maybe," Kazuaki muttered. "Maybe not." He pushed himself away from the task at hand. "We should send a letter to Nico. If time stops here with us in it, we need to send word so he can free us if worse comes to worst."

"Sound thinking, Captain," Kal dusted himself off, though it was of little use. His hands were far too covered in soot, and the action only served to dirty his attire more. "The only problem is any paper and pen within our reaches has long since burned to the ground. Not to mention, the nearest post—"

"Belay that," Kazuaki muttered, ripping a piece of his clothing off with his teeth. He clutched the makeshift parchment and, reaching down, grabbed an iron fire poker that survived the blaze. After dipping it in the available soot surrounding him, he scrawled a short message onto the cloth, the black ash a stark contrast to the pale color of the linen. "You seem to know Vadim's home town well," Kazuaki said, glancing at the ambassador. "Where's the nearest post?"

"Captain," Bermuda's hushed voice sliced through the tension as she shuffled up to him. "Set of eyes at 3 o'clock."

Without moving his head, Kazuaki utilized his limited peripheral vision to spy the onlooker from his or her place behind the skeleton of a charred building. Small frame, covered in filth, no visible weapons. He deemed their spy to be of little threat. "Ignore it for now," he replied. "We'll deal with it if need be."

"I really think we should be heading toward the fire," Rennington interjected, an anxiousness in his character. Every once in awhile, echoes of far off screams were carried on the wind. They gutted his ears. "I know we need to find Vadim, but ... shouldn't we look for survivors until recruits arrive?"

Kazuaki squared his shoulders, finding only small shreds of sense in Rennington's request. He did not share the soldier's dutiful concerns toward the peoples' well-being, but they needed someone to tell them where Vadim may have gone. As a last resort, before they hurled themselves into another perilous situation, he turned. "You," Kazuaki thrust a finger toward Mimir, "you're of a supernatural sort. Use your godly perceptions to tell us where Vadim is."

Mimir, scratching singed chunks of material with his fingernails, looked toward Kazuaki. "Hm? I don't know. I'm a lesser god, Captain, not a fortune teller."

Kazuaki's face fell flat. "That didn't stop you from knowing Northwestern was in a bad state back at Panagea's center."

Mimir chuckled, twisting his head so it hung in an inhuman state on his shoulders. "It didn't, did it?"

The captain glowered, unimpressed with the lesser god's attitude.

Jernal, silent in his prisoner-like state, dared to take a step forward. "Come on, Mimir. Let's just get this over with. If you know where Vadim is, spit it out," he urged.

The creature straightened, clapping his hands together once. "Now, now, Commander ... where's the fun in that?" he asked with a wide, mocking grin. "But truly. I do not know."

Granite's dog clawed at a patch of the debris before it lifted its head, its ears swinging forward on its skull. It stared in the direction Bermuda had indicated earlier. Taking a few quick sniffs, the beast trotted over to the stranger who watched from the shadows, stopping several feet away to investigate further with its nose.

"Beast," Granite, aware of the creature's location at all times, effortlessly pushed his way through a crowded room of burnt belongings and climbed into the open road. "Leave it."

The dog's tail wagged, undeterred from its curiosity.

"Go away," a hushed voice pleaded from behind the wreckage. "Scoot! Scoot on!"

The dog continued to stare, tongue lolling out the side of his maw. When the voice addressed him, his tail swayed faster, until his entire rear shifted from side to side with excitement.

"I said leave it, beast." Granite joined the dog at its side, unable to stop himself from glancing at the cowering child who attempted to hide from them earlier. "He doesn't bite," Granite informed, scooping down to pick the dog up. "Kids, anyway."

The child, no more than thirteen or fourteen years of age, peered up at the towering man from beneath her disheveled hair. She reeked of smoke, with holes eaten in some of her clothing to match the burns on her arms and hands. She tried not to breathe, too gripped by terror to react.

The beast wriggled in Granite's hands, begging with various whines to be returned to the floor. "Settle," Granite ordered, trying to hold on to the writhing animal without dropping it. When he realized the mutt's desire to get down was greater than his desire to fight with it, he grunted and lowered the canine back to the earth. "Fine. But you still have to leave it," he muttered to the mongrel.

Several quick strides later, Rennington joined Granite. He stooped to a knee to lower himself to the frightened girl's level. He assessed her with efficiency, though it was difficult to see her injuries through the layer of ash that clung to her skin. "Hello, love," he said in his gentlest tone. "Can I get you some cream for any of those burns?"

The girl withdrew farther into her cramped space, but her eyes never ventured far from the dog. With patience, the two men waited, until the wave of her shock succumbed to her need to receive assistance. "Th ... that would b-be most kind of you," she said, her words wavering and unsure.

Rennington held out a hand, an offering to remove her from her hellish environment. After a brief hesitation, she accepted his offer, and he pulled her into the opening. He opened his pack, rifling through it to find medical supplies. "You're a brave sort," he said while busying himself with his task. "What's your name, kid?"

The girl watched, sending cautiously fleeting glances to the other eight individuals who stood at a distance from Granite and Rennington. Her eyes lingered on Mimir, gripped by his unnatural appearance, before she tore her attention away from him and cleared her throat. "Hattie," she whispered, trying and failing to speak with more confidence.

"Well, Hattie," Rennington removed a clean cloth, and sprayed it down with an antiseptic liquid before he gently grabbed her arm, "the beast seems to have taken a shine to you. This might sting a bit."

Hattie winced as the cold cloth pressed down on her skin. She tried not to pull away, old enough to know medical assistance was a necessity in her current state. "I've never seen a dog before," she uttered, sounding on the verge of tears.

As if it sensed her agony, the dog padded over and licked her other hand. Hattie flinched. The beast licked more fervently, removing patches of soot in the shape of his tongue, revealing the girl's skin beneath. After several moments of his affection, she looked up at Granite. "He's friendly," she noted, less fear in her tone.

Granite stared down at her, his face giving away nothing. "Very," he replied.

When Rennington finished cleaning the wounds he identified through the grime, he returned his remaining supplies to his pack. "You got family around these parts, Miss Hattie?"

The girl swallowed. The beast continued to lick her hand. "I don't know if I do anymore," she admitted.

Jernal watched Rennington from his place near the others. His eyes narrowed, trying to make sense of the deserter's empathy. His memories of Rennington were all tied to his life as a soldier. His and his brother's desertion of the Southern military. It struck him as odd, to witness acts of kindness from a man he labeled a sinner.

"Look, Hattie, here's the thing," Rennington leaned forward as he pressed his palms into his knees, "I can't imagine witnessing the things you saw take place here. And it's killing me to ask you to relive the nightmares of what you saw, but ... do you think you'd be able to help us out with something?"

She stared into his eyes, taking a step forward into the beast. A shaking hand rose to rest on top of the animal's head, finding some solace in the softness of his fur. "I'll try my best," she squeaked.

A comforting smile claimed half of Rennington's face. "There's a fighter, right there. Can I ask, do you know how this happened?"

Hattie turned toward the beast, stroking his head. His beady eyes gazed up at her, black and welcoming, with a content tongue panting out the side of his jaw. "Mr. Canmore ordered the city to be cleansed, to pave way for new industry. New money," she explained, focusing on the dog to keep her voice from breaking. "I lived here," she expounded, gesturing with a shrug to the surrounding rubble in which she hid. "My parents always bragged about how close our residence was to the Time Father. They said it was the safest place to be in all of Northwestern."

Kal's brows knit together. He broke away from the larger crowd, calm as he approached Rennington, Granite, and Hattie. "You said Vadim did this?" he asked, needing clarification against her claims.

Hattie looked up, tensing at Kal's sudden approach. She threw her arms around the dog and pressed her body into his. "Y-yes, he did, I-I'd know him anywhere, I, I saw him almost every day because—"

Seeing his emergence ignited a terror in the girl, Kal stopped in his tracks and held up his hands. "Please, young lady, I mean you no harm. I extend my deepest apologies for frightening you. I just ... Vadim Canmore has never displayed such aggressive tendencies, and he's ruled Northwestern for nearly thirty years. Statistically speaking, your claim—"

"—is believable," Kazuaki interrupted. "Particularly if Mimir's claims are truthful, that lesser gods have invaded Northwestern."

Glowing eyes peered at Kazuaki, alight with pride and mischievousness. "I've always admired your perceptiveness, Captain."

Kazuaki scoffed and rolled his eye.

"Lesser gods?" Hattie swallowed the fear in her throat. She knew nothing of gods, but the hate in the captain's voice when he spoke of them invited an unforgiving picture in her brain. "Can ... can they make people go mad?" she queried, sinking further into the comfort of the beast's neck.

"That's about all they do," Kazuaki muttered, glaring at Mimir.

Hattie's fingertips curled into the mutt's fur. He sat, allowing her anxiety to spill into him. Several tears escaped her eyes and slid down her cheeks. She sniffed, wiping her wet face off in the animal's shoulder. "My mother went mad. She raved about wanting us dead. That only death would spare us from the hell the future promised. My father tried to stop her ... but she already choked my little brother before he realized what was happening."

Hattie turned to keep her voice from muffling, but she still hugged the mongrel tightly. "There were footmen everywhere. Some were keen to follow Vadim's orders ... to cleanse ... other footmen tried to stop him. Like they knew he was wrong. Some stood in the fire and willingly burned. Others ran. There was so much confusion." Her eyes began to well up again, her bottom lip quivering. "I … I ran. But no matter how far I ran, the smell of burning bodies followed me. I came back when I saw the flames moved on, but …"

Seeing the pain in her eyes at reliving the memory, Rennington decided to end it. "That's all well and good, Miss Hattie. You've been a big help. Thank you."

The girl nodded, sniffling once more. The dog flopped its neck back to lick the tears and discharge from her nose.

"So Vadim lives," Bermuda announced, pushing her hair out of her eyes. "At least, he was alive when this happened."

"We still need to get to a post." Kal looked to his comrades, then down at the cloth Kazuaki gripped in his fist. "If Vadim is a victim to the same mental turmoil that plagues the citizens of Panagea, he could do even more damage than he already has. Northwestern will need reinforcements to find him and contain his wrath."

That and Kazuaki surmised Nicholai was probably having a panic attack waiting for a response on their position. "Right. Granite, Penn, Kal … board the airship and take the girl to whatever town isn't drowning in flames. Find a post. Mail this," he ordered, grabbing Kal's hand and forcing the cloth into the man's palm.

Penn bristled. "None of us are familiar with piloting the airship, Cap—"

"You single-handedly guided the sea ship from the Southern coast to Brechita," Kazuaki reminded him. "You can do this, too."

The cook hitched a shoulder. "If you say so," he murmured. "Just don't be sore if something breaks off during landing." He turned his back to return to the airship, followed by Kal.

Hattie looked up at Rennington, still holding strong to the mutt. "The flames are heading east. The others fled to towns westward. You might find a post there."

The soldier nodded and tried to flash an uplifting smile. "Thank you for all your help, Miss Hattie. Where is the safest place we can take you?

With a small shrug, the girl shook her head. "I don't know."

"I'm sure these guys will figure something out," Rennington whispered, thumbing toward Granite, Penn, and Kal. "You didn't hear it from me, but Granite's a softy. Penn has heaps of knowledge on making do with little. And Kal's an ambassador," he said, rubbing his thumb and fingers together. "The man's packing the bank of the entire Southern division in his hands. I'm sure he'll set you up good and proper."

Hattie tried to smile, but the moment passed swiftly. "Can he come with me?" she asked, looking at the dog.

Rennington looked up at Granite.

The giant man nodded. "He goes where I go," he murmured. "If you're coming with me, so is he."

Weak legs straightened as Hattie looked to the others. She took several steps toward the airship, following the beast's guidance, before she turned around. "Follow the flames," she instructed, wiping a final set of tears from her streaked cheeks. "Mr. Canmore went with the fire."

Kazuaki nodded to the girl. She followed after Penn, Kal, Granite, and the mutt as they approached the airship. The captain waited until they were out of earshot before he looked to what remained of his crew. Revi, Bermuda, Rennington, and Brack perked up, awaiting his instruction.

Jernal withdrew, still unwilling to take orders from the man that once tried to kill him.

Mimir stared after the fire in the distance, an aloof look on his face.

"Right." Kazuaki dug his heels into the black earth and spun. He watched the smoke attack the sky in the distance. The scent of burning bodies that Hattie spoke of earlier assaulted his sense of smell. No doubt countless corpses awaited in the ash, but there was only one body at the forefront of his thoughts. Follow the flames. That's what the girl said. "Let's go find Vadim."

CHAPTER FOURTEEN

"Which lesser god did you decide to summon first?" Nicholai walked. As the branches overhead tried to knock his hat off his head, he tucked it under his arm.

"I thought it best if we start with Dimjir." Umbriel's lithe body slipped into the shadows of darkness provided by nightfall. "We will gain no greater sympathy than from the God of Mercy, himself."

Nicholai nodded. They continued to trudge deeper into the newly grown forest, amazing in its expanse for how young it was. His boots sank into the soft soil beneath him as he stopped. He moved to rest his hands on a moss-covered steam car, abandoned earlier due to mechanical failure and reclaimed by the liveliness of nature. The metal was almost fully engulfed by wilderness, integrating the steel, copper, and brass components with the neutral tones of the woods.

Umbriel stopped, sensing his halt. She turned to him, taking several alarmed steps toward him. "Nicholai? Are you all right?"

He hadn't eaten. He hadn't slept. Failure to accomplish anything resembling productivity plagued him. Nicholai rubbed at his eyes with his thumb and middle finger, trying to banish the growing migraine in his brain. "Yes," he said, attempting to sound reassuring. "I'm just ... worried. About Kazuaki. And the others. I can't believe Nordjan contracted Jernal to free Mimir from his well."

It was one of many things that bothered the Time Father as of late. Kazuaki's fate, and Nordjan's hand in it. The strange looks shared between the Northern Time Father and Edvard. The whispers ... the horrid thoughts that tried to dominate his mind. The fear of the lesser gods returning. The suicides. The murders. The awkwardness of warding off Avigail's advances. Maintaining his division. Warding off the continued assassination attempts, the unflattering mail, the guilt that remained because of Darjal's death, figuring out how to live a life absent of Lilac.

The weight of everything piled on the man's shoulders. The burden was heavy. He opened tired eyes to find Umbriel's apprehensive stare looking back at him. Nicholai urged a compulsory smile to appear. "I'm sure he's been in worse situations before," he added. "I just ..."

"I care about him, too," Umbriel said, her hair almost aglow in the light of the overhead moon. "Trust that he'll be okay, Nicholai. He has hundreds of years of experience at his disposal, not to mention Bermuda, Revi, Brack—so many companions to keep watch over him."

"Yes." Nicholai coughed into his hand and slicked his hair back, attempting to wake himself up. He needed to remind himself there was no sense in worrying about an immortal man.

Far from the eyes of Nenada's citizens, he drew in a deep breath. "So ... Dimjir ..." He looked to Umbriel and grinned. "Let's get this soiree started, shall we?"

She tried to return his smile, but it faded as soon as it appeared. "I must warn you, Nicholai, if we *can* get Dimjir to appear ... he might look rather haggard. The lesser gods wither in the absence of prayer. I have no clue how long he must have disintegrated before now."

Nicholai's eyelids felt heavy. Her words seemed far away, but he tried to dig his claws into the situation and hold on. "I see. So he may not even answer our prayer?"

"Perhaps not." Umbriel lifted her head to the indigo sky above. The stars were all but blocked out from years' worth of pollution and smog, but she tried to imagine they were there. "I just want you to brace yourself. He may look like death incarnate."

Nicholai nodded. "Of course. If there's anything I can do to help ..."

"Just focus," she said, but soon realized, by the state of him, that her request was asking a lot. "And pray for mercy."

A short, disparaging chuckle escaped him. "That shouldn't be too hard."

Umbriel flashed a sympathetic smile and closed her eyes, dipping her chin to her chest. She poured all her concentration into her plea to Dimjir, hoping he surfaced with the same ease her mother did. But no guarantees existed in the ways of lesser gods. It was much easier to summon Naphine; the blood they shared strengthened the urgency of Umbriel's requests. With Dimjir, she hoped the sheer desperation behind her prayer would be enough to beckon him.

"Dimjir, God of Mercy, please hear our prayer. We request your presence."

Nicholai tried to focus, but his efforts wavered with crippling fatigue. The only sound that accompanied them after Umbriel's request was the occasional trill of a night bird and the howling of an unsettling wind through the leaves.

Minutes ticked by. Dimjir did not appear.

Umbriel sighed. She licked her lips and focused harder, lining her thoughts with candid resolve. "Dimjir, God of Mercy, we strongly wish for your presence with unmatched urgency. Please, appear before us."

Her efforts gained more of nothing.

The two stood, silent in the woodlands. The towering trunks of black trees reached up and all around them. An occasional leaf fell from the branches above, twisting in the air until it settled at their feet near all its fallen brethren.

"Dimjir," Umbriel tried a third time, her voice coated with more anguish than it held previously, "I beg you."

"Is it possible," Nicholai asked, opening one of his eyes to steal a glimpse of the Earth Mother, "that he is too weak to surface?"

Umbriel sighed a second time. "It is possible ... though I had hoped our prayer would give him enough energy to at least appear this once."

Nicholai swallowed. He did not wish to tell the people of Southeastern about the threat of the lesser gods without having a ring of hope to back his statement up with. "Are there no other lesser gods we could pray to?" he asked.

Before she answered him, a rustling sounded to their right. The pair turned, gazing at the godly figure who appeared out of nowhere, who exuded omnipotence even in the darkness of night. Dimjir pressed his staff into the ground, a masculine picture of health. Curled locks flowed to his shoulders, his bronzed skin wrapped over well-toned arms and legs. He looked nothing like the frail, weakened picture the Time Father or Earth Mother concocted in their heads.

"I extend many apologies at my delay," Dimjir said, bowing to them both. "I have been ... very busy."

Though Nicholai knew the purpose behind their nightly escapade, instinct made him withdraw at Dimjir's sudden presence. His metal fingers gripped into a fist, prepped by a predisposition to strike a defensive pose, but he loosened the digits when he realized their prayer was a success.

"Dimjir," Umbriel stepped forward to greet him. "You seem well." She scanned his body, perplexed by his condition. "Quite well, in fact."

"Yes." He glanced down at his body as if it surprised him, too, before he returned his eyes to Umbriel. "I am well sustained. People pray to me frequently as of late, whether they realize it or not. Unfortunately, there are many begging for mercy these days ..." His voice faded away as his eyes fell, filling with empathy. "Daughter of Naphine ... I did not expect to hear a plea from you."

Nicholai glanced at Umbriel after Dimjir gave her mother a name, then returned his attention to the God of Mercy. "Thank you for coming."

Dimjir issued a nod to Nicholai but was quick to redirect his concentration back to Umbriel. "What can I do for you, Earth

Mother? I only ask that you make it quick. Many remain who still cry for me."

His confession pained her. It only cemented her worst fears: the gods had been ravaging people in places far from their eyes. "I'm afraid your workload is a direct result of why we summoned you here, Dimjir. Word on the wind is the lesser gods have invaded Northwestern with vengeance in mind. Can you not talk sense into them, tell them that the men and women of today are not the same people who shunned them years ago?"

Dimjir's expression told her all she needed to know. It was not the answer she sought.

Nicholai recognized the look. He forced himself off the steam car that he had leaned on for support. "Dimjir, please—I know without the prayer of the dead and the dying to sustain you, you will undoubtedly fall to the wayside once more, but—"

"Mankind's suffering is not my end goal, Time Father." Dimjir frowned, appearing insulted by Nicholai's assumption. "I, myself, have begged for mercy from the lesser gods seeking revenge. I adore mankind's prayers, yes, but clemency flows through my veins more than greed."

Nicholai tightened his jaw, feeling a rising sense of shame. "Of course. I didn't mean to imply otherwise. I'm sorry, but my heart bleeds for these people."

Dimjir nodded as an act of forgiveness. "I understand. Unfortunately, it seems the only mercy found in this world right now is from me ... and mankind already has mine in droves. They have my pity, as well, for all the damage the vengeful lesser gods have caused."

Nicholai felt his stomach sink. Dimjir verified his already high concerns about the state of Northwestern.

The God of Mercy recognized his disparaging look. He drew his shoulders back. "Please, have some hope. It is not all of the lesser gods who harbor a hatred for humanity. While we are all wounded for how people have mistreated not only us but Panagea, only a small handful have enacted a violent endeavor."

Umbriel's brows knit together. "Who among them, Dimjir?"

The lesser god turned to face her. "The God of War. He thirsts for such things. The God of Revenge, as clearly, it's in his blood. The God of Metal ... it is rumored something precious to him was recently stolen by a group of men, renewing his disdain. The God of the Underworld, who craves more spirits to fill his residence. Goddess Havidite, who is spurned by the destruction of the land. The Goddess of Animals, and the Goddess of Water, they share Havidite's rage at the mistreatment of Panagea. And ..." He paused, hesitant to tell her. "And the Goddess of Love, I'm afraid."

Naphine. Umbriel had her speculations, based on their last encounter, but she had hoped her mother would have a change of heart. "I see ..." she whispered, curling her fingernails into her palms.

Dimjir wilted at her reaction, knowing his message caused her grief. "For all those who are vengeful, Umbriel, there are just as many who forgive humans for their treacherous behavior. And even more who remain too weak to choose sides."

Nicholai raised his gaze from the floor and found the God of Mercy. "How is it some of these gods have regained their strength? I struggle to believe any man in Panagea would pray for war. We only just ended one."

The being gave a sympathetic face. "It is the stronger lesser gods and goddesses, I'm afraid. Havidite and Pymlena have grown in power with the resurrection of man's interest in crops. The Goddesses of Harvest and Water became resilient enough to influence others to pray to those they thought would share their cause."

Nicholai listened, rubbing his chin as he attempted to form a solution in his head. When none came, he sought Dimjir's advice. "Is there anything we can do?"

The God of Mercy gripped his staff. "Hold fast to sanity. The others and I are doing what we can. We outnumber them for now, but they try to grow their army more by the day, and, sadly, those of us who do not condemn mankind ... we're no match for their wrath. They not only have the omnipotent weaponry necessary to end our lives, but the skills to do it as well." Dimjir sighed, casting his eyes downward. "Those who sympathize with mankind are not warriors. We are beings of peace. We know they would sooner massacre us than let us stand in their way."

Umbriel nodded. "Of course, Dimjir. We understand. We do not want any of you to put your existence at risk."

The God of Mercy lifted his staff. He pointed it at Nicholai, making sure to find the mortal's tired, wavering gaze. "You, Time Father. You must be the most cautious of all. They are after the division leaders. They know men and women exist who are too mentally and emotionally sound to relent to their trickery. They believe if they cannot manipulate them through intrusive thoughts, they can influence those who have power over them. One way or another," he paused, returning the end of his staff to the earth, "they will not stop until they decide humanity has suffered enough."

Umbriel peered at Nicholai. He looked lost in the night, staring ahead at Dimjir as if he still tried to absorb the impact of his message. The man had endured many psychological pressures as of late. Umbriel bit her bottom lip. She hoped his wherewithal was more powerful than the unrelenting attacks that awaited him.

Dimjir brought a hand to his temple, frowning as he closed his eyes. "I must go," he informed. "The screams ... they grow louder with each passing second."

"I know the feeling," Nicholai muttered under his breath. "Thank you for everything, Dimjir. Gods-speed."

The God of Mercy extended a nod to both Time Father and Earth Mother, and with the wind and the blink of an eye, he was gone.

Abandoned to the darkness once more, the pair stood. Umbriel found Nicholai's face. Riddled with calm acceptance, she hoped the man took Dimjir's warnings seriously. "Are you going to be all right?" she asked, rare desperation in her tone.

With his boots planted firmly on the ground, he stared at a nearby rock. He heard them, now. The hushed calls. The articulated chatter. The corrupt malevolence, the depraved way feelings of acrimony slithered through each neuron in his brain tissue. The soft, inclement touch of loathing as imagined hands stroked his cranial nerves, beckoning him to relax. To sleep. To let them take over so that he might revel in sweet, sweet rest.

Nicholai closed his eyes. With his last thread of volition, he swept them away. "I'll be all right," he reassured her for what felt like the hundredth time. Without opening his lids, he felt her apprehension. The Time Father summoned an artificial smirk, hoping it would soothe her. "I promise."

His words were empty. He tried to fill them with meaning, but he had little of himself left in the shell that was his body. Umbriel drew her shoulders back. She needed to act soon. To help him. To save him.

If only she knew how ...

CHAPTER FIFTEEN

Bermuda grunted against the weight of the body in her arms. As Rennington lifted the pillar that once pinned it to the ground, the woman dragged the unidentifiable person from their prison. Cleared from the wreckage, she put a finger to the individual's neck, not harboring much hope, given the number of deep burns infecting the victim's tissue.

No pulse. Dead, as she suspected. It seemed the charred land beneath the pillar was not only the person's prison but their final resting place.

"Another gone," she called out as Rennington set the fragile pillar back on the ground.

The team had swept across Vadim's hometown of Striburn for what felt like an eternity. Fatigue bit at their bones into the tenth hour of hauling corpses from the burn barrel that was the city. They followed the flames, as instructed by Hattie. The fire was not far ahead of them, and though they were anxious to arrive at the forefront, they stopped for any visible bodies located along the way. Though they had dragged dozens from various scorched structures, there were no survivors.

"We're wasting time," Revi growled, consumed by an eagerness to return to Southeastern. "Assuming they weren't crushed or burned to death, the smoke inhalation alone would be enough to kill anyone we're going to drag from these pits."

"Come on, Rev," Brack bent down to lift a large piece of rubble off a set of unmoving legs. As he leaned in to press his soot-covered fingertips against the fallen person's neck, he added, "where's your sense of compassion?"

Revi glowered at Brack, unamused.

The Rabbit witnessed his disdain and laughed. "Too right, mate, I forgot you hadn't any to start with!"

"It's protocol," Rennington muttered, analyzing his surroundings to try and locate more bodies. "Soldier's duty."

Revi scowled. "Since when? Imagined duties aside, you're the only soldier here, Rennington."

"Nah, mate." Rennington dusted his hands off when he was satisfied that the area he patrolled held no potential life forms, as the only corpses he found were already rendered to bone fragments. "There's Jernal," he said, gesturing toward the Northern footman.

The commander blinked, surprised by Rennington's admission. He did not know what to say, having expected much more animosity from the man he had once tried to imprison. " ...He's right," he finally said, clearing his throat. "Service before self, we stand— "

"—even in the shadowed land," Rennington finished. The motto of the Southern soldiers had been embedded in his head since he and Iani were boys.

Jernal stared, both tense and staggered. He lifted his chin, suspicious eyes on Rennington, but the cold, brown irises softened after several moments passed. "That's right," he said, lowering his arms to his sides.

"If you two are done kissing one another's asses over the mutual selling of your souls to the governments," Revi muttered, readjusting the pack of supplies over his shoulder, "we're almost to the flames. Let's get a move on."

Kazuaki listened to his crew bicker with little concern. They had saved no lives. Revi was right; their time here had been nothing more than wasteful. Before he opened his mouth to force the group onward, the sound of the airship's propellers filled his eardrums.

Bermuda lifted her hand to her eyes to shield her vision as she watched it approach. "Brace yourselves," she uttered, taking a step back. "If Kazuaki can barely land that thing ..."

Penn found fortune that the others were too far away to see the look of absolute terror on his otherwise cynical face. His knuckles turned white from the intensity in which he gripped the wheel, his slender arms quaking as he tried his best to hold it in place. The wheels spewed out from the bottom at just the right time, the giant ship rattling the earth as it struck the uneven terrain.

Like thunder beneath their legs, the giant ship crawled forward. It sliced through the fallen debris of Northwestern with little effect, tossing chunks of charred remnants out of its path. Kazuaki watched, absent of emotion as the tip of the airship collided with the skeleton of an unstable building. What managed to survive the fire soon collapsed, falling to the ground.

The crew stood, unmoving, waiting for the dust to settle. They heard the ramp lower through the cloud of disturbed ash and Penn emerged, waving his hand wildly to fan the powder out of his face. Granite, Kal, and the mutt were quick to follow.

"Nice and hard, just the way I like it!" Brack shouted, knowing full well Penn harbored insecurity about the unevenness of his landing.

The cook's brows fell flat on his face as he wrinkled his nose. "Feck off, Rabbit. Like you could do any better."

Brack's uproarious laughter was a stark contrast to the dismal surroundings of burnt bodies and buildings. Kazuaki eyed the filth attached to his airship's nose before looking over the rest of the vessel's body. The condition met his standards. He turned to Penn. "What of the girl?" he asked, voice rough.

"Bart's wife set her up with some money and a place to stay," Penn muttered, thumbing toward Kal. "Said he'd find a foster family for her when he returned to Southern."

Kal shot daggers at Penn for his less than diplomatic description, but the chivalrous man chose not to comment on it. "How have things been here, Captain?"

"Slow." Kazuaki turned to face the fire. The occasional ember floated near them on the smoke-scented wind. "We're bypassing the debris now and heading straight to the source. We need to find Vadim."

Kal nodded, rolling up the sleeves on his nicely pressed shirt. "To the ends of the earth and all that, Captain. Let's go find him."

If Kazuaki was surprised by Kal's eagerness, he did not show it. Rennington frowned as Kazuaki started for the fire. "What of the survivors?"

Kazuaki did not turn around. "There are none."

Mimir, who had been slithering in and out of the destruction as if it were a playground, leaped off a beam and landed in a crouched position. He busied himself spying on Kazuaki the entire time, analyzing the immortal's curious behavior at stopping and searching for living people. It was unexpected, but he enjoyed the distraction.

Lifting his face to stare at the flames ahead, a sullen look took over him. Mimir knew what awaited them there, and he was not keen on arriving. But the lesser god could not stop the captain. He did not belong to him. Not yet.

Straightening to a stand, Mimir traced the captain's footsteps. Kazuaki felt his proximity. It irritated him beyond reason. Coupled with the tension emanating from Rennington at having to abandon potential survivors, the immortal walked with a briskness that he hoped would leave his annoyances behind him.

Silence gripped the throats of all who strode closer to the flames. It took the better part of an hour to arrive at the head. Kazuaki's eye narrowed as the heat from the fire attacked his skin. The dull, ethereal glow of chaos melted over his and the others' faces, accentuated only by weak screams rising from engulfed homes and businesses.

Bermuda jerked to the side as a smoldering woman bolted past her, running as fast as her blistered legs could carry her. Embers fell from the sky like burning snowflakes, settling at the feet of those who watched men and women scatter like a colony of ants.

Brack drew his lips back in disgust as a man climbed a smoldering beam, ignorant to the fact that the skin and tissue on his hands sloughed off with each touch.

"To Donius, God of War!" he cried as the flames ate through his muscles and devoured him whole.

"Gods be damned," Kal breathed, tightening his jaw as he witnessed the chaos that reigned around them. "This is madness ..."

Revi slid his pack off his shoulder and removed several oxygen masks, tossing them to Granite, Brack, Bermuda, and Penn. He slid his own on over his face, his voice distorted behind the material as he turned to Rennington. "We didn't anticipate you coming," he admitted. "The only mask we have left is the captain's."

"Take it," Kazuaki muttered, motioning Revi to hand the object off to Rennington. The smoke irritated his lungs and he felt the deprivation of oxygen like any mortal would, but overall, it served as no threat to his existence.

Rennington caught the mask as Revi tossed it to him, but he turned his attention to Kal without delay. "Ambassador," he said, holding the device out to the man, "Bartholomew would never forgive me if I didn't return you unharmed."

Kal hesitated to accept the offer, but he knew the limits of his body. "You're a good man, Rennington." He slipped the mask on over his face before he turned to face the flames once more.

Rennington drew his arm up, shielding his mouth and nose with his sleeve, though it did little to help.

Jernal mirrored him, forced to do the same. His eyes watered from the sting of the smoke. "It's not as if we can just charge in there," the commander said through a short cough. "What's your plan?"

Kazuaki narrowed his eye. He scanned the horizon, searching for the man who followed the flames.

"Captain—" Bermuda lifted a hand, her voice robotic behind the mask.

Kazuaki trailed the direction of her finger, shielding his vision. He saw him. Standing valiantly, encircled by fire but miraculously unharmed. A mountain of papers was gripped in his hands, some singed on the edges after creeping too close to the heat. Vadim.

The Northwestern Time Father halted from his depraved act of watching his people disintegrate around him. With a slow, eerie turn, he pivoted on his heels, his shining eyes locking onto that of the captain. No footmen protected him. No sanity lived in him. He raised his chin and shouted, "Ambassadors! They've been expecting you!" he cried, his voice competing with the roar of the crackling flames.

Kazuaki's expression flattened. He walked through the fire toward Vadim, fists clenched.

Brack arched a brow, holding his mask to his face. "Who?" he wondered out loud. He assumed he knew who he meant, but no lesser gods were in sight.

Though it should have been impossible for Vadim to have heard him over the violent disorder, the Time Father stretched his arms out to the heavens. "The gods are all around us!" he cried, his voice cracking from smoke inhalation.

The captain pushed through the flames, scowling as the temperature threatened to burn holes in his long jacket. Sweat dripped down the sides of his face until they disappeared in his beard. When he neared Vadim, the Time Father lowered his arms. "All hail—"

A swift punch ended his statement. "Snap out of it," Kazuaki growled as he loomed over Vadim's fallen body.

The Time Father propped himself up on his elbows and rubbed his jaw, testing to see if it had been dislocated. It popped when he opened his mouth, but he still sneered up at the immortal. "I'm sure they'll be most excited to see you, Captain."

Kazuaki looked unimpressed. His eye flicked to the Chronometer around Vadim's neck, putting him in mind of his objective. He reached down, grabbed the Time Father's leg, and hauled him without mercy, back toward the others. Though he cared little about the value of Vadim's life, he did not want the pressure of locating a suitable Time Father on short notice, should the current one find himself cremated.

"Show yourselves!" Vadim howled as his back dragged against the heated grounds of his once-proud city.

Kazuaki dropped Vadim's leg when they escaped the intensity of the blaze. Bermuda scanned the captain for any signs of physical distress while Rennington scoured the area for signs of life. His face fell at the sight before him. Unadulterated annihilation. The ravenous hands of the fire left nothing untouched, snuffing out any previously heard screams.

"What do we do with him?" Brack asked, giving Vadim a light kick in the ribs. "He's off his rocker."

"We should get him to safety," Kal suggested, kneeling beside the wild man. "Vadim—find your senses, your people need you!"

Kazuaki stared down at Vadim, an ever-present scowl on his face. He lifted his eye to steal a glimpse of Rennington's dejection. The soldier's heart died in the fire with those people. At first, he surmised this Rennington was far different than the one he remembered. The one who slaughtered footmen who stood in the way of his orders with ease. But when Kazuaki called forth all instances of the Platts brother's morality, he decided, no, he was the same. Rennington mourned the loss of these people much in the same way he lamented the children Darjal once ordered him and his brother to put down. He frowned. "We'll scan once for survivors," he muttered. "Be quick. Ten minutes and not a second more. Then we'll deal with Vadim."

Rennington turned a wide-eyed stare to the captain, his disbelief exposed. "Right," he nodded, feeling invigorated even against the smoke that choked his lungs, "ten minutes."

He turned, but his feet did not venture far. Rennington staggered back, recoiling from the sudden presence of the body that appeared before him. His eyes narrowed as he coughed into his sleeve, sweeping his other arm out instinctively to protect those behind him. "What in the feck are you?" he breathed, hostile.

The majestic woman before him smiled. "I am everything mankind made me to be," Havidite replied, her voice silk against the rage of the surrounding turmoil. Her full, ruby lips slid into a smirk. "I am the harvest. I am the nutrients in the earth. I am the food in your stomachs and the coins in your pockets," she purred, her wings folding behind her. "I am Havidite."

"Everything but humble, it seems," Bermuda hissed, withdrawing her weapon on instinct, though she was certain she stared into the eyes of an untouchable goddess.

"It took longer than I thought it would for you to find Vadim," Havidite said, tilting her head as she stared down at the man. "I've been waiting days in Northwestern to see what mankind's answer to our retaliation would be." Her bottom lip stuck out, mocking them. "I see without the gods' help, it is as pathetic as I expected. You must be the smallest collection of ambassadors I have ever seen."

"Don't know who fed you your information, lady," Brack uttered, looking at the members of the crew, "but the only ambassador here is this guy." He thumbed toward Kal.

A frown scuttled onto the goddess'ss face. "Are you not here to beg for our forgiveness? For the safety of your divisions?"

Kazuaki scowled. "I beg for nothing."

Havidite assessed him, from the patch covering his eye down to his battered boots. "I had hoped to watch you plead for clemency. It is the least you could do after how you've treated us. For how you treated Panagea." She sighed. "No matter. I awaited your arrival for a purpose beyond begging. Return to whoever sent you. Tell them your mission to appease the gods has failed. Warn them of the consequences they will suffer for their actions. The consequences you see here," she said, sweeping her arm out to showcase the destruction. "Leave no detail out. Paint this picture in their minds, down to the very last drop of blood you see on the ground. You will spread my message across all of Panagea," she paused, leaning down to pluck an anemone flower from the earth. She extended the hand that held it, gently gracing the side of Kazuaki's face, "won't you, Mr. Hidataka?"

Many bristled at Havidite's boldness, Bermuda and Kazuaki alike, but none more so than Mimir. He stepped out from behind Granite, glowering at the Goddess of Harvest. "Withdraw your efforts, Havidite," he hissed. "He belongs to me."

"Premature ranting," Kazuaki spat, swatting Havidite's hand away from his face. "Try all you wish, demon. I've hardened myself to the tricks of your kind."

A frown creased Havidite's otherwise perfect face. "A pity." She ripped her attention away from Kazuaki and cast wrathful eyes down to Mimir. "Bite your tongue, you little imp, or I will bite it for you."

Brack couldn't stop a grin from dominating his face. "That's my kinda woman."

"Oh, really?" Havidite's scrutiny toward Mimir fell aside as she laid licentious eyes on the Rabbit. "I have a feeling I could be *all* the woman you needed," she purred, stepping toward him to caress a hungry hand over his chest. "Your own personal goddess ..."

"Rabbit," Kazuaki glared at Brack with a cautionary tone. "Don't. You don't know where it's been."

A full, bottom lip inched out as Havidite pouted. "Does he always talk to you like that?" she asked, sliding her fingers up and around Brack's neck as she pushed the others away, pressing her body against his. "Most improper. I think you need a new leader, love. Someone who would treat you right."

Brack arched a brow. He met her eyes, the hair on his arms standing on end at the silken pressure of her touch. "What if I wanted you to treat me wrong?"

Havidite smirked. She leaned in to whisper into his ear. "In all the right ways ..."

"I ain't gonna lie, darlin'," Brack grinned as the warmth of her breath slithered into his skin. "That *does* sound lovely."

Kal's eyes widened. Jernal appeared to adopt a new alarm as well. The soldier reached for his falchion, prepared, should Havidite turn Brack against them after she invaded his thoughts.

"Doesn't it?" the goddess said slowly, seduction pouring from her like an untamed river. "Abandon yourself to me, and I will introduce you to all you desire."

Jernal positioned himself defensively.

Kal took a step away.

Havidite seemed pleased with herself, matched only by the look of sly pleasure plastered on Brack's face as the goddess slipped his oxygen mask off with her hands.

"Rabbit," Kazuaki said again, more forceful the second time. He did not seem concerned. On the contrary, he looked infected with incurable irritation. "Stifle yourself."

"Shh," Havidite placed a finger on Brack's lips, his mask dangling in her other hand. "Pay no mind to him ... you only have eyes for me, now."

Brack didn't move as she settled her soft skin onto his mouth. But it didn't last long. He pinched his lips together, trying to contain the obvious laughter he held inside his stomach. In moments, the corners of his mouth curved upward, his eyes alight with mischievous devilry as he finally released his long-held amusement. "Gods-damn, lady!" Brack laughed, hysterical as he wiped a tear from his eye. He doubled over, placing his palm on his knee to steady himself from the flood of his pent up delight. "You'd have fecked me right here and now, in front of all these people! You're a naughty goddess, aren't you? Oh, I'd pray to you all right—hell, I'll be chanting your name later tonight at the very least, I'm sure of it!"

Havidite's face twisted into one of initial confusion, followed by disgust. She realized quickly that Brack had taken her for a ride; her expression reflected her poisonous irritation. "You'll have wished later you *did* fall into my favor," she said, voice calm, though her loathing remained present. "You all will. But right now, I have too much of a need for you. Go forth, and spread the word of what you witnessed here today. Tell the Time Fathers. Tell everyone."

The crew stood, braced but silent. Kazuaki made no moves. Though every part of him shouted to reach for his sword, to plunge bullets into her chest, to take some form of action that involved spilling the blood of his enemy ... he knew his efforts would be in vain. It was an uncomfortable feeling. "We will leave when Vadim is lucid," he muttered instead. The captain felt a disdain that his eventual movements mirrored what Havidite seemed to want. Why she wanted trusted division voices to spread the word of the lesser gods' destruction, he did not yet know.

Havidite lifted a single shoulder, tucking her chin into it as a feigned coyness washed through her. "Oh, Captain, try all you wish. Waste your efforts. Men are predictable. Incapable of change. Even if you manage to attach your leeches and draw out his infection, the thoughts he has still weave into his chemical makeup. You can spend hours returning him to his former state, but know it would only take a moment for me to manipulate him again."

"What's your end game?" Bermuda approached, unafraid, knowing full well Havidite could inflict no physical harm. "Your revenge against men is purposeless. How far do you plan to take this?"

Havidite inclined her chin. Her wings stretched behind her, making her appear larger, bolder. "We will take this as far as you took it with us. As far as you took it with Panagea. She is but a husk, now, as you, too, shall become. An eye for an eye. A tooth for a tooth."

"I once heard from a reliable source," Kazuaki started, glaring down at Mimir, "that an eye for an eye leaves the whole world blind." He flicked his attention back to Havidite, apathetic. "Having been born of men's imagination, I am not surprised that your end goal is riddled with flaws that you are sightless to."

Havidite's breasts rose and fell as she let out a dramatic sigh. "Your words fall on omnipotent ears, Captain. Men may have created us, but they were too foolish to know, at the time, the power of their minds. They created something far more than themselves."

"No." Calm, Kazuaki stared at the goddess. "Men created exactly what you would expect them to. Inflated, overestimated versions of themselves. You were birthed from imperfect minds. Man's deficiencies weave through you. That you cannot see it for yourself only proves my point."

The goddess huffed. She lifted her hands, smoothing her perfect hair through her fingers. "You're right about *one* thing, Captain. We were birthed from imperfect minds. But we are far greater than you can even conceive."

"Are you, now?" Kazuaki's low voice rumbled against the still-crackling fires before them. "What will happen, then, when you have consumed the minds of all those who believe in you? When you trick them into throwing themselves on the pyre, or the stake, or the sword when they have run their course of usefulness? What of it, when you have swept through the divisions and killed all of Panagea's people?" He narrowed his eye. "Who will pray to you then?"

Havidite looked unaffected. She only smirked. "You lot may harbor enough conviction to keep yourselves from kneeling, but soon, you will see ... we won't need the weak to pray to us. When you're all that's left, you will *beg* for our favor, as you did countless years ago." Her wings rose above her, the feathers splayed. "We will correct the barren wasteland that you have made of Panagea. Prepare for war, Captain."

A burning wind tossed Kazuaki's hair behind him. When it finished, his unkempt, raven strands fell back around his jaw. "Wouldn't be the first time," he muttered.

His detachment earned him a vehement glare. Havidite threw her shoulders back and spun. Her wings stretched and whipped with the movement of her body, and in a single, fluid sweep, she was gone.

The mask she had held in her hands clattered to the earth. Her absence was felt, as the goddess commanded much presence. Brack looked down at Vadim and pressed the tip of his boot into the division leader's ribs to see if it gained a reaction. Vadim only stared, blank eyes shimmering with the golden glow of the flames. The Rabbit lifted his gaze to Kazuaki. "What do we do now, Cap?"

There was much to consider. They couldn't leave Vadim to his madness. He was too vital to the Northwestern division. But they needed to tell the other divisions to send whatever aid they could spare to the cities that continued to burn.

They also needed to warn Nicholai. Though Havidite did not shed much light on her plan of attack, Vadim's corruption remained a clear indication they were after the division leaders. If they couldn't claim the minds of all Panagea's people, Kazuaki was certain they'd try their damndest to make puppets of those who controlled them on a governmental level. One way or another, they would rain ruin down upon mankind.

"They know they cannot destroy everyone who prays to them, or they will fall once more from an absence of worship," Kazuaki announced. "In any case, we'll be of no help here. Plucking thousands of bodies from burning buildings is a job for a horde of footmen. We need to put our focus on Vadim."

Granite reached down, seizing Vadim beneath his armpits, and tossed him over his shoulder. "Where do you want him?"

Revi watched the Time Father flop over, open eyes motionless to match the rest of his body. "We should go back," he said, not attempting to disguise his desire to return to Southeastern. "It's only a matter of time before they finish with Northwestern and invade other divisions. We need to be there if Nico—"

"Nico will have to take care of himself for now," Kazuaki interrupted. Though he knew the Southeastern Time Father was vulnerable with Darjal biting at his mental wherewithal, they had no choice. He needed to trust Nicholai's ability to preserve his sanity. "We need to drive sense back into Vadim before we can leave Northwestern."

"We're stuck here until he's lucid?" Revi growled, thumbing toward Vadim. That was a death sentence. The man was crippled with madness.

"Your daughter waited ten years, Revi." Kazuaki found the man's eyes, challenging him with his own. "She can wait a little longer."

Tensed muscles betrayed Revi's dissatisfaction with Kazuaki's answer, but his respect for the captain kept his temper in check. "How do we cure him?" he murmured.

"I've scoured autobiographies and memoirs of Vadim Canmore," Kal offered. "I've studied his practices, his ruling tendencies. I might be able to pry him back into sanity by utilizing some psychological tactics."

"Jeeze," Brack laughed, patting Kal on the shoulder. "You and Bart really are feckin' soul mates. Cut from the same scholarly cloth, you two are."

"Fine." Kazuaki turned to Granite. "Take Vadim to the airship. Let Kal have a go at him. Hand your masks to Rennington—" He looked to the Southern soldier, knowing full well he wouldn't find rest until he lived up to his duty. "He and Jernal are going to scour the town for survivors. Revi, Penn, Bermuda, Brack ... scout ahead. Commandeer a vehicle, if you can find one that hasn't burned. Try to warn the next town over. Maybe they can stay ahead of the fire. If we have any success with Vadim, we'll pick you up on the way."

Jernal tensed, stepping back as he caught the oxygen mask Kal tossed to him. He stared down at it for a moment before he lifted a disdainful look to Kazuaki. "I don't take orders from criminals."

"You'll take orders or you'll take bullets," Kazuaki stated simply. "Which do you prefer?"

Mimir grabbed Jernal's arm and tugged him toward Rennington. "Come now, Commander. I don't want the Captain killing my second-best. Let's go look for body parts. It will be like we're right back at the well."

The commander deflated but knew when to back down to spare his existence. Kazuaki almost took his life once before; he doubted he'd have any qualms claiming it now. "Fine," he muttered, teeth clenched. As soon as the Southern soldier secured the mask he had acquired from Granite over his head, begrudgingly, he followed after Rennington.

It was difficult to spy movement from writhing bodies when the majority of the motion around them came from whipping flames. Rennington's eyes narrowed to slits as he tried to combat the effort of peering through the thick smoke. The sight around him was a discouraging one. He found plenty of bodies, but none held even a small fraction of life.

Jernal reached down to lift a large, flat piece of debris. He cursed upon discovering it was made of metal and clung to most of its heat. The commander flung his hand and wrist several times as if it somehow soothed the burn.

Mimir seemed at home amongst the chaos. The shadowed lesser god launched himself onto a fallen beam, high above the ground. His skills were inhuman. Despite the residual heat still emanating from the steel pole, he perched his bare feet upon it, looming over Rennington and Jernal like a hungry vulture.

His head tilted, farther and farther, until he eyed Rennington in a nearly upside-down state. "I must admit my surprise, Mr. Platts, that the captain would let you look for survivors," he said, knowing full well that no lives remained in the land of fire.

An initial hesitation climbed through Rennington's body, starting at his boots and stopping short of his throat. He did not enjoy Mimir's presence. Though he wasn't present at the well the day the lesser god took Bermuda's hand and Kazuaki's eye, his hatred existed as though he had been. "Yeah," he finally muttered through his mask, feeling it was best to appease the creature and end the conversation, rather than risk ignoring Mimir and inviting additional incessant chatter. "Me, too."

"He doesn't seem like the caring type," Mimir added, destroying Rennington's hopes that that was the end of their discussion.

The soldier tore his attention away from the smoldering chunks he sifted through. He looked up in just enough time to spy Kazuaki, Kal, and Granite returning to the airship with Vadim. Bermuda, Revi, Penn, and Brack bore through the wilder flames, forcing their way into the next town over with as much speed as they could muster. "The captain is guided by a very ... unique moral compass," Rennington said to Mimir, before returning his attention to the task at hand.

Jernal's ears perked at Rennington's statement. As he busied himself searching for any signs of life, he couldn't help but analyze the Southern soldier's testimonial. Despite his best efforts, he found truth in it. Jernal did not know what to make of Kazuaki Hidataka. He hated him. He was a criminal. And yet, here they were, trying to assist those who fell into Northwestern's hell pit. He became more perplexed by the captain with each passing hour.

"I see ..." Mimir lifted his scrutiny from Rennington as he peered into the orange horizon. "How very ... unexpected. Some might even say his true north points to a kindness of sorts."

Even in the macabre situation that Rennington found himself in, he laughed. "Never thought I'd hear Kazuaki and kindness in the same sentence," he said, pushing aside the remnants of an incinerated vat.

"Yes, well ... whether god or human, life still shines pearls of wisdom on us with each rise and fall of the sun." A slow smirk came to Mimir's face. His misshapen teeth looked as though they had no business on his face. "It's up to us to utilize that knowledge when it comes."

Every vertebra in Rennington's spine felt dipped in an ice bath. Mimir had uttered ceaseless nonsense since he appeared at Panagea's center. The soldier grew accustomed to his pointless chatter. But this time ... something in his tone ... something in his words ... it caused an uninvited chill to creep into Rennington's otherwise unshakable bones. He had no idea what the demon meant, but he was certain he did not want to find out.

CHAPTER SIXTEEN

Darjal had boasted a grandiose space during his reign over the Southern division. The splendor was lost on Bartholomew. It seemed impractical, given the limited space his division already suffered from. Large buildings required more energy to heat. More hired hands to keep clean. More of everything, in a world that had little to give as it recovered from its previous devastation.

The scholar sat in near darkness. Two tall candles flanked his sides. Cheap, efficient light sources were his preferred option. Until Southern recovered from the substantial damage it had endured throughout Panagea's suffocation, he'd bear the unnecessary trimmings of this place. This architectural reconstruction of Darjal's ego.

Only after much of his division was rebuilt, would he employ skilled laborers to deconstruct some of the more pointless components of this place. Until then, he bathed in candlelight and tried to keep the place as tidy as possible.

Bartholomew grew accustomed to the occasional draft. The spacious room in which he sat had many. But as a cold, unnatural wind blew up against his back, a frown crossed his face. His fingers tightened around the quill in his hand as he carefully looped the 'y' in his last name, finishing his signature on the ordinance before him.

"I knew one of you would come," he said without turning. "But I must admit, I didn't think it would be so soon."

Naphine tilted her head from behind him. She folded her wings neatly. The soft, golden feathers matched her faultless, buttery hair. "Then you're an intelligent man," she said, her voice emerging from the shadows like a false beacon of light.

"More observant than intelligent, at least in this case. I suspect Kazuaki and the others have already figured it out for themselves that the gods are after division leaders." Bartholomew dipped his quill into the ink well, sliding his current ordinance aside and reaching for another that needed his approval. "It's nothing more than common sense. As soon as Mimir announced your kind had taken over Northwestern, it became a matter of putting a very small puzzle together. Especially with Vadim's absence." Bartholomew shrugged, multi-tasking as his eyes scanned the contents of the document before him. "All signs pointed to division leaders as your primary targets. And why wouldn't we be? You're smart enough to dissect the hierarchy of people. You know who can best control those you can't."

A smirk found its way to Naphine's lips. "I see why they made you a division leader," she complimented, crossing her arms over her chest. "I suspect your intellect means you'll make it difficult for me to corrupt you."

"Difficult?" Bartholomew arched a brow, though he had yet to turn toward her. "My dear, it will make it impossible."

Finding his refusal to meet her eyes a small slight, Naphine sauntered toward him, peering over his shoulder to view the document he analyzed so closely. "You seem awfully sure of yourself," she said as her eyes darted from left to right, soaking in the text.

"Very sure. With only a small margin left to account for human error." He slid the document aside without signing it, reaching over to grab the one he validated previously. With precision, he folded the paper over itself, ensuring it would fit in an envelope. "How many of my people have you corrupted already?" he asked, nonchalant.

"Oh, darling, mankind was corrupt long before I got here," Naphine answered, finding boredom in his political duties. As she straightened herself to an upright position, she added, "but to answer your question, not as many as I'd have liked. These people still revere Darjal. It makes it difficult to manipulate their thoughts in *my* favor."

"I see." Bartholomew reached over and grabbed an envelope, and carefully slid the document inside. He knew why she shared her plans so freely. It was meant to be an insult. To not only stir fear into him, but to let him know that to her, he was, and never would be, a threat to her success. He did not buy into it. "I suppose Darjal is doing enough damage. There's probably not much slack left for you to pick up."

Naphine scoffed, placing a hand on her hip as it jutted out to the side. "The only damage Darjal is doing is to himself. He's too busy trying to corrupt Nicholai Addihein to pay any mind to his worshipers. Honestly, I have no idea why these people pray to him. He hasn't answered a single prayer since becoming a god." She reached over, picking up a brass paperweight from Bartholomew's desk, scrutinizing it with unimpressed eyes. "His selfishness will be his undoing. When they realize he offers them nothing, they will give him nothing in return. Mankind is very good at that." She set the trinket down. "*Then* I will 'pick up his slack'."

Bartholomew reached over to melt wax onto the envelope's back. His mind ticked rapidly at Naphine's mention of Nicholai. He knew of the Southeastern Time Father's plight. He wanted to resent his people for revering Darjal. It crippled his ability to assist Nicholai with his problem. But he could not. Not even for a moment. One second of weakness was all it would take for Naphine to capitalize on it. "You may be waiting a while," he finally said, pressing the Southern seal down into the pliable wax. "These people have admired Darjal for generations. It very well might take generations of flouting on his part to force a new tradition."

Naphine laughed, all silk and self-assurance. "Oh, my dear ... I have all the time in the world."

Bartholomew only nodded an acknowledgment of her reply. He placed the letter in a pile to his right before reaching over to grab yet another document seeking his approval.

Naphine watched him closely, the glow of the candles molding to the shape of his body. She slid her back against Bartholomew's desk, fluid in her movements as she lifted herself and glided her buttocks onto the top of the table to sit. She found the man's nonchalance impressive, and curious. "Are you not even a little afraid?"

Another request for financial aid. Bartholomew crunched some numbers in his brain, trying to recall the exact amount the treasury held before his last issuance of funds. "Fear stems from an absence of knowledge," he said, lacking ego. "Of which I have plenty to spare."

"Your knowledge of the gods is limited," Naphine interjected, crossing one leg over the other as she leaned back on her palms.

Bartholomew frowned. After deducing the importance of the project before him, he decided he would not be able to comply with their request for aid. He moved the paper over to a different pile. "I know as much about lesser gods as I do about every other of Panagea's fairytales."

A well-shaped brow rose on Naphine's flawless face. "How can you call me a fairytale when I stand before you?"

"You're a figment of men's imagination," Bartholomew said bluntly, grabbing a piece of parchment to write a formal letter of rejection. "You're an idea. Nothing more."

Her chest heaved once as she emitted a tiny chuckle. "Ideas can be the most dangerous things of all."

"A very judicious observation." Bartholomew scrawled his written reply, returning his pen to the well for more ink. "But sound logic and an open mind remain the best weapons against such things."

"You think so little of us, Bartholomew." Naphine pointed her toes straight as she bounced her crossed leg over her other. "It hurts. To be thought so little of, by those who created you."

The Southern Time Father continued writing. "Lesser gods were created out of mankind's desperation. Desperation is an emotional response. I've never been an emotional person."

A sly grin spread across Naphine's lips. "Oh, darling, now I know that's not true."

Bartholomew paid her little mind. His pen danced across the paper, the fine tip sliding smoothly with each new letter formed.

Naphine was not deterred. She touched his wrist and smiled. "You may be able to steel your thoughts from manipulation, Bartholomew Gray, but I can still see through your mind as though it were glass. And I spy, with my little eye, an emotional response by the name of Kal Rovanas."

The tip of his calligraphy pen snapped. Bartholomew stared at the parchment, unsure how he found himself gripping it so tightly, that it caved under the weight of his scrawling. He cleared his throat and opened a drawer, to retrieve an undamaged writing utensil. "Kal has no power over the people of Southern. He is of no use to you."

"Oh, my dear," she leaned over, and slid her palm up his arm, "you're smart enough to know that regarding this matter, you're very, very wrong."

Bartholomew finally met her eyes. From behind his glasses, he glared. He could tell his reaction satisfied Naphine to no end.

"Don't beat yourself up too much. You can't hide these things from the Goddess of Love, darling." She patted his arm and slid off the table with a sigh. "It might take some time, Bartholomew, but rest assured ... I always get what I want."

With that, she vanished, a gust of wind snuffing the candles out around Bartholomew's body. She left him to the darkness, in body and mind.

* * *

Elowyn had inherited all of Eastern's countless problems when she took over as its Time Mother. The most populated division, when compared to the others, came with a mass of challenges. The late leader, Avital, boasted of the numerous facilities he'd constructed in his limited space. The only thing that crippled the environment, more than the claustrophobic amount of people, was the constant supply of smog pouring from smokestacks across Eastern in droves.

The oxygen quality was laughable. The ground cracked and crumbled, depleted of anything resembling nutrients for years. Her people wandered, driven by their jobs and necessity, with masks strapped to their faces and goggles glued over their eyes. It was an endeavor to get from point A to point B without rubbing elbows with the oppressive collection of inhabitants in every Eastern town.

The natural disasters of Panagea's past claimed many lives from her densely populated division. They still struggled to find proper plots in which to bury their countless dead. Many businesses went unbuilt, selling their property to the government, as Elowyn attempted to not only cut back on the environmental damages of mass-production but the issue of not having enough land for vital endeavors.

There were issues with which she still struggled. But her greatest success filled her constituents with hope for the future. Her newly constructed medical facilities were unprecedented in their quality. Though many of her people were plagued by the aftermath of diseases caused by environmental decay, and the blasphemous gap between the wealthy and the poverty-stricken, superior medicines were never far from anyone's reach.

It was her greatest achievement.

But for how remarkable the hospitals were, they filled at an unprecedented rate. The number of patients requiring mental assistance quadrupled. Victims of unexpected, violent attacks from friends, neighbors, and family members burned through many of the supplies. Doctors, nurses, and volunteers were afraid to go to work. People deteriorated into beasts, influenced by gods who bred viciousness in their brains.

Elowyn paced the room of her chambers. She couldn't let these supernatural creatures deter her. The woman already struggled to prove herself capable in a patriarchal society. She'd be damned if these beasts stripped her of the respect she worked so hard to earn.

"Miss Saveign." Huric, one of Elowyn's most trusted footmen, leaned on his halberd for support. "You should sit. You can think just as clearly in a chair, you know."

The Time Mother frowned and shook her head. "It helps my blood flow," she muttered, gripping her dark hair in her fingers. "I know there's a solution, Huric. It's on the edge of my brain. I can fix this."

Huric became well acquainted with Elowyn's overconfidence throughout her many months as Time Mother. Though he did not share the majority of the other footmen's opinions that she was ill-fit for the job, he often worried about her inability to show any shred of weakness. He understood why she kept her vulnerable state on lockdown. The first sign of inability on Elowyn's part would surely ignite a rise in the already high levels of protestors she dealt with daily. Though Elowyn had gained much esteem, people still viewed women as fragile things. Elowyn fought hard to contest that stereotype, often at the cost of her health. Huric tried to smile, to ease her concern. "I'm sure you'll figure it out, Miss Saveign."

"Thank you, Huric." Elowyn crossed her arms over her chest. She forced herself to look at him. "I appreciate your unwavering support."

Huric nodded. His smiling face faded into one of caution when a strange sound met his ears. "Do you hear that, Miss Saveign?" he asked, looking to the window.

Elowyn paused. The low reverberations of timed pounds rattled through her tower. Disgruntled voices sounded below. "More protestors, I imagine," she murmured as she traipsed over to the window and stuck her head out.

Below, a group of footmen stood. They rose their halberds, smashing the blunt ends into the concrete ground surrounding her residence. Her eyes narrowed. "Soldiers?" she said aloud, having never witnessed a rebellion amongst her men, despite the whispers that some favored following a division leader with a Y chromosome.

Huric strode over to her side, a look of bewilderment on his face as he stared down at the roaring men. They threw their bodies and weapons into the door of Elowyn's home, clear in their efforts to destroy the barrier that barred them from entering. "I don't understand," Huric said, his brows furrowing. "They look—"

"—possessed," Elowyn finished. Her eyes widened as she backed away from the window in time to avoid an unexpected round of gunfire. The plague that claimed her people had infected her soldiers. Those sworn to protect her. "Shit."

Elowyn Saveign did not take lightly to running from a fight. It went against every piece of what made her the woman she was. But pride could kill a person if they weren't careful enough. Elowyn had no qualms sacrificing her life fighting for what was right. But sometimes, it was wiser, more noble, to live to fight another day.

The Eastern Time Mother darted around the room, stuffing loose medical supplies into a bag. She tried to concentrate against the rising voices and the pounding thuds. Her fingernail scraped down her face, exasperated, as she threw the pack over her shoulder. "We need to get to the first floor, Huric. It's our only chance."

The footman did not ask questions. It did not seem wise to put themselves closer to the threat, but he trusted Elowyn. He believed in her. "If that's what we gotta do," he said, throwing open the door, "then I'll lead the way."

"Good man." She followed him as they abandoned the place she called home. Quick feet trampled down the seemingly endless staircase. One flight. Two flights. Three flights down. Adrenaline powered both Time Mother and footman through.

The men raged outside. They threw their bodies into the door with the beat of war drums. Just as Huric's boot touched the marbled material of the first floor, the door gave way under the pressure of the mob.

Dozens of footmen burst inside, halberds raised, hatred living on their faces. Saliva dripped from their open mouths as they shouted, filling the room with their bodies.

Huric instinctually shoved Elowyn into the nearest room before prying eyes spotted them. The wooden shaft of his halberd pressed into her stomach as he flattened her against the wall. "Miss Saveign," he whispered, without taking his eyes off the threat, "which room do we need?"

"The library." Her words were hushed. Strained. A sea of men awaited them in the entrance hall. To make it across the room to the library without being detected bordered on suicidal.

Huric winced. A dangerous mission, indeed. A small handful of footmen fled up the stairs, hungry to find the object of their hunt. Elowyn's heart raced. Almost a year of tedious diplomacy made the feeling unfamiliar. But she knew the organ could withstand the pressure. After years of living with Kazuaki Hidataka, there wasn't much her heart couldn't handle.

"They're fanning out," Huric observed with caution, his head hovering just a sliver around the corner of the door. "Checking other rooms. I count nine standing in the entrance hall."

Elowyn bit the inside of her cheek and closed her eyes. "Then I will issue nine letters of condolence to their families." She slipped twin daggers out of her boots. One for each hand. She knew their actions were not bred of their own minds. At least, not mostly. But there was no way to spare them. Not with the time she had to work with before they came for her head. "On the count of three."

"Three." Huric rolled around the corner, bringing the blade of his halberd down onto the shoulders of an unsuspecting soldier. The metal ate through the nerves and laid into the bone. The man crumbled, shrieking under the force.

Before his comrades turned around, Elowyn lunged around the corner. She ran, launching herself off the fallen body for leverage, and drove both daggers into opposite sides of her opponent's neck. Blood painted the wall when she removed them. She had little time to react before she needed to dodge an advance.

Huric swept the floor with his weapon. It drove into the exposed shins of two footmen, severing a foot from one and tearing the tendons of another.

Elowyn was lucky to avoid an aggressive swing before she drove steel into an artery. The sound of the halberd clattering to the floor echoed off the walls.

She thought they'd have time to eliminate all nine. They did not. The fiendish cries from the dead and the dying summoned those who spread out earlier. It drew them back to the entrance hall like a wounded siren.

Huric reached for the library door and threw it open. "Miss Saveign!"

The Eastern Time Mother panted. She watched as a horde of men spewed down the staircase, a waterfall of flesh and iron. Elowyn ran into the library and reached out for Huric's hand to pull him in with her, but he refused, using the rod of his halberd to force her farther into the room.

He downed another aggressor, the closest to them before he backed into the room himself. With his free hand, he threw the door closed, just as a bullet fled from the barrel of its gun.

Huric shoved his halberd through the open handles of the newly locked door. An insurance policy, should the lock fail them. The door rattled under the pressure of the men outside. "What now, Miss Saveign?"

Elowyn rushed over to a window and threw it open. She then ran behind a desk and threw up the hidden entrance on the floor. The entryway to the catacombs below was exposed. "These lead to the nearest coast. Get in."

Huric's brows knitted together. He did not attempt to disguise his surprise. "How long have those ...?" The man served the Eastern division for years and was never made privy to the existence of any underground catacombs.

The faux-wood of Huric's halberd cracked as it bent. His eyes flashed to the door. They were seconds away from entering.

Elowyn's eyes pleaded with him from fifteen feet away. "Huric! Hurry!"

The soldier stepped back. A blade cut its way through the door, making a window for the soldiers to see. Huric's broad body blocked the vision of those seeking entry. He did not wish to remove focus from the door. He did not wish to draw attention to Elowyn's position. He couldn't move unless he wished to risk giving away her hiding place. "Go, Miss Saveign."

"Huric!"

"Go!"

Another blow to the door. Elowyn lowered herself into the catacombs as a second halberd made a larger hole. She ground her teeth together as she lowered the hatch, burying herself in darkness.

She heard every sound of the scuffle above. She had no doubt Huric fought with valiance. The only solace Elowyn took from that moment, was that the noise of the exchange above was short. She hoped with every ounce of her heart that Huric did not suffer long.

Footsteps clamored above her. The sound of shifting furniture. Books being tossed from their shelves. Pages ruffling. Confusion. It took all of her volition to still her strenuous breathing. To quiet the scream that hid in her throat over the loss of Huric. To still the rising rage that tempted her to burst through the door and slaughter as many as she could. But what difference would that make? What sense was there, to seek revenge on men who barely knew what they did?

Their voices were muffled. Scarcely audible through the thick layer of stone flooring that protected her. Elowyn listened as best as she could.

"She must've fled out the window," a footman guessed.

"She won't get far. We should return to Pymlena."

"Without the Time Mother? That would displease her."

"Pymlena is all-forgiving. She will guide us to our new objective with mercy."

Elowyn did not know who Pymlena was, but her racing mind held an educated guess. Her nostrils flared as she tried to breathe quietly. She heard several men grunt as they lowered themselves out the window. No doubt an attempt to track her. Others continued searching the room. Some left, their footsteps leaving the library behind them.

She couldn't move. Her back pressed against the cold, carved rock of the catacombs. Where was there to run? Who was left to trust? Those crippled by the lesser gods' madness looked every bit the part of regular men and women. No identifiable factor remained to pick them from a crowd, save for the clear absence of conscience.

The only remaining individuals Elowyn trusted with her life lived outside Eastern territory. She couldn't chance leaving. Not with the looming fear that she might not return. Putting the remainder of Eastern's stable people in even more danger simply wasn't an option. Not for Elowyn Saveign.

In the bitter chill of the underground, she felt something warm fall on her face. Though she couldn't see in the surrounding darkness, she felt the liquid trail down her forehead, over her eye, down her cheek, until it reached the corner of her mouth. It tasted of iron. The blood of Huric rained down on her through the thin cracks made by the hidden door. Too cautious to move until the sound of the footmen above faded away, Elowyn Saveign stood in shadows and blood. Holding her breath, she counted the seconds until she started her new life as Eastern's underground leader.

CHAPTER SEVENTEEN

The torn cloth smelled of fire. It struck Umbriel's sensitive nostrils in an unforgiving manner. She stared down at the make-shift parchment for what felt like hours, though it had only been moments since it was hand-delivered by a diplomatic courier. Scrawled in soot across the textured fabric, the ominous message haunted her:

NW in flames. Need assist.

-K.

The woman curled it into her fingers as she stared out the open door. Nicholai had finally found rest in his bed. His deprived body needed it greatly. Though Umbriel knew he awaited word from Kazuaki with incurable impatience, she did not wish to wake him. Not just because he needed sleep ... but because Nicholai Addihein needed one less thing with which to concern his already fragile mind.

She eased herself back into the house, careful to close the door with as little noise as possible. Her hand rested on the knob while she thought.

Disturbing Nicholai was not an option. But leaving Kazuaki's message unheeded wasn't either. Umbriel glanced over her shoulder, her eyes falling on what little she saw of the Southeastern Time Father through the small crack in the door leading to his room. Her eyes then flicked to the official stationery at his writing desk.

She could handle this herself.

Umbriel set the torn cloth on the small table near the door as she crossed the distance to Nicholai's table. Delicate hands seized his quill and dipped it in the nearby ink. With equal parts care and haste, she started to pen a sanctioned decree, diverting Southeastern soldiers to the Northwestern division.

Avigail crept out of the kitchen, her eyes on Umbriel as she bent over the desk. She seemed consumed by her task. The young Houton daughter lifted a cup to her lips and took a silent drink before her attention fell on the tattered fabric of Kazuaki's letter.

Her eyes narrowed. She scanned the contents. NW. Northwestern. Signed with only a K. Avigail gasped quietly. It must have stood for Kazuaki. The man her father followed into the pits of the Underworld.

Umbriel searched through old documents that cluttered Nicholai's usually meticulous station. She studied his signature, taking mind of the common loops and structure of the individual letters. Her hand lowered to her formal order, where she forged the Time Father's name.

After stuffing the letter into an envelope, she turned, jumping at the unexpected sight of Avigail before her. Umbriel blinked, taken aback more so by her surprise than Avigail's presence. That she was unable to sense her company caught her off guard. Then again, as concerted action consumed most of her focus, broken concentration was to be expected. "Avigail—I'm glad you're here. I need to tell you something."

The girl stiffened. She gripped her cup tighter, fearing the worse from Umbriel's lips. Did it have to do with Kazuaki's letter? Did it have to do with her father? Her heart threatened to destroy her ribs as she whispered, "What is it?"

Her reaction seemed strange. Unwarranted. But Umbriel hadn't the time to assess it. "I have something very important I need to do," she said, clutching the sealed envelope in her hand. "Please, watch over Nicholai until I return. I wouldn't ask this of you if it wasn't a time-sensitive matter. I will send Malcolm over to help you. Can you do this for me?"

Avigail scraped her front teeth against her bottom lip, waiting for the ball to drop. But Umbriel made no mention of Kazuaki or her father. "Is everything all right?" she asked, nervous.

"Everything is as it is," Umbriel said as she walked passed her, and stopped at the door. When she spied the cloth with Kazuaki's message on the table, she seized it in her hands, burying it in her palm. "But we do with it the best that we can." She smiled, in the hopes of banishing the young woman's obvious fear. "Can you do this? Not just for me, but for Nicholai, as well?"

Avigail opened her mouth to speak, paused, and looked over her shoulder toward Nicholai's room. "I ..." She watched him sleep, knowing full well he needed the rest, just as much as Umbriel knew. A frown crossed her face. She returned her eyes to the Earth Mother. "Yes. Sure."

Umbriel smiled once more. She reached over to give Avigail's shoulder a gentle squeeze. "Thank you. I'll make haste." With that, she stole one final glimpse of Nicholai and whisked herself out the door.

Avigail stood in the silence of the main room, with only the mocking sounds of a ticking clock to accompany her. She saw that letter. There was no denying the severity in which it must have been penned, given the material used and the worrying message it held. She pictured her father, surrounded by fire, following Kazuaki and the crew into demanding circumstances to do ... whatever it was that Revi Houton did.

He saved Panagea, she remembered. Nicholai had admitted as much to her. Avigail's father was a key component to reintroducing nature, destroying time-honored faults within the archaic system, and ... and throwing everything to the wayside to do it, family included.

Avigail clenched her jaw. The sound of her teeth grinding together did little to rattle her. It wasn't only what Nicholai had said. Umbriel's words filtered through her mind, too. Her confession about her own father. That she wished she had more time with him. That he made mistakes, like any other person, as was the human condition. That above all else, she would have loved to have one more moment with him ...

Avigail hated Revi Houton. But she loved him, too.

Without realizing what she was doing, her feet carried her into the small room that Nicholai and Umbriel had let her stay in. She shoved her few possessions into her backpack and strode to the kitchen. Perishable and unperishable foods alike fell into her bag without delay, but food would only get her so far. She couldn't get to Northwestern fast. Not without money.

A small attack of conscience bit at her. But Avigail was accustomed to handling the incessant feeling; her upbringing forced her into many situations where she needed to make debatable decisions. She lived with the demons who plagued her for most of her life. They were almost family at this point.

She crept over to Nicholai's desk and pulled open a drawer. Nothing of use. She tried another. No go. When her hands tried the third, Avigail discovered a small satchel that clinked when she pushed it aside. It was the undeniable sound of rattling coins.

Careful hands eased it out of its hiding place, and she spilled the contents into her palm. It was all Southeastern currency. She had hoped for a variety to get her through Northwestern when she arrived. But beggars couldn't be choosers. Or in this case, thieves.

Shoving the satchel into her pocket, Avigail headed for the door. Before she opened it, she paused. A slow craning of her neck returned her gaze to Nicholai, sleeping in the little space across the room. Despite Umbriel's gentle but firm chastising, she couldn't deny her feelings for the man. Lust, love, or otherwise, the teenaged heart did not dissect and analyze. It only felt. And she felt she couldn't leave him without a note to apologize for her thievery, and a vow to pay him back.

Taking a cue from the Earth Mother, Avigail scrawled a quick message on a piece of paper littering Nicholai's desk. She entered his room with caution, swallowing, fearful that she might wake him. Shaking hands set the note on his bedside table.

She took one final glimpse of him. Attractive, even in his state of deterioration. She would have liked to have been his.

For a moment, she almost lost her nerve to go ... but Avigail's heart had called out for Revi Houton for ten long years. It only belonged to Nicholai for a few short weeks. She mouthed the word 'goodbye' and slipped out the door.

A tinge of guilt crept into her veins when Avigail recalled her promise to Umbriel. But it was fine. Nicholai would be okay, she thought, as she exited the Addihein homestead and headed for the nearest steam train. Umbriel stated she'd send Malcolm right over.

She would not let her father run swiftly into death's open arms. Not without ... closure? An apology? Forgiveness? Avigail didn't know what she wanted from Revi Houton. But she knew it wasn't supposed to end like this.

She remembered her father saying he'd accompany Kazuaki to Vadim Canmore's home town. Striburn. She didn't know where that was, but she'd find out along the way. A man as well-known as the Northwestern Time Father couldn't hide his location from everyone.

Vacant eyes spied Avigail as she left the Time Father's home. The lifeless orbs followed her form until it disappeared. The body they belonged to licked at his lips as he edged himself out of a small alley facing Nicholai's house. Confident feet strode toward the door.

The man loomed outside the Addihein household, glancing to his left. To his right. When he saw little to no witnesses, bony fingers reached for the knob and turned it. With ease, it followed his commands. Rushed teenagers rarely had the foresight to lock doors behind them.

The door squealed as it opened, unoiled for far too long. A boot heel hit the ground first, followed by the tip. One foot entered, then another. A second protest from the door echoed as the man slowly shut the entrance.

Click. The throw latch fell into the strike box, indicating it closed behind him, though he did not turn to verify this. His focus was too consumed with the other door. The one across from him.

The one containing the slumbering body of Nicholai Addihein, Southeastern's Time Father and primary target of his mission.

His strides were unhurried but purposeful. The quickest route to any objective was a straight line. A large hand pushed the second door open further. He stared down at the man on the bed. Disheveled, still donned in his traditional garb, vest and all. It almost looked as if he'd simply passed out.

The man's head tilted as he watched Nicholai's closed eyelids flicker. A dream, he supposed. By the look on the Time Father's face, it did not appear to be a pleasant one. The stranger's hands lowered into his pockets. He removed the syringe that hid inside, lifting it closer to his face. His thumb gave the plunger a little push. Just enough to see if the liquid contained inside, was indeed ready to spill out the tip. It was.

Without speaking, the man lowered the syringe, wondering where the best place was to facilitate injection. Did it need to hit a vein? He wasn't sure. He should have asked Ameyar to be more specific. But it was a calculated risk, angering the God of the Underworld.

With little more than an uneducated guess to guide him, the man decided on the arm. Perhaps luck would befall him, and he'd hit whatever he needed to fulfill his objective. As the tip hovered an inch from its target, the front door behind him opened.

A pumping shotgun was a very identifiable sound. The man spun around, as Malcolm pointed the weapon at his face. If the old man was surprised to see the intruder, it was dominated by protective indignation. "Back the feck away from my son-in-law," he growled, a precise aim on his mark.

The stranger stared at the barrel. He blinked decisively, and absent of fear, turned around, back to Nicholai's arm.

Malcolm Finn grew up in a loving home. He was surrounded by the warmth of family and friends daily. He had lived in a supreme state of affection for his entire existence. Blessed with adoration from his wife, and his daughter, Lilac, Malcolm Finn had no history of violence. He barely raised his voice. No temper to speak of. And though he was certain Lilac's spirit would have delighted in Nicholai's company, he did not hesitate to shift his aim and pulled the trigger, sparing the life of the man who loved his only daughter.

Shot pellets shredded the assailant's leg. He would have crumbled under his weight, had the sound not jolted Nicholai from his unsettled rest.

The Time Father's metal hand clawed into the throat of his aggressor as he pulled the body down.

His lips peeled back like an animal.

He positioned his own body over the stranger.

Heated thoughts flew to the forefront of his newly wakened mind.

The stranger had no time to throw his arms up in defense. Before the Time Father quelled his dark thoughts and replaced them with his true self. Tranquilizers emerged from his mechanical forearm. They rammed into the soft underjaw of his foe without mercy.

Saliva spewed from the stranger's mouth as he released a sound of agony. Malevolent eyes locked onto Nicholai's, who only now started to showcase alarm when he realized what he'd done.

For a moment, he thought it was only a nightmare. One of the many he endured since Darjal's death, where he found himself staring down at the lifeless body he destroyed. But the body beneath his was tangible. He jerked his arm back, stepping off and away from his victim. "I—what—" Nicholai panted heavily, his heart pounding as panicked eyes darted from the poisoned man over to Malcolm.

"Ameyar ... save me," the man gasped through a clenched jaw, as the liquid spread through his limbs. His eyes started to roll into the back of his skull as he slipped in and out of consciousness. He tried to lift a hand, but only his fingers twitched as he succumbed to the sedative, and his tensed muscles relaxed him to oblivion.

Nicholai's chest expanded and collapsed as he ran flustered fingers through his hair.

Upon seeing the threat eliminated, Malcolm set the shotgun down, leaning it against a wall as he strode over to Nicholai and grasped his shoulders. His brows creased over his concerned eyes as he tried to command the confused Time Father's attention. "Nicholai—are you all right, son?"

Emerging from a powerful state of sleep clouded his mind; his brain struggled to piece the events into some semblance of order. When he could concentrate on the objects laid out before him, when the haze dissipated, Nicholai met Malcolm's gaze. "I ... believe so," he uttered, running his hands over his torso as if to reassure himself he hadn't suffered any irreparable damage. "What ... did I do?" he asked as he glanced at the fallen man on his mattress.

"Nothing you shouldn't have," Malcolm reassured him. He released Nicholai from his grasp and took a step toward the anesthetized stranger. "Do you recognize him? Another hired attempt on your life?"

Nicholai tried to swallow, but his mouth was too dry. The result of days of unintended dehydration. The name Ameyar repeated in his mind, over and over, spoken from the lips of his would-be assailant. "I don't think so," he said, rubbing the back of his neck.

Malcolm frowned. He shifted to face Nicholai. His expression was stern, though his voice pleaded for honesty. "Look, son, be straight with me. I know something serious is going on. I may be an old man, but I'm not senile."

The little sleep he had received minimally helped his condition, as Nicholai called forth his memories of Panagea's current state of affairs. The lesser gods. Mimir's ominous message regarding Northwestern. Darjal. And now this; this strange man, donned in common threads, bearing little to no resemblance of a trained assassin, spewing names from his mouth that bore the ring of godliness. Nicholai found Malcolm's gaze. "You are far from it, my friend. As you know, I announced to Southeastern's journalists last night that the lesser gods are making monsters out of otherwise good people."

"I'm not talking about the lesser gods, Nicholai." Malcolm straightened himself, knowing, as well as any other inhabitant of

Southeastern, what terrors waited to manipulate the minds of fragile men and women. Nicholai's announcement had spread like wildfire. "I'm talking about you, specifically. You're not yourself."

"Yes, well," Nicholai agreed with little fight. He did not have much in the way of energy to argue. "I've had a lot on my mind lately."

"I should say so." Malcolm turned to the body on the mattress. "Does this man have anything to do with it?"

Nicholai followed the eyes of his late lover's father to the bedridden assailant. Against every tortured thought that rattled him, he emitted a short, depraved laugh. "Malcolm ... I honestly can't tell you whether he does or does not."

Unsatisfied with Nicholai's answer, Malcolm clenched his jaw. "In any case, we should get him out of here and into a Nenada jail cell, before he does any more damage. I can go find a nearby footman."

"Yes. Thanks to you, I do not think he'll be—" Nicholai paused. He jerked his head behind him, looking out of the bedroom door. "Where's Umbriel? Avigail?"

"Calm down, son, calm down," Malcolm lowered his hands as if it would help deescalate Nicholai's rising panic. "Umbriel is the one who sent me here. She seemed like she had something terribly important to do. You know, I don't know that I've ever seen that girl in such a state. She's usually so composed ..."

Nicholai breathed a sigh of relief at the news of Umbriel's safety, though the back of his mind wondered where she went off to in such a hurry. "And Avigail?"

Malcolm parted his lips to speak, but stopped, and shrugged. "I'm sorry, Nicholai, I didn't see her when I entered."

The Time Father bolted out of the room, throwing open the entryway to Avigail's temporary residence. He scanned the contents, noticing immediately that what little belongings she had were gone. "Damnit—" He dashed out, and into the kitchen, though he knew before his gaze settled on its interior that she would not be there. "Damnit!"

Before he crossed into Umbriel's room, the last place in the small homestead she might be able to conceal herself, Malcolm emerged from the bedroom. He held a note in his hands. "Nicholai." His face looked grave as he held it out to the man.

Quick hands seized the letter and scanned it without delay. It was short and to the point. She took his money. She promised to repay him. A hurried mention of her gratitude. Nothing more. He lowered it to his side and collapsed back into the wall. "She's gone. Revi's going to kill me."

"Perhaps she told Umbriel where she was going," Malcolm said, trying to be helpful, though he doubted the validity of his own words.

"No," Nicholai shook his head. "She would have said something in here. No mention of where she's going. No mention of when she'll return. Only that she will."

Malcolm's lips tightened. "Just focus on the last sentence, then. That she'll return."

Nicholai closed his eyes. His grip on the paper tightened. It creased under the pressure. "Right," he whispered, trying to pull forth any will he had reserved inside him. "Did Umbriel at least say where *she* was going?"

"She did not." Malcolm returned to his shotgun and picked it up. "But she clutched an official document in her hands. Signed and sealed in wax with the Southeastern emblem. I venture she was off to the post."

Nicholai frowned, wondering what Umbriel would be doing with an official letter he did not recall penning. "Then I'll meet her there. Thank you, Malcolm. You've ... quite literally saved my life."

"And I would time and time again, my son. Now go. I'll send someone to deal with this mess," he said, referring to the body.

A quick nod came from the Time Father before he rushed out the door. His feet carried him quickly. He felt the scrutinizing stares of the residents whom he passed. The ones who once bid him hello without a second thought. They shied away now. They lived in fear after his announcement yesterday. News of the lesser gods infiltrating not only Panagea but peoples' minds, spilled from his very mouth, with no calming follow up to accompany the announcement.

The people of Southeastern did not have the burden of living in the fear of Panagea's crumbling state. While natural disasters withered the other divisions, these people had lain dormant, stilled by Nicholai's dishonorable decision to stop time. They did not have to harden themselves to terror, like the people of the other seven divisions. It was new to them. Fresh. And he felt it in every hushed whisper as he walked to the post to find Umbriel.

He needed to get a hold of himself. He felt less like Nicholai, and more like Darjal, with each passing hour. That he had attacked his assailant with such violence was not who Nicholai Addihein was. He suspected, had it been actual poison in his vials instead of a sedative, he still would not have stopped himself at that moment. He would have taken another life.

The realization rattled him. But a deep, well-timed breath shoved it to the back of his already crowded conscience. He'd deal with it later. Personal problems ranked second to the issues plaguing his city. His people. His division.

Nicholai Addihein would never, not on his life, whether by the influence of lesser gods or otherwise, let the people of Southeastern down again. Not if he could help it.

CHAPTER EIGHTEEN

"Your progress is slow."

Kal closed his eyes, his fingers coming to the tips of his temples as he endured yet another one of Kazuaki's countless pushes for results. "I'm well aware that we're not making much progress, Captain. With all due respect, your constant reminders don't breed a particularly conducive environment."

Kazuaki paced the floor, his hands behind his back. They had strapped Vadim to a chair in Granite's cabin many hours ago. Though the Northwestern Time Father occasionally tried to force his arms free from their restraints, the knots at his wrists and ankles kept him anchored in position.

The captain knew his rants offered no assistance. But his drive to expedite the time they spent fixing Vadim had peaked. To calm the unusual overflow of restlessness, Kazuaki filled his lungs with air and turned away.

"Vadim," Kal leaned forward, gripping both arms of the chair, "your division is burning. The buildings, the factories, Northwestern's precious exports—"

"—the people," Granite murmured. Though he did not care much for the state of human affairs, he found Kal's efforts to focus solely on the financial devastation rather odd.

Kal lifted his eyes to Granite. "Yes," he added. Though his word lacked conviction, Granite witnessed care in the ambassador's gaze. He didn't highlight the people's plight as an asset for recovering Vadim's lucidity, but Granite saw the compassion in Kal's face. His heart bled for those lost.

Vadim, whose head hung loosely, with his chin embedded in his chest, shot up. He found Kal's attention. He grinned. Then, he spit in his face.

Kal jerked back and closed one of his eyes. A disgusted hand raised from his side. He scraped the saliva from his skin with his middle finger and flicked it off. "And they say there are no gentlemen left," he muttered, removing a handkerchief from his pocket to clean his hand.

Kazuaki spun on his heels and gripped the chair's sides. He dipped it back, balancing it on two legs, as he shoved his face into Vadim's. "I will rip those ear canals open lest you start listening!" he growled, drawing back an arm to enhance his threat.

"Captain," Kal crossed his arms over his chest, unamused, "while I appreciate your extensive history in forcing results from your adversaries, we're trying to condition his brain to be *less* violent. I hardly think throwing more fuel on the fire is going to be useful."

Despite the low rumble of dissatisfaction that came from his throat, Kazuaki returned the chair to all four legs. He was slower to tear the face of his rage away from Vadim, but eventually, he managed it. Kazuaki glared at Kal instead. Though irritation lived in his stare, the ambassador reminded him of Bartholomew. Sensible. Levelheaded. Skills Kazuaki had yet to master in his hundreds of years of living. He said nothing, but shifted, allowing Kal the benefit of space to work further on Vadim.

The ambassador stood, looming over the Northwestern Time Father. "Picture it, Vadim. Drained treasuries. An absence of goods or services to replenish the currency that will flood past your borders and never return. No people left to pay your taxes. Your division will fail. Your failure is a reflection of you."

Vadim glared at Kal. He scoffed, haughty as he uttered, "Northwestern burns to pave the way for more profitable endeavors. This purge is an investment."

"This is no investment, Vadim. This is a scam. You fell for their con game, my friend. You need only open your eyes to see they took everything from you. Yes, you've leveled the industries, the homes—you've initiated your step one, but with what money will you rebuild these more 'profitable endeavors'? Your division treasury already boasts dismal numbers; we're coming off the worst environmental devastation in Panagea's existence. *All* the divisions are tapped. I don't know what financial gain the lesser gods promised you, but it is fictional. It does not exist, Vadim. And with your land in ruins, it never will."

It was only a moment. A flicker. A small, infinitesimal flash of clarity. Fear. But Kal caught sight of Vadim's returning sanity. Regardless of how short-lived, he took it as a sign of hope. "We're reaching him," the ambassador announced, excited.

Kazuaki glanced at Vadim, who had quickly reverted to his inattentive, manipulated state. The captain scowled, unconvinced. "One moment of stability will not help."

Kal stared at Vadim, shrugging. "Psychological remedies take time, Captain."

"Of which we have none." Kazuaki suspected Nicholai edged closer to the same fate as Vadim with each passing hour. Though he trusted the Southeastern Time Father's volition, he was already fighting off the mental advances of Darjal. Throwing the efforts of more lesser gods on top of it would eventually break any man.

The sound of footsteps summoned the captain's attention. He smelled them before they entered the cabin. Rennington, Jernal, and Mimir arrived, reeking of smoke and death. Rennington removed his oxygen mask, a clear outline of where the device had been secured over his face, where untainted flesh met the skin sullied from ash and soot.

He tossed the mask onto a nearby table and collapsed into a chair, exhausted. Nobody had to ask. The look on his face said there were no survivors.

Vadim's eyes narrowed when he spotted the three newcomers. "Is that my city I smell on you?" he asked.

Rennington glared. "Your city. Your people. Your failure."

Vadim's questioning gaze fell to the ground. His pupils darted around the floor, brows together as if trying to make sense of something.

Kal took to a knee to find the bound Time Father's level once again. "Vadim?" he asked, hoping to penetrate Havidite's manipulation.

The haggard man's gaze locked onto Kal. He portrayed a certain horror. A revelation. It lived on his face for some time. Kal allowed him to come to terms with it. When he thought Vadim had suffered enough in his soberness, the ambassador opened his mouth to speak, but it was too late. Vadim reverted into influenced submission once again. The reality of his actions was simply too painful to face.

"We're chipping away at him," Kal said with a sigh, pushing back off the chair to face Kazuaki again. "His moments of lucidity are getting longer. I'd wager that I can break him in a few more hours, but I cannot make any promises as to how long he will remain stable."

"I'll take that bet," Kazuaki grumbled, throwing his concentration to Rennington and Granite. "I'm piloting the ship to the next town over. We're picking up the others. With any luck, Kal will have made enough progress with Vadim in that time that we can leave him somewhere safe. I need you two on lookout. If you spot any of the crew, alert me immediately."

Granite nodded, swooping out of the room with his dog in tow. Rennington, who had just eased his tired legs into a sitting position, goaded his bones to stand once more. "You got it, Cap."

"What about me?" Jernal's voice was unexpected, as everyone stood in the small confines of the cabin. He was not accustomed to purposelessness; though these people weren't his superiors by any means, Jernal's character did not allow him to stand idly by. "What should I do?"

Kazuaki arched a brow. He expected little participation from Nordjan's militant rat. The captain reached down, grabbed a bucket and mop, and hurled it at Jernal. "If you want to make yourself useful," he said, "you can scrub the shit off the deck."

Jernal caught the objects in his arms as Kazuaki left the room. He glanced down at the unwelcome, metal pail, a frown on his face. Many years had passed since his rank dictated a necessity to perform mediocre tasks. He should've expected that these societal rejects wouldn't use him to his full abilities.

Mimir snickered. "The squeaky wheel gets the grease, Commander." He glanced over his shoulder at Jernal, closed both of his glowing eyes as he smirked, and then trailed off after the captain.

Positions were assumed. Rennington dangled off the airship's ledge, clinging to a rope for support, as his eyes scanned the ground below. The challenge of seeing small bodies through thick smog was great, but the soldier did not shy away from it. With Granite on the opposite side to increase their chances of spotting the others, Jernal relented to the captain's demands, and begrudgingly scrubbed the deck.

Scarred hands guided the ship away from the wreckage that Penn had crashed it into previously. The sea of Havidite's flowers was more visible from the air. Red was the perfect color. Her own garden of spilled blood.

Kazuaki was silent as the vessel crawled through the tarnished sky. He enjoyed that silence for only a moment before the irking sound of Mimir's feet on the staircase accosted his eardrums.

"What do you want?" the captain growled without turning around.

Mimir came up beside him. "For someone who has no qualms slaying men, you certainly seem to like them an awful lot."

Kazuaki balked at the ridiculousness of Mimir's statement. "Have you traded your eyes away too, demon? Your insight seems based on blindness."

"Oh, Captain, do not be ashamed." Mimir lifted his chin and closed his eyes, delighting in the feel of the wind on his face. There were no winds in the hole that was his well. "For not unlike you, I, too, harbor both a love and a hatred for the curious little collection of bones wrapped in flesh."

More incessant jabbering. Kazuaki remembered it from his time spent at the well years ago. He did not respond to Mimir's ramblings. Instead, he continued to guide the ship deeper into

Northwestern territory, waiting to hear the call from Granite or Rennington.

Mimir found his stillness amusing. His shoulders shrugged around his neck until his arms settled back down at his sides. "A change. A shift. Changes happen every day, Captain. We are helpless to them. Just as you are helpless to the lesser gods now, am I right?"

A muscle in Kazuaki's jaw twitched, but that was his only response.

The lesser god held out his hand, enjoying the feel as the wind guided his hand up and down on the current. Mimir smirked. "You're a man of myths and legends, Captain, are you not? Have you ever heard the story of Ameyar?"

Kazuaki knew the name. Though he hoped his admission would buy him a free pass from what he was certain would be a cryptic, nonsensical story, he doubted it. Still, the captain muttered, "The God of the Underworld."

"The God of the Underworld, indeed," Mimir confirmed as he stared out into the sea of clouds and gray plumes. "He who lived in total darkness, beneath the land for centuries ... condemned there from the moment mankind first craved the comfort of knowing where a soul went after death." Mimir chuckled. "People are a bit mindless that way, aren't they, Captain? They had entire realms with which to traverse after their journey in the physical world ended ... and instead of trusting that, they built their own prisons. Imaginary walls to contain their spirits for eternity. All for the sake of temporary comfort."

Kazuaki did not comment.

His unresponsiveness did not deter Mimir. "Ameyar came to the surface one day, as he often did when he was gathering souls for the Underworld. He was to take a young man. Barely into adulthood. Death by disease, as was common back then, you know. Ameyar approached, but the deceased's sister hurled her body over the corpse. She wept. She begged Ameyar not to take her dear brother." Mimir tilted his head. "Humans are enthralled by death, but continuously recoil at its necessity. Fascinating creatures."

Kazuaki drew in a slow breath, to keep himself from losing his temper. Mimir's prattling was endless.

The lesser god continued. "He gazed down at her tear-soaked cheeks. Her puffed, rosy eyes. Even in her sorry state, he fell for her. She defied everything he ever was. As people loathe themselves for what they lack, Captain, so too, do the gods. He saw her uncontaminated love for her brother. He wanted to taste that purity for himself. So, he made her a bargain. He wouldn't take her brother to the Underworld, on the condition that she went in his place. Of course, she thought this meant Ameyar would spare his life ..."

It was Mimir's final sentence that finally snagged a small thread of interest in Kazuaki. Though he did not remove his eye from the course ahead, a long-awaited response finally escaped him. "He didn't," he guessed with near certainty.

Mimir shook his head. "No. He did not. Much as men want it to be so, people do not come back from the dead, Captain. No amount of prayer, or bargains with gods, will ever make that so."

The universal truth. Kazuaki knew it well. He turned the wheel, guiding the airship slowly to the right. "A god who tricks people into making agreements to benefit only himself," he started, squaring his shoulders. "Sounds like someone else I know."

"I'm flattered that you're thinking of me, Captain." Mimir stood on the tips of his toes, to get a better view of his surroundings. Northwestern still burned as far as the eye could see. "When she fell into the Underworld," he continued, "she learned of her brother's death. He was stuck in Purgatory. Unable to enter any afterlife, as per the deal she made with Ameyar. Beside herself with regret for her foolishness, she turned her spirit into light. A beacon. To guide her brother to her, should he ever lay eyes on her as he wandered aimlessly through nothingness. She figured the Underworld with her was better than Purgatory alone. No matter what Ameyar tried, he could not snuff her. The human spirit, bathed in love, is a powerful force, indeed."

Kazuaki's grip on the handles of the wheel tightened. Mimir's tale put him in mind of that moment in Aggi Normandy's home. The music from the phonograph spilled out around him, in the dark, with Bermuda pressed up against him. The moment she ripped out his cursed eye. An eye he tried to rip out many times himself, only to have it grow back into the empty socket. With a cleared throat, he shoved the memory aside. "What's your point?" he muttered, the propellers of the airship swirling the dull fog around them.

Mimir puffed out his chest. "Don't you see, Captain?" He dipped his head back and closed his glowing eyes, bathing in the abysmal, dead grays of the sunless sky. "Eventually, light finds its way to even the darkest places."

Kazuaki's eye tapered. Mimir was an enigma. He knew dissecting the lesser god was an uphill battle, for each unburied truth only revealed ten more complexities he didn't care to stomach. He opened his mouth to see if the creature might put himself to actual use and serve on lookout duty, but Rennington's voice rose up from below deck.

"Captain! Comrades off the starboard bow!"

Mimir stretched his neck out to see. Kazuaki's gaze followed. He spied the movement of the stolen steam car first, watching as it kicked up black dust with its tires. It seemed the town below had only just been touched by the heat of the wildfire. In the time they had spent working on Vadim, the crew seemed to have a difficult time getting ahead of the destruction. But as Kazuaki had watched a horde of people abandon their soon-to-be engulfed homes and businesses, crawling across the uneven grounds like a condensed tidal wave, he deemed their efforts a success. Some lives spared were better than none.

They must have spied the airship from the ground. The steam car came to a halt. Revi, Brack, Penn, and Bermuda raised their arms, guiding the vessel to their position.

As Kazuaki lowered the airship for pick up, Bermuda grabbed someone from the crowd of fleeing people. A terrified woman, holding a bundle of cloth to her chest. An infant, the quartermaster guessed. "You know how to use one of these things?" she asked, thumbing toward the steam car.

The panicked woman only nodded. Bermuda threw open the door. "Get in then. It's all yours."

The woman did not argue. A faster exit was a welcomed gift. The rate at which she threw her body into the vehicle was intense, but she still managed to keep a tender hand cradled over her infant as the car rattled off, following the crowd away from the approaching flames.

"Oi, Cappy! Perfect timing!" Brack shouted as Kazuaki struggled to find a spot to land.

He cursed Northwestern's clustered architecture. The propellers of the airship spun, keeping the large craft hovering above, but no open space presented itself. "Lower a rope!" he barked to Granite, as his arms locked the wheel in its place.

Absent of a verbal reply, Granite took measured, purposeful steps toward a supply crate and threw it open. He seized a suitable length of rope and tied it around his torso, content to serve as a stable anchoring point as he hurled the end over the ship's side.

Brack was the first to catch it. He held it out to Bermuda with a grin. "Ladies first."

The quartermaster rolled her eyes and scaled the rope, making short work of the task. Revi, Brack, and Penn followed suit. Before all four had successfully placed both feet on the floorboards, Kazuaki increased the airship's altitude, not wanting to loiter close to the heat of the approaching flames.

Bermuda had already made it on deck when Revi and Brack hurled their bodies over the ledge. "How did it go with Vadim?" Revi wondered, obvious hope in his tone that they'd be able to depart Northwestern swiftly.

"Kal's working on him now," Rennington informed the man, peering over the ledge to see if Penn made any progress. He watched as the cook muttered obscenities under his breath, slowly hoisting himself up the rope. Often the one to stay back with the ship, Penn had not developed the same endurance his comrades had. Rennington grinned and cupped a hand to his mouth. "Aye, Elmbroke, you need an assist?"

"Feck off, Renn!"

The Southern soldier snickered, swatting Granite's chest with the back of his wrist. "Come on, mate, pull him up. I've watched enough people suffer today."

Granite, emotionless, grabbed the rope. With one arm reaching out after the other, he dragged Penn's small body up with minimal exertion. When the cook finally emerged over the railing, his seething eyes fell on Rennington. "I had it," he muttered, smacking collected ash off his clothing.

"Yeah, yeah," Rennington laughed as Granite untied the rope from around his torso. "Whatever you say, mate."

Bermuda swept across the deck as the crew fell back into their responsibilities. She climbed the stairs to the captain at the wheel, only giving Mimir a fraction of her attention before she directed her words to Kazuaki. "It took most of our time just to get ahead of the fallout," she said, wiping her forearm across her cheek and chin. "We alerted the town to vacate. Told them to spread the word, but," she shrugged, "it's chaos down there, Kazuaki. I don't know how many of them will stick around to warn their neighbors unless they have family or friends there."

Kazuaki looked her over. She was coated in a heavy layer of residue from her labors. A streak of skin appeared across her face where her arm smeared the scum away. "It's fine," he said, finding perfection in her ruin. "You did everything you could."

"Yeah, well," her sigh turned into a cough as she tried to free some debris from inside her lungs, "I hope it was enough."

The two fell into an extended exchange of eye contact. It would have continued, had Kazuaki not become painfully aware of Mimir's cheeky grin. Even in his limited peripheral vision, it mocked him.

"Captain!" Kal threw open the cabin door to the main deck. He glanced up to the man at the wheel, shadowing his eyes with his hand to help him better see. "It's Vadim. We've made a breakthrough."

"About damn time," Kazuaki muttered, his shoulder blades tensing under his long jacket as he made a dramatic turn of the wheel. "Where's a safe place to drop him off?" he yelled down to Kal.

The ambassador rubbed the back of his neck, his expression betraying his uncertainty. "I don't know that such a place exists, Captain. No matter what town he's in, Vadim is susceptible to their return."

A tensed muscle twitched in Kazuaki's face. They had to leave him in Northwestern. He was bound to his division. With little options, he guided the ship in the direction opposite the fire's path. They'd get him as far away from the lesser gods' reign of terror as they were able. It was all they could do.

* * *

Kal strode out of the small, shabby building, readjusting the tie around his neck as he did. Night fell. Though they carried Vadim far from the fire, the amount of land that burned still showcased a soft, orange glow in the distance. Almost like a permanent setting sun.

The ambassador sighed and grabbed the rope that dangled from the hovering airship. He gave it three tugs, the indication from below that he was ready to be brought aboard.

Granite responded to the call, raising him back to the top of the airborne craft's deck. He grabbed the ambassador's arm and set him down before winding the rope around his hand and elbow, to return it to its place in the storage crate.

"Well?"

Kal spun at the sound of Kazuaki's voice behind him. Though he expected an interview from the captain, he still startled at the commanding nature of the man's presence. "Well, he seems back to himself. He put up quite a fuss at having to reside with the industrial working class. I told him the odds of any blue bloods taking him into their residence is nearly nonexistent, given the risk that would put them in. He should count himself lucky the laborers took him." Kal sighed, exhausted. "He's probably safer here, anyway. The lesser gods know he's a material man; I'm sure the factory belt will be one of the last places they look, should they feel the need to exploit him again."

Kazuaki glanced over his shoulder to be sure Revi fared well in keeping the airship piloted. Even at a distance, the man seemed irritated but capable. He turned back to Kal, his thoughts returning to Vadim. "Do you think we can trust he'll stay coherent?"

A hesitation followed. "We have no choice. Even if we found a suitable, level-headed replacement, without another Time Father to willingly initiate the new recruit, we'd be unable to strip Vadim of his Chronometer and bind it to another. I know it's not ideal leaving Northwestern under his control given his current record, Captain, but we're fortunate to have Vadim at all."

Kazuaki nodded. Kal was right. They'd done all they could here. It was time to return to their respective divisions, and hope the aid the Time Fathers and Mother sent to this place would be enough. "Prepare for departure then," he said, turning away.

Kal watched him go. He looked back at the crumbling structure he left Vadim inside and frowned. It was a pity to leave him here. Kal feared not just for the Northwestern Time Father's sanity, but for the people who shared the building with him. Their sense of patriotism to their division welcomed Vadim to share in what little they had. The ambassador hoped their kindness wouldn't be what killed them.

"Revi," Kazuaki climbed the steps to join the disgruntled father. "I can take over."

"Get some rest, Captain." Revi turned the wheel, guiding the airship back to Southeastern. "I wouldn't be able to sleep, anyway."

Kazuaki paused, his fingers winding around the rails. He studied Revi. The graying hairs and weathered face did not age him, but living with the apprehension of not knowing his daughter's well-being the last handful of days, certainly had. He knew the man volunteered to pilot the ship because he felt none could slice the skies apart as efficiently as he could. The offer stemmed more from anxiousness than the generosity of spirit. "I'm sure she's fine, Revi."

Revi only grunted a reply.

Kazuaki frowned. He couldn't deny he needed sleep. "I'll relieve you in three hours," he said, turning and descending the stairs.

The walk to his cabin was a quiet one. Contemplative. He found gratitude in it. Quiet moments were few and far between now, with Mimir constantly up his ass. Kazuaki closed the door behind him and threw his long jacket off before collapsing into his hammock: a replacement for the one that sank into the sea with his long lost ship.

The netting cradled his tired bones in all the right places. He closed his eye and relaxed into it; the one familiar comfort that followed him for years on end. All the physical ingredients for rest were present. It was the goings-on prodding his brain, which kept him from falling victim to sleep.

The state of affairs differed greatly from the last several years. There wasn't much Kazuaki Hidataka could not solve with a simple swing of a sword, or a well-timed bullet flying from a gun's barrel. But against the gods, he was helpless. He could slay those they brought under their influence, sure, but the gods were slaying them anyway. Those people were pawns. Single-use tools easily cast in the garbage when they ran their course of practicality. But the people weren't the problem. The lesser gods were.

And they were untouchable.

A slow squeak from his door's hinges made the captain scowl in the darkness. "Gods dammit, Mimir," Kazuaki snarled to the shadows, "can I not have a single hour of rest to myself?"

The door closed. He felt a presence in the room. "It's me," Bermuda's voice sounded; only a dusky figure in the corner.

"Bermuda?" Kazuaki swung his legs off the hammock's side and sat up, concerned. "What's wrong?"

She let out a short laugh. It was music. "What isn't?"

The captain's shoulders eased upon the realization that nothing, aside from the norm, immediately needed his attention. "An understatement," he whispered to the dark. "What can I do for you?"

Bermuda tilted her neck to the right, then to the left, banishing any stiffness from her spine as she strode over to the captain and sat down beside him. Her small body sank into the mesh. She rested her arms on her knees as she leaned forward. "We've seen a lot of terrible things together, haven't we, Kazuaki?"

The immortal felt his blood shift as if each cell was injected with helium. She'd never know what it did to him when she called him by his name. "We have."

"The things I saw down there, in that city ..." She shook her head. "It was chaos. The absolute evolution of human ruin. I watched flesh peel away from the bones of wild men, barely aware of their actions. I saw people begging for their lives as they were slaughtered by their friends, neighbors, husbands, wives, brothers, sisters. I saw others, who chose to die in the heat trying to return sense to their loved ones, rather than attempt to live a life without them. I heard the raw screams of pure agony, as some learned those they cared for had already perished in the next town over." Her voice was low. Detached, but still clinging to an undeniable piece of emotion. "Worst of all, Kazuaki ... I listened as the air burned with the regrets of lives unlived."

He listened. With the whole of his eye on her, he said nothing.

"I know we've seen it all before. I know we'll see it again." Bermuda reached over, without restraint, and placed her still soot-covered hand on his. "Death can't find you, Kazuaki. Blessing or curse, either way, you are spared from what I saw today. But one day ... one day, it will come for me. And I will not die like those people." She squeezed his hand. "I will *not* die with regrets."

His pulse quickened. He felt it in his throat. The savage beating of his heart. They had both toyed with this moment, he knew. But the safety of fantasy, the necessity of it, kept both of them in check. Bermuda challenged the barrier with her words. She challenged *him*. It was a battle he knew she'd win if she continued. The one arena in which he stood no chance. "I would never let anything bad happen to you," he said, a feeble attempt to redirect the conversation. "Not again."

"A noble gesture ..." Bermuda found him, her eyes on his. "But life is full of uncertainties. One day, you'll have no choice." She pulled his hand toward her, gripping it as she rested it on her chest, over her heart. "I will fight whatever problems face us until my dying breath. As long as there is blood in my veins, I will see to it that we do what must be done. But I'm tired of fighting this. I'm tired of fighting us."

His hand pressed into the exposed skin of her chest. He could not stop himself from spreading his fingers outward, just for the chance to grace the smooth line of her clavicle, as it spread toward her shoulders. "Bermuda," he hung his head, knowing the only chance he stood at a successful resistance was to avoid the temptation of seeing her offered body before him, "I won't deny my covetousness ... but this is a precarious path."

A smile cloaked half her face. She leaned toward him, slowly, her voice hushed. "As it turns out, I have a lot of experience with precarious situations."

He exhaled until his lungs winced and lifted his head. Her face was inches from his. She still smelled of fire, but also lust, and somehow, the sea. As if the salt and the wind embedded into her. It was intoxicating. "Tell me, with absolute certainty, if this is what you want," he said, feeling the last bits of restraint dissolve from his bloodstream.

"Ye—"

His hand slid up her neck and into her hair. Before she could finish, his lips were on hers. Years of pent up avidity broke through him with no control. The desire, the animalism, the appetite for which neither had any ability to harness, guided Kazuaki's hands around her waist and pulled her toward him.

In a moment of swiftness, he stood from the hammock, taking her with him. Her legs wrapped around the sides of his body, holding herself up as nimble fingers pried at the various buckles of her clothing. A soft glow from outside the cabin window illuminated their carnal entanglement. Whether from the moon or the still-burning fire sweeping the horizons of Northwestern, they did not know, and in the heat of the moment, they did not care.

CHAPTER NINETEEN

Several routes existed that Umbriel could have taken on her way to the post, but Nicholai remained certain his odds of running into her were better if he kept to the main road. He coughed into his arm at an unwelcome burst of coal dust carried on the wind. A stabbing of sand particles accosted his eyes. He wasn't sure how much sleep he got, but from the protests his body voiced, he figured it wasn't enough.

Umbriel's identifiable silver and lavender strands gave away her position as she stepped out of the post. They somehow caught the sun, even as it struggled to pierce through the clouds. A small gasp escaped her when she turned the corner and saw him. Umbriel knew immediately, by the look on his face, he was not happy.

It was a rare occurrence for Nicholai to catch Umbriel off guard. The moment was only matched in infrequency by Umbriel catching Nicholai with a less than pleased expression. The two stood for a moment, staring at one another, in their scarcely seen states, until Umbriel ventured the first words.

"You're mad," she said.

Nicholai glanced around at the patrons who slowed their strolls to observe the Time Father and Earth Mother huddled outside the post. He cleared his throat and gently took her arm, guiding her to a less visible location. "I'm not mad," he replied, a bit too irritably to sound convincing. "I'm disappointed. Malcolm says you had official documents in your hands—did you send something off under the guise of my approval?"

"You needed the sleep," Umbriel interjected, calm but firm in her reply.

Nicholai sighed, removing his hat to sweep his hand through his hair. "What you did is a capital offense, Umbriel. I know you're from a different time, but that's not how things work around here now."

Umbriel stood straighter. "I am sorry, Nicholai. But contrary to what society wants to believe, the world hasn't changed that much."

The Time Father turned his head away from her. He tried to collect his countless scattered thoughts and organize them but to no avail.

"We received a letter from Kazuaki," she explained, wrapping her arms around her torso as she readjusted which leg held her weight. "Well ... a cloth. He and the crew are alive, but he indicated a need for assistance. I've been watching and helping you with the political side of things for almost a year now, Nicholai. I know your habits. You would have sent whatever help Southeastern could spare, bearing in mind that we need to keep plenty of footmen for ..." She paused. Her voice lowered. " ...any impending deity-related crises."

Nicholai fixed his gaze on her, his brows furrowing. "Kazuaki sent word? And you didn't wake me?"

Umbriel closed her eyes and reached out to grab Nicholai's shoulders. When she opened them again, she made sure to find his dispersed focus. "Listen to me, Nicholai. Northwestern burns. I can only surmise it is the work of the gods. Now, I know what horrors weigh down on you. I know you want to save your people from this hell that awaits them. I know part of you went with Kazuaki and the others to Northwestern, dividing your already divided mind." Her grip squeezed to ensure she had his attention. "But you *need* to take care of yourself. You are drained. You are weary. I can replenish and replenish you until I have devoured every last speck of energy within myself, but your body still requires sleep. Nourishment. There is simply no way you can save anyone if you cannot even save yourself."

He felt the pressure of her fingertips as they buried into his ligaments. It seemed excessive, but she needed to make her point. His heart bled for Northwestern and its chaotic state, but he could not dwell on it. Instead, he cataloged it into the back of his mind with his growing collection of qualms. He needed to center himself. Nicholai inhaled deeply and nodded once. "I know. You're right." He rubbed the back of his neck, announcing an even greater concern. "Avigail is gone."

"What?" Umbriel's eyes widened, alarmed, and she looked over his shoulder as if she might somehow find the young woman standing there. "When? She can't have gotten far, she was there when I left— "

"She left a note. She didn't say anything, just that she would eventually return."

"Did Malcolm not see her leave? Or have any idea which way she went?" Umbriel's voice was steady, but Nicholai detected her hidden worry. "I sent him straight over as soon as I left."

Nicholai held up a hand to try and calm her. "He didn't. I know it sounds grim, but it may have been better that she wasn't there. She was fortunate enough to avoid an unwelcome confrontation with a hired hand of sorts."

The horror on Umbriel's typically serene face only grew at his announcement. That she had only left him alone for such a short time and so many terrors befell him, made guilt nip at her ankles. She knew it was ridiculous; guilt was a useless emotion, incapable of solving anything. She tried to shake it off, but it stuck like an embedded thorn. "Where is the person who attacked you now?" she asked.

"Malcolm is alerting some footmen to remove him from the house. He's tranquilized, no threat anymore."

"Another assassination attempt?" Umbriel guessed.

"I can't say for certain." Nicholai shrugged a single shoulder. "I think if he meant to kill me, he could have. He uttered something strange before he surrendered his consciousness. A name, I surmise. Ameyar, was it?"

Umbriel's face lost some of its color. "The God of the Underworld," she whispered, sliding her hands off his shoulders to raise her fingers to her lips in thought. "Dimjir said he was among the few lesser gods who wished to exact their revenge. Ameyar must have chosen Southeastern as his territory."

"The Underworld ..." Nicholai blinked and rubbed his eyes, exasperated. "I suppose the God of Harmlessness would be asking for too much, wouldn't it?"

"You joke, Nicholai, but Ameyar is not to be taken lightly." Umbriel's expression shifted, unamused.

In spite of everything, Nicholai laughed. "What would you have me do, Umbriel? If you don't laugh ..." He shook his head. The only other option was to curl up into a fetal position and damn his bad luck. "On the positive side, at least things can't get much worse."

Tiny bells chimed as the post office's door opened and closed. A courier, dressed in his official regalia, started down the cobblestone streets of the main road leading to Nicholai's homestead. He paused when he caught sight of the Time Father and Earth Mother tucked into the building's exterior corner. The man arched a brow, finding it unusual the two would hide away from the public in such a manner. He chalked it up to the whispered rumors of the two's scandalous relationship with one another and cleared his throat. "Uh, excuse me—I ... had hoped to catch up to Miss Umbriel Dasyra before she wandered too far, but ... um ... I see you're both here, anyway."

Nicholai stiffened under the scrutiny of the courier's gaze and climbed out of the shadows with a forced smile. "Ha, yes, well ... here we are," he said, stumbling over his words. "What can I do for you, Mr. Nowen?"

The courier flashed a contrived grin. "Right. I forgot to mention when you dropped off the letter, Miss Dasyra," he fished into his satchel and handed the document to Nicholai, "I was going to send this back to the Addihein homestead with you. But I see your unexpected presence has ... saved me a trip."

Nicholai kept up his smile, perhaps a bit too forcefully, and with the letter pinched between his fingers, gave the courier a salute. "Right. Thank you. Well done, Mr. Nowen. Will that be all?"

The courier coughed, radiating awkwardness, and nodded. "Y-yes. That will be all, Mr. Addihein. Good day to you, sir."

Nicholai watched as the man strode down the street, off to carry on with his deliveries. Umbriel stepped out from the corner, her attention on the sealed letter. "What is it?" she asked, almost too apprehensive to question its contents.

The Southeastern Time Father broke the wax seal, unfolding the cream-colored parchment into his hands. His eyes darted from left to right as he scanned the contents. The paper fell at his side, still clutched in his hand.

Umbriel took on a worried appearance. It did not take a keen observer to know by the look on Nicholai's face, that it did not hold good news. She forced herself to ask, "What does it say?"

A warm breeze brushed up against Nicholai's skin. He couldn't look at her. He barely felt the letter in his hand anymore, as a numbness crawled up his fingers and arm. It threatened to consume him in his entirety, but like everything else, he muscled over it, trying to drown the doubt in his surplus of optimism. But this ... this was a difficult one to hold down. "It's from Eastern," he said. "Elowyn is missing."

* * *

The environment was sterile. It was a coveted quality for a mental hospital. The white walls, with the white floors, with the white trim, the white desks, the white uniforms worn by the staff ... it was enough to send a strange chill up a man's arms. And it did.

Edvard Addihein composed himself soon after the short shudder swept through his bones. Unstimulating. That's what one would call this environment, he decided, as he waited in a hallway outside a patient's room. Absolutely lacking in anything that might evoke a single feeling whatsoever.

"This one is probably your best bet, Mr. Addihein," a well-dressed gentleman said as he approached Edvard from behind. He tapped his finger on the door as he peered into the iron grates that fell over the small window. "She's one of the few who will talk. The others ... well, over half of them won't even eat or dress themselves unless they're forced to do so."

"What's her name?" Edvard asked as he stared at the woman, hunched over in the single, decrepit chair the room held.

"Uh ... 245, 245 ..." The man flipped through several documents he held in his hands. "Esther Hiddle. Came in about a week ago. Sharpened a point on a metal weather vane she had on her roof and stabbed a mail courier with it. Insists the God of Metal required it."

Edvard frowned. Without removing his eyes from her, he asked, "Required it for what?"

The man shrugged, tucking the papers under his arm. "She didn't say."

The Western Time Father closed his eyes. The woman emitted an aura he did not find particularly welcoming. He did not wish to enter. But whole cities burned. In and out of Western, flames crept through Panagea like a tsunami. The occasional rainstorm silenced some, but it was not long before others burned in their place.

Though Kazuaki Hidataka took a crew to Northwestern following the events at Panagea's center, he had yet to hear anything from Vadim.

Nicholai reported citizens panicking in numbers unheard of. Those who feared the announcement of the gods' presence wished to flee, but the terror lived everywhere.

Aggi Normandy had begrudgingly started to quarantine those who passed extensive psychiatric evaluations, in an attempt to keep the sane people safe while he struggled to find a solution to save the corrupt.

Nordjan prepared his cognizant soldiers for a battle against his own people. A battle he did not wish to enter. Though the cold tactics of Northern seemed questionable to some, Edvard knew Nordjan loved his people, but he didn't know what to do. He responded with the only thing familiar to him: force.

Emont of Southwestern hadn't responded to any letters.

Elowyn of Eastern was missing.

His division suffered a similar fate. He needed to get to the root of the problem. He needed to know how to end this madness. And there, sitting in a rotting chair on the other end of an iron wall, was his best bet at doing so.

"I know it looks inhumane, Mr. Addihein," the hospital operative frowned as he dug out a key to open the door, "but she's in shackles for her safety as well as your own."

Edvard nodded as the metal cage creaked open. "I understand."

"I don't know how much progress you'll make, but you're welcome to ask her whatever you'd like," he added as if she weren't there. He closed the door behind Edvard, sealing him inside. "I'll wait here until you're done."

Muscles tightened at the sound of the door closing behind him. Edvard stared down at the woman, who barely rocked an inch or two, back and forth in her seat. He tried to find compassion. He tried to remind himself she was one of his people.

Esther looked up at him. Her face couldn't be used to read her mind. It was too wild, too unpredictable. An otherwise sweet looking woman, neatly dressed, holding tight to a handkerchief that she crumpled and uncrumpled in her hands. Edvard approached, stopping several feet away. His eyes followed the chains that started at her wrists and ended at a metal clasp dug into the wall.

Her skin bore marks of self-injury. He spotted dried blood underneath her fingernails, to match the clawed out tears on her arms. For a brief moment, he wondered if they tried to use drugs as an effective means of sedating her, but these were professionals, capable psychiatrists of the Western division. Edvard ventured a guess they had tried just about everything.

It was this knowledge that made him feel the part of a fool for coming. But still, he had to try.

"Hello, Esther," he said, his voice seeming loud in the otherwise silent room.

She smiled. It was a smooth grin. If he hadn't known she murdered a man with a weather vane, he would have found it pleasant instead of off-putting. "Hello, Time Father," she replied, ceasing her rocking.

Edvard cleared his throat. "I understand you are ... a ward of the God of Metal?"

Her smile broadened. "You understand correctly."

The Time Father's hands slipped behind his back as he loomed over her. He tried not to appear threatening in his stance, but it was difficult, with her chained to her place in the chair beneath him. "I would very much like to know your objective, Esther. Or ... the God of Metal's objective, if that is who you are acting for."

She seemed content by his word choice. "You were right to come with words and not weapons, Time Father. Olnos is unbeatable in the realm of metal and steel." Esther laughed as if she were privy to a joke Edvard did not understand. "Our objective is to undo the injustice of mistreatment."

"Mistreatment?" Edvard arched a brow. It had been a long time since he read up on anything regarding the lesser gods. Over thirty years. He knew that human beings were otherwise safe from their wrath, that the only thing a lesser could do was over-embellish an already anchored thought held by an individual. For Esther to have responded to Olnos' whispers, she must have shared his thoughts. "Do you feel as if you've endured mistreatment of sorts, Miss Hiddle? Before coming to this place, I mean."

She lifted her head. He better saw the claw marks around her temples and cheeks, but they were not her sole sign of suffering. Her eyes, sunken and hollow, paired with her pale, wasting skin, indicated malnourishment of sorts. A sickness. "We have all suffered, Time Father. Gods. Humans. Panagea. Men used gods for their gifts and favors, with no actual care for their long-term state. They were abandoned as soon as they ran their course of usefulness. Panagea is much the same. We have sucked it dry. Used it for all it was worth." She squeezed the handkerchief in her bony fingers. "It's just as the elites and blue bloods of Panagea use us for physical labor. They leave us to our squalor. It's only a matter of time before we, too, are forgotten and abandoned when we run our course of usefulness ... like our omnipotent companions before us."

Edvard listened, his jaw subconsciously tightening with each additional word she spoke. "We do the best we can by all of Panagea's people," he said, though his words lacked conviction. He recognized the societal divide. He'd seen it his entire life.

"No ..." Esther adopted a coy smile and raised a shaking hand, extending a finger in Edvard's direction. "Olnos hand-picked you, Time Father. He told me that everyone says those who used the gods and forgotten them have all died out ... that a new generation of people has been born, free from the sins of their ancestors. And yet, here you remain. You've buried your sins by playing the part of a fair leader to your people. Maybe so much time has passed that you've genuinely forgotten your egregious act of injustice. But history never forgets."

The Western Time Father's veins filled with ice. He exhaled sharply, caught off guard by her statement, then swallowed and turned to face the operative standing outside the metal prison. "Leave us be."

The man, who had not paid much attention, straightened at the request. "Excuse me? With all due respect, Mr. Addihein, shackles or not, she's a dangerous—"

"That's an order," Edvard stated, his voice booming off the claustrophobic walls of Esther's cell.

A long pause followed. Hesitation lived in the man's actions. One did not disobey the instructions of a Time Father. "Yes, sir," he said, obvious in his reluctance to relent. But acting on command, he slowly walked away.

When Edvard turned his attention back to Esther, she grinned from ear to ear. "You know of what I speak," she whispered.

A stillness followed. But soon, Edvard dug his hands into his pockets as his eyes hit the floor. "How could I forget?"

"See how quick men are to exchange guilt for comfort?" Esther licked her lips and leaned back in her chair. "This is why we follow the gods. They are absent of the same fallacies that follow mankind. They will lead us to something better."

"They're leading you to your deaths," Edvard interjected, his hands balling to fists safely inside his pockets.

Esther's face iced over. "Look deep into the world in which we live, and you will see, in some cases, death is better."

He did not want to believe it. He refused. "They're killing you. Making you kill each other."

"They're saving the world, Time Father. Panagea can no longer endure mankind's mistreatment."

Edvard's nostrils flared as he tried to suppress his voice. "They're just using you to get what they want."

"How can you chastise their actions, when they mirror your own?" Esther's brows rose on her scarred, emaciated face. "Worse, perhaps, that you not only used the gods for their gifts, but you betrayed your wife in the process."

Edvard's eyes fell to a close, gentle at first until he squeezed them with fierceness. He did not care to pick apart the details on how she knew. As he remembered, the gods were full of surprises. "I made a mistake," he murmured.

Esther only grinned. "Which part was the mistake, Time Father?"

He pulled his hands from his pockets and rubbed his face, leaving his fingertips resting on his exasperated jaw. "Seeing the damages the gods have caused ... at this moment, I am no longer sure."

"Oh, Edvard," Esther smirked, addressing him by name for the first time since he entered her room, "they're only getting started."

CHAPTER TWENTY

The airship floated above Southeastern, having sliced through all of the Northwestern division, leaving the bulk of the fires behind it. The occasional plume of smoke rose from the land below, but they did not stop. There was nothing they could do. It was a fool's paradise to think they could save everyone from the lesser gods' wrath.

Kazuaki opened the door to his cabin and closed it behind him. A man of his word, he had tried to pry Revi away from the ship's wheel three hours into his shift, but the man refused to relent. Kazuaki did not object. Revi's obstinacy afforded the captain more time to acquaint himself with the curves of Bermuda's body: war-torn, but flawless, nevertheless. The reality of her exceeded every fantasy.

There was no sun present to shine down upon him, but he could not shake the satisfaction from his traditionally rigid body. It had been a long time since Kazuaki Hidataka experienced a dominating sense of excellence, stranger still that it followed an abysmal visit to Northwestern. But even the heavy uncertainty of Panagea's fate did not weigh the captain down. Not today.

"Mornin', Cappy!"

Brack's shrill voice pierced through Kazuaki's reverie, like a sword through flesh. Kazuaki closed his eye, as if that would somehow bar the Rabbit's words from penetrating his brain and ruining his faultless morning, but to no avail.

"Did you hear the news, Cap?" Brack arched a brow as he bent over to grab a crate he had every intention of moving to the storage area. "Strange things happenin' on board since we left Northwestern."

Kazuaki cocked his head to the side. Puzzlement did not often find its way to his face, but he could not disguise his confusion. "Such as?" he asked, baffled that anything newsworthy could happen aboard his ship without his knowledge.

The Rabbit shook his head, assuming a look of apprehension as he cradled the box under one arm. "There's been whispers ... of a rare creature spotted on this very ship."

Confusion shifted to skepticism. Kazuaki narrowed his eye. "Really," he muttered flatly, his single word more a statement than a question.

"Indeed, it's true," Brack confirmed, nodding to emphasize his statement. "A being as legendary as it is scarce," he added, injecting a dramatic level of tonality in his words.

Kazuaki caught on quickly. His expression shifted to a glare. "Don't say it—"

"The beast—"

"Rabbit—"

"—with two backs!"

"Belay that!" Kazuaki barked, clenching his fists as Brack erupted into volcanic laughter. He did not know how he knew. It was as if Brack Joney could smell lascivious activity from a mile away. "Rabbit, I have no energy for this today."

"I reckon not," Brack chuckled, his lips pressed together as he tried to keep his amusement trapped inside. Unable to resist, he added, "Gave it all to the quartermaster last night, aye?"

"Go on!" Kazuaki scowled, thrusting an arm in the direction of the airship's storage. "Distance yourself from me now, before I hurl you over the ledge."

Brack continued to snicker as he approached the entryway leading to the storage room. He paused in the open door, turning over his shoulder to look at the captain. "Hey, Cappy?"

His eye twitched. Kazuaki clenched his jaw and rubbed his temples. Though he suspected he'd regret it, he muttered through clenched teeth, "What, Rabbit?"

A wide grin split across Brack's face. "On a scale of one to ten—"

"Go!"

"Right," Brack sunk into the staircase that led below deck. The sound of his laughter echoed up the flight of steps, taunting Kazuaki until he reached the bottom.

Kazuaki shook his head and crept toward the edge of the airship, his hands behind his back as he peered out at the horizon. He recognized some of the landmarks below. They would arrive in Nenada at any moment. Revi certainly pulled his weight navigating the vessel home quickly.

The man must have run on fumes. He did not once see him partake in any of the food Penn had prepared since they left Vadim. Kazuaki needed to relieve him, whether he wanted to or not. He couldn't have a half-mad man, disparaged by sleep deprivation and starvation, trying to land an airship the size of a small factory.

He spun around and into Mimir, who sniffed at him like an animal. "Ugh," Mimir wrinkled his nose, and he drew his neck back as if standing close to Kazuaki edged him toward illness. "Captain. You reek of testosterone and pheromones."

Kazuaki's jaw tightened as he pushed passed Mimir, preferring to ignore him rather than drive himself mad with the knowledge that he could do him no physical harm. He headed toward Revi to take over the landing.

"Control yourself in the future, Captain! You have a lot on your plate!" Mimir shouted after him, cupping a hand around his mouth to help his voice travel. "Humans," he muttered to himself. "Whether modern times or ancient, they sure love their copulating and their orgies."

"Revi." Kazuaki climbed the steps to the main deck where the man stood, gripping the wheel. "I'm here to relieve you."

"I got us this far," Revi murmured, showing no indication of moving.

"And your efforts are as appreciated as they are temporarily terminated." Kazuaki shoved him aside and took over the wheel.

Revi grunted at the physical force of the captain's body ushering him aside. He scowled, annoyed, but as he curled and uncurled his fingers, he realized a stiffness lived in them from his hours-long endeavor of holding fast to the wheel.

It felt strange to walk. His legs stabbed at him as soon as he moved, urging him to sit, to relieve the pressure of having to hold up his body for another moment. "Fine," he muttered. "Nenada is just ahead. I'll prepare the ship for landing."

Kazuaki did not protest. If Revi's prerogative was to work himself into oblivion, it was his decision to do so. As long as he wasn't responsible for landing the ship.

Kazuaki spied the familiar territory of Nicholai's home town ahead and prepped the airship to decrease its altitude. "All hands on deck!" he shouted, his order carrying through the ship with the same magnetism it always had. "We're taking her down!"

Landing in Southeastern was a much easier process than anywhere else, given Nicholai's generosity in preparing a practical space for the airship to return home. As the vessel lowered to its place, propellers whipping in their predictable fashion, Kazuaki felt a small sense of relief ignite inside him that Nenada was here to greet them. After the chaos in Northwestern, he almost feared the small town might have perished in a sea of flames.

The ramp lowered. The crew exited. Mimir and Jernal were the first off. Granite's dog barreled down shortly after, happy to set foot on solid ground again. As the other crew members departed, they gazed into the faces of Nenada's people.

A few wandering eyes from passers-by fell in their direction. Bermuda arched a brow. Their expressions seemed fearful. Skeptical. As if the people wondered whether they brought chaos back with them, or comfort.

Revi ignored them. He strode across the lot, making a line for Nicholai's homestead. The door opened before he approached, and

Umbriel stepped out, but before she said anything, he eased her aside and walked into the residence.

"Avigail?" he called out, looking around.

"Oh, Revi—" Umbriel extended an arm toward him, but Nicholai beat her to the punch when he stepped out from behind one of the bedroom walls.

"Revi ..." The Time Father took a deep breath and held it. He held a note in his hand. "Welcome back."

The Houton man's eyes tapered. He did not like the way Nicholai and Umbriel flanked him. Nor did he like the obvious absence of his daughter. "Where is she?" he asked, already knowing he wouldn't enjoy the answer.

Nicholai cleared his throat and took two steps toward Revi, holding out the note. "She left. But, she did indicate she'd be returning—"

Revi tore the note out of Nicholai's hands and scanned it. The Time Father knew when he finished, as soon as the look of devastation crept into the man's eyes. "You were supposed to watch her," he growled, lifting his venomous gaze from the note.

The Time Father held up his hands. "I tried, Revi, I did. We both did. We had no idea she even entertained the idea of leaving. She seemed content here."

With thoughtlessness bred by fatigue and anger, Revi grabbed Nicholai's arms and pushed him up against the nearest wall. "I trusted you," he snarled, an unruliness in his eyes.

Umbriel approached to intervene, but Nicholai stopped her with a look. "You're entitled to your anger. I'm sure you're feeling—"

Revi pulled him forward just to slam him into the wall once more. "Do not tell me what I'm feeling, Nico! You can't even begin to grasp it," he seethed, his shoulders rising as he lowered his head. He tried to steady himself. He knew his actions were unwarranted, but Revi Houton was familiar with rage. It served him well over the last decade. He did not know much else, other than to lose himself to it completely.

"Revi," Rennington's voice sounded through the door. He entered the room and put a hand on the man's shoulder. "Come on, mate. You know Nico. He would've stopped her if he could've."

"We're all worried about Avigail," Nicholai added, still pinned to the wall by Revi's aggression. He made no move to free himself, and instead waited for Revi's anger to pass. "But I'm afraid ... she isn't the only one missing."

By now, the others had gathered closer to the open doorway. Umbriel stepped aside, allowing Brack, Penn, Kal, Bermuda, Granite, the dog, and Kazuaki to enter. The small home filled up quick. The Earth Mother's eyes fell on Jernal and Mimir as they stood outside.

"Do come in," she said, motioning them inside. "We'll make room."

Mimir beamed as he joined the crowd. Jernal, however, looked less than pleased as he squeezed his body into the claustrophobic space. "Awfully small quarters for a Time Father," he murmured, trying not to touch anyone.

Nicholai ignored him. "Elowyn has been reported missing. But Eastern's time still ticks, so wherever she is, she's presumably safe."

The news did not settle well with anyone, but Rennington, in particular, showcased a deep concern. "E.P ..." His eyes narrowed. "How long has she been gone?"

"I've only known about it since yesterday," Nicholai announced. "Emont is also unresponsive. I fear something may have happened to him, as well."

"We've surmised they're after the division leaders," Umbriel interjected. "Ameyar sent someone to try and place a claim over Nicholai."

Kazuaki caught Umbriel's eyes. "We've concluded the same. The Goddess of Harvest had Vadim. Northwestern is in dire straits. Towns all over are in flames. There wasn't much we could do."

"With all due respect," Kal stepped forward, standing tall, "I must announce my departure. If what we fear is true, and the lesser gods are targeting division leaders, it is of utmost importance that I return to Southern with efficiency."

"Right." Rennington sighed, sweeping a hand through his hair. He feared for Elowyn's safety, but he was duty-bound to protect Bartholomew. To protect Southern. "I'll take you there straight away, Kal. But Nico ..." He turned, pointing a finger at the still-held Time Father, "if you hear anything about E.P., and I mean *anything* ... you alert me straight away, you hear?"

Nicholai tried to force a comforting smile. It was only half successful. "You'll be the first to know."

"Thanks, mate." Rennington patted Revi's shoulder, a silent urge to release Nicholai. He then turned to Kazuaki and held out a hand. "Captain. Always a pleasure."

The immortal seized the offering, nodding. "Give Bartholomew my regards."

"And a big ol' hug from the Rabbit," Brack nudged Kal with his elbow, grinning.

The ambassador chuckled, issuing a polite nod to Brack. "Yes, well ... it was a pleasure to meet you all. I wish it were due to better circumstances," he said as he backed out the door. Rennington joined him after he finished his farewells. Kal smiled, once. It was genuine. "Gods-speed to you all."

The Southern soldier led the ambassador to the nearest steam train as the others remained inside. Bermuda closed the door after they disappeared, not wanting to risk the infiltration of prying ears. "So," she started, glancing at Umbriel and Nicholai. "What can we do? I doubt Vadim will remain stable. If the gods require him again and find him hiding in the industrial district, I don't think he'll have the ability to stop them from manipulating him again."

"And we had no luck with Dimjir," Umbriel added, tucking strands of hair behind her ear. "He claims only a small handful of the lesser gods harbor resentment, but they are amassing more followers by the day ... and, unfortunately, they are the most volatile of them all. The other lessers hold no grudges with mankind, but do not wish to take up hands against humanity's tormentors, as they could easily slay them."

In the heaviness of the room, Brack laughed. "Slay them? I thought gods were immortal."

"To a degree," Mimir chimed in as he leaned up against a nearby wall. "Just as man can kill man, god can kill god. If you ask me, Dimjir is wise not to meddle with that lot. It's one thing to possess a weapon hand-forged by the lesser gods from the realm in-between ... it's a whole different challenge entirely to get close enough to those warmongers to use it."

Kazuaki visibly delighted at Mimir's confession that gods could die. A bit too much for the lesser god's comfort. But before either could speak, Umbriel interjected.

"There's no way we could acquire a weapon from their realm. Only lessers, themselves, can bring one of their holy creations into the physical world. But I do have another option for us to try ..."

The others perked with interest, save for Revi, who still drowned in apprehension for his daughter's fate. He finally managed to release his grip on Nicholai, allowing the Time Father to cast a curious eye toward Umbriel. "What option is that?" he asked, having heard nothing of it until this moment.

Umbriel pinched her lips together. "The lesser gods are after the Time Fathers and Time Mother. They know they can't influence every man, so they're attacking society's hierarchy at its top-most level. If they're going to crawl to the highest chain of command, then so, too, are we."

Mimir bristled and drew away from Umbriel. His glowing eyes widened. "You wouldn't ..."

She ignored him. "I will not mislead any of you. This will be a very dangerous undertaking. If you do not wish to take part, there will be no assigned blame."

The crew exchanged glances with one another before returning their questioning eyes to Umbriel. Brack was the only one anxious enough to ask, to avoid lingering in the crippling wait. "What is it we have to do, exactly?"

* * *

" ...Mushrooms?"

Bermuda did not attempt to hide her skeptical expression at the small pieces of fungi that Umbriel held out in her palm. The Earth Mother made a large show of ushering everyone into the deepest part of the woods, reiterating the countless cautions they needed to take, and emphasizing the importance of having a firm hold on individual certitude. But now, staring at the rather unimpressive looking creations Umbriel grew from the ground, the impact lost its punch.

"Not just any mushrooms," Umbriel informed. "They're Pneuma bisporus. Otherwise known as the Spirit Mushroom."

Mimir was quiet. He gazed at the fungi with a certain level of consideration, while the others huddled in a circle around the Earth Mother. The lesser god stroked his chin as he sat on a moss-covered piece of shrapnel, silent in his musings.

Nicholai stared, accompanying Bermuda and the others in their state of disbelief. He opened his mouth to speak, stopped, thought, and then opened it again. "Ah ... Umbriel, it's ... it's not as if I don't believe this will help, but ..." He rubbed the back of his neck, not wanting to come across as unreceptive, "but, how, exactly, will this help solve our problem?"

"You needn't concern yourself with this particular task, Nicholai." Umbriel offered him a gentle smile. "I'm sorry. But your mind is currently too fragile to participate."

"Excuse me?" A single brow rose on the Time Father's surprised face. "What do you mean? I intend to help. This affects my people."

"It's not debatable, Nicholai." Umbriel tilted her head, sympathetic to the man's anguish. "The Spirit Mushroom is a dangerous tool, used in archaic times to expand an individual's consciousness. Its effect is as profound as it is temperamental.

Once the mushroom is ingested, the chemicals released will trigger a reaction in the brain, washing away your preconceived limitations of the physical world, as it relates to the unseen realms. It will open the door to places in which lesser gods weave in and out of; where many went to wait out their weaknesses when mankind allowed them to fall away from existence." She turned to the others. "Our primary goal is to find the Unnamed. The Being responsible for creation. If your resolve wavers even a hair from its objective, if something else clouds your mind from your goal, you will fail to find It. And you will be lost to the manipulations of wherever your mind ends up. I can say with great certainty, you will be taken to a wonderful place. A place the gods who remain there will make you never wish to leave. And that is where you will stay, trapped between realms, until your physical body perishes. You're too vulnerable, Nicholai. I'm sorry."

"I'm not—" Nicholai paused, sighing. "I know Darjal has been in my head. I know, in a few instances, I haven't been ... 'myself'. But I need to do this, Umbriel. The more of us who participate, the better our odds are of reaching this Unnamed and requesting Its assistance."

"The Unnamed does not play favorites in the affairs of men or gods," Mimir chirped from his place in the corner. He busied himself picking the petals off a small flower he found on the ground. "It only abides by universal law, none of which the lesser gods are breaking. You're wasting your time."

Revi paced, restless, as the others discussed the plan. Dried leaves crunched under the force of his boots. "This is pointless," he growled, stopping to face the others. "What the hell is this thing supposed to do for us anyway? We can't defeat the gods ourselves, so what, we invite an even more omnipotent one into the shit storm that's Panagea?"

Umbriel frowned, more from frustration born of the circumstances than Revi's attitude. "I understand it sounds desperate. That's because it is. The Unnamed created mankind. Perhaps It will take pity."

"I doubt It feels pity," Mimir muttered, twisting the now destroyed flower between his fingertips. He flicked the stem away, bored with it. "It didn't feel anything when it condemned me to that well."

"When you find It, if you find It," Umbriel said, casting Mimir's words to the wayside as she looked out across the others, "beseech It. If It will not help on Its own accord, perhaps It will show us the way to help ourselves."

"Fine," Bermuda said, holding out her hand. "Shell out the mushrooms, then. Let's find this thing."

Umbriel curled her wrist inward, pulling the contents in her palms back toward her chest. "It is not as simple as all that, Bermuda. We need someone to stand vigilant and guard us. With the lesser gods running amuck, and the men and women of Panagea falling victim to their manipulations, we cannot be too careful, even out here in the forest. The Spirit Mushrooms will render us paralyzed. We will, in all essence, leave our physical bodies behind. The only way to return is through sheer force of will."

The quartermaster drew her shoulders back and inclined her chin, looking out over the collective. "Any volunteers?"

"With respect, Revi," Umbriel interrupted, resting a gentle hand on the unstable man's arm, "I believe you should sit this one out, too. Your head and heart are clouded with concerns for Avigail. I suspect the gods would capitalize on that heavily, should you not reach the Unnamed."

The man scoffed and lifted an arm as if that would somehow sweep away her cautions. "No, if this thing is all-knowing, I want in. Maybe It can tell me where Avigail went."

Umbriel shook her head. "It is your very concern for Avigail that will prevent you from reaching the Unnamed. It's best if you stay guard."

Even the Earth Mother's supernatural serenity could not calm Revi Houton. He tried to temper himself, but his growing rage was evident. "If I stand a chance at finding her— " he started, through clenched teeth.

"You have no chance," Umbriel interrupted, blunt, but kind. "Your mind is chaos, and understandably so."

"Revi," Kazuaki snapped his eye toward the man. "Stand guard. You'll be a hell of a lot more useful to Avigail if you're not trapped between realms."

The man closed his eyes. His fingers balled into tight fists and shook with boiling rage. He wished to hurl his arm into a tree but stopped himself. Sense lived in the captain's statement, but it did not make accepting it any easier. Standing watch demanded much of him, with only his imagination of what happened to Avigail left to keep him company.

He almost hoped they endured an attack. Circumstances as they were, Revi itched for a therapeutic release. Slamming his pent up aggression into the body of an attacker would be welcomed. Though he said nothing, Kazuaki sensed his acceptance.

"I'll guard," Granite offered, crossing his hulking arms over his chest. It's what he was best suited for. That, and he did not wish to abandon consciousness, knowing Mimir showed an avid interest in his dog. His trust for the lesser god was nonexistent.

"I can stand guard," Jernal said, having stood quietly against the trunk of a tree as the crew laid out their plan. "I've had enough of gods and god-related things. The last thing I want to do is enter their realm."

A scoff from Kazuaki deflated the soldier's offer. "We're not going to make it that easy for you to off us," he muttered.

Jernal's eyes narrowed to slits. "If I wanted to off any of your crew, I'd have done it by now."

Ire lived in the captain's face. He glared at Jernal. "Say that again," he started, taking a step toward him.

"Easy, Captain," Mimir clambered from his spot and wedged himself between Jernal and Kazuaki. "The commander will issue no harm to your ..." He glanced at Bermuda and made a face. " ...belongings. I will make sure of it."

Kazuaki's gaze flattened. "Somehow, that doesn't make me feel any better."

"Captain," Granite's booming voice commanded attention. "I got it."

It was with a lingering hesitation that Kazuaki scrutinized Granite's offer. He knew the behemoth could handle Jernal alone; even greater were his odds that Revi would be present to serve as an additional hand. Though it did not sit well in his gut, he withdrew his apprehension upon the realization that he had little choice. "All right."

"Umbriel," Nicholai stepped forward, "I still think you're making a mistake. I can help."

She spun around and laid her hands on his face, cradling his cheeks between her palms. Warmth radiated from her. Her eyes found his. "Nicholai, you have an incredible heart and a passion for assisting everyone. I know you want to believe you can do this, but you are the Time Father of the Southeastern division. The risk is too great. If you were to fall to the tricks of the realm in-between, if you were to lose yourself to that place, Southeastern would be in a terrible position. I know you love your people. It is *for* your people that you cannot contribute."

Nicholai saw the determination in her. He knew he could not change her mind. That it stemmed from genuine concern for his well-being was of small comfort, but he surrendered with a small nod.

Umbriel offered him a comforting smile before she turned toward the others. "Our chances of reaching the Unnamed are small. If you find yourself elsewhere, amongst the lesser gods, they will do anything necessary to trick your minds into staying. Take heed. Nothing is as it seems. Focus on the Unnamed. If you don't make it, you must wake yourself. Ignore the fantasies. Focus on returning to your body. Please, my friends, hold tight to that knowledge. It may be the only thing that gets you out alive."

Bermuda held out her hand once more. "We know the risks. Come on. Let's get this over with."

Umbriel drew in a large breath and placed a small handful in Bermuda's palm. Then Kazuaki. She approached Brack and Penn, then tilted her head. "Are you two sure you wish to partake?"

Penn shrugged, apathetic as he held out his hand. "I've eaten worse things."

Umbriel smiled. She saw through his detachment as if it were glass. His hand shook with a nearly invisible fear, but he projected none in his mannerisms. Penn Elmbroke knew he was of little use in hand-to-hand combat, but he did not shy away from rising to any occasion that benefitted his chosen family. "There you are then," she said, placing the Spirit Mushrooms in his palm.

Brack smirked when she gazed at him. His face held a cockiness to it. It differed from his usual self-assuredness. "You're aware of the dangers, Brack?" Umbriel hovered the fungi over his waiting hand, hesitant to give it up.

"Don't worry about me none, love," Brack winked. "Not my first go with Pneuma bisporus."

Umbriel blinked, perplexed by his admission, but she did not have time to explore it further. She placed the mushrooms in his hand and turned to the others, cradling the remainder of the harvest in her palm. "All right. Good luck, everyone."

Kazuaki stole a glimpse of Bermuda from the corner of his eye. As if she felt his gaze upon her, she turned to it. He knew she was a capable woman. More than most. But he couldn't shake the growing feeling of concern that she might lose herself to a faux world, should she fail to reach the Unnamed. "Don't ... forget to come back," he whispered.

Half a smirk formed on the quartermaster's lips. Her eyes reassured him. "They could never hold me," she whispered back, throwing the mushrooms into her mouth.

Nicholai watched as the crew consumed their hallucinogenic morsels. It was a slow wait for the ingredient to take hold. Umbriel eased herself down into a sitting position and appeared to meditate.

Brack showed an obvious absence of fear. He hunkered down and laid on his back, crossing his arms behind his head to serve as a makeshift pillow. With one leg bent at the knee, he laid his other over it, bobbing the foot up and down, carefree as he waited for the aftermath.

Kazuaki watched Umbriel. Having no experience with the product, he thought to follow her lead, but the pose she assumed wasn't his forte. He felt the weakness grow up his legs as the paralysis started to take hold. He lowered himself to the ground, his back pressed up against a gnarled tree trunk for support.

Bermuda seated herself on the opposite end of Kazuaki's tree, resting the waning muscles in her neck against the bark. Her head bobbed as immobility crept through her. It was a strange thing to surrender herself to vulnerability. She despised the feeling of weakness in much of its forms, but the necessity outweighed the detestation.

Penn's eyes darted back and forth, assessing the others. The more his limbs ceased to respond to his brain's commands, the harder his heart thundered in his chest. He tried to steady his breathing, tried to remind himself this was for his comrades. Though not of his own blood, he'd die for them. And for a moment, he thought he might.

Penn was spared his horrifying thoughts as he slipped away from consciousness with the others. It was quiet then, with nothing more than the sounds of the beast's tail wagging through a pile of dead leaves and Mimir picking absentmindedly at something beneath one of his fingernails.

Nicholai honed his focus on the lesser god. He wasn't sure if he was always so unobservant, due to lack of sleep or whatever else, but he could've sworn the creature did not have fingernails before.

When the others showed no signs of responsiveness, Revi glanced at Granite. The behemoth stared at him, both knowingly, and unamused. "Don't," Granite instructed.

Revi bared his teeth, like an animal. "If eating those things can lead me to Avi ..."

"Don't," Granite repeated, his order simple and firm.

Revi approached Granite, unafraid. He stared up at him. Though Revi touched six feet in height, Granite easily had an extra foot on him. His voice dropped and took on a coarseness. "Are you going to stop me?"

Granite's face did not change. Save for his steady breathing, he did not move at all. "Easily."

Nicholai observed the men bicker. He stole a glimpse of Jernal, who had his back to the arguing men, the only one who served his duty of protecting the unresponsive bodies. His eyes were on the forest, consumed by his task of keeping vigilant for threats.

The Time Father flicked his eyes over to Mimir. The lesser god seemed absorbed by his task of removing whatever unsightly things hid underneath his nail bed. Nicholai took several quiet steps over to Umbriel's fallen body. He lowered to a crouch, staring at the remaining mushrooms that sat in her limp fingers.

It was getting easier to push the guilt away. He'd had much practice smothering the horrid culpability he lived with over Darjal's death. But the guilt he'd have to add to the growing pile if he did not attempt to help the situation ... the situation he created ... he did not trust his ability to oppress that.

With swiftness, he palmed the mushrooms and stood, readjusting his vest as he glanced at Revi and Granite. They continued to argue. He took several paces away and sat, popping the mushrooms into his mouth and swallowing them down before he changed his mind.

Umbriel stood a chance at making headway with this Unnamed ... but Kazuaki, Bermuda, Brack, Penn ... he respected them all greatly for varying reasons, but their skills rested in things aside from diplomatic appeals. If there was a man who was right for this job, a man who could implore pity from the Unnamed with the right words ... he hoped it was himself.

In the near distance, Nicholai thought he heard Revi relent. He must have realized he'd stand no chance at making it past Granite. Just as well. There were no mushrooms left to take.

The dizziness was hard to get used to. Nicholai hoped it wouldn't last long. It felt very much like the fatigue he tried to ward off for the last week or two, however long it had been. The days seemed like one long, drawn-out blur. He couldn't remember.

The weight in his eyelids pulled them closed. They opened only for a moment, a flicker, when he felt rustling leaves nearby. A figure crouched near him, but he could not focus. For a moment, Nicholai thought it was the beast, and awaited an uninvited tongue to find its way to his cheek. But the familiar voice of Mimir whispered into his ear instead.

"Safe travels, Time Father. I must say, I admire your courage. Very inspiring." Mimir grinned, though Nicholai was too far gone to see the look on his face. "I may pay a visit to the lands in-between, myself."

It was the last thing he remembered. That, and his overwhelming intention to find the Unnamed, to beg for a solution to the hell he unleashed on Panagea.

CHAPTER TWENTY-ONE

The gulls were cawing, as they always did. It was strange the way they screeched, though. Bermuda remembered hearing them her entire life, particularly when she and Kazuaki claimed the small piece of land the ocean cupped on all sides. It was almost as if her brain didn't recognize the sound. Like she'd never heard it before. But that was impossible ...

The gulls always cawed. She was sure of it.

She sat on a large, flat rock that jutted out of the sand. It was an odd place for a rock to be, but she adored this spot. Her legs carried her here almost every day.

Bermuda saw the horizon line of Panagea from the small island where she and the captain made their home. Close enough to visit, yet far enough away to keep peace and freedom at the forefront of their daily life.

The smooth surface of the boulder always warmed under the sun. It felt amazing on the soles of her bare feet. The temperateness radiated up through her ankles and into her legs. Whenever her feet first hit the rock, the warmth spoke to her so much, that her toes curled involuntarily, as if trying to scrape more comforting heat into her skin.

A boat bobbed up and down with the waves, tied to a small dock she and Kazuaki crafted by hand, not far from her sitting place. She smiled at the memory. There was a lot of swearing involved, as neither of them was a craftsman, but sheer determination and hard work eventually brought it to fruition.

Bermuda closed her eyes and inhaled. Salt. She loved the scent, and the air was full of it. A cool breeze blew her hair aside while a more energetic wave crashed her rock, spraying droplets of the sea onto her exposed legs and feet. It was a wonderful reprieve from the sun's rays above.

Movement on her right caught her attention. Bermuda glanced over her shoulder, watching as Kazuaki stooped down to join her on the rock. He eased himself down slowly, donned in the casual attire of a man with no responsibilities. He joined her in looking out at the ocean for a moment, before he turned to the woman, his black hair tied back to stay out of his eyes.

His eyes. Bermuda tilted her head. There was something ... off about that. His irises still reflected every bit of the man who kept her heart. That soothing sea green. The kind of green that showed in the waters during thunderstorms. Everyone always considered the ocean to be blue, but Bermuda did not share their opinion. Kazuaki held the ocean in his eyes ... the jade of the deep wave, with the white sea foam of his corneas surrounding it.

He smiled at her. It was that rugged kind of smile that wasn't really a smile at all. But it was classic Kazuaki. The only way he knew how to show contentment. His expression was candid. He slid his hand toward her, a silent invitation to enjoy the touch of one another.

Bermuda felt her stomach soar, even at the slightest touch of his skin on hers. She returned his smile and looked down as she slid her left hand over his. Flesh on flesh. That, too, was off.

Her delight faded at the sight. Umbriel's warning flashed through her thoughts. She knew, then, and sighed. "Shit ..."

Kazuaki frowned. He tilted his head. "What's wrong?" he asked, voice low.

Bermuda closed her eyes and allowed the mild devastation to sweep through her. His voice was perfect. Down to every small pitch and inflection. The false Kazuaki the gods had made for her was seamless in almost every way. "I didn't make it," she forced herself to say.

His unscarred hand slid over hers, engulfing her delicate fingers in his. "To where?"

The warmth from his palm felt so real. "To where I'm supposed to be," she said.

Kazuaki frowned, but a dim laugh followed. He lifted his hand and gently raised her chin with it so that he could find her eyes. "This is where you're supposed to be."

His gaze had the wonderful ability to stop her heart in its place. For a moment, she considered how happy she'd be to die here. It almost had her. But her lips pinched together, and she shook her head. "Yeah ... someday. I'd rather it be real when I get there, though."

He seemed confused by her response but said nothing. She breathed him in; the feel of his hands on her. The look of him: happy. She rarely saw Kazuaki in such a state since she met him. Her head turned to soak in the place that the gods had made to trap her. This small slice of perfection. They did a terrifyingly stunning job. As much as she wanted this fantasy to be her reality, it wasn't.

They were broken, the two of them. They fell apart together. One-handed, one-eyed, scarred physically, emotionally, and every place in between. Every knife wound and bullet hole was a memory that didn't exist in this place. She wasn't willing to make that trade-off. Bermuda preferred to be perfectly imperfect, an incomplete person who found another incomplete person ... not necessarily to fill in the pieces they were missing, but to feel understood and accepted in knowing they weren't alone.

She placed her hand on his and squeezed. She hoped the others made it. With a final inhale to savor the scent of the sea, Bermuda honed her focus. Though it was one of the more painful endeavors she ever faced, she left her paradise behind and returned to her body that waited in the forest of Nenada.

* * *

Penn glanced down at his pocket watch, a simple thing, made of simple materials. Nothing fancy. He only needed it to tell the time. A crowd gathered around the building behind him, and when the doors opened, they started flooding inside. The excitement was tangible. Plays were a wonderful distraction from reality. It was this very reason that he met his parents here every Sunday to take in the matinee show.

They were right on time, as they always were. His mother's hat was the first thing he looked for. Penn could always spot the soft, white feathers bobbing up and down as she took her tiny steps in the fancy shoes she constantly wore to Sunday plays. The way she took her strides said the footwear was uncomfortable, but she was not afforded many opportunities to dress up. She delighted in it whenever she had an excuse to, whether or not it was convenient.

The two approached, his mother's arm weaved into his father's, as they joined him on the walkway outside the playhouse. "We didn't miss it yet, did we?" Though they were never late, Penn's mother always feared she missed the first several minutes of the show.

"You're good, mum," Penn smirked before he turned to his father, a well-dressed man in a suit his wife made him wear. Penn knew the elder Elmbroke preferred the feel of loose-fitting clothes to the shackles of the one luxurious suit he owned. Only well-trained eyes could spy the various stitches and patchwork that had been performed on the outfit. It was much more economical to repair good things than to buy new ones.

"What's this one about, then?" Penn's father turned to the playhouse and adjusted the glasses on his nose.

"It's a recreation of an archaic tale, I believe," his mother replied as she rifled through her shoulder bag to find the clipping she removed from the newspaper. "A man travels through various parts of the Underworld to find and save the love of his life."

Penn's father chuckled and shook his head. "That's a fantasy for you," he said, as he ushered his wife and Penn into the building. "Everyone knows nobody comes back from the dead."

The elder Elmbroke's opened the door, stopping and turning when they realized their son did not follow them. He was stuck in his place, staring at them with a look that was both love and crippling realization.

Mr. Elmbroke arched a brow. "You all right, son? I know the premise sounds ridiculous, but it'll still be good fun."

Umbriel's words ran through his mind. He tried to hold tightly to them, out of fear he might lose them again. It was incredible how easy it was to misplace her caution. Penn lifted his eyes from the ground and found his father's gaze. "Yeah, I'm ... I'm okay," he said.

His words seemed sincere, but Penn's eyes held a sadness his mother couldn't ignore. "You can't lie to your mother, dear. What's wrong?"

Penn had to look back at the ground. It was easier than looking at the confusion in his mother's face. "I have to go back."

"Home?" she asked. "You'll miss the show, dear. Why is it you need to go back? Did you forget something?"

"No, I ..." Penn grinned despite his grief. He still couldn't bear to look at her. But it was nice, hearing her voice. "I have to go back because you're just figments of my imagination."

The Elmbroke's drew their heads back, aghast at his accusation. Mr. Elmbroke tilted his head, concerned. "Are you sure you're all right, son?"

"I assure you, dear, we're quite real," Mrs. Elmbroke added with a faint chuckle, unsure if her son was making a joke she did not understand.

"No," Penn sighed, honing in on a speck of dirt on the walkway outside the playhouse. It was amazing how much detail the gods threw into his fantasy. Even down to a speck of dirt. "You're not."

Mr. Elmbroke's brows furrowed on his face. His mustache scrunched up into his nostrils. "What makes you say that, my boy?"

Penn smiled at the speck of dirt. "Because. This is everything I've ever wanted. Simple get-togethers and shitty Sunday plays that nobody really wants to see. Nothing special. Just the company of each other. This is how I always pictured it. Word for word. The perfect recreation of my happiness."

"My dear," Mrs. Elmbroke approached him, placing a hand on his forehead to see if he felt hot, "you're not making any sense. This *is* life."

"Nah." Penn closed his eyes. Her hand on his forehead, it felt real. It was strange since he didn't remember what his mother's hand felt like. He was much too young when she passed. But if he ever had to envision it for himself, and he had, this was exactly what it would've felt like. He wanted to reach out and hug her, to experience what that might have felt like, too, but he knew if he did, he would never leave. "Life is never this perfect."

"Son, do you need to see a doctor?" Mrs. Elmbroke tried to find his gaze, but he avoided it.

By now, Mr. Elmbroke approached as well, standing alongside his wife. "We can take you to Dr. Harner, he's right down the road."

It was funny. He knew he never heard that name before in his life, but he still remembered every visit he ever had in Dr. Harner's office. His will to leave weakened. He had to go before it vanished altogether. "It was good to see you both. I would've liked to see the play, but ..." His mouth shifted into a sad grin. " ...if I walk through the doors, I know I won't come back out."

Mrs. Elmbroke's voice broke. She sounded scared. "Son?"

"Love you, mum. Love you, dad. Next time I see you," he said, "I'll stay longer."

* * *

The first thing Umbriel heard was the sound of running water. A stream. She opened her eyes and light flooded her vision, temporarily blinding her of her surroundings. It took several blinks before shapes became discernible. Even still, it looked as though she were in an unfocused land. Every object wavered in structure as if distorted by a constant-moving wave.

She didn't see anyone when she first looked around. It brought her sorrow, but not surprise. Arriving at the Unnamed took an incredible amount of mental focus and self-assuredness.

"'Ello, love."

Umbriel's skeleton nearly leaped out of its skin prison at the sound of Brack's voice. She spun in fright, a hand on her chest to steady the rapid beating inside it. "Brack!" she announced, a sigh of relief following. She delighted that she was not alone, but couldn't hide her disbelief. "I ... I ..."

"—took a while, but you made it. No worries, I wasn't waiting long."

She forced a smile, smoothing out her hair. "I'm glad you're here," she said, exchanging incredulity for relief. They stood at a fork in a river. Both directions seemed to span beyond their eyesight. "We've made it halfway. We must—"

"—follow the river to the ocean, I know." Brack pushed himself off from the tree he leaned against and stretched his arms over his head, yawning. "Which fork you want to chance, m'lady?"

Umbriel blinked. It was not often she found herself at a loss for words, but Brack's lackadaisical self-assuredness met her with unexpected vigor. The Earth Mother tried to leave the feeling behind her, but for the half of her that shared godly blood, the other half of her remained human, and her curiosity burned. "I'm not sure," she admitted. "I heard it changes all the time."

"I'd venture a guess that so long as you believe you'll get there," he started, choosing the one on the left and striding down the embankment with confidence, "you'll get there."

Umbriel smiled. She followed after him, the world around them rippling from the ground to the sky. "You seem poised here, Brack. Care to share your secret?"

"No secrets between friends, love." Brack smirked, squinting his eyes to try and see better through the out-of-focus world. They had only walked a short while, but when he looked behind him, they had traveled miles from their starting point. He directed his attention back around and nodded with a laugh. "There we are."

Umbriel followed the finger Brack lifted, to see a large figure sitting at the base of what she thought was a tree. It was hard to tell, as she could focus on neither. They rippled, like objects held deep beneath the water. It was easy to make out a shape, but details, fine points, the specifics of what she looked at, lived in a constant blur of fluid motion. "The Unnamed," she breathed, taking a step forward. "You're here."

If the being had a face or a facial expression, neither traveler saw it through the distortion. Its voice rattled their lungs, a powerful reverberation that seemed to rise from the ground they stood on. "I am here because you came looking for me ... and there is nowhere I cannot be."

Brack grinned, clapped his hands, and shook his head, amused. "Cryptic. I love it."

Upon realizing she showed no signs of respect, Umbriel quickly took to a knee and bowed her head. Her silver hair spilled around her shoulders and touched the ground. "Thank you for allowing us the honor of your presence. I am certain you know why we've come."

"Yes," It said. "I do."

"Panagea needs your help." Umbriel lifted her head to take in the unfocused being. "The lesser gods are ravaging her people. Men and women are being manipulated into behaviors they only briefly entertain the thought of. It is chaos."

"Yes," It said. "It is."

Umbriel bit her bottom lip. "I know you created Life. I hoped you would take action against those who tried to destroy it."

The Unnamed said nothing. It shifted slightly but otherwise did not move.

"Oi, you hear us, mate?" Brack arched a brow, crossing his arms over his chest. "Don't want to rush you, but we're in a bit of a time crunch here."

"You want me to stop the lesser gods from manipulating men," It said.

Brack shrugged. “I mean, that would be a hell of a start, yeah.”

“The lesser gods came to me with a similar plea hundreds of years ago. They begged me to remind mankind how much they loved them. They feared the aftermath of being forgotten.”

Umbriel winced. The history of the lesser gods was not a pleasant one. If they sought help from the Unnamed all those years ago, they clearly did not receive it. “You … you will help mankind, won’t you?” she asked, already fearing Its reply.

“I could help,” the Unnamed replied. “But not unlike the syringes mankind used to combat hypoxia, the intrusion only keeps the ailments from crippling the body. The syringes … my interference … they combat the symptoms, but do not cure the disease.”

Brack scratched at the mutton chops that grew on the sides of his face as he raised a brow. “So, that’s a no, then?”

“Please,” Umbriel laced her fingers together. “So many lives have been lost already.”

“Yes,” the Unnamed replied. Umbriel thought she detected a hint of pity, but she couldn’t be sure if it was there, or if she only wanted to believe it was there. “I know.”

“Well, shit,” Brack rubbed the back of his neck, and for the first time since Umbriel met him, he wore no visible signs of enjoyment. “That’s a bit irresponsible, isn’t it? I mean, why create something if you only plan to let it die?”

“I made no plans for mankind. I only made them to live.”

“And I’m not saying I lack gratitude for the whole creation thing,” Brack said, holding out his hands to defend himself. “I’m only saying it’s a wee bit cruel to allow such a colossal difference of power to exist, don’t you think? How the hell are we supposed to fight gods?”

A noise emanated from the Unnamed. Almost a sound of consideration, though not quite. “When I created human beings, they were all birthed from the same materials. Skin. Bones. Tendons. Veins. Blood. Atoms. You are all crafted from the same recipe. You were all equal until you decided you were not.

You created the division of powers. Just as you created the lesser gods."

Brack winced under the weight of the Unnamed's response. For once, the Rabbit was rendered silent.

Clutching one hand to her chest, Umbriel got back up to her feet. "I don't understand. You interfered once. You punished Mimir, you shackled him to the well for his sins against mankind. The lesser gods are harming men, is this not the same?"

The light around the Unnamed continued to ripple. "Mimir interfered with mankind's free will. Life is a series of decisions and choices. These are not meant to be taken away."

"But life is?" Umbriel asked, trying desperately to understand. "They're making men and women destroy each other!"

"The lesser gods only exaggerate thoughts mankind already harbors within themselves," the Unnamed replied calmly. "If they had no violent thoughts to aggrandize, the lesser gods' influence would be useless. You wish to punish the lesser gods, but the crime belongs to mankind."

Umbriel's eyelids fell to a close. From the depths of her heart, she fought to understand the Unnamed's detachment, but could not. "These people are born of you," she uttered, her voice cracking. "How can you not want peace for them?"

The Unnamed paused. "It is all I have ever wanted for them," It finally said. "But there are not enough of them who want it for themselves."

The Earth Mother stood, defeated. The Unnamed would lend no assistance. Her suggestion had only served as a hazardous disaster. She hung her head, hoping the others did not suffer because of her proposal.

Brack walked over to Umbriel and gently took her arm. "Come on, love. It is what it is. We got ourselves into this mess, we can get ourselves out of it."

She peeled her eyelids open, her lips pursed as she looked at Brack. Unshed tears of desperation glazed her pupils like glass. The people of Panagea were running out of time. Umbriel couldn't help but feel a thread of responsibility, having hoped to invite the lesser gods back into their lives all along. Her purpose was to protect Panagea. To uphold the Earth Mother's code. To stand for everything her sisterhood died for, by reintroducing more Earth Mother's back into Panagea. But all she gained for her efforts was failure. "I don't know what else we can do," she whispered.

"Oi, chin up, lady." Brack smirked and pretended to gently punch her shoulder. "Panagea coexisted with those lesser gods once. How's about we give round two a go before we reduce ourselves to tears, aye?"

His confidence brought a smile to her face. Umbriel took a deep breath and wiped at her damp lashes with the back of her wrist. "Of course, Brack. Where would I be without your unwavering assurance?"

"Nowhere I'd wanna be," the man said with a laugh. He turned to the Unnamed and saluted It. "Right-o, mate. Sorry results, but it was a pleasure nonetheless, I'm sure."

"Yes," the Unnamed replied, steady in Its tone. "It was."

Brack turned back to Umbriel and extended an arm. "Right. That's that, then. What do you say we get out of here and go figure out how to solve this little problem, eh?"

Umbriel tucked her arm into his and nodded. "I'd like that very much."

* * *

Kazuaki wondered if this was the afterlife. It felt like it. At least, what he imagined the afterlife would feel like. It was dark. For some reason, he expected it to be. Kazuaki doubted the light of the sun reached the afterlife. But there *were* stars above him. How stars could reach the afterlife but the sun could not was beyond him.

It didn't matter much. He felt too at ease to care whether or not things made sense. He simply laid in his strange, out-of-place hammock, hanging between two trees, in the middle of nowhere, with only a giant, black sky above him.

It was silent. A treat for the weary soul who had traveled through one too many lifetimes. A complete, unadulterated instant of genuine peace. He closed his eyes and reveled in it, pleased to have found utopia after many years of searching.

The moment lasted an eternity. But eternities were apparently very short in the afterlife. His brows came down over his closed eyes. Something in this piece of perfection was missing. It gnawed at his skull. He couldn't remember until it gnawed at his heart instead.

Kazuaki shot up out of the hammock.

This place wasn't paradise. It was one component short. He checked his surroundings. It felt like she was here. The selfish part of him wished she was, but the part of him that loved her ... if this was, indeed, the afterlife, hoped she didn't arrive prematurely.

As if the environment bent to his every whim and desire, he saw her on the horizon. Bermuda. A vision even at a distance, standing confidently on a boulder facing the ocean. Her back was to him, but he knew it was her.

Kazuaki swung his legs out of the hammock and started to walk toward her. She must have sensed him coming. Bermuda turned and flashed one of her cocky smirks in his direction. It beckoned Kazuaki with its charismatic allure. He found himself grinning as he closed the distance between her, an honest expression of serenity.

He had only made it halfway toward her when he felt something collide with his stomach. The clatter of clanking metal met Kazuaki's ears, as his arms instinctively reached out to catch the objects that had been thrown toward him. A set of ethereal katars, emblazoned with intricate carvings he was not familiar with; so polished they almost glowed in the darkness. They were not built by the hands of a man. His eyes narrowed, and he looked to his right.

Mimir panted, a maniacal look on his face. "Time's up, Captain. Hold these for me, would you?"

Kazuaki panicked. He looked up, catching sight of Bermuda one final time before Mimir pulled him out of his nirvana. He felt cheated. He never got to touch her. Whether she was real or not, the look of horror when she recognized that he was being ripped from her world felt all too authentic. It embedded itself into his mind.

He opened his eye to the physical world. The real one. It was in a state of waking, with the others around him either having already abandoned the other realm or just coming to. Kazuaki sat up and rubbed his throbbing head as the light of pre-dawn touched through the trees. He wasn't sure how long he was out. It felt like only minutes. But the obvious passage of time as related to the sun's position told him otherwise.

When he realized where he was, Kazuaki quickly turned to view the woman behind him. Bermuda sat, clearly suffering through her own aches and pains that the Spirit Mushrooms left in her head. But she was awake. She appeared to be fine.

The captain glanced over to Mimir. The lesser god held the two katars in his hands, swinging them around like a child with a toy. He stabbed a leaf and held it over his head as if he had ran an enemy through and victoriously presented him to a crowd of imagined onlookers.

"Mimir, no, have mercy, we love you!" the lesser god said, distorting his voice to sound like a terrified child. His voice returned to normalcy as he added, "You're too late, ha!" He swirled the katars and the leaf around before he realized the captain was staring at him. Mimir grinned. "Good morning, Sunshine. I got you a gift."

Kazuaki narrowed his eye. He lifted his hand and touched the side of his face. The familiar piece of faux-leather he kept over his socket fell under his grasp. That paradise ... it felt factual. His brain had a hard time realizing he was back to where he started. Or where he was all along. "What is that you have there?" he muttered, his voice making the throbbing in his head more persistent.

Mimir scraped the leaf off one katar with the blade of the other. His immaturity faded and his face grew serious. "The answer to your problems, Captain. I hope you remember that *I* helped you when the Unnamed did not."

"It didn't?" Kazuaki threw his focus over his shoulder toward Umbriel, Brack, and Penn. "Did any of you make it?"

Penn shook his head, stuck in the same mental fog as the others.

Brack grinned, but his apathetic shrug did not match the spiritedness of his facial expression. "Yeah, Cappy, we did. 'Fraid the little bugger is right, though. The Unnamed ..." He shook his head. "It's a true neutral, mate. We're on our own with this one."

Kazuaki's huffed. He expected as much. Solutions were rarely ever as easy as that. "Did everyone make it back, at least?"

Granite, Revi, and Jernal surrounded Nicholai's body as it sprawled out in the rust-covered leaves on the woodland ground. He was still, with only a shallow rise and fall of his chest visible from where the others sat. Revi tore his eyes away from the Time Father, an admitted concern accompanying the restlessness that lived on his face since Avigail left.

"Not everyone ..."

CHAPTER TWENTY-TWO

The sound of her blade as it dragged across the smooth surface of the rock was one Elowyn grew familiar with over the unending days. She made her home in the catacombs that ran below Eastern, enduring endless nights of sightlessness in the darkened tunnels. The Time Mother dedicated all of her hours to following it to the coast; her fingers trailed along the cold, damp walls, acting as her most important sense in the place that stripped the usefulness of sight, sound, and scent.

It almost hurt when she witnessed that first pinhole of light at the base of the catacombs. Elowyn had wandered in the dark for so long, her eyes struggled to adjust to the reintroduction of sun. But she persisted. She persevered. It took more than a long hike through the shadowed land to deter Elowyn Saveign.

She didn't remember how many days she walked through those tunnels, but she knew when she emerged, finding the cockboat full of supplies hidden on the shoreline was a top priority. Driven by thirst, as sucking the small amount of rainwater that leaked into the cracks of the catacomb walls did little to sustain her, she waded waist-deep into the embankment and clawed her way through the rocks. The second the last stone fell away and exposed part of the boat hiding behind it felt every bit of a miracle.

Elowyn did not wander far from the mouth of Eastern's catacombs. Not yet. She needed to regain her strength, which she did slowly, thanks to the contents of the cockboat. She had enough non-perishable food to last for many weeks, and a small device with which to purify whatever water she needed. Duty-bound fingers wound her Chronometer each day. Though she fell from the public eye, her responsibilities to Eastern did not.

The blade dipped low as she ran it along the stone. The rock fit well in the palm of her hand, and while it did not accomplish the task of honing her knife with the same level of efficiency a sharpening stone would, the smooth surface, worn away by years of abuse from the ocean's waves, did well enough. She continued to scrape it along, sitting cross-legged in the mouth of the catacombs, overlooking the ocean.

Eastern was so densely packed that she heard the familiar sounds of industry carrying on above her. The occasional hiss of bottled-up steam being released. The squealing of unoiled wheels from passing steam cars. Her people were not far from her. She hid nearly in plain sight. Elowyn contemplated leaving her hiding spot several times, but each time she considered it, something cemented her feet to their place.

It was not just industry that sounded above her. The scents and sounds of the lesser gods and their destruction waged on as well, in the form of guttural cries from people being ran through. That, and the depraved ranting of men and women who were unmistakably manipulated by the gods.

From what she heard, the footmen of sound mind tried their best to keep up with the aftermath. It tore her apart, sitting in her safe haven while her ears burned with the clamors of their skirmishes. She wished to help them. But Elowyn had to remind herself that she put her people in even greater danger by putting her life on the line.

The lesser gods wanted her. That much she knew. Elowyn remained confident that even if they found her, they could not corrupt her mind. She did not wish to make any goals they desired easy for them to attain. In any case, the woman had other plans.

She held the sharpened blade up to her eyes and squinted, inspecting it for perfection before she lowered it and stared off in the direction of Southeastern. It bordered her division. Assistance lived there in the form of the captain and the others. It was frustrating at first, knowing help was so close, and yet so far. There was simply no way she could cross the border on foot, travel to Nenada, find the others, amass a following, and return to Eastern in less than twenty-four hours.

This was one endeavor she'd have to go alone. For now.

The working class of Eastern still met her governance with some resistance. Understandably so. They grew up in generations of belief that only men could lead others to greatness. That politics and battle were not places for the 'fairer' sex. She scoffed to herself as she grabbed hold of her black locks, which had grown out since her initiation into division leadership. With her other hand, she rested the newly sharpened knife against it, and it one quick swipe, the hair fell away.

Elowyn did not care much for shaping it to suit the modern woman's fashion trends. She just needed to change her appearance. Otherworldly gods might be perceptive enough to see beyond her camouflage, but she would not hand her position to them on a silver platter.

After gathering the cut strands, the Time Mother traipsed over to the waters and peered down inside. The ocean off the coast of Eastern did not make for a suitable mirror. Runoff from the countless factories had left the water a rather murky color. She tossed the cut hair into the waters and ran her fingers through what little remained, to shake out any loose strands.

Imperial clothing would not do. If the public knew anything about Panagea's society of elites, it was that hand-to-hand combat was not in their forte. She reached into the crate of belongings in the cockboat and removed a thick blanket, meant to keep fleeing division leaders warm in the cruel chill of the ocean winds. It was a material that lacked in aesthetics, built instead for endurance. With a few alterations, it would be perfect.

By the time the sun decided it had enough of bringing light to a darkening world, Elowyn completed her necessary modifications. She shed her regal garb and slipped her new garments on over her head. The stitches would hold, she decided, as she ran her fingertips over them. Sewing cloth differed from sewing gaping holes in human flesh, but the medic made do with the skill set she possessed and the medical supplies from the cockboat.

Even in the evening hours, Elowyn still saw the dense clouds of smoke that Eastern's factories poured into the atmosphere. It heaved a strange shadow over the land. Her reign had been short; she had much to do to fix this place. But for now, she had to make sure her people survived long enough to live in it.

She stooped down where the waters lapped up against the hardy boots she pulled from the cockboat. Elowyn dipped her hand into the mud and rubbed it between her hands, thinning it out before she used it to smother her hair. The thick coating of auburn muck served as another element to her disguise. The less she looked like a division leader ... the easier it would be to weave through the public unnoticed.

The blade Elowyn used to sheer her hair found its place back at her hip. She needed more weapons if she were to amass a proper resistance. There was one place she knew of that would serve as a starting point: the gun-toting maiden that nearly shot them all on the river banks last year, when they floated up onto Eastern's shores after the loss of the captain's ship.

Mairyn Catteral.

Elowyn pulled her body up from the confines of the catacombs for the first time in weeks, letting the polluted haze of lamp light fall over her form. Only some of the lanterns were lit. The lamplighters of Eastern likely feared the repercussions of roaming the streets at night. Elowyn frowned. She did not delight in the knowledge that her people lived in dread. She needed to make this place safe.

Amongst the fearful, the brave always lingered. She would search all of Eastern to find them. Memories of the time she and the crew rallied the inhabitants of the Southern slums flooded her mind. So many valiant people, unafraid to sacrifice their lives for change. The lesser gods mistook humanity for a weak collection of organisms. Perhaps even mankind bought into that lie. Elowyn Saveign would remind them they were wrong.

The medic was no stranger to organizing an opposition. People needed to know they could fight back. They made the lesser gods. They fashioned them into invincible creatures. As such, they believed that's what they were. Invulnerable. Unbeatable.

As Elowyn walked deeper into the murky environment of her division, under the guise of a nameless wanderer who appeared as nothing resembling Eastern's salvation, she had every intention of challenging that myth.

* * *

Avigail stepped off the steam train, her fingers trailing on the smooth, black surface of the locomotive before she traipsed too far to touch it anymore. She did not yet make it to her destination. The tracks cut through the whole of the Southeastern division and made it as far as the high part of Southern.

While the border to Northwestern lived only sixty or so miles away, the Houton daughter could not make it by track. The trainmen announced that it was the end of the line. The condition of the railroad was too far gone, whether by the natural disasters of Panagea's history or by the new threat of the lesser gods, she wasn't sure.

There were many whispers from passengers onboard the locomotive. Speculations were as endless as they were varying. She didn't know much about the threat of the lesser gods before her departure from the Addihein household ... but after the many hours spent in the company of others on the steam train, she certainly knew more than she had before.

Knowing her father was in the heat of it all, she found none of it comforting.

Avigail adjusted her pack over her shoulder as she distanced herself from the station. It was an interesting visual journey. Trees thinned out the farther she traveled from Nicholai's home town. Southern had several small patches of wilderness, but they were few and far between when compared to the Southeastern division. It was a shame when the trees disappeared from her sight. She found them comforting. They reminded her that Nicholai had stepped foot there, whether recently or otherwise, as he was the only one who could have grown them to that height. For whatever reason, being in a place the Southeastern Time Father had walked offered her some semblance of security.

If she couldn't make it to Northwestern by train, Avigail would resort to the other method of travel that served her well over the years. Hitchhiking. It was not as glamorous, and twice as dangerous, but it did hold effectiveness she couldn't deny. Hitchhiking was well over half the way she ended up in Southeastern at Nicholai Addihein's doorstep in the first place.

The young woman approached the nearest road that looked healthy enough to accommodate traffic and glanced in both directions. Buildings, some upright, others not, flanked her viewpoints on all sides. Avigail spotted the movement of people, but passing steam cars were few and far between. She tightened her lips and started down the main road, in the direction of Northwestern. She could at least walk until one happened by.

Avigail had ventured through Southern before, but never through this particular area. Her first quest to find her father stretched out over a year and carried her through several divisions, but the uppermost part of Southern was a foreign land to her. It was strange how the makeup of a division could differ so widely from the whole of itself.

The various towns and villages of Southern she had wandered through previously endured heavy losses from the natural disasters. Bartholomew Gray had accomplished stunning things in his short rule, however. Large parts of the devastation were under repair by hired hands. It seemed his influence did not stretch to the farthest parts of Southern yet, or the chaos she witnessed before her was too fresh for him to have had any chance at correcting it.

People walked around her as if they didn't notice that half of their buildings were in a state of disrepair. Avigail wondered if they had just grown accustomed to it. What a thing to get used to, she wondered to herself. Obliteration. Ruin. They seemed so disassociated from it all, the jagged roads, the upturned stone that once served as walkways, the shaken factories, the shattered homes. The people of this Southern town seemed oblivious to it all. Or accepting. She wasn't sure which haunted her more.

Avigail's ears perked when she heard an approaching steam car. She held out her thumb, cliché but custom in the hitchhiking business. The sound of the car's engine indicated a deceleration. She had high hopes. The woman turned, watching as it slowed beside her.

She performed a quick assessment of the couple in the car. Mid-forties. Man and assumed wife. Simple wedding bands on each finger. Standard to degraded clothing. Somewhere between working poor and lower-middle class. Low threat level. By the looks of them, she would have guessed them for common laborers, but the fact that they had a steam car threw her off. The automobile was often a luxury most plebeians did not attain.

"Where you headed, little miss?" the gentleman driving the steam car asked as he hung his arm out the window.

Avigail put on her best smile, trying not to appear like an inconvenience. "Northwestern," she replied. "Any town will do."

"Hop on in," the man said, motioning her to take a seat in the back.

Avigail delighted in her luck as she found a spot in the steam car's rear. Hitchhiking was an unexpected game. That she managed to find a ride so quickly was a rare and wonderful thing. Better yet that it appeared these people had no ulterior motives. "Thank you," she said, settling down in the back.

"Of course." The wife smiled and readjusted herself before her husband turned the vehicle's wheel and carried on. "It's no trouble. We're heading to Northwestern ourselves, actually."

"Oh?" Avigail leaned forward, resting her forearm on her knee. "What brings you both up there?"

"Worry, I'm afraid," the woman admitted, frowning as she stole a glimpse of her husband. "We've heard rumors about the state of Northwestern." She seemed hesitant to share the knowledge so freely with Avigail but decided if the young woman was venturing to that part of Panagea, it was best she knew the speculations of its alleged condition. "Our son and daughter-in-law live in Bricklemore, a small town within its borders. We haven't heard hide nor hair from them in two weeks. We were lucky to be able to borrow this vehicle from a dear friend to go check on them."

"That's very sweet of you," Avigail said, unable to contain her mild jealousy at the appearance of parents who traversed the world for the knowledge their child was all right. "I hope your bravery rewards you and they're okay."

"Oh, bravery's nothing to do with it, dear," the mother replied, smiling as they drove through a destitute part of town. "It's a necessity, really. A parent needs to know their child is all right."

Avigail forced a smile. "So I've heard."

"I'm Everly," the woman said before gesturing to her husband. "This is Thom. We're happy for your company, dear."

"Avigail," the Houton daughter replied as she leaned back in her seat. She did not get any foul reads from the pair and did not mind participating in harmless small talk. "It's nice to meet you both."

The three traveled for some time along the crippled roads of Southern. The steam car jostled over the uneven terrain, its absence of shock absorbers making every bump all the more noticeable. Pleasantries exchanged between them. As pleasant as strangers could converse.

The closer they got to the Northwestern border, the more things seemed to deteriorate. Avigail looked out at the wreckage of the city that laid beyond her window. Some of it still smoldered from an apparent fire that died not long ago. She frowned at the sight of it. And the smell ... there were certainly casualties. The scent in the air left little doubt.

"You aren't scared?" Avigail asked as they drove passed a confused-looking mother, clutching a bundled object in her arms. She guessed it was an infant. Things appeared grimmer the farther they crept toward Northwestern. It gave credit to some of the rumors she heard the other patrons whispering about. She wondered if some of the disordered people she spied outside her window had fled from the very place they tried to enter.

"Not to enter Northwestern, no," Thom stated.

"Only that we'll find there's a solid reason our son hasn't responded to our letters," Everly added.

Avigail did not know their son, nor their daughter-in-law, but she had good intuition. In this case, she wished she didn't. In the short time since she met them, the woman knew these people lived on hope, but she suspected a valid cause existed that their son did not answer their mail. Based on the circumstances of things outside her window, Avigail speculated they weren't going to find a comforting end to their travels. She kept her fingers crossed that her journey would have a different ending. "I'd be terrified," she admitted, pushing some hair out of her eyes.

"Yes, well," Everly smiled as she leaned back in her seat, "things seemed pretty grim last year, too. We were among the many people living in the slums of a town called Avadon. A large part of Southern's nearby working poor had flocked there after the disasters wiped our houses from the face of the land. The late Darjal Wessex showed no signs of repairing residential properties, funneling all his money into the restoration of damaged churches and that gods-forsaken iron ship." She shook her head at the memory. "We had all but given up hope when Nicholai Addihein and his companions came to our aid. They are the true gods among men. Knowing people like them are out there ... well, it gives us something positive to hold on to."

Avigail perked at the mention of Nicholai and the others. She'd heard brief mentions of the story they referenced, but never from someone who had actually dwelled in the Southern division while they swept through. "You met them?" she asked, leaning forward again in her seat. "What was it like?"

"It was ... reassuring." Thom guided the steam car around a corner with a slow crank of the wheel. "All seemed lost there, for a while. Living under tarps, covered in the smell of the dead and the dying. It was abysmal." He shook his head at the memory. "Those people ... they brought hope to that place."

"Do you remember the dog?" Everly asked with a laugh. "Oh, that creature was wild! The children threw rubbish for him to chase after all day and he never seemed to tire."

"And Umbriel," Thom added with a fond smile, "I don't know that I ever saw her without an aura of genuine affection around her. She gave her heart to everyone there, regardless of their status or state."

"Yes." Everly sighed at the reminiscence, a tender smile on her face as well. "Her warmth was almost inhuman. I've never seen another person love so much."

Avigail sat back in her seat, her eyes falling to the floor. She knew of what they spoke. Though her feelings for Umbriel were tainted by perceived interpretations of the Earth Mother harboring feelings for Nicholai, she truly reflected the heart of a saint. Despite Avigail's attempts to discredit her, Umbriel remained, undoubtedly, one of the kindest people she ever knew. "She sounds lovely," she uttered, not caring to dive into the short history she shared with the Earth Mother.

"And Bartholomew Gray," Everly beamed at his name, "I still fawn at the idea that I was *this* close to a future Time Father," she said, holding her thumb and index finger an inch apart from one another. "He is truly a wise and wonderful man."

"They all were," Thom agreed, nodding to further cement his approval.

Avigail could not let the opportunity pass her by. These people lived in the company of her father. Apprehension took hold of her before she spoke; she did not want to learn anything she might regret later. Her fingers dug into the cloth around her knees, but she cleared her throat and dared herself to ask. "What about Revi Houton? What was he like?"

"Mr. Houton?" Everly blinked, trying to beckon the memory forth. "Yes, I remember him. A quiet man. Very hard working. He did much of the work restructuring the slums, removing dangerous debris, clearing out the bodies and all that."

"Yeah," Thom joined his wife in her recollection, jostling a bit as the steam car ran over a jagged hole in the road, "it didn't take an observant person to look at that man though and know he had some demons in him."

"Even still," Everly interjected, coming to the rescuc of Revi's honor, "most of us have demons. It's how we live with them that makes us who we are. And Revi Houton, if I'm not mistaken, was an honorable man."

"Through and through," Thom agreed. "Particularly good with the children, if I recall."

Everly smiled. "Now that you mention it, yes. He was. I don't know that I ever saw him smile, but when he was with those kids ... he looked every bit the contented type. You would have liked him, dear."

Avigail swallowed and once again fell back into the cushion of her seat. Her arms laid in her lap as she lived in the tales the two told. "Yes," she finally said, taking in a deep breath and letting it out slowly. "I think I would have."

CHAPTER TWENTY-THREE

Tick. Tick. Tick.

Clocks surrounded him. Large, towering things. The faces read 1:02. Though their presence would have seemed surreal in any other occasion, Nicholai did not find it strange. Complex mechanisms such as these brought him an abnormal sense of comfort. He adjusted his vest as he strode through the endless valley of enormous cogs and gears, a peacefulness surrounding him.

He felt at ease. Each part of every machine had a purpose, and each action had a predictable reaction. Everything made sense here.

Nicholai climbed a towering set of stairs that wrapped around an impossibly tall grandfather clock. Where they led, he wasn't sure, but ascending them felt right. Almost as if a reward of sorts awaited him at the top. He didn't know how he knew. He just did.

Though climbing each step took the form of a physical effort, Nicholai experienced incredible relaxation through his entire body. He didn't remember feeling stressed before, but if he had, it would not have lived inside him long. Not here. Worries melted away in seconds in this perfect place.

Only several steps to go. He followed after his intuition until he found himself at the top of the stairs. The soles of his boots rested on large sheet of transparent glass. He saw every cog and component below him that made up the giant clock on which he stood. But that wasn't what captured his attention.

Nicholai's head tilted to the side when he spied an elegant figure across the clear floor. Her back was to him, but even with her facing away from him, he knew her form well. He memorized it for years.

"Lilac."

The woman spun, her red hair bouncing around her jawline as she offered him a smile. "Hello, Nicholai."

Her eyes were the feature that ignited him most. Nicholai took several steps toward her until she was near enough for him to wrap his arms around her waist. A curious feeling crept over him. The environment where he stood, which by all accounts reflected a perpetual dreamlike atmosphere, felt entirely normal. Lilac's presence, however, struck him as uncharacteristically odd. He delighted in seeing her, as he always did. Her proximity lit his heart on fire. But for whatever reason, holding her body tight against his felt ... impossible. It made him want to grip her forever.

"I've missed you," she said, leaning her forehead against his.

Nicholai chuckled, closing his eyes to further soak in the warmth of her existence. "I didn't go anywhere."

"Of course you didn't," Lilac laughed, giving him a gentle squeeze as she nestled further into him. "And you won't, will you?"

A permanent grin found its way to his face. She had that effect on him. "I can't imagine anywhere else I'd rather be."

"Good," she whispered, smirking as she shifted to rest the side of her cheek against his. "Very good."

The heat of her skin on his awakened him. Nicholai pulled a deep breath into his lungs, content simply to hold her. His eyes opened, staring off into the horizon behind her. He blinked once, twice, challenging his eyes to adjust as he attempted to focus on the clocks in the background.

The faces. They all read 11:44. His eyes narrowed. He could've sworn it had just been minutes after 1:00. How over ten hours passed in what felt like such a short period baffled him. But as

Lilac burrowed herself into his chest, he felt the desire to make sense of it fade.

"Come with me." Lilac smiled as she pulled out of the embrace and held his hands in hers. "I want to show you something."

"Of course." Nicholai returned her show of affection, hopelessly belonging to the woman who stole his heart. He squeezed her hand once, then gently pulled out of her grasp to extend his arm. "Lead the way, m'lady."

A charismatic giggle escaped her as she pulled him along, but they did not get far.

From the sky, a woman descended. Soft, gray wings flapped behind her as she lowered herself to the glass; the tips of her toes bending when they met the smooth surface, until the whole of her feet laid flat. The creamy pallor of her flowing dress contrasted wonderfully with her delicious cocoa skin. She smiled. Her eyes, though sunken into her seemingly malnourished face, were orbs of compassion.

Nicholai parted his mouth to speak, to ask who she was, but before he uttered a word, the supernatural woman extended a shaky, bony hand and gently swept it through Lilac's body.

The tangible firmness of Nicholai's lover gave way under the motion as Lilac turned into nothing more than smoke, swirling around the stranger's forearm as she continued to brush her away.

He felt her fingers in his. And then she was gone. Nicholai took a step back, his eyes darting wildly as a gust of wind carried what was left of Lilac Finn away. "Wh-what did you ...?" He forced his attention to the mysterious being before him, lost in a combination of confusion and shock.

"She wasn't real, Nicholai." The winged woman's voice echoed around him, reverberating up through his ankles and into his bones. Though the words felt like a touchable force compared to others, they were filled with gentleness and a strange weakness. "I'm sorry."

"Who are you?" Nicholai's brows furrowed as he took a step back. He still did not know what was happening and found himself unable to initiate a suitable response. Was Lilac dead? Did this woman kill her? Was she ever really alive at all? Countless questions floated through his brain at a rapid pace, but he only managed to get a few out. "How do you know my name? Where's Lilac?"

"She is dead, Nicholai." The woman seemed disheartened by the obvious pain in his eyes. "It is a hard truth to accept, but it is a universal one. The dead ... they do not return."

"She's not ..." He started to disagree, to challenge this brazen woman's statement, but his words fell short, as did his breath. "She's ... not ..."

She couldn't be. Lilac Finn was never dead. But he couldn't form those words. It was almost as if his tongue knew they were false. Nicholai drew in a deep breath, and he reached up to grab his hair as if pulling on the strands would somehow wake him from this terrible dream.

The woman reached over to place a hand on his cheek. Her skin was cold, but the touch steadied him instantly. Steadied his pulse. His anxiety. He remembered, then.

Yes. Lilac Finn was dead. He recalled the exact moment when the bullet pierced her skull. The exact moment when her body hit the floor and Rodgie bemoaned his crimes. He remembered everything.

"Are you the Unnamed?" Nicholai asked, unable to tear his gaze away from hers.

"No, child." She smiled, brushing her thumb over his cheek with platonic affection. "I'm afraid you didn't reach the Unnamed. Do not fret. It is very difficult to do."

He was unsuccessful. Nicholai winced at the realization. The Southeastern Time Father did not enjoy writhing in self-pity, but it was getting harder not to feel the pressures of failure after repeated failure. His jaw tightened as he tensed under the weight of her touch. Nicholai thought he would find her bold contact uncomfortable, but the energy that originated from her dismissed any apprehensions. "Who are you?" he asked again.

"Someone who loves you." She lowered her hand and tucked it behind her back. "Someone who is here to help you return home."

It was then Nicholai realized innumerable eyes were surrounding them. What was once a land of non-threatening, albeit oversized clocks and open space became a claustrophobic environment of yellow, glowing orbs. The eyes did not have faces. Instead, they floated in the endless expanse. They did not appear friendly.

The woman followed Nicholai's gaze to the sea of eyes surrounding them. She frowned. "They know I've assisted you. It's time to go. This is no place for a human."

"No, wait," Nicholai ripped his focus from the looming threat and found her face again. "I have questions—"

"I am sorry, child." Her voice was soft, coated in a sadness. "They are not for me to answer."

Additional features started joining the eyes. Flaring nostrils took shape. Mouths, some with jagged rows of teeth, others without and somehow still appeared menacing. Skulls, muscles, and sockets formed around the eyes until each had an entire head to belong to. The creatures, some humanoid, others a combination of mythological beasts pieced together by imagination, advanced toward the pair. They defied gravity with each step, walking on nothing.

Nicholai frowned, holding his ground. "If they're not for you to answer, then who do I ask?"

The woman drew her skeletal shoulders back as she adopted a defensive stance. "You are better off not knowing, love."

"I'm getting really tired of people making these decisions for me," Nicholai muttered, clenching his hands into fists. "Please—you said they know you helped me—even if I can't ask who you are, can you help with the lesser gods destroying Panagea?"

She paused. Empathy swarmed her, dominating her entire being. The creatures drew closer. She parted her lips to speak, but a distorted voice from the crowd halted her speech.

"Epifet!"

She looked up. Her eyes widened. "I'm sorry—" She held up an arm to defend herself, and reached out to seize Nicholai's shoulder with the other.

One of the monstrous creatures leaped forward. The Time Father vividly remembered the weight of the panic behind her fingers as she dug them into his skin and shoved him away.

Then he woke.

In bed, with Umbriel, Brack, Granite, his dog, and Jernal in chairs at his side, Nicholai sat up from the mattress, covered in sweat. His hands flew to his chest to inspect for his Chronometer. Tensed shoulders eased at the familiar touch of the metal. He held it in his palm for a moment, to reassure himself it was still there before he slid a hand through his hair and tried to catch his breath.

"Nicholai—" Umbriel sat upright in her chair and leaned forward, reaching a hand out to rest it near him. "You're awake."

"Just in time, too," Jernal murmured, his arms crossed over his chest as he leaned back in his chair.

"Too right, that," Brack laughed, giving the footboard of the bed a soft kick with his boot. "Damn near terrified the piss out of me, mate. We were a good three hours away from being feckin' frozen in Southeastern if you couldn't wake your ass up."

Nicholai blinked and looked down at his Chronometer. It was true. He had been unconscious for over twenty hours. The man shook his head and tried to make sense of things, though he knew that effort was in vain. It felt as though he had only lingered in the other realm for mere minutes. "I'm sorry ..." He rubbed at his face before resting his hands in his lap. "Truly. I never meant to put you all in that position."

Umbriel's lips pursed together. Despite her attempt to conceal her anger, it remained visible on her face. "Then you shouldn't have."

Her words cut him. Nicholai never witnessed Umbriel in a state of irritation before. Though a tempered lividness hid in her stare, he still found relief at the sight of her well-being. "I'm ... glad you are okay," he admitted, turning to Brack shortly after. "You as well, Brack. The others," he started, looking back and forth between those who gathered around his bedside, "Kazuaki, Bermuda, Penn ... are they all right?"

Umbriel sat back in her chair, still unable to disguise her crossness. "Everyone is fine."

Granite's dog placed its front paws on the bed, its tail wagging. It made several little efforts to jump onto the mattress but was ultimately unsuccessful. Granite reached over and picked the aging dog up to set it on the bed.

"Did ... did you make it?" Nicholai arched a brow, reaching over to pet the beast as it thrust its muzzle into his palms. "To the Unnamed?"

Brack shrugged. "Yeah, mate. Umbriel and I found It. But the Unnamed is a no go."

Nicholai's shoulders fell. The dog licked his hand. "I see ..."

"You discredited my warning." Umbriel stared at Nicholai, the weight of her gaze unsettling.

He knew she was upset. It did not take a scholar to fit the pieces of that puzzle together. "I thought I could make it," Nicholai confessed, leaning back into the pillow behind him. "I wanted to help, Umbriel. I need to do something other than sign documents that disperse financial aid to those who wouldn't need aid to begin with if I hadn't damned Southeastern last year. And I certainly do not wish to send my comrades into dangerous situations just to clean up errors that are my own doing."

"Your reckless behavior almost doomed the people of Southeastern once again." Umbriel's words were sharp but honest. "Three hours, Nicholai. Three hours separated all of Southeastern's people from reliving the same fate you condemned them to last year. You're lucky you made it back at all."

Nicholai grimaced. He wished to offer her some form of comfort but ventured a guess she would not welcome it from him in the heat of the moment. For each fresh injury that her words delivered to his ego, the true salt in the wound was the truth behind her statement. It was a big risk. And it did not pay off. "I know, Umbriel. I apologize. It was ... foolhardy, at best. Honestly,

I don't even know that I would've made it back were it not for ..." He paused. Nicholai absentmindedly scratched behind the dog's ear as he tried to recall the name. "Umbriel ... does the name Epifet mean anything to you?"

The Earth Mother cocked her head to the side, confused. "Epifet?" Her brows rose as she shrugged a shoulder. "Yes. She's the Goddess of Fertility."

A frown crossed Nicholai's face. He pegged her for a lesser goddess, in that she roamed the in-between, where a majority of the deities hid when they fell from mankind's memory. But the Goddess of Fertility? Why in the world would she assist him? "Odd," he mumbled, patting the dog as its tongue lolled out the side of its mouth.

Perhaps she was simply one of the more compassionate lessers. Nicholai recalled Dimjir admitting in the forest that not all the gods harbored grudges. He was thankful she appeared. Were it not for her, he likely wouldn't have come back. It felt too good, being in Lilac's presence. Though it made him wonder, if his false reality was as alluring as all that, Kazuaki, Bermuda, and Penn must have had their own stories about their faux utopias.

"Where are the others?" Nicholai asked, wondering what the next plan of action was now that things with the Unnamed failed.

* * *

The stillness of Malcolm's greenhouse was the perfect place for a secluded conversation. When the students left for the day and Malcolm retired to his bed, the humid environment proved to be welcoming. Kazuaki stood, palms on a tabletop lined with several small succulents, as he stared across it to look at Mimir. The lesser god perched himself in a chair, one hand on each of the katars.

Kazuaki's stare possessed weight. His fingers dug into the table. "Weapons."

Mimir nodded. "Yes."

"That you stole."

"Yes," Mimir chuckled, shaking his head as he let out a low whistle. "They are going to be mad."

"From the other realm. Forged by lesser gods."

"You're doing very well keeping pace with the circumstances, Captain."

Kazuaki wrinkled his nose. His eye fell to the katars Mimir held in his grasp. "I can ... *kill* ... gods with these?"

"Yes, indeed," Mimir said, stroking the carved blades of the katars. "Weapons made by gods to use against gods."

Bermuda listened from outside the main door, her back pressed up against the wall as she sat on the ground. The opening was ajar only an inch or two, enough to allow her the luxury of listening in. She kept quiet, not wanting to disturb wherever the conversation headed.

Kazuaki remained skeptical. Anything that spewed out the mouth of Mimir was likely tainted in half-truths. But even if it was only a partial certainty, it remained a fractional step closer to a solution than they were before. "Fine," the captain muttered, reaching his hands out to grab the weapons. "Hand them over."

"Tut tut, Captain." Mimir slid the katars back toward himself, a devious grin on his face. "You of all people should know by now how this works."

A low growl rumbled in Kazuaki's throat. He knew what the lesser god implied. A barter. "What do you want?" he murmured.

"I want us to be *friends*, Captain." Mimir smirked. "But even as friends, you must understand why I'd hesitate to give you these."

Kazuaki squared his shoulders. "You don't want me to slaughter you with them."

"Precisely." Mimir traced one of the patterns with his index finger, finishing it to completion before he returned his focus to the captain. "So, that's the deal. I'll give you the katars, on the condition that you cannot use them to kill me. But ... you must also keep me safe. As you can imagine," he paused, snickering, "the lesser gods will be pretty cross with me for taking these."

Hesitation followed. A victim of Mimir's trickery in the past, Kazuaki did not want to rush blindly into any more foolish situations. His gut told him it was a mistake. That he should never partake in a barter with a lesser god again, particularly one as divided and unpredictable as Mimir. He stood up straighter, clasping his hands behind his back, and paced the floor.

Bermuda heard his boots on the linoleum as he traipsed back and forth. Though she couldn't see him, she pictured the look on his face. One of torment, she guessed. It was a hell of a decision to make. Trust a lesser god, or remain a victim to them.

"You're in a good position, Captain." Mimir watched him closely as he wandered the small room. "You may be immortal, but you're still a man. The lesser gods are bound by law not to hurt you. Not without incurring the wrath of the Unnamed, at the very least." He tapped his nail on the blade of one of the katars, his pupils shrinking to tiny dots. "It's a golden opportunity that I hope builds a ship even better than the one you lost at sea." He grinned maniacally. "A *friend* ship."

Kazuaki appeared unamused by the joke. He shook his head, incredulous. With his back to Mimir, he whispered, "What makes you think I'll trust you on this?"

The lesser god's enjoyment melted away. He leaned his elbows on the table and sat forward, his voice lowering. "The world burns, Captain. As word spreads, the lesser gods will further reintegrate themselves with the physical realm. With humans. When they learn of the potential the lessers bring, mortals won't be able to stop themselves from praying. Men love shortcuts too much. Given time, the gods will be everywhere, crawling like weeds over the whole of Panagea. Unless you stop them."

Kazuaki ground his teeth together. A muscle in his jaw twitched as he slowly spun around, facing Mimir.

The lesser god met his gaze. "I know you don't trust me, Captain. That's wise. But in this instance," Mimir's words fell to a whisper as his head tilted, "what other choice do you have?"

CHAPTER TWENTY-FOUR

The porch steps of the Addihein household were not the quiet place Revi hoped they would be. Nicholai's house lived too close to Nenada's countless other residents. It made sense for the Southeastern Time Father, whose heart seemed capable of holding a limitless supply of human kindness.

But sentiments like that were lost on Revi Houton.

The time the crew spent in Southeastern dominated any other length of time he stayed in one place. Second only to when he and Arabella lived together, anyway. They were young when they fell in love. Naïve. It was a time when the innocence of youth clouded the heaviness of life's realities.

He remembered the day he met her. Barely into adulthood at nineteen years of age, Revi stumbled upon the woman bathing in a nearby creek. She was a product of the working poor. Luxuries such as bath water were not permitted to everyone in Revi's home town. It was not uncommon to stumble upon someone washing in the polluted stream waters, but to happen upon a maiden as beautiful as Arabella ... the memory brought a nearly invisible grin to Revi's lips.

She shrieked and hurled a rock at him for his obvious staring. But he caught a flicker of amusement in her eyes as she threw it. She was stunning in her own right.

Young adults were not proper examples of upholding responsibilities. They gave accountability away for the thrill of lustful endeavors. Arabella quickly fell pregnant. She was not yet twenty when she gave birth to Avigail.

Revi remembered the thrill of being a father. Though each new child born brought a sense of pressure that accompanied the joy. A jack of all trades with no particular skill set, he spent most of his life toiling away in a parts factory while Arabella stayed home to tend the children. She offered to work, to relieve some of the obvious burdens she saw in Revi's face each night he came home after a fourteen-hour day, but he refused. He did not want the kids to grow up without the full-time love of at least one parent. They deserved all that and more. Unfortunately, love did not pay the rent nor put food on the table.

Tension between the two grew worse with each passing day. The children grew larger, hungrier, requiring more as one after the other went into the educational system. Though their costs rose, his pay remained the same. Coming home each night, staring into the sunken eyes of loved ones who went without, but made no fuss ... it ate away at him. None of them ever uttered a word of dissatisfaction, but Revi Houton had enough for himself to fill that dismal factory he gave his life to day in and day out.

He remembered how each of his children looked the day before he left. Their faces were burned into his memory. Even Arabella, who aged gracefully despite the number of children her body housed and nourished. Things between the two of them were not perfect, but he adored her. Loved her. It was the love that made him leave. At least, that's what he told himself in the beginning. It became too hard, looking at their emaciated faces day after day, knowing he should have done better by them.

It took quite a few years after he left to realize exactly how foolish his thought process was. It was not love that made him leave at all. It was weakness. It was hatred. Hatred for himself. Hatred that he could not give them everything they deserved. And with Arabella's growing belly, knowing he would soon add another face to the sea of those he disappointed ... Revi Houton crumbled.

He left them every coin he had to his name the night he left. It wasn't much. He took nothing from the kitchen. The only thing he took was his unadulterated disgust with himself, and he carried it with him ever since.

Revi shook the memories out of his head, returning himself to his physical place on Nicholai's porch. The town of Nenada seemed to stare back at him, judging. It was not a bad town. Better than most he had experienced in his lifetime. But right now, absent of Avigail, it was no place he wished to be.

Each person who dared to walk too close to his sitting place earned a dagger in the form of a scowl. They moved along quickly after that. The fierceness of Revi's animosity seemed to sting even more than a bullet might. Fresh off the memories of his past, he was in no mood to appear approachable to civilians.

Oncoming footsteps behind him made his ears pulse. Revi heard the door to Nicholai's homestead open, creaking all the way. The noise irked him. Those hinges should have been oiled long ago. Lapses in the material condition of things would not fly like that if they were still aboard Captain Hidataka's ship.

Penn grunted as he eased himself down into a sitting position beside Revi, leaning back onto one of his palms. In his free hand, he held a half-eaten pear, pilfered from the kitchen Nicholai and Umbriel shared. At first, he said nothing, only picking at a stubborn piece of the pear's skin that wedged itself between his teeth. When he finally freed it with his tongue, he spat it out in front of him, startling a woman who happened to be passing by. She cast him a look of disgust, to which he cynically tipped his beret.

Revi hunched forward, his elbows on his knees. He adopted the look of an angered statue, carved out of frustration and not much else.

"So," Penn started, taking another bite of his pear. With a full mouth, he uttered, "Captain's pretty keen on testing those katars Mimir stole from the other realm."

Revi grumbled something inaudible.

"I venture a guess it'll come easy at first," Penn continued, swallowing the mouthful of food down. "Soon as those bastards realize he's got a weapon capable of killing them though, it'll be a feckin' game of cat and mouse."

Revi's head fell between his legs, but it only lingered there for a moment before he pulled in a deep breath and ran his hands through his salt and peppered hair. "Captain knows I'll do what I can. Not a day went by spent with that man that I didn't give him everything I had."

"Right." Penn inspected his pear, and upon realizing he'd eaten most of the flesh from it, he tossed it carelessly onto the cobblestone before him. "Thing is, it's hard to be of use when your head's elsewhere, isn't it? Gonna get yourself feckin' killed if you're not paying attention."

Revi glared at Penn, clamping his jaw. But the man's temper faded when he concluded some sense lingered in Penn's observation. "I just need to know she's all right. Or where she went," he muttered, his fingers digging into his palm.

A brow arched on Penn's face. He looked unimpressed by Revi's admission, but Penn always showcased a perpetual appearance of dissatisfaction. He leaned forward, matching the Houton man's posture. "Let me tell you something, Revi. Avigail sought you out. She had no money, no resources, and yet, she still managed to find you." He frowned. "The environment she grew up in wasn't ideal, but it made her smart, and it made her tough. I'm sure wherever she is, she's fine."

The brooding eyes of Revi Houton focused on the pear carcass tossed aside by Penn. He needed something to hone in on that was not the questionable faces of the passersby or his imagination. "I know," he murmured.

Penn's gaze flattened when he realized Revi did not pick up on the entirety of his subtle message. "I'm also sure that if she traversed half of Panagea to find you once ... she'd probably try to do it again."

Something in Penn's tone prodded Revi to sit up a little straighter. He peeled his eyes away from the pear, casting an uncertain look in his comrade's direction. "What are you saying?"

An eye roll followed Revi's inquiry. Penn counted off the sequence of events on his fingers. "I'm saying she knows you went to Northwestern. She knows it was dangerous. She probably got an even better idea of the danger since we left, what with lesser gods running around manipulating people like it's the end of the feckin' world or something." His hard expression softened, but only minutely. "I'm just saying ... if my folks were still alive ... even if they did dump me off in some shithole ... I'd still put my life on the line to make sure they were okay."

Revi's mouth felt dry. The wisdom of Penn's words burned him. It all seemed so obvious now. "You think she went to Northwestern," he said, trying to recall all the information he had given her at Panagea's center.

He got it. Penn pushed his beret up further on his head with a small nudge from his thumb. "I'm only saying that's what I would do. And whether I like it or not, your whiny ass daughter and I are cut from the same cloth."

Revi's eyes narrowed to slits and he fought the initial uprising of offense that boiled through his arms. But a slow breath helped him settle. The words about his daughter were unflattering, but he wouldn't expect any different from Penn Elmbroke. He recognized the man's confession for what it truly was: a helpful gesture.

He rose from his spot on the porch steps and looked down at his comrade, who sat just as swaggering and conceited as he always did. Though Revi did not offer him a smile, his words held an honest coating of appreciation. "Thanks, Penn."

The man waved his wrist as if it was no big deal. "Yeah, yeah," he muttered, getting comfortable once more in his spot on the porch. "Go on, then. Gather your shit. Captain's going to be pissed you're leaving, you know."

Revi scoffed. It would take him very little time to acquire his belongings. He'd need some supplies from the airship, but experience aboard it left him with the knowledge of where everything was. He could be on the next steam train within an hour.

Penn was right, though; Kazuaki likely wouldn't be pleased. Especially with the terrible timing. The captain was out for the blood of the lesser gods, now. Still, Revi knew the immortal would bite his tongue. If the captain's behavior last year was any indication, when he abandoned an entire uprising to track and secure a rouge Bermuda, Revi knew he'd understand. Some people just held more precedence than others. And to Revi Houton, his daughter held it all. Even if it took ten years to learn, he would spend the rest of his life holding himself to that.

* * *

"You ... want to use me?"

Kazuaki stared at Nicholai from his chair in the Addihein household. His elbow settled on the Time Father's desk, with his fingers splayed on the right side of his face to hold it up. He nodded. "Yes."

"As bait?" Nicholai asked.

"Yes."

The Southeastern Time Father blinked, sitting back in his chair. He draped his arm over the object's back and cradled his chin in his hand. "I'm keen on helping, Kazuaki, but I thought, perhaps, you might find a use for me as something more than a piece of meat, placed under a box trap, held up by a stick."

"Don't be ridiculous." Kazuaki leaned back in his seat. The fragile material creaked under the weight of his frame. "Nobody uses box traps anymore. They're completely ineffective."

The captain's words were lost on Nicholai. "You know what I mean."

Kazuaki stared at Nicholai for a moment, impatiently tapping his finger on the side of his jaw. "They're after the division leaders, Nico. Vadim was already a victim. We can only surmise the same fate has befallen Emont and—" He paused. It was brief, but Nicholai caught it. Kazuaki cleared his throat. "—and Elowyn. You were attacked once already. We know they'll try again. Right now, they're busying themselves manipulating countless thousands of people. None of us stand a chance at getting them to tear themselves away from their reign of terror. But you ... to them, you're a worthy prize. You're our best shot at getting one to physically manifest itself."

The clock hanging on Nicholai's wall mocked the silence with its incessant ticks. Normally, the Time Father found the sound comforting, but after his experience in the realm in-between worlds, the constant reminder of passing seconds troubled him. "But it wasn't a lesser god who sought me," he interjected, holding out a hand. "It was only a random man under the influence of one."

"They know the hierarchy of mankind," Kazuaki said, narrowing his eye. "Your voice has resonance. Perhaps, if you pray to one, one will appear."

Nicholai parted his lips to speak but halted. His attention fell on the set of katars leaning against the wall beside Kazuaki. Polished steel that defied its age, they shimmered with an otherworldly essence expected of a weapon forged by gods. Still, Nicholai frowned. "And what if a lesser god *does* appear ... and these weapons Mimir gave you are nothing more than some sort of cruel joke?"

Kazuaki huffed. "It wouldn't matter. They can't hurt us."

"They seem to be doing a lot of damage for creatures that can't cause harm," Nicholai murmured. He leaned forward in his chair, his gaze stern as he studied Kazuaki. "I'd prefer not to welcome *any* chaos to Nenada if I can avoid it. In fact, I'd rather the whole of Southeastern stay as far away from lesser gods as possible."

"Get your head out of your ass, Nico. They're already here," Kazuaki snapped, slicking strands of black hair out of his face. "And like a plague, they will continue to spread if we do not stop them."

The Time Father closed his eyes. The knowledge that Kazuaki was right battled with his desire to keep his people safe. What kind of leader invited harm to his home town? Then again, what kind of leader said no to a potential solution for the whole of

Panagea? If Mimir spoke the truth, and Kazuaki could, indeed, slay the lesser gods ... it would be the beginning of a long endeavor to wipe their wrath from Panagea. But killing ... it almost felt as if he was back to where he started with Kazuaki Hidataka in the first place, begging him not to use violence as a means to an end.

But were lesser gods actual men and women ... or were they only physical manifestations of mankind's ideas, hopes, and desires? Nicholai's conscience labeled them as individuals, but a small part of him had no qualms removing them from Panagea forever.

Then again ... it was hard to tell if that thought stemmed from himself, or the callous influence of Darjal. The being prodded at his brain ceaselessly as of late. He felt him in every ounce of blood pumping through his veins. In every step he took. In every minute gesture. He was getting harder and harder to ignore.

The Time Father thought about what Umbriel would say. That it was dangerous. That he was already fragile. That inviting a lesser god to infect him with even more mental pressure than Darjal already unleashed daily was foolhardy and thoughtless. Nicholai could already see the disappointment on her face. He'd already left so much there in the last several weeks. But unless they did something, there was no end in sight for disappointments all around.

Nicholai's eyes opened. He had to do this. For his people's well-being, first and foremost. But if it also helped him get one part closer to removing Darjal from his head, he would do just about anything. "All right," he relented, glancing at Kazuaki. "I'll do it. But give me a chance to talk with whoever we summon first. I know things didn't go well with Dimjir, but it's never too late to try and reason with them instead."

Kazuaki glared, as he always did. What he felt in that moment, Nicholai could not tell. The captain never gave much away. "I'll give you five minutes."

He'd take it. It was four minutes longer than he thought he'd get. "My only other condition is that we wait for nightfall."

Nicholai glanced out the window, taking note of the sun's position in the sky. Though he could have looked at his clock, much like the ticking, he found the face left a sour taste in his mouth. "We'll wait for the residents to take to their beds. If we're going to be summoning lesser gods to gallivant around Nenada, the fewer people awake for them to control, the better."

Kazuaki nodded once more. That would give him time to prepare the others and himself. "Fair enough." He pulled himself out of his chair, grabbed the katars, and strode across the room, leaving the Time Father to whatever political duties he wished to wrap up before nightfall.

The captain swept fluidly through the room and reached his hand out to open the door to the porch. On the other side, someone beat him to the punch.

As the door swung open, Kazuaki fell into Revi's sight and he stepped back, not wishing to run into him.

"Captain—" Revi stared, holding tight to a series of travel bags.

Kazuaki eyed him, from his boots to the supplies draped over his shoulders. The bags were full, fit to accommodate a man for quite some time. His gaze flicked to Revi's face. "Going somewhere?" he asked, his tone unenthusiastic.

The Houton man's shoulders drew back, despite the weight of the provisions he packed to accompany him. "I have reason to believe Avigail went to Northwestern," he said, with little other explanation.

He didn't need to elucidate. Kazuaki knew immediately what he insinuated. "Northwestern is a big division. It won't be easy finding one girl among hundreds of thousands with only one set of eyes."

Revi knew what the captain implied. His search for Avigail would be a solo mission. He expected as much; Kazuaki was guided by his own set of morality. While Revi was certain the captain's respect for humanity wavered at the best of times, ultimately, he knew Kazuaki would answer Panagea's call for help. One could not place an enchanted weapon in the hands of the immortal and expect him not to use it. "You're right," he murmured, "but it'll be much easier than sitting on my ass for another ten years, living on hope alone that I might see her again."

Kazuaki studied Revi's face. He scrutinized his posture down to the last subconscious twitch in his fingertip. Then he nodded. "Then go. We all know hope is useless, and nothing to wager on."

Revi affirmed the captain's statement. His eyes fell to the katars at Kazuaki's side. In a temporary wave of regret at abandoning his comrades in a time of need, he forced himself to face his superior once more. "Good luck. With the gods."

Kazuaki lifted one of the katars and set it gently against his shoulder. With a stern face, he muttered, "Never needed luck."

A small smirk appeared across Revi's mouth. Kazuaki's classic dismissal, masked with a thick veneer of arrogance, gave him all the amnesty he needed from his guilt. With or without him, the captain would be fine. He always was. "I'll return," he said. "As soon as I find her."

"Well," Kazuaki motioned him off with a quick jerk of his head, "you know where we'll be."

Revi nodded, amending the series of travel packs he held with a quick rotation of his shoulder before he left. He felt no need to make additional farewells to Bermuda, Brack, and Granite. His departure was only temporary, anyway. Penn and the captain would fill them in. Right now, his only focus was finding the nearest steam train.

When Revi ventured out of earshot, Nicholai walked up behind Kazuaki, a concerned look on his face. "He's going alone? Shouldn't we send someone to accompany him?"

"No." Kazuaki stood with his back to Nicholai. "That would only slow him down."

* * *

Anxiety often made time tick by faster than usual. Nicholai could have sworn he was back in the in-between realm, as the hours flew by without remorse since the decision was made to summon a lesser god. After an in-depth discussion with Umbriel, who was predictably displeased with the danger Nicholai put himself in with this endeavor, they settled on one of the gods Dimjir named as being among the few vengeful: Madros. The God of Revenge.

The Earth Mother did not shy away from putting her disapproval on full display. But every worry he saw in her eyes, he knew was borne of compassion. Of fear for his well-being. It was after some time that she relented. Umbriel cared for Nicholai, but she also cared for the people of Panagea ... and if Nicholai could somehow pull mercy out of Madros and end the reign of terror ... if he could harmlessly invite lesser gods back into Panagea, that she might see another Earth Mother again in her lifetime ... it was worth the risk.

A soft rain misted his arms. He delighted in the small pleasure. Nicholai rolled the sleeves of his shirt up earlier, finding the anticipation of the evening's events made him work up a sweat. Standing under flickering lamplight outside his home, he glanced in all directions. As predicted, much of Nenada was asleep. The last of the lamplighters retired to their homes. It was now or never.

Mimir stood in the doorway of Nicholai's home, spying the man's back from the open entrance. "I extend to you the best of luck, Time Father. You'll understand if I do not take an active part." A slow but undeniable smirk danced onto his face. "As you can imagine, I do not wish to be within striking distance of any vengeful lesser gods. Your mortal blood holds the antidote to their axes and swords," he paused, sliding his hand up around his neck as if he feared his head might detach from his spine, "but mine does not."

Nicholai glanced over his shoulder, surprised Mimir made even a small appearance. "Yes," he said, his face betraying the confusion he felt that the lesser god addressed him at all, "I understand."

He blinked, and Mimir was gone. The others took to their hiding places as well. Where they hid, Nicholai did not know. He was not made privy to their location as an insurance policy. If Madros did infiltrate his mind, it was pertinent that Nicholai possessed no knowledge of the whereabouts of the others. They needed all the help they could get to keep Madros in the dark.

"Right," he said to himself, looking down at his hands as if they held an answer to a question he didn't know. "Okay." Nicholai inhaled, rubbed his palms together, and hung his head. "Madros, God of Revenge ... I am Nicholai Addihein, the Time Father of the Southeastern division. I understand your kind are out for the division leaders. I seek council with you, that I might quell your lust for retaliation." He frowned, realizing the idiocy of his statement in pursuing exoneration from the God of Revenge. Nevertheless, he persisted. "Um ... please."

The only response to his plea was a well-timed gust of wind. It blew more tiny rain droplets onto Nicholai's face and neck. He cleared his throat and tried again. "Madros, God of—"

"I'm here," the voice uttered, sounding as though it stood inches from his face, but Nicholai could not locate him. "Say your piece, so that I might bathe in the amusement of how truly pathetic it is."

Nicholai's spine arched at the sudden onset of chatter. He steeled his nerves and reached up to grab the brim of his hat; holding something helped keep his hand steady. "I understand you feel betrayed by mankind. You have every right to feel so. Being abandoned by those you love, those who are supposed to love you ..." Nicholai frowned. "It is ... not a good feeling."

From the shadows cast by tall street lamps, a movement occurred on the ground. Nicholai squinted as the dark shape peeled itself off the cobblestone, manifesting in the form of a demon-horned beast. Madros snorted, his breath forming around his mouth in a translucent mist that died shortly after it was born. "What do you know of it, Time Father?" His eyes glowed, piercing Nicholai's retinas with the savagery of their brightness against the black that surrounded him. "You are a man of power here.

Humanity bows down to the division leaders. You are adored by all you rule over."

"Oh, boy," Nicholai winced, scratching the back of his head, "you've never been involved in politics, have you?"

Madros' nose wrinkled as he shot a rapid breath out through his nostrils. "Do not insult me by striving to comprehend the motive behind my vengeance. Simply know it is just."

"No, no," Nicholai held up his hands, "I ... I get it. After my mother's death, my father—eh, you might know him, if you're out for the other division leaders and all that ... you know, he, he left me with my grandparents. Didn't visit more than once a year, if that." Nicholai shook his head. "It does sting a bit, being forgotten. But ... I can honestly say I never contemplated mass genocide."

"Do not mock me, young Addihein." Madros inclined his chin, glaring down at Nicholai from his massive height. "You compare one man's adoration to that of hundreds of thousands. It is not the same."

"Try telling that to an eight-year-old," Nicholai murmured under his breath, wincing at the memory. "Look, Madros, it's neither here nor there. The point is, you feel slighted. Understandably so. What can I do to fix that?"

Madros frowned, unamused. It reminded Nicholai of a facial expression the captain might have made. The rain intensified, spilling down onto the lesser god's shoulders, which looked as though they were carved of rock. Small hisses of steam sizzled around him with each droplet that touched his unnatural skin. "There is nothing you can do."

Nicholai pinched his lips together, a single brow raising on his face. "Yes, that's what everyone keeps saying."

Madros chuckled. The sound boomed like thunder, to match the rain. "Your companions are wise to say such things. They are perceptive, to see through your worth like glass, transparent and fragile."

"I don't think they—" Nicholai paused, unsure how he found himself in this conversation. He intended to plead to Madros for mercy, but somewhere his objective fell off course. He frowned, fairly certain it had much to do with the lesser gods' abilities to manipulate people. He hadn't even realized Madros had done anything. "—they don't consider me all that useless," he finished, compelled by a supernatural desire to complete his sentence.

"These are the same lies we told ourselves," Madros rumbled. "When fewer and fewer men and women offered up their prayers, we deceived ourselves into thinking as you do. That they still saw use in us. But even gods are wrong sometimes, young Addihein. As are you."

He felt it, and he didn't. That single second of doubt. He relived every disagreement shared with Kazuaki. Every reservation voiced by Umbriel at his ability to assist with the lesser gods' infiltration. Every disregarded opinion he ever announced, every overlooked, omitted, unheeded thing he shared amongst the captain and the crew. His comrades. At least, they were supposed to be.

These people were the ones who were supposed to trust him most. They were from two different classes of Panagea, but after he got to know them, their variances never dissuaded Nicholai from respecting every one of them. The sentiment was not always shared. Or so it felt ... particularly as of late. They treated him like glass, as Madros said, more than an esteemed member of their party.

Yes. He was glass to them. Brittle and dispensable.

He shouldn't have been. Nicholai Addihein was capable of devising solutions. If only they weren't present to stifle his success, he could easily achieve what Panagea needed. If only.

The twin blades of the katars pierced Madros from behind. One for each lung. A guttural sound escaped the lesser god's mouth as he arched his back. His head quaked as he strained to look over his shoulder, to see what had happened, but his movements were hindered by the rods of steel penetrating his form.

"Im ... possible," Madros stuttered, a slow trail of blood seeping past his tongue, slithering down his neck, where it nestled into a jagged crack in his skin.

Kazuaki huffed. He placed his boot against Madros' back and kicked the body off his blades. The lesser god staggered forward, trying to catch himself, but was unsuccessful. He collapsed onto the cobblestone, his fingers scraping against the ground beneath him.

Kazuaki approached, resting the tip of the katars in front of Madros' face. He lowered himself down into a crouched position, the rain pelting his long jacket, washing the blood of the god down the polished steel, where it diluted into nothing more than a pink wash near Madros' fallen head.

The lesser god's wild eyes traveled up the tainted blades to Kazuaki's hands. A man's hands. Hands that had no business wielding a weapon forged by gods. "Where ... did you get those?" he gurgled, wrath and unreleased blood poisoning his words.

Kazuaki glanced at the katars before he looked down at Madros. More iron-red liquid from the two gaping holes in his chest seeped out from beneath him, commingling with the blood washed away from the blades. The captain hitched a shoulder. "Doesn't matter much now, does it?"

With the last of his fading strength, Madros reached out and gripped the captain's boot. He dug his nails into the aged leather, snarling as the contact allowed him to scour Kazuaki's brain for the information he wanted. Though his grip on the immortal's footwear weakened, the rage in his throat was very much alive. "Mimir," he hissed, releasing the boot and curling his fingers into a fist.

His knuckles did not strain in that shape for much longer. Little by little, the pressure behind each finger gave way as Madros' life slipped from his imagined body. When Kazuaki was certain he passed, he stood to his feet.

"Well done, Nic—"

The captain flinched. He felt a sharpness in his neck. He rested one of the katars against his leg as he raised his hand, grabbing the dart that stuck out of his skin. Kazuaki ripped it out. His eye contracted as he inspected the object with confusion. It didn't take long for him to figure out what it was.

He turned his eye to Nicholai. The Time Father's arm was still raised, the slot where the dart exited his metal limb still open. He looked wild, standing there in the rain, living in the chaos Madros bred in his brain. He looked every bit the part of a demon standing there, his shoulders rising and falling with each labored breath.

"Gods dammit," Kazuaki muttered, his arm falling to his side. Unable to balance the katars against his body any longer, they clattered to the cobblestone beside Madros. He felt the paralysis claim his legs. It brought him to his knees. "Nico—"

The Time Father retracted the opening where the dart released. He scowled at Kazuaki, wearing a disgusted look that the immortal captain had never witnessed before. It looked unnatural on the kindhearted man's face.

"Nico," Kazuaki tried again to reach him, but his spine's ability to hold his body upright faded. He barely felt his cheek hit the stone ground, the dampness of the accumulated rain only resonating as a scarcely recognizable cold. His nerves stopped processing sensations. Like the rest of him, his tongue failed to move.

The last thing Kazuaki remembered was the one thing the dart could not paralyze: the overwhelming sentiment of anguish at the mental collapse of Nicholai Addihein. If the gods could ruin the unwavering resolve of the Southeastern Time Father, the man who Kazuaki came to respect as being immovable in his ethics ... that only meant one thing.

Nobody was safe.

CHAPTER TWENTY-FIVE

"Shit, shit, shit—"

Brack burst out from his hiding place inside a steam car he picked the lock on prior. He nearly tripped over his legs when he saw the captain collapse to the ground. It was a sight he'd never witnessed before, and one he never intended to witness again. He slid to his knees and inspected Kazuaki, finding the empty vial belonging to the dart close by.

"Nico!" Brack spayed his fingers and held his hands out in a shrug of confusion. "What the feck, mate?"

Umbriel, who watched from the partially pulled curtains in the Addihein household, threw the front door open and assumed a defensive stance on the porch. "Brack, be cautious," she warned, her eyes wide. "I fear Madros has broken through his last shred of fortitude."

Brack arched a brow, turning back to face Nicholai, who threatened him with nothing more than an ominous glare. "I see," the Rabbit muttered, keeping a keen focus on the manipulated Time Father.

Bermuda ran out from an adjacent alley, cursing as her eyes stumbled on Kazuaki's fallen form. She had watched from the sidelines out of caution and regretted it fully. "We'll have to secure him," she instructed to Brack, removing a short dagger from the place it was stashed inside her boot, "as we did with Vadim."

Brack spied Bermuda's dagger, only taking his focus off Nicholai for a moment. "Well, we can't feckin' kill him—"

Bermuda glared, tightening her grip on her small blade's handle. "Why do you think I grabbed the dagger instead of the gun?"

Having heard the commotion of Umbriel dashing out into the forefront, Jernal filled the doorway with his body, leaning his palms on the frame as he stared outside. "What the hell is going on?" he asked, incredulous, as he saw the body of Madros, and what appeared to be the body of the immortal Captain Kazuaki Hidataka on the cobblestone streets of Nenada.

"Nico's a wee bit possessed at the moment," Brack informed him, removing a dagger from his hilt. "You could make yourself useful and get out here; we gotta restrain him and get him inside."

Jernal did not need to be told twice. He rushed out the door, wincing only at the surprise of the cold rain from above. "It's three against one, it shouldn't be too hard."

"Four." Granite rounded a corner behind Nicholai's house, his eyes on the Southeastern Time Father.

Brack smirked as he looked at Jernal. "Don't be so sure. You ever tried fighting a man before with restraint? Hard not to kill a fecker."

Jernal shook his head, a look of disgust on his face. As a soldier, he had destroyed his fair share of lives, but he detained far more than he ended. "He's a pacifist with no weapons. This is going to be a cakewalk."

"He still has three darts left," Bermuda cautioned, edging her way to Nicholai's other side. She saw the Time Father's eyes follow her, though his head did not move. It sent a chill through her veins. "Enough to even the playing field."

"This is ridiculous," Jernal muttered, removing the handcuffs he kept at his hip from when he served as a footman in Southern. "Just hold him down."

Bermuda was pinned by Nicholai's focus. She felt frozen. It was as unsettling as it was unusual. At that moment, Granite's dog ran out the door that Jernal left ajar, barking as he descended on Nicholai, absent of any fear. The Time Father's gaze shifted to the canine, tearing away from Bermuda.

Brack took full advantage of the distraction. He bolted toward Nicholai and tackled him to the ground, feeling the full force of the unforgiving stone beneath them. "You know I love you, mate!" he shouted, holding tight to the Time Father as he writhed under his grasp. "But this is for your own good, so I ain't gonna go easy on you!"

Without a word, Nicholai opened the shield on his forearm. The metal splayed out, cutting into the arms Brack wrapped around him. The sting made the Rabbit release him. Freed from the man's hold, Nicholai struck his shield into his attacker's nose and shoved his body away from his.

"Son of a bitch!" Brack dropped his dagger, his hands involuntarily coming up around his already swelling nose. Blood from split skin and his nostrils collected into his palm, though the rain was quick to wash it away. "Fecker packs some punch for a pacifist!" he scowled to Jernal, his words muffled as he held his hand around his injury.

Nicholai scooped up Brack's dagger, surprisingly light on his feet. He turned toward Jernal, Bermuda, and Granite, making sure not to have his back to them. He flipped the small blade around in his palm until the handle settled well into his grip.

The desolate look in his eyes said he might kill them. Of that, Bermuda had no doubt. She couldn't gamble on the hope that the Time Father's cognition would return by his own will. "Nico." She didn't take any steps toward him, not wanting to breed additional panic in the already unsteady man. She tried to remember what Kal said regarding Vadim's reformation. She needed to appeal to his character. "Look at Brack. Look at what you did to him. That's not who you are."

Nicholai responded with a contemptuous stare. It was eerier than if he had said anything. Vehemence seemed so misplaced on him.

Penn, the last to appear, came up behind Umbriel after exiting the house. He stole a glimpse of her, immediately getting a feel for the desperation behind the situation. The captain was down. Nicholai was possessed. "Feckin' shit," he muttered, reaching down to scoop a few rocks into his palm. The closest non-lethal objects he found. "Oi, Nico—"

In his peripheral vision, Nicholai flicked his eyes to Penn.

"Catch." The Elmbroke man whipped a rock toward him, having earned much experience throwing stones in the wayward home for orphaned children.

Nicholai looked unamused as he lifted his shield. The rock bounced off it without damage.

Capitalizing on another distraction, Bermuda leaped forward. Her small blade bit into the side of his knee.

Nicholai seethed. He spun, clipping the temple of her skull with his shield before he dropped.

Bermuda fell to her palms, swearing as she raised her free hand to the side of her head. Warm wetness met her skin, a blunt contrast to the cold rain from above. It bled profusely, as head wounds did. She rolled away from him and righted her position to a stand.

The attack seemed to hinder his movements, but it did not dampen his quiet ferocity. He did not grip his injury. He simply let it bleed.

Granite removed a small blade, taking a cue from Bermuda. He feared neither shield nor dart. Granite assumed he could take at least two of the three injections Nicholai still housed in his forearm before he fell. But the Time Father had other plans.

Nicholai raised his arm. The blade Granite held corroded. The behemoth dropped it with haste, not wanting to end up like a crippled heap of dust as the late Darjal Wessex did back in Avadon. He growled, angered by his inability to restrain the rogue man.

Brack's eyes flicked to the fallen captain, his finger still applying pressure to his split nose. He spit out a mouthful of blood that had washed into the back of his throat. "Bet Cap's wishing he didn't teach Nico how to defend himself now."

Bermuda scowled. She dug her heels into the wet stones beneath her. "We're done playing nice. Umbriel can heal his wounds. Just bring him down, so long as it's not an instant fatality."

"Aye aye, quartermaster!" Brack pulled a pistol from his hip, but before he aimed, Nicholai rusted the device in his hands. "Gods dammit!" The Rabbit cursed and chucked the weapon aside. "His feckin' parlor tricks are hard to beat, love."

From the porch, Umbriel steeled herself. "He can't keep it up forever." Every year of his life he gave away into corroding the weapons weakened him. She already saw the Time Father's posture stagger as his breathing became tortured.

Granite rotated his shoulders and charged. His first swing missed and earned him a stab in the arm. Nicholai was quicker, but the massive man had endurance. An exchange of attacks met Nicholai's shield. Then he landed a hit.

His fist met the Time Father's ribs, some of which buckled under the force. Nicholai wheezed sharply, but wild desperation slid the dagger across Granite's exposed torso before he staggered away.

Granite huffed, his gaze flicking down to the crimson that stained his shirt. It wasn't deep. It could have been. It was almost as if Nicholai showed some restraint.

Umbriel couldn't watch any longer. She walked off the porch, approaching Nicholai from behind. Adrenaline was the only thing keeping his body upright. His leg bled, his ribs were surely broken, and he'd given much of his life into destroying two weapons. He wouldn't last. His body could not keep up with his mind. He didn't even hear her quiet footsteps until she was right behind him.

"Nicholai."

He turned. Like lightning, his arm came toward her, the dagger stained with Granite's blood still clutched in his palm. Umbriel did not move. He caught her eyes. The blade stopped just before it met the skin on her neck.

"Nicholai," she said again, pleading with the man through eyes that took every ounce of willpower to calm.

His arm quaked. She saw pain in him beyond the physical injuries he suffered. A small piece of the Time Father's true self flickered to the surface of his pupils. Nicholai's jaw clamped, a rasping sound of agony spilled a gush of saliva through his gritted teeth.

He suffered. He wanted to destroy her. His body wanted to know what it felt like to puncture her jugular with the blade. But a minuscule thread of sanity, which he gripped onto with broken bones, strengthened under the ethereal connection of Umbriel's gaze. It would not last long.

Bermuda brought him down. The pair hit the cold cobblestone and wet fingers pried one of the darts from his exposed metal panel. The quartermaster jammed the tip of the needle into his neck, cringing when Nicholai's dagger found a place in the meat of her shoulder.

His rapidly beating heart carried the vial's liquid through his veins faster than it would have otherwise. Nicholai tried to push himself up, but the blade clattered to the ground and he gripped his side. It burned each time he inhaled. It radiated through his chest. The sting in his leg throbbed, but the effects of the sedation soothed the ache. Soon, he couldn't feel his legs at all. Then, he felt nothing and collapsed.

Umbriel reached a hand up to the place on her neck where Nicholai almost gored her. There was no time to dwell. "Jernal."

"On it." The soldier strode over, securing Nicholai's hands behind his back and cuffing them.

The Earth Mother knelt, her knee in a puddle of rain as she laid her hands on him. She was quick to restore his lost years, quicker to mend the torn flesh surrounding the gaping hole Bermuda left in his knee. Umbriel did what she could for the swelling tissue attached to his ribs, but there was nothing she could do for the broken bones. "Take him inside. Please."

Jernal nodded, grunting as he threw Nicholai's limp arm over his shoulder. He'd carried his fair share of fallen soldiers before; the effort was well within his skill set. As he dragged him back into the Addihein household, Umbriel kept her place on the ground, taking in a few bottomless breaths. She gave much of herself to Nicholai. She needed a moment to recover.

Bermuda slipped her blade back in her boot, sweeping her hands through her drenched hair. She tried to scrub away some of the blood from her temple with the water, but for every swipe of her fingers across the wound, more scarlet liquid escaped. "Brack, Penn, help me get the captain inside, too."

The men nodded, each taking up opposite sides of Kazuaki's arms. It was an endeavor; not only had the rain weighed down the immortal's long jacket, but he was several hundred pounds of muscle and dead weight.

Bermuda closed one of her eyes, the rainwater making a pathway for her blood to spill into her cornea. The body of Madros still laid on the earth. They couldn't leave it there. Civilians waking up to witness the towering corpse of an unearthly creature would surely ignite a panic. "Granite ... I think you're the only one who might be able to lift him."

The man nodded, his dog running circles around him as he approached Madros' carcass. The lesser god dwarfed even Granite in his mass. Though his stomach still leaked from the nip of Nicholai's dagger, he reached down to seize the lesser god's arm. It crumbled under his touch.

Granite's eyes shifted into slits. He watched as the rest of the lesser god's body collapsed into ash and smoke. The fierce downpour from the sky collected the dust into a puddle, where it dissolved into the pool of rainwater accumulating in the streets. Without a word, he seized the katars Kazuaki dropped earlier, relieved the endeavor of finding a place to bury the corpse of a massive creature was taken care of.

His long strides carried him over to Umbriel, who remained kneeling. He placed both katars in a single hand and extended his free one to her. "Need an assist?"

The silver-lavender strands of Umbriel's wet hair clung to the sides of her face. She looked up, her eyes falling on Granite's offering. "Thank you," she said, accepting. After he helped her to her feet, she laid one hand on his torso, another on his arm, both places that had been ripped open by metal. In moments, the wounds were closed.

"Thanks," Granite muttered, his voice dark but grateful.

Umbriel offered a weak smile. "Of course."

By the time the two made it back into the Addihein household, the others had placed Nicholai in his bed. Jernal readjusted his shackles, choosing instead to chain one wrist to a bedpost. The other was secured to the opposite post with a metal chain.

"We'll need to figure something else out when he wakes up," Brack said, leaning against a wall. "He'll just rust those chains the second he comes to."

Umbriel felt an unnatural weight in her chest. Her heart was crushed seeing him like that, a prisoner in his own body, fettered to his bed like an unlawful beast. She turned away, unable to look at him, and walked into her room.

The unconscious Kazuaki occupied her bed. Bermuda sat in a chair she pulled up beside him, her head bowed as if she either lived in deep contemplation or a state of concussion.

"Bermuda," Umbriel's gentle voice swept into the quiet room. "Might I heal your head wound and your shoulder?"

The quartermaster's eyes slid open as she lifted her head. She blinked, touching her temple once again. The blood was still warm. Still fresh on her fingers. "Yes," she said, standing. "I nearly forgot about them."

Umbriel took several steps toward her and reached out, regenerating the damages suffered by her flesh. Her arm fell loosely to her side when she finished. Flaccidity infected her muscles. Umbriel hoped she maintained enough energy to correct Brack's split nose. After a large sigh that she hoped would bring much-needed oxygen into her lungs, Umbriel's eyes fell to Kazuaki. "You two stay as long as you need."

The quartermaster recognized the Earth Mother's fatigue. She saw it frequently aboard the ship when the woman drew out the poison left in her heart by Mimir. "If you need to rest," Bermuda started, "let me know. We can move him."

"No, no," Umbriel shook her head, holding up a hand. "It's really all right." She smiled. It was frail. "I'll see to Brack. Get some rest."

The Earth Mother slipped out the door and closed it gently behind her. Beads of sweat formed around her brow, her complexion pale, an accompanying clamminess glistening on her skin. She gave a large portion of herself away tonight, but walked up to Brack and raised a hand to correct the bridge of his nose.

The Rabbit held up his hands and took a step back, a reassuring grin on his face. He witnessed her fatigue. "Save your strength, love," he said with a level of charming confidence. "I hear maidens are into blokes with scars, anyway."

She knew his gesture stemmed only from kindness and concern, but Umbriel did not fight him. On the contrary, she was relieved. The woman offered him a smile and gave his arm a gentle squeeze before she crossed the distance over to where Nicholai laid. She sat on the edge of the bed, frowning.

He fought the lesser gods' whispers off for a long time, but Umbriel knew he was a ticking time bomb. They were relentless. Even still, Kazuaki ran Madros through. The God of Revenge perished. She shook her head. "I just don't understand. As soon as Madros' life energy depleted, his hold over Nicholai should have turned to ashes with him."

Mimir, who stood in the corner of Nicholai's room with his arms crossed over his chest, lifted his chin. "Hm?" He only gleaned some of what occurred, having holed up in the Time Father's bedroom out of a need for safety. If any of the lesser gods would have sought revenge for his efforts in stealing the katars from the in-between, it would have been Madros.

He pushed his body off the wall and leaned over Nicholai's unconscious form. The lesser god extended a finger and gave his body a poke in the ribs. By accident or cruel intention, none were certain. It was with some luck Nicholai remained unconscious and paralyzed, unable to feel the weight of the lesser god's jab on his broken bones. Mimir leaned closer still, his nostrils flaring as he sniffed the Time Father.

Umbriel watched him with caution, a skeptical look glued to her tired face. Jernal, Brack, Penn, and Granite shared in her suspicion, each throwing watchful eyes on the lesser god as he inspected Nicholai's figure.

Mimir craned his neck and placed a finger on Nicholai's forehead. "Ah." He tapped it several times, nodding his head as he did. "Madros only planted the seed, but Darjal watered the tree."

Umbriel felt her heart stop, but she kept a steady outward appearance. "I see ..." She felt Darjal's wrath from the moment he found Nicholai. Though she never saw him, his presence never ventured far. His lust for judgment was insatiable. How Nicholai managed to restrain himself from gutting her in the throat, she would never know, but an exhausted hand slid over to the Time Father's leg. She gripped it and closed her eyes. The woman had nothing to give him. No energy left. But she wanted to feel him in her hands, to reassure herself that although Darjal consumed him, he was still here. Somewhere inside his manipulated brain, the empathetic Nicholai Addihein remained.

"Can't we just kill Darjal, too?" Brack asked, breaking the silence. "I mean, we got the katars. And we got practice. Already killed the fecker once."

Mimir returned to his spot near the wall. He leaned against it, casual in his movements. "I doubt it. If Darjal bore witness to Madros' slaying, he is now aware our dear captain possesses a weapon capable of destroying lesser gods. I should think it will be quite difficult to get him to manifest himself now."

Penn made a face, sliding his hands into his pockets. "Hard to kill what you can't see," he muttered.

Mimir snapped his fingers and pointed at the Elmbroke man. "Precisely."

"He'll be fine," Umbriel reassured them, though her words were more for her benefit than for theirs. Her fingers embraced his leg tighter. Though she did not often need such luxuries, it brought her comfort to touch him. To feel him present, though he remained unaccounted for. "I'll make sure of it."

In Umbriel's room, Kazuaki's eye bobbed open, unsteady. His surroundings lived in a blur. Instinct compelled his hands to reach for his side, to seize a weapon, any weapon, but his movements were languid and unmanageable, still hindered by the effects of the powerful sedative. When he felt a distinguishable absence of hard metal available, he tried to sit up.

"I'd take your own advice and belay that," Bermuda said from his side, resting a hand on his arm to steady him. "I removed your weapons. Didn't want you rolling over on a dagger while you slept."

Her voice. It had a sedating effect. Edgy muscles eased as he collapsed back into his spot in Umbriel's bed. His chest rose and fell shallowly as he turned his head to face her. Clear vision returned slowly, but Kazuaki was quick to locate the dried blood caked on the side of her face.

An unsteady arm raised from the bedside. Though his fingers shook, he took care to gently part her hair to the side, offering him a better view of her injury. But where he expected a wound to be, there wasn't. "That belong to you?" he asked, his voice slurred as he nodded toward her crusted crimson stains.

Subconscious desire made her lean into his touch. It kindled something in her, a continuous craving for the feel of Kazuaki's hands on her body. Despite the situation, she found a wry smirk slip over her face. The way his words melted together, weighted down by the poison still present in his veins, and still, his concern shined through. "I've lived through worse."

His arm hovered for as long as he was able to convince his body to hold it there. Kazuaki brushed his thumb over her cheek before gravity pushed his limb back to the bed's side. "Madros?"

"Dead." Bermuda leaned forward, resting her elbows on the mattress to put herself closer.

Kazuaki's voice sounded hoarse. His eye turned to the ceiling. "And Nico?"

Bermuda hesitated. Her face shifted to a downcast state. "Alive. Restrained. Not himself, I'm afraid."

She watched Kazuaki's eye close. The immortal was flawless at containing his sentiments deep within his brain; he trained himself to imprison anything that might serve as something someone could exploit. But here, now, with his actions dulled, she bore witness to his grave disappointment.

"We corrected Vadim," she said, her tone delicate. "We can correct Nico, too."

Kazuaki opened his eye. He continued to stare at the ceiling. "He shouldn't have fallen, Bermuda. He's willful. Determined. But he did. He did because he believed what Madros said to him ... even for a moment ... how we treat him ... devalue him ..." His words rolled off his tongue, lumbering and incoherent, but sincere. "He fell because what Madros said was right."

He was still lost in a mental fog. Bermuda winced. Though lacquered in tranquilizers, his words held a tinge of truthfulness. Still, she did not wish to cause him any additional burdens. "He'll find his way through the dark. He's persistent."

Kazuaki tried to raise his head, but it only lifted several inches before he allowed it to collapse back into the pillow beneath him. "Yes," he murmured, his words rough. "That he is."

Bermuda slid forward and laid the side of her head on his chest. The sound of his beating heart provided its own sedative effect. As his chest bobbed with each breath, she peered up at him. "So, you've killed a god. What do you intend to do now?"

Measured movements shifted Kazuaki's arm as he slid his hand up the side of the bed, slow to trace the line of her spine before it stopped in the softness of her hair. He held it there, gently burying his fingers into the auburn strands. She heard his heart beat faster. "I intend to kill some more."

Bermuda grinned underneath his touch. She couldn't help but find amusement in his anesthetized state when the ancient walls Kazuaki Hidataka built over the years crumbled away. But her smile was quick to fade. "Kazuaki. Do you trust Mimir?"

His hands stroked through her hair, slow and gratifying. "No."

The quartermaster closed her eyes. "Neither do I."

"He is a nuisance," Kazuaki muttered. "But he is powerless to harm us ... so far as I know."

Bermuda lived in the quiet of Kazuaki's touch. A haven in which she abandoned the afflictions of the moment. It wasn't until she felt the captain looking about the room that she crawled out of her temporary reverie.

"This must be Umbriel's room," Kazuaki murmured, a brow arching on his face.

Bermuda lifted her head from his chest, gazing about the small, four-cornered chamber. Potted plants lived in almost every nook, ranging in variety from wild grasses to exotic blooms. The quartermaster chuckled. "What gave it away?"

Kazuaki's head turned to the right. He spied a small bush growing near the bedside opposite Bermuda's chair. A familiar burst of red. It lived in the farthest reaches of his memory, in a time when a majority of Panagea's plants had all but withered away. But this one ... this one he remembered, though four hundred and some odd years separated him from the last time he saw one.

His free hand slid across the sheets, extending to the shrub. Though thorns dug into his calloused fingertips, he made no signs of discomfort as he plucked the rose from its place. Umbriel would not find pleasure in his actions, but the Earth Mother was a forgiving sort. Idle hands spun the short stem between his fingers and thumb, taking in the sight of something he long thought to be extinct. "This reminds me of you," he said, studying each scarlet petal.

The quartermaster's eyes settled on the flower. She tilted her head as a soft laugh escaped her. "Gods, how much sedative is in those vials?"

"Mock me if you must," Kazuaki said, his voice low as he venerated the rose with an admiring eye, "but it's true. It's a faultless creation. Bewitching. Sung of by poets and scholars alike. Its bloom is commanding ..." His look of contented introspection faded. "And fleeting ..."

He tightened his jaw, not satisfied to dwell on the pain of Bermuda's mortality. The captain cleared his throat. "It looks fragile at first glance ..." Without hesitation, he pressed the pad of his thumb into one of the thorns, just enough to feel the needle-like sting. "But if you're careless, it will still make you bleed. A baleful beauty."

Content to remain there and listen to the sounds of his pacified musings, Bermuda returned her head to his chest. She reached over, delicate as she took the flower into her metal hand. "What's it called?"

"Rosa Othello." The words slipped off his tongue, unhurried and unenergetic. "Most just called it a rose."

She brought it to her nose and drew in the scent. It smelled of rain and wind that crawled through the leaves of Southeastern's forests. Though the thorns were a threat to skin, Bermuda did not wish to part with the plant, and it did not bother her nerveless, metal fingers. "So, Captain," she wondered out loud, peering up at Kazuaki past the burgundy petals, "what do you want to do now?"

He sank his fingers further into the enthralling sensation that was her hair. She felt a ravenous hunger in his touch, and for a moment, she knew where his mind went. But pleasures of the flesh played second fiddle to necessity. Though it wasn't easy, Kazuaki calmed his impious thoughts. There was plenty of time for rendezvous later. With any luck, again, and again.

"Let's restore Nico's sanity," he whispered, his eye on the ceiling once more. "Then, let's slay some feckin' gods."

CHAPTER TWENTY-SIX

Elowyn trudged through the waste of Eastern for miles. Mud tainted by chemicals cast off from the division's countless factories marred her from head to toe. She kept close to the coast, not only to reduce her interactions with those who might be a threat but because that was where the homestead of Mairyn Catteral dwelled.

She was no stranger to the hardships of travel. Elowyn had powered through more horrid conditions than this. Her time spent as a medic to the Northern military ensured that. Now, though, she drove her legs through sheets of muck instead of banks of snow.

Flashbacks triggered with each parallel to her past. Screams of civilians trailed down from the mainland and into her ears. Poor, unprepared people, brought down by the hands of their manipulated family members and neighbors. There were too many for her to stop and intervene. It was a tough lesson she had learned from the battle of Northern and Northeastern.

The shrieks of her people echoed the cries of the fallen soldiers in her past. It was a sound that never left a person's brain, no matter how many years it sat there, collecting dust.

Elowyn used to be a crusader. She risked her life on the battlefield more than once, dragging mangled bodies back to vehicles that carried them to the safety of her tent.

She couldn't save them all then. She couldn't save these people now. Not yet, anyway.

The shabby condition of Mairyn's humble home came into Elowyn's vision when she crawled over a final hill. It looked just as it did when she and the crew washed up on Eastern's shores last year.

Muscles in her legs pulsed from their extensive journey. Her lungs ached from breathing in the still-tainted oxygen of the Eastern division. But her destination only rested several long strides away. That knowledge alone helped convince her throbbing limbs to approach the door and knock.

Elowyn waited. She didn't deny the heart palpitations she experienced in the vicinity of Mairyn's home. The Time Mother wondered if the gun-toting maiden would shoot first, impelled by the conditions as of late to take no risks. But after much thought, Mairyn Catteral remained the only person in Eastern she trusted.

Elowyn only hoped she hadn't fallen to the gods.

Her knock earned no response. Before she lifted her fist to try again, Elowyn's ears perked at the familiar sound that came from behind her: the undeniable noise of a lever-action cocking on a shotgun. She remembered it well.

Elowyn made slow, careful movements when she raised her hands above her head. She did not wish to encourage any rash decisions. "Hello, Mairyn."

"You've got ten seconds to explain to me how you know my name and what you're doing on my property."

Elowyn turned, unhurried and gradual, to portray no sense of danger. When she finally spun all the way and found Mairyn's eyes, she said nothing.

The woman scrutinized Elowyn for the longest seconds in the Time Mother's life. She couldn't tell what went through her mind. Elowyn's heart battled the fear inside her, until Mairyn slowly lowered her rifle, and balanced it to rest on her shoulder. "Well, well, well," she said, seeing through the filth into the eyes of Elowyn Saveign. "Look what the tide dragged in."

"I hate to impose," Elowyn uttered, lowering her voice. "But I find myself between a rock and a hard place. You're the only one I can trust."

Mairyn looked over her shoulder, scanning the horizon for any watchful eyes. When she was satisfied with the lack of onlookers, she reached passed Elowyn and opened the door to her home. "Get inside."

The Time Mother nodded and slipped into the confines of Mairyn's dwelling. She shivered once, her body's way of banishing the adrenaline that boiled through her. Now, in the relative safety of Mariyn's home, she felt as though she could ease her shoulders some.

"I knew you weren't dead," Mairyn muttered, resting her shotgun against a wall. She put a kettle on the stovetop and ignited the heat. "Word is spreading you abandoned Eastern. Have a seat."

Elowyn glanced at one of the mismatched chairs that flanked Mairyn's table. Her legs were grateful to relieve themselves of the burden of carrying her weight. She sank into the hard material, indebted despite its lack of padded comfort. "That's ridiculous," she replied, resting an elbow on the tabletop beside her. "If I did, time here would have stopped."

Mairyn stood on the tips of her toes, reaching into the highest cupboards above her to find several cups. She examined them as she pulled them from their resting place, blowing dust out of the unutilized vessels. "People believe what they want to believe. And what they want to believe, as they have for generations, is that women are unfit to lead."

A look of disgust frosted over Elowyn's face. "Yes, I'm aware. Those voices have raised loud and clear. But there are just as many who thought I was doing well."

"You were." Mairyn set the cups down on the table and returned to digging through her cupboards. She pulled out a manufactured sugar substitute, along with a synthetic tea, and placed them near the cups. "I don't know much about the demons invading this place," she started, having only heard of the gods since Elowyn made her public announcement that they invaded Panagea weeks ago, "but I venture a guess that they're happy to feed fear to people. If what you said in your declaration is true, and they can only control the thoughts of those who don't have mental strength, I'm sure they'll look for other ways to rattle those of sound mind. Your disappearance, for example."

Elowyn's eyes closed. It was a mixed feeling. The reprieve brought to her from the simple action, allowed her body to think she might rest. But Mairyn's observations were swift to banish any extended release. "I think I have a solution," Elowyn said, her words tired, but forceful. "I just need to amass some competent people who can get me into one of Eastern's medical laboratories." She knew just the one. The most advanced of them all. The first one she helped finance the moment she took up leadership of Eastern.

"You'd get in pretty easily if they knew you were the Time Mother. Just lord your title over them," Mairyn suggested, glancing at the kettle as it started to produce a weak whistle.

"The lesser gods are after me. Half of Eastern still hates having me as their leader. As I stated before," Elowyn said, her voice trailing off as she revisited the loss of her dear companion, Huric, "you're the only person in all of Eastern who I would put my life in the hands of. I can't let anyone know who I am, let alone where I am. They already tried to come for me once. The risk is too great."

Mairyn removed the kettle from the stove. She walked over to the table and popped two of the artificial teas into the cups before she doused them in the heated water. Steam swirled upward, wafting around the kettle until she returned it to the stove. "Do you really think you can help Eastern?" she asked, finding Elowyn's eyes as she sat down.

The Time Mother met her penetrating stare. She did not waver. She wanted Mairyn to know the belief behind her statement. "I do."

A small nod came from Mairyn's head. She slid her cup closer toward her and exhaled a gentle breath over the top to cool it. She seemed to mull over something before she took a small, considerate sip and set it back down. "There is a rebellion gathering in the town of Brendale. Mostly footmen who haven't been turned by the gods. Go to them."

Elowyn's brows scrunched together. She laced a finger into the handle of her teacup but did not take her attention away from Mairyn. "How do you know that?"

Another small sip from the hot tea kept Mairyn from answering immediately. Just as well, she did not seem eager to share, as the memories attached to her statement brought her discomfort. "Mr. Catteral patrolled Eastern for almost twenty years. When the riots broke out over the families who were sent to Southern for the construction of Darjal's ironclad, he felt for them. All the complaints were diverted to the footmen. He saw everyone's pain, their confusion, their pleas for their family members to return to them. He said they just wanted answers. But he didn't have any to give them. So he went to find some."

Elowyn's head tilted to the side as she dragged her cup toward her. The warmth that filtered into her weary hands felt nice. "Where did he hope to find them?"

"Edgar was a no-nonsense man. He wanted to go straight to the source. Avital York, himself."

A lingering sense of doom infected Elowyn as she watched Mairyn relive her tale. She wondered whether it was wise to allow the woman to continue, but she did. Mairyn did not seem to bend to weakness, no matter how painful.

"He was on his way to Avital to ask about the status of the families. On the way, he saw a riot form outside the Time Father's stead. Scared people, acting out of pain. They were trying to break through Avital's residence with force. He tried to stop them because he was always a soldier first. A man of Eastern." Mairyn's face steeled. Her grip on her cup intensified, to the point Elowyn detected a small quake in the liquid that was inside it. "They saw his uniform as a symbol of solidarity to Avital. Avital, who they despised. So they killed him."

Elowyn was no stranger to death. Even still, Mairyn's story drained the color from her cheeks. "I'm ... so sorry, Catty."

Mairyn did not react to her condolences. She only stared ahead, focusing on nothing. "He was a good man, my husband. He knew unanswered questions raised fear, and fear raised violence. 'It's only their flight or fight response', he said. A by-product of all people. He said it wasn't their fault. He would have forgiven them. He was good at pardoning others." Her gaze trailed over to the shotgun she leaned against the wall. Elowyn saw a quiet rage reflecting in the woman's eyes. "I suppose it's true what they say. Opposites attract."

The two women sat in silence, the only movement coming from the steam of their cups before it faded into the air. Elowyn did not know what to say. Her eyes scanned the floor as if it would give her some insight. As expected, it did not.

"In any case," Mairyn cleared her throat, lifting her tea to steal another cautious sip, "the surrounding footmen of Eastern tried to get the families of their brothers-in-arms to find shelter with them in Brendale, for protection. But I have children to raise in this fecked up world, and I know the world will give them nothing." Her voice iced over, matching her eyes. "No shelter. No hand-outs. So I stay, to give them all of myself, and hope with everything I have they will learn through witnessing, that they can provide for themselves. They can be their own heroes." She shook her head. "It's the only way they'll stand a chance."

Maternal instincts were lost on Elowyn, but she found sense in Mairyn's sacrifice. The Time Mother offered a small nod of approval. "That's very noble of you."

Mairyn sighed, reaching over to a drawer from her chair. She removed a small box and set it on the table, opening it with ginger fingers. "They're slow to trust, the footmen of the rebellion. They're keen on protecting those in their circle, so they won't accept just anybody." With delicate movements, she pulled a medallion from the box, clinging to it lovingly for only a moment before she slid it over to Elowyn.

Hesitant hands abandoned her tea to reach over and lift the medallion from the table. It had weight to it, bearing the Eastern insignia in heavy gold. Elowyn traced the engraved edges, where a path of text curved around the circular medal. "Bravery, valor, and strength manifest, a symbol of honor for Eastern's best," she read aloud. High praise from the Eastern division. Mairyn's husband had to have done something incredible to have earned it. "Mairyn ... I can't accept this."

"I don't wallow in the values of trinkets, Miss Saveign. That medallion belonged to Edgar, but it won't bring him back. Take it. Find the men of the Brendale rebellion. Tell them Catty sent you."

Elowyn stared at the medal for a moment before she slowly curled her fingers around it. She held it to her chest, turning her eyes to Mairyn. "I don't know what to say."

The woman's face betrayed none of what she felt. "That's not all you'll need." Mairyn slid her chair out and disappeared into the small room attached to the kitchen.

She was absent for some time, but when she returned, a handful of clothing and armor obscured her from Elowyn's view. Mairyn placed it all on the table with a grunt, wiping the back of her wrist across her forehead. "Listen, they're good boys up there. Good men. But regardless of your status, if you walk in there as a woman, they will offer you safety and nothing more. Generations of old thought have fed lies to their minds. If you want to be heard ... you need to immerse yourself in their world."

Elowyn spied the contents of the table. Pauldron armor for her shoulders. Metal bracers attached to plated gloves for her forearms. Iron greaves for her feet. A fauld to protect her waist and thighs. A closed helm. A breastplate that lived inside the navy blue fabric of a long jacket, emblazoned with six brass buttons and straps. The materials on the table told an even greater story of what the military had expected of Edgar Catteral. To require this much protection, Eastern must have revered him as an incredibly capable man.

Still, Elowyn did not understand what Mairyn implied. She reached out to touch the large pauldron, sliding her fingertips over the weathered plate armor. "What do you mean, immerse myself?" she dared to ask.

"Like it or not, you're entering a man's world, Miss Saveign." Mairyn grabbed the helm and slid it down over Elowyn's head. "It's time to play the part."

Elowyn felt the weight of the helmet settle onto her skull. It protected her on all sides, allowing no gaps. She frowned, turning to Mairyn. "It'll never work."

"It'll have to." Mairyn slid the rest of the armor toward her. "I know it's not ideal, Miss Saveign. I know it's downright insulting. But if you want to help your people ... if you think you can," she paused, taking a step back to take in the sight of Elowyn, "you'll have to make some sacrifices. I'm sure your dignity is only the start."

The Time Mother reached up to touch the steel that surrounded her head, a look of contemplation settled over her. It was not ideal. But Mairyn was right. She knew the ins and outs of Eastern's footmen far more than Elowyn did. Her short reign over the division paled in comparison to Mairyn's intimate familiarity through her late husband. She drew in a deep breath, tried not to feel completely defeated, and nodded her head. For her people. For Eastern. "All right. I'll do it."

Mairyn nodded as well. She slid back into her chair as Elowyn took the armor to the nearest room and fitted her way into each piece. The greaves were several sizes too big. She accounted for the difference by stuffing cloth into the sides. The fauld fit loosely over her narrow hips, threatening to slide off at any moment. Elowyn threw more thick clothing over her body to add bulk to her frame, giving the fauld something to cling to.

The gloves and bracers nearly fit. It was easier to disguise the discrepancy by keeping her fingers clenched at all times, so they did not risk sliding off. Elowyn slid her arms into the long jacket, which reminded her much of Captain Kazuaki's attire. The pauldron armor was the final piece, secured over her small shoulder. It was with some luck it had buckles and straps, unlike the rest of the components; though it was huge and gave her the appearance of broad shoulders, she adjusted it with relative ease.

The helm was just about the only thing that fit properly. With a flick of her finger, the lightweight steel visor came down over her face, disguising the femininity of her features behind it.

She emerged, holding her arms out at her sides. The armor felt cumbersome, but she remained confident she could adjust.

Mairyn tilted her head, inspecting Elowyn for authenticity. The heftiness of Edgar Catteral's armor gave the Time Mother the appearance of a warrior. So long as she never removed her disguise in front of the Brendale soldiers, none would be the wiser.

"It's perfect," Mairyn said, a difficult to detect sadness coloring her words. "Just one more thing."

Elowyn watched from behind the slits of her visor as Mairyn vanished into a different room. She returned, holding a towering halberd in both her hands. The official weapon of the Eastern military. "Here you are."

Armored hands reached out, accepting the staff of the halberd and bringing it to her side. She dug the blunt end of the stick into the floor and took a subterranean breath. "Well?"

Mairyn nodded, approving. "You certainly look the part. Here are the instructions to Brendale's rebellion," she said, slipping a piece of paper into Elowyn's iron palm. "Good luck."

Elowyn bit her bottom lip. She summoned no words that would capture the gravity of her gratitude. The mass of her armored body made the floor creak as she approached the door and stood in the frame. "Thank you, Catty. I won't forget this."

Mairyn watched as Elowyn stepped outside and turned to face her. "Don't. Don't ever forget," she said. "Not me, not what I've done for you ... but what *you* need to do. For these people, much as I hate them with everything I am. For this place. And when you return to your position of power—and I hope you will—remember to never, ever, let this happen again."

It was a lot to live up to. Elowyn nodded, fearing no pressure. "I'll do my best."

"I know you will."

Mairyn watched her go. She lingered in the door frame for a long while, recalling the last time she witnessed Elowyn Saveign and her comrades vanish from her property line. Much had changed since then.

When Elowyn faded completely from sight, Mairyn disappeared back into her home, closing the door. She swept over to her shotgun and seized it, then crossed the distance to the table and sat. Gentle hands laid the weapon across her lap, freeing them up to curl around the heat of her teacup. She took a sip, eyes on the door, and waited.

Mairyn Catteral knew that the odds of the next entity to waltz through her doorway being a welcomed thing was slim to none. Not in Eastern. Not these days.

With any luck, if Elowyn Saveign was successful, someday Mairyn could stare at that door without concern, and put her apprehension to rest, just as she did her husband.

CHAPTER TWENTY-SEVEN

Rennington released a grunt as he shoved the delirious civilian against the walls of Bartholomew's residence. Though the raving madman's cheek pressed tight against the rough stone structure, he still managed to spew several curses off his tongue. The soldier forced the man's wrists behind his back, holding them with such a fierceness that his fingers turned blue.

"Justice will prevail," the man spat as Rennington struggled to hold him still and shackle the iron cuffs around him. The coarse texture of the walls outside the Southern Time Father's home scraped the top layer of skin from his cheek as he slid down the exterior. "Naphine will bring righteousness to this place!"

When Rennington heard the satisfying click of the shackles falling into place, he pulled the man from the face of the wall. "Yeah, yeah," he muttered, having a much easier time maneuvering the body about now that it wasn't flailing its arms like a threatened animal, "so I've heard."

"She is the one who truly loves us!" the man shrieked. Rennington pulled his lips back in repugnance as he handed the cuffed individual off to a fellow soldier. "Naphine, Goddess of Love! Shine a light on the false adoration of our Southern Time Father, Bartholomew Gray!"

"Where do I take him?" the footman asked, one hand on the shackles while the other pinned the writhing man by the back of his neck.

Rennington frowned, running a frustrated hand through his hair. Seacaster's institution was full. The institutions bordering the city were at maximum capacity. They had sent the overflow to Eastern—with Elowyn's strides in medical advancements, they had more suitable facilities, more space, but since her disappearance, all transfers ceased.

The prison was not the right place for this man; he was no criminal in his right mind. Callouses on his hands pinned him for a hardworking man. While the condition of his clothing pointed to a class of the working poor, Rennington did not lump the underprivileged people of Southern into stereotypes. He jailed his fair share of blue bloods, too ... but they had enough money to escape the confines of a prison cell with relative ease. With little other choices, the soldier groaned. "Take him to the penitentiary. Make sure he has a single cell, so he's no threat to others."

"Penitentiary is filling up quick, sir." The footman dug his boots into the ground, to better hold himself steady against the floundering man's movements. "I can't promise him a single cell."

Rennington cringed, scratching the back of his head. "Just do the best you can, soldier."

"Yes, sir."

He watched as his brother-in-arms dragged the howling man away and shoved him into a steam car with several other footmen in back. "Naphine!" the man continued to wail, his head to the sky as if the heavens would open up and deliver her to him, "save me!"

Another wince from the Southern soldier betrayed his discomfort. Rennington never thought he'd miss people chanting for Darjal. But as time went on, and more and more people fell under the influence of the lesser gods, the late-Southern Time Father's name did not surface as often as it used to.

He felt an admitted sting of guilt for wishing the Darjal enthusiasts would return. Rennington knew from the conversation at Panagea's center that the newly ordained lesser god was an inconvenience to Nicholai. But he knew what to expect from Darjal's worshipers. They were easier to handle, predictable.

Just single-minded people, obsessed with finding and destroying the Southeastern Time Father.

The others ... the people obsessed with the old-world gods ... they were fixated on killing everyone. Including themselves.

Southern fell further from her graceless state. The division had barely begun to recover from the devastation of last year's events. Much of the land still suffered in a state of disrepair, with the skeletons of businesses and the ghosts of homes littering every street corner. While it was true some improvements were made, the land was slow to heal. Finances were drained. Much thought needed to be poured into where investments would be made.

The few signs of progress that Southern had lived through came to a standstill. Bartholomew did his best. He continued to govern with sound logic and reason. But the men and women available to employ his corrections were in short supply, and dwindling more with each passing day.

Rennington had hope in the beginning. Upon comparing notes with Bartholomew, Southern's state of infection was relatively low when likened to the other divisions. Eastern's status was abysmal. At least, the latest report they received from Elowyn was. Rennington only imagined what it was like there now. It made his chest tighten, thinking of what Elowyn must be enduring ... or what she had endured.

He tried not to think about her in the past tense.

The soldier knew from experience Northwestern lived in turmoil. More so than his beloved home division. But for how long? It felt as though the statistics were catching up with the others. Restraining the barbaric became harder and harder as their numbers grew. Some footmen were turned. Others simply left. Rennington wanted to harbor grudges, but he couldn't. He remembered a time when he, too, abandoned his duty to the Southern military.

It was hard to watch the descent. His division loosened into uncultivated savagery before his eyes. The place he and his brother had grown up in reflected few precious similarities to the nostalgic land he remembered.

One of the few things that brought him comfort in these times was knowing Iani was buried close by. Though his brother was long gone, he felt him in every takedown. Every act of integrity. Every effort he made to keep Southern what it was when they were boys: home.

Iani's presence, whether real or imagined, was enough to get him through the hard days. Rennington felt he brought a sense of honor to his brother and the Platts name. It was a name that, if he were being honest with himself, needed a little restoration.

The soldier kept watchful eyes on the town center as he pressed his back up against the wall of Bartholomew's home. An eager hand positioned near the falchion at his hip, ready to sacrifice everything for the man he believed would keep Southern afloat.

Inside the residence, Bartholomew hunched over his desk. It was a place he became accustomed to over the past weeks. With his elbows on the table, his sleeves rolled up, and his head in his hands, he loomed over a parchment, though any onlooker could see his focus was not on the text.

Kal watched him from the open door to his study, a saucer and a cup in his hands. It pained the ambassador to see his lover in such a sorry state. It was not a look Bartholomew Gray wore often. He slipped into the room, quiet in his movements, and carefully placed the small plate and cup beside the Southern Time Father's arm.

Bartholomew hardly acknowledged Kal's presence. When the ambassador leaned forward to see the scholar's eyes were closed, he knew why. "I wish you'd get some rest," Kal said, reaching over to give Bartholomew's arm an affectionate squeeze. "You know ... in a bed. With a mattress. And blankets. Pillows. You remember pillows, don't you?"

The Southern Time Father startled at Kal's sudden appearance. He readjusted the glasses over his face after rubbing his eyes. "Yes," he nodded wearily, "I know. But I'm afraid sleeping brings more harm than good these days."

"Here." Kal pushed the tea toward him. "Compliments of your friend, the Earth Mother. She sent it some time ago. I cannot say for certain what's in it, but it might help you relax."

Bartholomew put on a worn-out smile. He lifted the tea to his mouth and drew in a small sip. The subtle herbal flavors coated his tongue. The liquid pleasantly warmed down to his stomach. "Thank you, Kal."

The ambassador met his gratitude with a smile of his own. "Would you care to elaborate on why you haven't come to bed as of late? I have my speculations, of course, but it might help to discuss it."

Careful hands lowered the teacup back to its saucer. Bartholomew adopted a look of exhausted contemplation. "Naphine haunts my dreams. She speaks of her growing army. In the vision, she says they will descend on Southern as soon as Darjal falls from power." He shook his head, rubbing his temples. "It mimics what she said when she appeared to me earlier, when you were in Northwestern, with the captain and the others."

Kal listened, a gentle hold on his tea. "Do you believe them? These nightmares?"

Bartholomew hung his head, pushing his sliding glasses up his nose, as his eyes drew to a close. "There is logic in her words. She says the people of Southern have long been conditioned by Darjal to seek the favor of a higher power. As soon as they realize Darjal will not answer their prayers, they will grow eager for a new god, or gods, to follow. In the dream, she assures me they will have plenty to choose from ... after the gods finish slaying those who they feel parallel an equal retribution for mankind's past sins against them."

A pensive countenance took over Kal. He tried to exchange it for something more reassuring. "They're just dreams, Bartholomew, I'm sure."

"Are they?" The scholar raised his gaze to his infatuate. "Or are they premonitions? I can no longer tell the difference. Whether it is Naphine trying to instill fear in me to make it easier to command my mind, or my subconscious manifesting images of chaos, either way, Kal, I can't help but feel she is gaining the upper hand."

It shattered the ambassador's being, watching the man he adored live in such mental anarchy. His brows knitted together, hoping to devise a solution to his ails. "You could always alert Mr. Hidataka to your concerns." Kal harbored hopes Bartholomew's old comrades would restore his sense of self. "They're quite the team, as you know. Very capable. I discovered as much in Northwestern. Perhaps their presence might bring you some peace of mind, if Naphine was, in fact, determined to surface in Southern."

Bartholomew pinched his lips together, nodding. "I suppose it couldn't hurt. As this also relates to Darjal, it may be of interest to Nico, as well. I feel he'll find himself dragged into this one way or another."

"Most wise," Kal said, patting Bartholomew's forearm. "I can draw up the necessary documents and send the letter straight away while you get some rest if you'd like."

A calmed grin tiptoed onto Bartholomew's face. The ever-present affection of Kal Rovanas remained a light in a darkening time. He shuddered to think what he would do without him.

The thought swept a restless agitation through Bartholomew as he remembered the cryptic words Naphine spoke to him concerning Kal. If his calculations were correct, and a chance remained that the Goddess of Love was, indeed, vying to infiltrate his brain, Bartholomew winced at the thought of the repercussions.

"Kal," he reached over, taking the ambassador's hand in his, "if my resolve should wither ... if my logic should cave to the gods ... I want you to run. Run far from here. There are catacombs beneath the city. You can—"

"Bartholomew," Kal chuckled, rubbing his thumb over the scholar's hand, "such folly, and from an otherwise intelligent mouth."

"I'm serious, Kal." Bartholomew's expression fell to one of grave significance. "Elowyn remains missing. Emont still hasn't responded to any letters. We do not know whether Vadim holds fast to his lucidity or fell to the gods again. Nico, too, is under mental attack. I have a strong belief in my abilities to withstand them, I do, but I am not foolish enough to eliminate the possibility of my failure entirely. It's not unwise to have a backup plan."

Kal withdrew his previous show of amusement. He knew Bartholomew's confession stemmed from a pained, loving place, and he did not wish to mock it. "It's not injudicious, no," he said, a serene smile on his face. "But it *is* foolish to think I would ever leave you to any fate that would ruin you."

Comforting words, though Bartholomew wished he'd reconsider. Regardless, he smiled. "Well ... let us hope it does not come to that then."

"You're a strong man, Bartholomew." Kal patted his hand. "I know you worry about your comrades, Elowyn and Emont. But remember that Aggi Normandy, Nordjan, Edvard, and Nicholai all remain, despite the lesser gods' efforts."

The scholar inhaled deeply, nodding. "Yes. I suppose you're right. Nico is an iron-willed man. So long as he hasn't caved to the gods yet, then hope remains."

* * *

Nicholai thrashed against the hold of the vines that confined him to the bed. They were Umbriel's replacement for the iron shackles that held him prior. The plants consumed a large portion of the room. As the others predicted, he tried to age them to their death to earn an escape, but the efforts only made the vines grow sturdier and longer.

Umbriel sat beside him, restoring the life force he gave to the vines with a sigh. She tried to stay ahead of the bruising on his ribs, as well. Unable to mend bone, each time he lashed out earned him more swelling surrounding the fractures. The pain didn't seem to slow him down.

She had lingered near his bedside for hours, working tirelessly to regain his wits with little success. Once in awhile, she'd catch glimpses. A flash of confusion in his cobalt spheres, or a small look of recognition. Even sounds of frustration, as if he tried in vain to free his mind from its hostage situation, but to no avail.

He allowed his body to suffer too long. Weakness from sleep and food deprivation, weeks' worth of accumulated stresses, and all of the other things that plagued Nicholai Addihein stifled his ability to overpower Darjal's influence.

"Nicholai ..." The Earth Mother laid her hands on his forearm. He ripped at his organic shackles with such force, the veins beneath his skin looked as though they threatened to burst. Sweat collected on his forehead. His fingertips turned an off-color in spots. The more he fought the vines, the tighter they got. "Please. You must try."

Feelings of helplessness were uninvited guests as of late. Umbriel could do little to assist him. Nicholai's predicament was in his psychological endurance. There were no physical issues for her to manipulate, no poisons for her to withdraw. All she could do was whisper words that might rise over the sound of Darjal's voice ... but her luck was transitory.

The door opening behind her severed her concentration. Umbriel spun around, taking in the sight of the captain. "Kazuaki," she gasped, standing from her chair. "I didn't think I'd see you on your feet so soon."

A small muscle in the immortal's jaw convulsed at the unflattering reminder that he'd been rendered unconscious. "Yes, well ... here I am," he murmured, clearing his throat. "I appreciate the use of your quarters."

"Of course," she nodded with a tired smile. "I hope you found it comfortable."

It was no hammock, but it served as a suitable substitute. Kazuaki entered the room farther, peering down at Nicholai, who finally stopped fighting the strength of the vines. "How is he doing?"

Umbriel bit her lip as she tucked some hair behind her ear. "I ... I catch glimpses of him now and again. But I'm afraid they are fleeting."

Not unlike the situation in Northwestern with Vadim. Kazuaki remembered it well. He clamped his teeth together, contemplating. Though he did not turn to look at her, he directed his words to Umbriel. "I'd like a moment alone with him."

The Earth Mother blinked, taken back by the captain's request. She saw no harm in it, but couldn't deny her surprise. "Of course," she said, striding over to the door. "If you need anything, just let me know."

A nod followed and Kazuaki listened for the sound of the door closing behind him. He stared down at Nicholai, his eye narrowed to a slit before he pulled Umbriel's chair toward him and sat down.

The Time Father lived in an unsatisfied state. His arms strung up on either side of him. He stared at the wall ahead, making no move to acknowledge Kazuaki's presence. Disheveled clothing draped over his body, mangled from the fight the evening prior. It was a surreal picture. Nicholai Addihein did not belong in this condition.

Kazuaki's eye shifted to the Chronometer poking out between Nicholai's shirt and vest. If worse came to worse, they could force him to wind it. He hoped it wouldn't come to that. "Look here, Nico," the captain started, sitting back in his chair and crossing his arms over his chest, "I won't pretend to understand what you absorb while you're under the influence of the lesser gods ... or Darjal ..." He trailed off, shaking his head. "Vadim was a bloody embarrassment. At least you're not prattling on endlessly about nonsense as he did."

Nicholai said nothing. He returned to the unrewarding task of trying to break free from his restraints. His fists shook as he attempted to force himself from the vines.

A wide, open eye turned to the ceiling as Kazuaki craned his neck back. He did not want to have this conversation. Already, unwelcomed feelings of awkwardness crept through his otherwise stoic body. His lips peeled back in a short, frustrated snarl before he dipped his head to face the Time Father once more. "What Madros said to break you ..." He paused, cringing. Another moment of contemplation powered him through. "I know why it did."

Nicholai paused long enough to lift his chin at the mention of Madros. It was short, and once several seconds ticked by, he returned to fighting the manacles.

Kazuaki continued, undeterred. "It's been a long time since I've been governed by another. Not since I worked for the ship that crashed on that island," he muttered. The one where he met that gods-forsaken mermaid who bestowed her curse of immortality upon him. "Since then, I've only ever governed myself and others. As time passes, you gain experience, and I've convinced myself that nobody alive holds more of that than I." Though he felt ridiculous, he forced himself to look at Nicholai's face. "I do not make many mistakes. But even with my capability ... I still find I made one."

The Time Father's absence of response made it easier to keep talking, but Kazuaki still looked over his shoulder to be sure nobody else listened. Satisfied they were alone, he uncrossed his arms and leaned forward, lowering his voice. "I was wrong about you. From the beginning, I took you for another self-entitled, piece of shit Time Father who cared more about lording his superiority over the common man than anything else. But you've proven otherwise. You are ... capable. Determined. A little too idealistic for your own good sometimes, but ... you care. And though Madros may have led you to believe otherwise, and my actions as of late only accentuated his words ... you have my respect."

Nicholai stopped thrashing. While he did not move the position of his head from facing the wall, his eyes crept over to Kazuaki.

The captain felt a small stab of optimism. Though it irked him to carry on, he did. "I discredited your ethics. As an ethical man, I'm sure you felt slighted." He frowned. "I won't pretend your code of morals matches my own. I won't even pretend that I think your ideas will be successful in the long-term. But I'd venture a guess that if anybody could prove me wrong, again, it would be you."

The Time Father turned his head to face him. Still, he said nothing.

Nicholai's lack of clarity was discouraging. Kazuaki waited for several moments, to see if he might speak, but when he said nothing, he clenched his jaw and stood. "Right. I'll send Umbriel back in."

Sliding the chair out of his way, the immortal approached the door. With his back to Nicholai, he reached for the knob. A familiar voice sounded behind him, coated in heavy repentance.

" ...Is Bermuda all right?"

Kazuaki turned. He assessed Nicholai as he laid in the bed. He looked the same as he did a moment ago, save for a shimmer of humanity in the blues of his eyes. The man seemed embarrassed. But lucid. "What was that?" Kazuaki asked, skeptical at first as to how long it might last.

"Bermuda. Brack. Granite." The color drained from Nicholai's face as he took on a look of unmodified indignity. He remembered splitting the bridge of the Rabbit's nose open. Nearly gutting Granite across his torso. Bashing Bermuda's skull and stabbing her shoulder. "Gods, I ... I was not kind to them."

The captain was quick to return to his seat. He recalled how frequently Vadim wavered, spurred by moments of stress. He needed to keep Nicholai as free from anxieties as he could if there was any hope he'd cling to his lucidity. "They're fine."

Nicholai appeared relieved by the captain's admission. "Good. Good." He took a deep breath and winced, the pain in his ribs radiating outward. An appropriate consequence for his actions, he supposed. Without complaint, he turned to the immortal, a new look of remorse on his face. "I'm sorry. I let them win."

"We can't win them all." Kazuaki's response held its traditional roughness, but an infinitesimal smirk stole over half his face. "For the one battle you lost, you won another. Did you know you're the first person to render me unconscious in at least fifty years?"

Amid everything, even in the face of the pain it caused, Nicholai laughed. He flexed his wrists, still held by the vines, but made no requests for freedom until he knew he could trust himself. "I promise not to spread that around."

"I'd appreciate that," Kazuaki murmured, straightening his posture. "I have a reputation to uphold."

The door opened without ceremony. Kazuaki turned, expecting to see Umbriel walk back in, but Mimir slithered his body through the open frame instead. His head cocked to the side, not at all surprised to see Nicholai regained his composure. "Hm. Took you longer to return to your senses than I thought it would," he uttered, unimpressed.

Kazuaki glared, leaning his arm on the back of the chair as he took in the sight of Mimir. "What the hell are you talking about? Just last night you said it would be difficult to get Darjal to manifest himself. That it would be difficult to kill him."

"Yes," Mimir chuckled, leaning against the wall to Nicholai's bedroom. "But what does his manifestation have to do with his strength?"

A brow rose on the captain's face as he scrutinized Mimir.

The lesser god snickered. "I have other news you might be interested in, Captain. While you were busy trying to reel in your primal human lusts in Bermuda's company last night, I opened my ears to the channel in which the lesser gods' voices travel."

Nicholai blinked, casting an uncomfortable eye toward the captain at the mention of his time spent with Bermuda.

Kazuaki was too inquisitive to care about such things. He glowered at Mimir, his tone dark. "What are you talking about?"

"I feared Madros may have sent a message out to the others before he died ... a thought beacon of sorts ... regarding my, ahem ... 'borrowing' of the katars." Mimir frowned. "He did, by the way. Discerned it through *you* when he grabbed your leg, so, thank you very much for that."

The immortal scowled, standing from his chair. "I don't give a damn about that. What does your supernatural bullshit have to do with Darjal? With Nico?"

"Oh, not much. Just that he grows weaker by the day. Darjal, not you," Mimir clarified, grinning at Nicholai. "For every continually unanswered prayer, he loses a worshiper. For every worshiper lost, he loses strength." The lesser god cupped his hands around his mouth and shouted to the air around him, "If he wants to continue being revered as a god, he needs to start doing some god stuff!"

Nicholai winced. Knowing Mimir shouted to an invisible Darjal invoked an unpleasant feeling. "Please, don't give him any ideas."

Mimir shrugged. "It won't matter soon. Word on the ethereal plane is that once Darjal falls, the lessers will command Southern. Those believers are wasted on Darjal, anyway. He's too green to know how to be a proper god."

Kazuaki squared his shoulders. His blood pressure rose. "What do you mean?"

"I mean a war, Captain. A blood bath. Southern is a religious division, always has been. It swims with people desperate for a god. Once Darjal is out of the picture, the others ... they intend to give them some. In Darjal's hometown of Seacaster, no less." Mimir paused, hitching a shoulder. "After they cement their retribution by making half the population slaughter one another, I mean."

Nicholai shot up in the bed, momentarily forgetting he was stuck to it. The stab of his broken bones paled in comparison to the dread raised by Mimir's confession. "What?" His eyes widened, his mouth dry. "Why?"

Mimir tapped the side of his head. "For multiple reasons, Time Father. They know they can't manipulate everyone. But it becomes far easier when fear is introduced into the mind. What better way to earn fear than by taking lives? If it happens to simultaneously heal a dying continent by irradiating the parasites infecting it, well ..." He glanced at Kazuaki with a grin. "Two birds with one stone, and all that."

The captain did not share Mimir's amusement. An immediate concern rose for Bartholomew's well-being. On the same hand, the timing couldn't have been better. If they gathered in one place, it would make it that much easier to slay them. "When are they planning the attack?"

Mimir smirked. "Oh, Captain ... I would guess Darjal has only weeks left, at best, before the people of Southern forget him in his entirety. That's why they chose Seacaster, you see. There's morbid poetry in invading his hometown, the birthplace of his rise to godliness." He turned his attention to Nicholai. "Lucky break for you, aye, Time Father?"

Nicholai looked horrified. Kazuaki appeared prepared for the moment, but the Southeastern Time Father was not. Another year of bloodshed and lost lives. The clincher, though, was the location of the invasion. Southern. He felt a sinking in his chest. Nicholai wished to go with them, to assist, to ensure the people he came to love met no foul ends ... but as the Chronometer ticked against his chest, he lived with the sorry reminder that he was bound here, to Southeastern.

Despite Mimir's words, he did not feel very lucky at all.

CHAPTER TWENTY-EIGHT

"I ... I'm glad I didn't stab you in the neck," Nicholai uttered, shifting awkwardly as he stood outside before Umbriel.

The Earth Mother placed her fingertips on her lips to stifle an inappropriate laugh. "I'm quite pleased you didn't as well, Nicholai. Thank you." She stood back to admire him. "It's good to see you reacquainted with your old self," she said, fixating on the clinging aura of fatigue the man still grasped. "For the most part."

Questioning eyes flitted to the airship, which the others prepared for departure since dawn's arrival. After Mimir's confession, they did not know how much time they had before the lesser gods made their move on Southern. The captain and crew decided it was best to go now, rather than wait and risk missing their opportunity. Nicholai cleared his throat, fixing his gaze on Umbriel once more. "Are you sure you have to go as well?"

Umbriel nodded without hesitation. "I do. I know you believe the fault rests with you regarding the lesser gods' return, but ... this is my doing. I knew the reintroduction of nature would bring about their reappearance in Panagea. In my desire to rebirth the Earth Mothers, I fear I've made some hasty mistakes. I must see to it that I heal any, and all who I can, that might suffer under my mother's wrath."

Nicholai listened, knowing full well he would have done the same thing. It did not make it any easier to accept. "I understand."

A soft breeze blew her weightless hair around her shoulders. She wore her familiar smile, but it fell a shade as she tilted her head. "Will you be all right?"

"I think so," Nicholai replied, gently rubbing the tender skin where his fractured bones remained. "Darjal's whispers are fading. And even if there are more assassination attempts, it turns out Malcolm is a total renegade with a shotgun, so ..."

Umbriel laughed at his joke, her smile returning in full force. "Good luck, Nicholai." She reached out and grabbed his hand, giving it a light squeeze. "I'll see you when I return."

He watched as she pulled away and headed to the airship ramp. The Time Father adjusted his shoulders, the weight of his Chronometer around his neck feeling heavier than it ever had prior. "I'll be here," he said to himself, unmoving as clouds rolled in above.

Mimir came up beside Nicholai, his shadowy hands behind his back. He stood tall, taking in the sight of the others as they prepared the airship for take-off. Nicholai turned to face him, opening his mouth to speak, but paused when he saw Kazuaki walk by.

"Kazuaki—" Nicholai took several steps forward to catch up to him, glancing at the katars the captain held over each shoulder. "I ... just wanted to thank you, before you left. For what you said earlier. When I wasn't myself. It helped."

The immortal stared, a brow arching over the eye socket that hid beneath his faux-leather patch. "Don't mention it," he muttered, readjusting his grip on the katar handles. "Ever."

Nicholai blinked, relenting with a small nod. "Yes, I know."

"Nico." The captain locked onto his eyes, a stern look on his face. His tone eased. "I meant every word I said."

A relieved grin stole over the Time Father's face. Rather than further agitate the captain with any excess words of sentiment, he yielded, motioning him toward the airship. "Good luck."

"I don't believe in luck," he murmured, looking beyond Nicholai's shoulders as Mimir fell into view. Halted by contemplation, Kazuaki eventually walked passed Nicholai, coming to stop in front of the lesser god. "Mimir."

The being perked, his ears delighting at the sound of his name coming from Kazuaki's mouth. "Yes, Captain?"

"For my own sanity, I need to know ... are you coming with?"

Mimir held up his hands and shook his head. "Not this time, I'm afraid." A swift grin found its way to his face. "Simply too risky for me. A division swimming with angry, vengeful gods ... and little ol' me, the thief of the weapons that will slaughter them. I will miss you, Captain, but my company is not a good fit for this particular endeavor."

"That's a relief," Kazuaki growled beneath his breath. A slow pause followed, and he drew his shoulders back. "Mimir. Alerting us to the condition of Northwestern ... risking your life to steal these katars ... warning us about what awaits Southern ... these were all good things."

The lesser god tilted his head to the side, feigning obliviousness. "What are you trying to say, Captain?"

Kazuaki rolled his eye. He intended to make him say it. "I'm saying ... perhaps first impressions are better left in the past. I will not say your constant presence has been without mental anguish on my part, but ... if you mean to continue favoring us with your help ... I guess I could get used to it."

A shimmer swept across Mimir's glassy eyes. "Captain," he uttered, clasping his hands together, "that is the single nicest thing anyone has ever said to me."

A look of irritation returned to the immortal's face. "Right." He turned around, returning to the airship. "Don't get used to it," he called out, his back to Mimir.

It was a feeling of bliss. Earned admiration from the heart of a legendary man. It was all Mimir ever wanted. He basked in the moment, feeling like a new god all over again. The warming memories of mankind's adoration resurfaced in his brain. This was happiness. He remembered it now.

Jernal stepped up beside Mimir. Along with his military guise, he wore a standard expression of disappointment. "Why can't I go with them?" he asked, attempting to cling to his masculinity, but obvious in his dejection. "My wife and kids are in Southern. If the lessers are planning a war, they could be in danger."

"Southern is a big division, Commander." Mimir dismissed his concerns with a flick of his wrist. "I am confident the captain can handle it. Besides, I need you here—what if I finally decide what to do with you?" he said, turning to him with a huge grin.

It provided no comfort. On the contrary, it caused Jernal to glower. More and more, he regretted his decision to release Mimir from his well. More still, he regretted accepting Nordjan's offer of employment. The Northern Time Father sent no soldiers in an attempt to release Jernal from his hostage situation. The commander bled duty to his superiors, but it was getting harder to offer blind service to those who continued to spurn him.

Brack and Penn set down the last of the crates of food they carried onboard, while Granite and Bermuda readied the propellers. The mutt sniffed at the box of food, its tail wagging with excitement as it pawed the sides.

"None for you, beasty!" Brack knelt and ruffled the sides of the dog's face. "Not unless you start doing your part around here and help with the heavy lifting."

A large, pink tongue tried to assault Brack's face. The man laughed, scratching beneath the dog's chin as he stood to his feet. "Feckin' Revi," he said, turning to Penn. "Smartass left at just the right time, aye?"

"In his defense," Penn muttered unenthusiastically, "he didn't know things were going to blow up to this level. Again."

Brack laughed, finding great amusement in Penn's nonchalance. "Right-o, I'll give him a pass on this one, then." He sighed, crossing his arms over his chest as he leaned against the exterior walls of the airship's cabins. "Hope that fecker's havin' more luck than we are right now."

* * *

Revi watched as a child nestled into the arms of its mother, who laid destitute on an unforgiving patch of broken flagstone. By the looks of things, she suffered from demanding turmoil. It was as if the Underworld opened up beneath her and she rested right upon it, with no concern for the discomfort of the pointed shards poking into her torn skin.

Her eyes were glassy. Vacant. From the short distance, Revi spied the stains of salty tears that stretched down her cheeks, spilling into the hollow of her throat. The flesh around her eye sockets swelled, outlined by a crippling shade of pink.

The child rubbed her hands over the tattered clothing covering her mother's arms. She patted her blistered hand gently, reassuringly. "It's okay, mama. Everything's going to be okay."

The mother did not respond. Revi was unsure how long ago she went into shock, but it was clear she lived in a state of cessation. Whatever things this woman witnessed, her brain no longer wished to comprehend them. It raised the white flag, shutting itself down, as a means of protection from further deterioration.

Years of wisdom did not live in that small child's eyes, but for however many years she walked the earth, she filled her days with love. The way she stroked her mother's hand, loving and calm, was perhaps the most heartbreaking thing Revi had observed on his endeavor to find his daughter.

And he had seen many heartbreaking things, indeed.

Children were stronger than most parents credited them for. The little girl, who sat with her broken mother, couldn't have been any older than nine. Perhaps she was, and malnourishment dwarfed her growth, but even still, the presence of youth lived in her. She projected it.

Revi remembered once when Avigail broke her arm. She had been playing in the busy streets with her brothers, Amadeu and Jacob. Natty lived in her mother's belly at the time, and the other children were merely thoughts on the horizon. He was not there to see it. The requirements of his job pulled him away from luxuries such as watching his children frolic. But he recalled how Arabella described it when he returned home that evening.

Avigail always tried to show up the boys. Though she was the oldest, Amadeu and Jacob had her beat in both height and weight. They were chasing after an old ball, participating in some game they had invented themselves. To flaunt her agility and prowess, Avigail bolted after it as it flew high overhead.

Arabella said her focus on that ball remained so, that it appeared as if she thought catching it might cement her legacy in the minds' of her brothers.

It was her intense focus that kept her from hearing the oncoming steam car.

Arabella remembered screaming, watching as Avigail shoved her arm out at the last minute as if her frail, little limb would be enough to stop a three-thousand-pound metal monster. The driver managed to stop in time, but not before it crippled her humerus, dislodging it from the shoulder socket and crumpling her forearm.

Avigail cried, of course. When Arabella finally convinced her legs to move and collapsed to her knees beside her child, she saw the agony that lived in the little girl's face. But as soon as Avigail spied her mother's overwhelming distress, she sucked in all visible signs of pain. She did not whimper. She did not whine. For Avigail, it hurt more to see her mother in discomfort, than it did to have her skeletal system shattered by a vehicle.

Revi hoped that strength carried through into her adulthood. He needed to believe it did, after what he saw.

The minute he crossed the border into Northwestern, the atmosphere shifted. For every living body he spied, three or four laid in the ruined streets. But even some of the living bodies lacked the characteristics of humanity. Their eyes were vacant, their movements lumbering, confused, and purposeless. It was as if their brains rotted from inside their skulls, leaving them absent of anything resembling a soul.

It was as if, once the gods occupied them, manipulated them, and used them to whatever ends they wished to use them for ... they left them. But they did not leave human beings. They left husks. Hollow shells of who a person used to be. Revi wondered if, like Vadim, they could find their way back with the right instruction. But there were so many. Too many. He had neither the time nor the ability to assist these wandering cases of empty mortals.

He decided he did have time to help two, though.

Worn-out boots, weathered from heavy travel, took him over to the young girl. He knelt beside her, trying to appear as non-threatening as possible. It was a difficult thing to do when one was surrounded by the smoldering wreckage of any living being's worst nightmare. The condition in which the gods left this particular Northwestern town was abysmal. In any case, he produced a gentle smile.

"What's your mother's name, kid?"

The small thing shriveled into the chest of her matriarch, but Revi saw a flash of bravery in her eyes. She swallowed, her hand placed tightly over her mother's. "Jessina," she squeaked, trying to sound more courageous than her dehydrated throat allowed.

"Lovely name," Revi replied, his tone soft as he tried to find the fallen woman's attention. "And you? Did your mother give you just as exquisite a title, then?"

The tension in her arms released, but not by much. "I'm Emmy," she said, marginally more confident this time.

"Emmy. Beautiful." He nodded, keeping a respectful distance away from the pair. "Have you a place you two were trying to get to?"

Emmy's eyes fell. She looked at her mother, hoping the woman would answer. She did not. "We were trying to get to the shelter. Mama said some good people made a place for us to go."

"I see." Revi stayed calm, though Jessina's condition troubled him. "Did your mama say which town this shelter was in?"

Emmy bit her bottom lip, still patting her mother's hand. "She ... said it was in Bricklemore."

He was not familiar with the town. Panagea was a big place, and Bricklemore rang no bells. But as Revi turned his eyes outward and assessed the direction in which the small handful of lucid others wandered, he crafted an educated guess where they needed to go. "Were you heading in this direction?" he asked, gesturing to where he saw other people walking.

Emmy nodded wordlessly.

"All right. Well, Emmy, your mama looks very tired." Revi tilted his head, trying once more to catch any signs of cognition in her. "Don't you think she deserves someone to carry her a while so that she might rest?"

Emmy nodded again, her pupils growing wide with a glimmer of optimism.

"You don't think she'd mind?" Revi asked, just to be sure.

"No, sir," Emmy shook her head. "She is very tired."

"Right, well ..." Revi slid one arm behind Jessina's back, the other beneath the bend in her knees. He lifted the woman up, who did not process the ability, or need to fight back, and cradled her against his chest. "She can sleep while we go the rest of the way then. How does that sound? Are you able to walk?"

Emmy stood. She grabbed her mother's hand, which dangled down at her side, next to Revi. "I can walk," she said with sureness.

"Strong girl." Revi walked, making sure to keep a low pace, as not to apply any additional stress to Emmy. "Do you know how far it is to Bricklemore?"

Emmy climbed over a small chunk of upturned ground, still clinging to her mother's limp hand. "Mama said it was only another mile or so before she was too tired to go on."

A mile or so. He had that in him. Revi readjusted his grip on Jessina as the world smoldered around him. The sun cast strange shadows on the streets as it shined through the broken structures that flanked them. He stepped over a puddle of something, what it was, he did not wish to know.

Nearly a week had passed since Revi entered the chaos of the Northwestern division. He did well to pass by those who grieved. It was easy to bypass the slew of lost adults. His heart did not bleed for them, and they offered him no insights into Avigail's location. He asked every articulate person he saw if they spotted her along the way, but to no avail. They were unable to help him, and in turn, he felt no desire to assist them either. But he couldn't find it in himself to leave Emmy to her fate. He did that to enough children already.

His objective was Vadim's home town: Striburn. Where that was in relation to Bricklemore, he did not know, as traveling on foot differed greatly than traveling by airship. But he remained confident he'd find his way.

The decaying land around them reminded him much of Avadon. The air collected the putrid, unmistakable scent of decomposing corpses. It was so thick, he tasted it on the back of his tongue. An occasional, far off scream punctured his eardrums, but Revi did not react. He'd heard enough screams in his lifetime to pass them off as nothing more than unflattering lullabies. While he hoped Emmy was not negatively affected by them, Revi also wished she did not share the same level of detachment he did.

But as the small child lovingly caressed her mother's hand with her thumb while they walked, he doubted she would.

Sheer determination goaded him to make the trek in less than an hour. Even with the burdensome weight of Jessina's lifeless body in his arms, Revi and Emmy crossed the shattered remnants of the unknown Northwestern town. The two advanced up a short hill, crafted by a mound of rubble, and gazed down at a tent city, sprawling across the expanse of what Revi assumed was the border of Bricklemore.

"I think we made it, kid." He glanced once at Jessina, to see if she recovered from her shock, but the woman had yet to regain herself. "Do you know anybody here?"

Emmy shook her head. "All's that's left is me and mama. But she said everyone here shared a common thread. That sometimes, even when bad things happen, communal chaos bonds people just as much as any bloodline does."

Revi could tell Emmy did not quite grasp the meaning of 'communal chaos', that she only repeated what her mother told her word for word. But he also knew she believed in the sentiment of her mother's message with her whole heart, whether she understood it or not. That alone dissolved her fear of the unknown. "All right. Let's find you both a place then, shall we?"

Emmy led Revi down the hill of wreckage, running into the streets that were lined with makeshift camps. Families of all sorts dwelled beneath tattered tarps and stretched sheets. The long walk made Revi's arms ache, but he held fast to Jessina, weaving through unfathomable crowds of people.

So many displaced. So many gathered. Though the situation that brought these people here was a depressing one, the aura that emanated from this place left Revi with a consoling feeling. He could leave Jessina and Emmy here and know they would be all right.

The scent of a public stew met his nose. It was much kinder than that of sun-blistered cadavers. He followed Emmy, who must have also followed the smell, to a group of people surrounding a rusted, iron cauldron. It sat over a pit of fire, surrounded by mismatched stones that contained the flames. The viscous liquid bubbled and boiled as he glanced inside it, still holding tight to Jessina's frail frame.

"From which part of Northwestern did you come?" an unidentified voice asked.

Revi spun, taking in the sight of an elderly man. Wrinkled, bearded, with liver spots spanning his face, he appeared as though he lived through several lifetimes of hell, but prevailed each time. "None," Revi replied, clearing his throat. "I've come to Northwestern in search of my daughter. Perhaps you've seen her?"

"We've seen many," the man said, his eyes flicking to Jessina. "Does this one need a bed to rest in?" He motioned for a young man behind him to step forward.

"Probably some water as well," Revi muttered, carefully sliding Jessina into the waiting arms of the man the elder summoned. "But I doubt she'll drink anything until she's had sufficient time to recover."

"Take her to the resting grounds, Ahlan, if you please." The old man gestured for him to carry her off.

Emmy followed after her mother. Before she wandered too far, she stopped and turned around. A smile lived on her face. One of strength. One of gratitude beyond her years. "Thank you, sir."

Revi nodded. "Any time." He watched as Emmy bounced after her mother, ignorant of the fact that anything other than a full recovery awaited her. He hoped her optimism would be rewarded.

"Tell me about your daughter," the elder said, lowering himself onto a raised chunk of rubble that served as a chair.

Revi inhaled, running his hands through his hair before his arms fell at his sides. They throbbed from the strain of carrying a grown woman across the expanse of several miles. "She's eighteen. Blonde hair that saw a touch of brown weaving throughout, cut to about her shoulders. Freckled face, a bit of an attitude. Strong. Resilient. Smart." He shook his head. "I'm sorry. I wish I had a photograph."

The man shook his head, a look of sympathy on his aged face. "I apologize, young man. Your description does not ring a bell. But many have found their way to Bricklemore, and more come in each day. Perhaps she is here somewhere, and if not, perhaps she will make her way here soon."

Revi tried to disguise his disappointment. Not one to be deterred, he straightened his spine. "Do you mind if I ask some of those who have taken solace here? This is the largest coherent group of people I've come across since I entered Northwestern."

The man stepped aside, extending his arm out as if he offered Revi the world. "Be my guest, young man. And thank you for your service to that woman and her child. May your good deeds be rewarded in time."

Revi frowned. He remained a non-believer of karmic things but wiped it from his face as soon as he was able. "Thanks," he murmured, slipping off into the collection of weary spirits who gathered in the tent city.

If karma had any intention of rewarding his good deeds, it did not happen here. After hours of interrogation, not one person gleaned insight into where Avigail may have been. Nobody claimed to have seen her. None thought the description sounded even vaguely familiar. It was with frustration that Revi came up empty-handed.

He wandered past the camps, to the outskirts of the collected mass of people. It grew difficult to keep the negative thoughts at bay. Revi wondered if Penn's assumptions held a degree of truth to them, or if they were only that ... guesses. Shots in the dark.

It was true, Avigail did traverse a large portion of Panagea to find him. She also expressed an incredible distaste for him from the moment she arrived. Revi lifted a hand to his nose, feeling the betrayal behind the force of her punch. It still stung, though it took place a long time ago. The man speculated the meaning behind the assault hurt more than the physical act, itself.

Avigail knew where he was going. She knew he'd enter Striburn. He still had a way to go before he reached it, but it wasn't unfathomable to think she might have wandered through this place on the way. Then again, perhaps she took a different route? Or perhaps the people of the tent city were far too consumed with their own concerns to have paid much attention to the presence of an otherwise unassuming girl?

Or maybe ... he only *hoped* she came looking for him.

Dismal thoughts aside, he couldn't get the message Avigail said to him out of his head. When he asked her how she found him ... and her response. *I looked*, she said. And that is what he intended to do. For as long as it took until he found her, he would look.

Revi stared out on the horizon, his eyes narrowing as the silhouette of two adult bodies came into his view. His spirit was not compelled to move. He did not care for their condition. They were close enough to the tent city to find refuge if they wanted it. And yet, his feet headed toward them, crawling over the uneven rocks and building remnants.

Their backs were toward him. When he got close enough, he found himself asking, "You folks all right?"

"We're fine, sir, thank you," the man responded without turning around.

He identified a hurt in his voice. A strain. The words did not match the tone. When Revi peered passed their shoulders, he spied a primitive mound. It was not one that took that shape by chance. A manmade structure, resembling a monument of sorts, perched on the damaged earth before them. A tombstone. Scrawled across the surface in soot from a fire long burnt out, a name, a birth date, and a death date. The deceased was only twenty-five years old.

"I'm sorry for your loss," Revi murmured, clearing his throat. "I'll leave you to your mourning ... if I could just ask one question, first."

The woman spun around. Her eyes resembled Jessina's, enflamed, with a ring of rose-colored skin surrounding them. Though a glimmer of life still lived in hers, unlike the woman he carried across the badlands. "What can we help you with, young man?" she asked, wiping the tears from her face.

"I ... I'm looking for my daughter," he started.

Her head tilted. Her face adopted a look of familiarity. "Your voice," she uttered, her words choked from the strain of misery, "and your face ... my gods," she breathed. "You're Revi Houton, aren't you?"

Revi blinked, taken back by her statement. "I am," he replied, both incredulous and cautious.

"Forgive my surprise, young man," Everly clutched her hand to her chest, gesturing to her husband. "My name is Everly, this is Thom. We were residents, in the slums of Avadon last year. You and the others came to our aid. You brought light to a very dark place."

Her admission caught him off guard, but he remembered his time in Avadon well. It was one of those memories one simply did not forget. "Glad to see you are well," he said, though immediately regretted the fallacy of his observation.

If his statement offended her, she did not show it. "You and those people did a fine thing," she said, nodding her head as she relived the reminiscence. "Thom and I will try our best to assist you in any way we can. What can you tell us of your daughter, Mr. Houton?"

"She's …" He paused, having recited the words a thousand and one times to the people within the tent city. "She's a spitfire. A head full of street smarts. Blonde hair, to her shoulders, with some browns cutting through it. Eighteen years old. She's—"

"Oh, dear," Everly stopped, exchanging glances with Thom as he finally turned around. "Her name … is it Avigail?"

Revi's heart dared to leap from his throat. He felt it quicken with his pulse as hope inflated in his chest. "It is."

"Gods," Everly shook her head, "now that I'm looking at you … yes, she looked just like you. She has your eyes."

"Do you know where she is now?" Revi asked, scarcely able to contain his anxiousness.

Everly bowed her head. "This was as far as we were able to take her. She said she was heading to Striburn. We told her the rumors that it was reduced to ash, that it was dangerous to go, but …"

Revi nodded, his gaze flicking along the ground as he plotted his next move. "Thank you. And … I'm sorry, for your loss."

"It's unnatural to bury your child," Everly said, her focus falling back to her son's tombstone. "It's just not right. I hope you find her, Mr. Houton. I hope you are spared from this. I would not wish it on anyone."

Revi squared his shoulders. "Neither would I."

"Here." Everly lifted her finger, pointing to a steam car that sat twenty feet away. "Take it. There should be enough liquid in the water tank to get you there."

Revi glanced over his shoulder, taking in the sight of their offering. It would cut down on his travel time greatly. But the gesture was too much. "I can't accept that," he said, taking a step back. "How will you two return home to Avadon?"

Everly smiled. She seemed at peace. "Take it, darling. It will ease the pain in our chests knowing it was used to save someone from the hurt we feel now."

Hesitation followed; Revi wanted to say no, to refuse, to let those who grieved for their lost son maintain their safe transportation back to their home town. But he also wished to find Avigail before any harm befell her. His eyes closed, and to his surprise, he found himself saying, "Thank you. If I can return it, I will."

Everly shook her head, holding up her hands. "No need for that."

Revi did not question her. He glanced at Thom, nodded a thank you to him as well, and bolted for the vehicle. It would take time to prepare it, to steam it up, to start the pilot—but it was still a faster alternative than his own two legs.

The effort it took to get the automobile moving flew by. Before Revi knew it, he rattled over the uneven environment toward Striburn. The tent city faded from his vision, falling farther and farther into the landscape behind him. High in the darkened sky, clouds crept in, disguising some of the light offered by the moon.

He hoped Everly and Thom would be all right. He could not fathom being in the same predicament they found themselves in. If any ill fate were to end Avigail's life, it would destroy him. Ruin him.

Before, Revi had the luxury of denial. Endless thoughts that his children were fine, that they lived a better life without him. But Avigail's reemergence into his life crushed that pipe dream and replaced it with reality. He couldn't live with himself if something happened to her.

As the steam car jostled over a rough patch of road, a frown crossed Revi's face. He knew, then, why Everly and Thom gave him the steam car. He knew why they reassured him there was no need to return it. They had no intention of returning to their home. Of returning to Avadon.

They, too, couldn't live with themselves, knowing the rest of their lives would be spent without their son.

CHAPTER TWENTY-NINE

Mimir stood outside Malcolm's greenhouse, admiring the exterior. The lesser god found it amusing that such a small building contained so many hidden varieties of plants. He liked it in there. It put him in mind of the days of old. When wildlife choked the hills of Panagea with bursts of floral sweetness. Colors spilled over every mountain peak and valley, coating the world in something other than bronze and iron, as it did now.

The lesser god did not mind the metal world. He did not mind any world that had people in it. Preferences teetered toward the archaic version of Panagea, as nostalgia had a way of flattering a mind, but this place was tolerable, too. It had Kazuaki Hidataka in it, after all. The immortal was, without a doubt, the most fascinating persona Mimir encountered in his centuries of living.

He missed the captain's presence. His constant looks of irritation. Though Kazuaki and the others had only been gone for a week, to Mimir, it felt much longer.

He busied himself by flashing wide grins at those who walked by, though there were only a few. The state of things terrified handfuls of civilians from wandering outside their doors unless it was deemed necessary. Those who made eye contact with him shuddered at his unnatural appearance and quickly moved on. It only dampened his spirits a little.

He did not need these people. He had the commander. He had the captain. The unfulfilled bargains between those two alone were enough to sustain him. Though, he wouldn't have minded a little of that old-world worship. It came in droves, then.

A feeling of being watched caused the lesser god to turn around. A small, knowing chuckle escaped him when he saw Darjal. The man did not look as grand as he had when they first met one another on the island that bore his well. It made Mimir grin. Darjal was a prick back then; for that, Mimir found his predicament amusing. "Well, well, well," the lesser god gleamed, puffing out his chest, "look what the crippling absence of prayer dragged in."

Darjal's wrinkled face leaked an allowance of emotions. Anger, frustration, confusion, desperation. Mimir ate it all like a four-course meal served at a sophisticated banquet. The weakening being stepped forward, his step more labored than before. "Why is this happening to me?" he growled.

Mimir did not bat an eye. "You know why this is happening."

A sound of unadulterated grievance spilled from Darjal's mouth. "I gave them everything! I spent decades giving myself unto them, lavishing them in the reverence of my churches, of my presence! How could they forget me so quickly?"

"You did do some of those things, yes," Mimir agreed, nodding. "But elegant churches and elaborate stained glass windows featuring you at your best, do not make you a god. Telling people you are godly does not make you a god. *They* made you a god. And you forgot to do the one, simple thing that cements that which you coveted into reality: you never answered their prayers."

"Their prayers were none of my concern," Darjal spat, shaking. "They ask for meaningless, earthly things. Money. Health. Good fortune. Things only central to those who dwell in the physical realm. I am a god, Mimir, not a puppet for them to use for requests."

Mimir snickered, shaking his head. He could not tell if Darjal rattled from ire or weakness, but he did not care. "That is all we have ever been. And that is all we will ever be. You may be a god, Darjal, but you still suffer from a very human ego."

The late Southern Time Father looked down at his hands. They quaked beyond his control. He closed his fingers into his palms, hoping that might steady them. Some of Mimir's words seemed to sink in. The prisoner of the well certainly had more experience being a lesser god than he had. In a rare act of earnestness, Darjal hung his head. "What can I do?" he asked, his voice low.

Mimir shrugged. "If you would have put as much effort into maintaining your status as you did into trying to kill the Southeastern Time Father, we may not be having this discussion right now."

The instability in his legs mocked him. It was so much more than a physical deficiency. Darjal remembered bits of mortality. He remembered the pains of injuries suffered. This was something far different. An internal failing. A feebleness that withered his soul, if, as a god, he had one left at all. It was as if he was being slowly swallowed by a snake that would eventually digest him in his entirety, leaving nothing behind but the stomach acid he melted in. "I don't want to be forgotten," he whispered.

Mimir did not move. He looked unquestionably commiserative. "Nobody does."

"I've dedicated my entire life to this," Darjal breathed, extending his arms out toward Mimir in a final act of securing his pity. "What can I do?"

Glowing eyes fell to the cobblestone. Mimir shrugged once more, with less effort. "The gods have been trying to figure that out for centuries."

Restless footsteps exited the Addihein household as Nicholai opened the door to check his mail. He hoped to have received word from the others. He removed a small stack from the iron box attached to the side of his home. The letters were fewer and farther between these days. The praises people sung of him dwindled with not only the infection of the lesser gods throughout Panagea but the announcement he made prior that no plans were yet in place to combat them. It was not a popular statement when he said the people needed to do their best to steel their nerves and minds until a solution was devised.

As he filtered through the letters, scanning for anything that might be from his companions, his eyes flicked up and outward.

He spied Mimir's back in the distance, near Malcolm's greenhouse. Though the lesser god stood far from his vision, his unnatural, shadowy color made him stand out from the common man. Nicholai winced. The public sentiment toward gods was one of turmoil. As far as the people knew, they were a thing to be feared. Allowing Mimir to run amok was not in Nenada's best interest.

"Mimir!" Nicholai called out, stepping off his porch to approach him.

The lesser god spun, taking in the sight of Nicholai as he neared. When he turned back to speak to Darjal, he was gone.

The Southeastern Time Father issued several awkward nods to the few passersby he encountered on his brisk run toward the lesser god. They watched him with cautious eyes as he neared Mimir and gestured toward the greenhouse. "Would it be too much to ask that you stay indoors?" he asked, a kind plea in his tone that was followed by a hint of exasperation. "I don't mean to offend, but I don't want the public to think I'm fraternizing with the lesser gods any more than they already do. The last thing I need right now is additional attacks on my life."

A smirk from the lesser god was Mimir's reply. "Of course, Time Father." With his hands behind his back, he waltzed inside Malcolm's greenhouse.

Nicholai glanced over his shoulder. He earned some questionable stares from those who saw him. "Everything's fine," he said, giving a friendly wave. "Nothing to concern yourselves over."

They did not appear convinced.

"Right. Well." Nicholai summoned as charming a grin as he could muster. "Good day to you both."

The citizens exchanged uncomfortable glances with one another before they carried on with their journey. Nicholai pursed his lips together and turned, slipping into the greenhouse door before he found himself in any other uncomfortable situations.

Inside, Malcolm tended to his indoor plants. With a watering can in hand, he delivered fresh liquid to the waiting greens, trying to avoid the intense curiosity of Mimir, who watched from barely an arm's distance away. The lesser god spent a lot of time in his greenhouse since Kazuaki and the others departed for Southern. While Malcolm was not particularly fond of him, his presence grew familiar. Tolerable.

Nicholai continued to shuffle the letters around in his hands until his eyes fell on one bearing the Western seal. He set the remainders on a table and tore the wax open, removing the parchment that laid dormant inside.

Having completed his task, Malcolm relieved himself of the watering can, traipsing over to a nearby chair. "What have you got there, Nicholai?" he asked, lowering his bones into the waiting padding of the cushion.

"It's from my father," he replied, distracted as his eyes darted from left to right to absorb the contents of the text. "He says he's been spending a lot of time with a particular woman in one of Western's psychiatric hospitals. He claims he's gleaned some insight into how the lesser gods are corrupting people. Statistics say those most easily affected are the working poor. The lessers seem to have capitalized on their feelings of disparity by comparing them to the indignities they, too, feel they've suffered."

"The elder Addihein is still alive?" Mimir arched a brow, raising his gaze from the plant that consumed his attention prior. He returned his interest to the leaves, rubbing the velvet shapes between his fingers as he muttered to himself, "I should have thought they would have taken him out weeks ago."

Nicholai frowned. "What makes you say that?"

Mimir peered out at the Time Father from behind the green flora. "Let's just call it a hunch," he grinned.

The lesser god's cryptic reply earned no appreciation from Nicholai. Mimir never shied away from an opportunity for ambiguity, much to everyone's annoyance. It seemed to be a trait shared by several lesser gods that the Southeastern Time Father had encountered as of late.

Nicholai glanced back down at the letter, thinking back to the time he spent in the in-between. While distractions diseased him, he could not get Epifet out of his thoughts. "Mimir ... when you told Kazuaki about the impending attack on Seacaster ... you mentioned you discerned that on a channel of sorts, shared by the lesser gods, is that correct?"

The being slipped out from behind the plant, slithering over to sit beside Malcolm. "More or less."

"How does that work, exactly?" The Time Father's brows drew together as he set the letter down near the others.

Mimir rotated his shoulders, stretching. "It is difficult to explain. It's a network of unspoken words. Feelings. Since we are all a creation of mankind, we are all connected by it, this spiritual frequency. Ways exist to prevent certain messages from traveling, but," he shrugged, "all in all, we are bound by a shared thread."

"Can I ask," Nicholai approached, taking a seat near Malcolm and Mimir, "what do you know of the goddess, Epifet? As a lesser god yourself, you must have some knowledge of her."

"Oh, Time Father," Mimir's voice faded. It almost sounded as if a strand of pity lived in his words. He smiled. It was not his traditional, cunning grin, but more of a sympathetic gesture. "I love humans. I do. And I despise them. But you ... you are truly one of the good ones. A genuine, benevolent soul. I will not burden you with the story of Epifet, that you might stay good a little longer. Panagea needs more of that. You have plenty of time to learn the horrors of mankind's ugliness as the world keeps spinning."

Nicholai did not extend Mimir the courtesy of hiding his dissatisfaction. "I've seen plenty ugliness in my day, Mimir." The Time Father raised his chin, his stare concentrated as he threw it toward the lesser god. "I just choose to believe it is temporary. We all have moments of ugliness, but deep down, people are inherently good."

Mimir's eyes crinkled as a smirk split across his cheeks. "Adorable."

As the tension in the room grew, Malcolm cleared his throat. He stood from his chair and clapped his hands together. "Who's for drinks?" he asked. Without awaiting a reply, he left the two to themselves, disappearing into a room in the back.

The front door to the greenhouse squealed as it opened. Jernal entered, his hair still damp from the shower he finished not minutes ago. It felt good to wash his body of the filth the last months brought him, but no matter how long he scrubbed, the soldier could not recapture a feeling of complete cleanliness.

He closed the door behind him, collapsing into the nearest chair. An aura of frustration lived over him, like a lightning-filled cloud that threatened to strike him down at any moment. The man's fingers flexed into the arms of the chair, the base of his nails turning white from the subconscious pressure he applied.

Mimir jutted his bottom lip out. "Not still pouting over your family, are you, Commander?"

Jernal shot a sharp look of daggers at the lesser god but said nothing. He said everything he wished to say already and more. Jernal asked Mimir countless times to let him accompany Kazuaki and the others to Southern. When the lesser god refused, he demanded it. When, still, the lesser god did not relent to his requests, he cast his dignity aside and begged.

Mimir did not concede.

The soldier tried to leave on his own. For each footstep that fell closer to Southern's border, an invisible weight around his ankles grew heavier, until it weighed him down so unnaturally, it felt as though his bones were a thousand pounds each. His debt to Mimir did not grant him the benefit of leaving. Supernatural efforts made it too difficult to accomplish. It was only when Jernal decided that he would die if he continued trying to make it to Southern that he finally yielded to Mimir's desire for him to stay.

He was not happy about it. And he made no move to hide that fact.

Nicholai matched Jernal's outward look of dissatisfaction. When Malcolm returned with three glasses of wine, he stiffened at the rigidity in the room. "Come now, gentlemen," he extended an offering to Nicholai, "your negative energy is going to seep into my plants."

An unenthusiastic arm reached out and accepted Malcolm's offering. Though Nicholai shared no interest in consuming alcohol, he did not wish to offend Malcolm. He knew how much work the man poured into crafting the wine. The botanist knew it was a favorite of Captain Hidataka, and therefore made it a priority to perfect a small harvest with Umbriel's assistance. A show of gratitude, to the immortal who saved the life of his son-in-law on more than one occasion. "Thank you, Malcolm."

Mimir reached his eager hands out, his eyes aglow with excitement. "I have not tasted an organic libation in centuries," he purred, saliva collecting in the pockets of his mouth.

A hesitation subsisted in Malcolm's face, but he eventually handed the lesser god a glass. Mimir put it tight to his nose and breathed it in before sliding his tongue down into the ruby liquid.

Nicholai wrinkled his nose. Seeing Malcolm only brought out three glasses, he handed his to Jernal. "Looks like you could use this," he uttered.

The soldier said nothing as he accepted it, and washed it down his throat in three large gulps. He wordlessly set the glass on a nearby table and returned to sulking.

The Time Father's appearance still matched Jernal's. Seeds of worry were planted in his gut since the others had left. Though he was never of a particularly strong use to them in battle, it seemed irregular not being beside them. Not knowing whether or not they were all right. His concern thrust memories of Iani's death into the forefront of his thoughts. Nicholai still remembered the look on the young Platt's brother's face when Carlo Angevin filled him full of lead.

His gaze moved to Mimir. Nicholai knew the lesser god lived in a constant state of awareness. He seemed to know things the others did not, balancing on a mystic thread that ran between realms. Though he still felt a level of discontent for Mimir's unhelpful response earlier, Nicholai couldn't help but ask, in the hopes of easing his anxiety, "Do you think they'll be all right?"

Mimir lifted his wine glass to his lips and tilted it back, savoring the liquid much more than Jernal did. When he finished his sip, he exhaled. "Do you want me to tell you the truth?" he asked. "Or do you want me to tell you what you want to hear?"

Nicholai scoffed and tried to cross his arms over his chest, but the movement only reminded him of his sore ribcage and he readjusted. He was edgy. Restless. The sound of Malcolm calmly sipping his wine in the corner was nearly enough to send him over the edge, but he tried to steady himself. It was of no use to act irrationally. He'd done enough of that already when possessed by Darjal.

Jernal sat in his chair, deflated. He exuded an unmatched sensation of wretchedness. A fierce combination of resentment, frustration, and uneasiness. The soundlessness around them only served to emphasize the shared dejection of both men.

It was too much to tolerate. After several minutes of living in the atmosphere created by both commander and Time Father, Malcolm set his glass of wine down. "Good gods, son." His eyes fell on Nicholai and he shook his head. "I haven't seen you this far from yourself since Lilac passed."

His words cut him, but only in a way that seized his attention. Nicholai knew Malcolm must have been serious in his conviction; it hurt the greenhouse keeper just as much as it hurt Nicholai when the subject of Lilac Finn rose to the surface. "I apologize, Malcolm. I'm just ... worried."

"Kazuaki is immortal, Nicholai." Malcolm frowned. "He'll be fine. And the others, they're human. From what I understand, the lesser gods cannot touch them."

"Malcolm speaks the truth," Mimir interjected, taking a considerate sip from his glass. "Mostly."

Like a screeching record, the three men whipped their heads toward Mimir. Nicholai crossed the room toward him, his hands pressing down into the arms of the chair Mimir sat in. He lowered his head, his voice uncharacteristically dark. "How so?"

If Mimir was affected by the proximity of Nicholai's face, he did not show it. He tilted the glass up, savoring the last drop of the crimson liquid before he set it back onto the table. "Well, Havidite will certainly be there," he said, chuckling. "And she *hates* Earth Mothers. It used to be that she, alone, was responsible for the success of plants, but when the Earth Mothers came to Panagea ..." He shook his head. "Oh my, was she ever livid."

"Havidite." The name rang a bell of familiarity. Nicholai's brows furrowed together as he searched his brain. Yes. Havidite. The Goddess of Harvest. The one responsible for the death of Jodathyn. The one who set this entire series of corruption into motion. "But she cannot hurt her," he said, hoping to convince himself. "Umbriel is ... is ..." He couldn't finish. Nicholai already knew what Mimir was going to say before he said it.

"—born of both gods and men." Mimir leaned back in the chair, relaxed. "As the blood of Naphine runs through her veins, so, too, does the ability for them to spill it."

"Kazuaki will keep her safe," Jernal muttered from his place in the chair. Whether he cared to admit it or not, the immortal showcased a surprising penchant for protecting those in his crew. Jernal noticed it even overflowed at times, into defending the lives of others.

"I am certain he will, too," Mimir nodded, "if the army of lesser gods they have amassed do not keep him too busy."

Nicholai released his grip on Mimir's chair, running his hands through his hair. It was already hell living with the knowledge that they were in danger before—but now, with this—Mimir dumped a tidal wave of doom upon him. Would Kazuaki know to protect Umbriel? If he thought lesser gods could not hurt humans, he might not. He stormed about the room, trying to collect his thoughts.

Malcolm caught him by the shoulders. Nicholai lifted his gaze from the ground and snagged the elder man's stare. "Nicholai," he said, holding him tight, "just go. Umbriel has made herself a daughter to me. I will not lose another."

"I ..." Nicholai felt a void in his chest. A hollow surface that only responded to the icy metal of his Chronometer against his skin. "I can't," he uttered, though his words lacked conviction. "I am bound to Southeastern. I ruined these people once, Malcolm, I, I cannot risk— "

"How many times have you left Southeastern this year alone, Nicholai?" Malcolm's voice was stern, sharp enough to be certain he penetrated Nicholai's wall of misgivings. "You are not the other Time Fathers. You know your time restrictions. You've nearly mastered them. Just go. Make it back before your twenty-four hours are up."

He seemed so sure. Nicholai hesitated. "And if I do not?"

A frown crossed over Malcolm's face. "I know the only thing that would stop that from happening is if the lesser gods succeed. And if they do, then Panagea is already doomed, whether her divisions are frozen or not."

It was all he needed to hear. Half of his heart had already left with them anyway. But it was not just for Umbriel and the others that Nicholai was struck with a sudden need to go. All along, he felt he was abandoning his people, putting them at risk for his carelessness again ... but Panagea had not yet recovered from the events of last year. Infection still plagued her. Their small collection of forests had only touched the surface of curing her. If Umbriel fell ... if the last Earth Mother perished ... Malcolm was right. His people were as good as condemned anyway.

"I'm going to need some transportation," Nicholai said. "The faster, the better."

* * *

"My cycle?" Rhirvin winced as Nicholai walked passed him, heading toward the machine's resting place in his backroom. He followed, carrying a guise of uncertainty with him.

Nicholai threw the tarp off the vehicle, running his hands over one of the smooth, metal bars that protruded out from each side. He lifted his head, finding Rhirvin's hesitant eyes. "Please. I would not ask if it were not a matter of great importance."

"I don't know, Nico." Rhirvin rubbed the back of his neck, straining as he cocked his head to the side. "I haven't even worked out all the kinks yet."

"You're an expert machinist, my friend. Your knowledge blows mine out of the water." Nicholai tried to flash an encouraging smile. "I'm sure it's fine."

Rhirvin cringed at the Time Father's display of reassurance. The heartening grin he wore only served to layer a sheet of guilt over the machinist if he were to refuse Nicholai's request. With a surrendering sigh, he uttered, "Please, don't break it."

Nicholai lit up at the sound of Rhirvin's submission. He circled the cycle, a hand on his chin, as he tried to quickly study the components. "Great—how does it work?"

"Gods," Rhirvin murmured, shaking his head. "You're going to break it, aren't you?"

"Rhirvin ..."

"Right, right," he pinched the bridge of his nose between his thumb and middle finger, sighing once more. He knew Nicholai recognized his way around machines; all Time Fathers were required to be expert mechanics on some level. But the sophistication surrounding his cycle was beyond anything mankind discovered yet. It was the pinnacle of design, speed, and function. While Nicholai would likely recognize the purpose of some components, he'd need an introduction to the innovative technology if he had any hope of not killing himself. "I'll give you a run through."

Nicholai perked and rubbed his hands together as if the action helped him concentrate. "Thank you, my friend."

A nod came from Rhirvin as he gestured to the cycle. "Here's the engine, clearly. It's liquid-cooled. No steam power from this baby." He patted his creation lovingly. "You'll find the rotary valves here ... the carburetor ... the throttle, for speed—"

"Great, great," Nicholai nodded, having a vague familiarity with some of what Rhirvin showed him. "And the brakes?"

The machinist shot the Time Father a questioning look. "Remember when I said I didn't work out all the kinks?"

Nicholai made a face. He scratched at the back of his head. "That ... seems like a fairly key component though, don't you think?"

"The braking system is flawed," Rhirvin informed him, kneeling beside the cycle. "Even at half its capability, the machine has too much power and speed for me to find anything that'll succeed in slowing it down at a good pace. It'll brake, but it takes a long time ... which is fine, if you know when you're coming to a stop and can make whatever calculations you need, but not so great if you need to brake in an emergency."

The knowledge was only mildly discouraging to Nicholai. He wrapped his fingers around the handle again and flashed the machinist a charismatic smile. "I'll try not to crash into anything."

Rhirvin freed a sound that was something between a scoff and a chuckle. "That would be nice."

Nicholai threw one leg over the cycle, careful not to show any indication that he operated with still-broken bones, and settled into the seat. He glanced down to familiarize himself with where everything was a final time. When he lifted his head, he found Rhirvin's gaze. "Thank you, my friend. Truly."

The machinist walked over to a chain hanging from the ceiling. When he pulled on it, the hanging door to his shop heaved upward, exposing the outdoors to the Time Father. Rhirvin extended a hand, a gesture for Nicholai to venture off into the wide world toward whatever it was he needed to do. Rhirvin had no intention of asking. He knew for Nicholai to request the use of his cycle, it was clearly something vital. "Good luck."

With a final nod, Nicholai lowered his goggles over his eyes and tossed his hat aside, knowing full well it would not survive the ride. He fired up the cycle's engine. The loud noise echoed off the walls of Rhirvin's machine shop, and without delay, he charged out the mouth of the building.

Rhirvin watched him go until he disappeared. With the cycle's speed, it only took moments. He shook his head, wiping his hands on a dirty rag he pulled from a belt loop. "So far so good," he muttered, pleased to see Nicholai did not immediately pilot the cycle into a wall.

The machinist's eyes weren't the only ones that followed the cycle's path as it exited the Southeastern town of Nenada. Perched on the roof of the greenhouse, Mimir stood as tall as he could, hovering on the tips of his toes.

When all that remained for him to see was a line of dust kicked up from the cycle's tires, he turned to Jernal, who he dragged up to the roof with him. "Pack your things, Commander. The time has come for us to follow."

The soldier's eyes fell under the shadows of his knitted brows. He knew something was up when the lesser god lugged him up to the roof, but he never expected an announcement like that. "I thought you said it was too dangerous for you to go to Southern?"

Mimir smirked. It was hard to see at first, but when a beam of moonlight caught the glistening saliva covering his teeth, it glowed. "He who risks nothing," he whispered, "becomes nothing."

Jernal frowned. Another dissatisfying answer from the cryptic creature. He turned his attention in the direction of Southern, shoving his chilled hands into his pockets. The soldier had no intention of arguing. He had been trying to get to Southern since he discovered news of the chaos that awaited it.

To return to the relative proximity of his wife and children was a great reward. Though they did not live in Seacaster, and were therefore safe from the initial onslaught of the lesser gods' invasion, Jernal doubted their security would remain. If Kazuaki Hidataka and the others were unsuccessful in their efforts to destroy the gods, it was best to have back up.

Terminating his contract with Mimir was a close second in the list of important goals to Jernal. He hoped the lesser god found a use for him in Southern. Something that ended his obligation to stay with the beast of burden. He glanced over at the lesser god, who met his annoyed stare with a pleasant grin. Jernal scowled.

He would give *anything* to be free of Mimir.

"How do we get there?" Jernal muttered, gazing out at the dust left by the cycle's tires. "We'll never beat him."

Mimir grinned. "Oh, Commander. As you are owned by a lesser god, you will travel like a lesser god."

Before Jernal figured out what that meant, Mimir seized his wrist. He felt every atom of his body shift, tugged on by a force he could not see. A panic prospered inside him at the uncomfortable feeling, and before he knew it, Mimir pulled him to Southern by a supernatural force.

CHAPTER THIRTY

The crew settled into Southern without much adjustment. Bartholomew's reassurance last year that they always had a home on his division's ground stood true. Kazuaki leaned back into one of the many ornate chairs that sat in Bartholomew's study, an amber drink clutched in his hand.

Sitting across from him, the Southern Time Father closed his eyes, holding his beverage of choice: a ruddy looking liquid Kazuaki could not identify. The two men allowed the luxurious cushions of the elaborately carved chairs to swallow them, relieving the burdens of reality, if only for a moment.

"Darjal had decadent taste in furniture," Bartholomew murmured to break the silence.

Kazuaki coated his tongue with a small blanket of alcohol and swallowed it down. His eye scanned the room. Vaulted ceilings towered above them. Elegant chandeliers dangled from custom scenery painted on the tiles. Fireplaces made of marble bordered the men on both sides. Even the trim lining the affluent flooring was excessive. The only thing that seemed out of place was the bookshelves: simple and linear in their design. Logical. Inexpensive. Likely brought in by Bartholomew earlier in his reign. "It's ... nice," Kazuaki said, his voice flat and lacking honesty.

"There's no need to placate me, Captain." Bartholomew gazed about the room in which he spent a large majority of his time and wrinkled his nose. "It's hideous. Nothing more than a lavish monument to his ego."

Half of Kazuaki's face swept into a smirk. He nodded.

"I would have removed it already, but that, too, would be a waste." Bartholomew frowned, resting his glass down on the arm of his chair. "Finances are hard to come by these days. Anything I threw away I would only need to replace."

Kazuaki nodded again. He'd heard Nicholai drone on about similar grievances while he tried to find the best places to send Southeastern's dwindling currency. "I imagine they are."

The scholar leaned his head into the chair's tall backing, his eyes floating to the ceiling. He knew he could turn this place around. Southern could become something better than it was. He could bring education to the people, who would in turn craft intelligent ideas to suit their division. To suit others. It had the potential. If only it had the opportunity. "Another war, Captain." Bartholomew lifted his glass and took a drink. "When will it end?"

Kazuaki's eye flicked over to the twin katars leaning against a rich, decorated wall. "Soon, with any luck."

Bartholomew fell silent. Kazuaki's appearance in Southern was only a partial surprise. When the captain came to him in his airship a week ago, with the crew in tow, he knew there was a reason. The Southern Time Father had hoped it had nothing to do with the nightmares he was having lately. The unspeakable ones involving Naphine and her army of slighted gods and goddesses. But before the captain stepped foot off the airship and validated his reason for coming, Bartholomew knew. He felt it in his core.

The pair discussed it briefly, but put it off for the time being, knowing with critical certainty that it needed to be acknowledged. Kazuaki could no longer wait. It was for that reason he requested Bartholomew's presence in the grand study. The captain speculated the scholar knew what he was going to say; Bartholomew's efforts to delay the inevitable with idle small talk was a sure indication. "Bartholomew ..."

The Southern Time Father sank farther into his chair, avoiding eye contact. He knew. "Yes, Captain."

Kazuaki leaned forward, resting his elbows on his legs. He did not wish to insult Bartholomew's intelligence by saying it out loud, but he needed there to be absolute clarity regarding the matter. "We're going to have to put some of your citizens down."

Bartholomew's grip on his glass tightened. "I've had the pleasure of knowing you for a long time now, Captain. I suspected as much." He slid the liquor closer toward him and spilled a considerable amount into the back of his throat. His eyes seemed vacant, but he kept his voice steady. "It's not their fault, you know."

The torment in the announcement of the man he respected cut him, but Kazuaki did not question his decision. "I know." He hung his head and stared at his boots before he raised his neck again. He tried to find Bartholomew's focus. "You're a man of intellect. You know there's no way to stop them all without putting the lives of the crew at risk. And I will not do that."

Though he did not look at him, Bartholomew nodded. "I know."

The cavernous room only highlighted the accompanying silence. It was so tangible, it felt as if it was its own presence in the room. The two men sat in the company of it, with only the sound of Bartholomew's ticking Chronometer at his chest eliminating complete gloom.

"In spite of everything, Captain," Bartholomew finally met Kazuaki's eye with his own, "it is good to see you happy."

A brow rose on Kazuaki's face. The situation was grim at best. Though he had no qualms taking the lives of men, he knew Bartholomew held a vested interest in his peoples' well-being. Kazuaki did not delight in playing a role in his comrade's turmoil. For Bartholomew to see happiness in him was strange. "What do you mean?"

"I've observed you in the week since you've all arrived," Bartholomew said, helping himself to another small sip from his drink. "You seem ... content. Fewer demons."

Kazuaki held fast to his look of skepticism, but he leaned back in his chair. "I've always respected your keen observation skills, Bartholomew."

Bartholomew shrugged. "I'm sure it has something to do with the fact that Bermuda has been sharing your bedchambers."

A quick hand raised to contain the mouthful of booze that nearly shot out of the captain's mouth. He coughed once, feeling the sting of jostled alcohol as it coated his tongue and burned the back of his throat. His eye watered a touch as he coughed again, wiping the liquid that managed to escape his lips off onto his sleeve.

"Take no shame," Bartholomew said with a light chuckle. "I remember the way you looked at her. It was only a matter of time."

"I was never as confident as all that," Kazuaki choked out, still caught trying to soothe the scorch in his throat. "I do not wish to sound morbid, Bartholomew, but I never had much optimism for either of us finding that kind of bliss. I venture that's why I took to you so quickly."

"Two doomed individuals from the start. And yet," Bartholomew stretched out the hand that did not hold his drink, gesturing to the room around them, "here we both are. Sometimes light finds its way to even the darkest of places."

"So I've heard," Kazuaki mumbled, his thoughts drifting back to the story Mimir told him. It wasn't long before they were replaced with memories of Kal Rovanas' actions in Northwestern. "I'm happy for you, Bartholomew. Kal is ... not unlikable."

The scholar smirked, with a look of absolute happiness. "I'm quite fond of him, too."

Kazuaki glanced at his drink. A small amount remained at the bottom of the glass, but he still smelled the high proof of the alcohol. He set it down on a nearby table. "No matter what happens ... knowing that we have both defied the odds and tasted happiness ..." He trailed off, shrugging. "Were it that I could die, I would die content."

Bartholomew's smirk evolved into a full-blown smile. Though he noticed Kazuaki set his beverage down, the scholar lifted his glass. "I'll drink to that, old friend."

* * *

The armory was not a comforting place. The high walls displayed an incredible array of weapons, ranging in all sizes and for all skill levels. Penn scanned the long-range arsenal. Longbows, crossbows, reflex bows, pistols, muskets, throwing axes, some kind of grenade that varied in appearance from the clay ones the captain carried on his person. A feeling of discomfort shuddered through the cook's bones.

Penn was no stranger to standoffs. His brazen, boorish attitude hurled him into more fistfights than he remembered, both before, and after his introduction to life aboard Kazuaki Hidataka's ship. He did not fear black eyes or broken noses; such things did not drain the life out of a man. But as he stole a glimpse of Brack, who joyously wove through the incredible assortment of weaponry, he knew he did not share the man's confidence in the face of all-out warfare.

Penn had yet to live beyond his mid-twenties. He did not develop the confidence with blades and bullets the other crew members possessed. His heart bellowed in his chest as his imagination betrayed him to the horrors that awaited him when the lesser gods attacked. He reached a hand out to grab a crossbow off the wall, unable to calm the subtle quakes in his nerves.

If his skillset matched the others, perhaps terror would have avoided him. He scanned the components of the crossbow, unable to concentrate.

Brack twirled about the armory, his arms extended out from either side of him. "What a collection, aye, boys?" He laughed, prancing over to various hanging guns to touch each one. "I thought Cappy had an impressive collection, but my gods! It's good to be a Time Father, ain't it?"

Granite reached out, sliding various implements into his belt. When he ran out of space, he placed other additions into the straps across his back and thighs. No space wasted, objects of destruction made their way into every available crevice.

Sensing the time of the lesser gods' arrival drew nearer based on Mimir's predictions, Bartholomew finally allowed the crew access to the room's contents. As his dog stood beside him, wagging its tail, Granite hoped they would have time to test some of the objects out before using them for their intended purpose.

"Revi is missing out!" Brack continued pocketing weaponry before he slipped over to the defensive objects, sliding a helmet on his head. "Oi! Does this helmet make me look like a warmonger?" He flexed his fingers until they resembled talons and took a challenging step forward. "Fear me, for I am the almighty Brack Joney! I shall smite thee from where ye stand!"

Granite's eyes rolled into the back of his head as he distanced himself from Brack. Careful consideration was given to the display of armor before him. Due to his unnatural size, not much fit. It did not bother the behemoth. The constraints of armor were not often utilized in his history of fighting.

Wandering eyes flicked over to Penn when Granite's mongrel let out an exasperated whine. Despite the cook's labors to camouflage his fear, Granite caught sight of it. It lived in every coaxed breath. Every wild darting of his constricted pupils. Every small bead of sweat that collected on his brow.

With Brack prattling on endlessly in the background about the remarkable assemblage of steel and lead, Granite crossed over to Penn and stood beside him. Penn felt his shadow before he felt anything else, turning his head away from the crossbow and up toward the towering man. "What?"

Penn reminded Granite of Iani. Scrawny. Sarcastic. But the younger Platts brother had something the cook did not: skill in battle. And even with that skill, he still fell to Carlo Angevin's gun in the events of last year. Granite did not wish for Penn to suffer the same fate. "I request a favor," he said, his voice somehow still booming despite the attempted softness in his tone.

Penn drew his shoulders back, obvious skepticism dominating his face where the fear used to be. "What is it?" he asked, a cautious brow arching upward.

"The beast is aging," Granite explained, glancing down at the canine who stood joyously at his side. "He should not be at the forefront of this battle. But if I leave, he will follow." The man paused, looking to Penn. "Unless I leave him with someone I can trust."

The cook shifted, offering his focus to the dog who barely came up to Granite's knee. Evidence of the mongrel's age lived in the white hairs around his muzzle. His leg, too, lost in the events of Avadon last year. Penn was not there to witness the fate of the footman who shattered the mutt's bones, but he heard from the others that it was gruesome enough to make even the captain nauseous. Granite loved the dog. Penn did not doubt he would do anything to keep it safe. While the offer to jump at the opportunity was tempting, the man hesitated. "You'll need all the hands you can get at the forefront," he muttered, his eyes still on the beast. "Especially with Revi gone."

"Penn. He is ten years old. If something happens to him ..." Granite's voice faded out, his words slow and calculated. He wiped away his dismal thoughts. "I am asking you. As a friend."

The beast's tail swayed lazily from side to side. Its pink tongue hung without care over the yellowing teeth that lived in its mouth. Penn frowned. For Granite to ask ... hell, for Granite to engage in a conversation that extended beyond three words ... Penn knew it was a matter of great importance.

He knelt, reaching a hand out to the beast. The animal sniffed it before layering a thin coat of saliva over the fingers. Penn slid his palm up the dog's neck, scratching where the ear met its skull. The mongrel showed clear evidence of arthritis; Granite's instincts were correct. It would likely not do well in the chaos that awaited them. Penn glanced up at Granite, protecting his vulnerability with an unenthusiastic look. "Fine," he muttered. "I'll watch him."

Granite nodded. He showed no irritation at Penn's brash inability to accept his offer without a feigned veil of irritation. He only cared that the beast would be safe. That Penn would be safe. "Thank you."

"You guys think Havidite will show up again?" Brack's voice shattered the tension that floated around the others. He came up to them, wearing a mismatched series of armor he plucked from the walls. "She probably will," he added, his arms stretching up over his head as he released a relaxed sigh. "Never met a woman alive who got a taste of the Rabbit and didn't come crawling back for seconds."

After he finished scratching behind the beast's ear, Penn stood and cast Granite a sample of his annoyance. "If he doesn't die in the battle," he muttered, "then please kill him so that I never have to hear him utter that sentence again."

"You'll have to beat me to it." Rennington's voice cut through the walls as he poked his head around the corner to the armory. He wore a grin as he stepped into the room, arms outstretched. "Long time no see, mates."

"Renn!" Brack ran to him and scooped him up into a hug. The metal adorning his body crushed into the soldier's ribs as he lifted him off the ground. "Been a long while since Northwestern, that's for sure!"

Rennington cringed as the hard steel dug into his skin. While compressed in Brack's embrace, he squeaked, "At least Southern isn't engulfed in flames. Yet."

"Ah, Southern will be fine." Brack set the soldier down, a reassuring sentiment in his statement. "Especially now that the old band is back together again."

"Except for Revi," Penn muttered, ever the crushing voice of reality. "And Elowyn. And ..." His words trailed off as he threw an awkward glance in Rennington's direction.

"Iani's here, mate." The soldier smirked, putting Penn's apprehension at ease. "Just took the lazy man's way out, is all. Ghosts get a pass on account of their inability to fire a gun."

A boisterous laugh from Brack's lungs resonated throughout the hollow armory. He patted one hand on Rennington's shoulder, the other somewhere in the middle of Granite's back, as he could not reach the top of the massive man's arm without looking ridiculous. "I'm sure they're all here in spirit." He reached over and grabbed a nearby pike, raising it high into the air. "For Southern!"

Rennington grinned. He leaned over to seize an adjacent halberd, raising that as well. "For Southern."

* * *

In the tallest tower of Bartholomew Gray's majestic, gothic home, Bermuda stood on a balcony. She balanced harrowingly on the railing. Her metal hand clutched one of four tall, wrought-iron beams that pierced the sky in each of the terrace's corners. The vantage point granted her an aerial view of Seacaster.

Umbriel stood beside her, though her bare feet rested on the flat surface of the balcony rather than teetering on the thin strand of the rail. The Earth Mother's hands rested behind her back, the fingers of one wrapping around the wrist of the other. High above the ground, the wind whipped with a fierceness, tossing her hair about her shoulders and back as she stared, unmoving, at the goings-on below.

The lifeless gray color of the clouds and sky matched the emotion of the town. People walked, their movements hindered by an identifiable caution even from the distance in which Bermuda and Umbriel stood.

Families huddled in groups as they ventured to the market for food, finding false safety in numbers.

Most who braved the conditions to attend their jobs traveled together. On the backs of most steam cars, some clutched various guns in their hands, while others drove the vehicle. Avoiding the workforce was not an option for anyone. The blue bloods and societal elites of Panagea, who owned the various factories, did not reward workers who shied away from their jobs.

The conditions for most were abysmal. Their choices were as limited as they were unappealing: face the dangers of those who wandered around with infected minds, waiting to plunge their daggers into the hearts of anyone who the lesser gods instructed them to kill ... or lock themselves in their homes and starve, where the risk of the madness waited to manipulate them, too.

The town center sprawled open, the most spacious place in all of Bartholomew's city. A pattern of stone circled outward from a central fountain; a monument meant to bring a sense of tranquility to a municipal that suffered much. The water that trickled from the shrine's spouts collected in a large basin, only to be pumped up and recycled: a never-ending flow of serenity.

The Southern Time Father thought the space created when countless businesses and residences had fallen to the ground would be better utilized as an open area. A place that did not invite claustrophobia and competition among people. He just wanted one beautiful place. One area where citizens could go to escape the oppressive nature of the buildings that survived.

While the monument was indeed beautiful, it failed to deliver anything resembling tranquility. Especially as of late.

The crew had taken turns watching the affairs of the townsfolk from Bartholomew's tower since they arrived a week prior. Each day that lived and died with no new activity bred more anxiety. Not knowing was the worst part.

Bermuda stole a glimpse of Umbriel in her peripheral vision. The Earth Mother wore a subtle look of desolation, though she hid it well behind a cloak of indifference. The quartermaster frowned, tilting her head to the side. "Can I ask you something?"

Umbriel blinked. The two women had lived in silence for so long, she almost startled at the sound of anything other than the wind howling in her ear. She gazed up at Bermuda. "Of course."

The quartermaster stiffened as she held tight to the iron post. "If you already summoned one of the lesser gods ... and you know that you cannot talk sense into them ..." Bermuda's stomach swirled as she paused. She did not know why the Earth Mother birthed such nervousness in her. Perhaps, she did not wish to see her get hurt. "Why did you come? I know you won't raise a weapon to any of the townsfolk, whether they're being manipulated by the gods or not ..."

The wind whistled through the open spaces of the fence that surrounded them. Umbriel knew Bermuda only asked out of concern. This knowledge painted a soft smile on her lips. "Because I brought them back here. I knew that they would come hand in hand with nature because the fruits of nature take time ... and most people suffer from undeniable impatience." Umbriel gazed back out at the town, a love living inside her eyes. "I thought I could bring Earth Mothers back. I thought it would be a good thing for Panagea. It used to be. But this time ..." She shook her head. "I thought the lesser gods' love for mankind would outweigh their feelings of betrayal. I was wrong."

"Well ..." Bermuda shrugged, following Umbriel's focus back out to the people below. "You don't need to beat yourself up over it. Bad things happen. That's the way of the world."

"It is," Umbriel agreed. "But it is critical that we see our failures through to the end. We must witness the consequences of them, that they might brand themselves into our minds. It is the only way we can ever hope to remember never to repeat them."

"That's what this is, then?" Bermuda raised her free hand over her eyes, shielding her vision from an unexpected ray of sunlight that penetrated the ashen clouds. "You're here to punish yourself?"

"No." Umbriel stared ahead, unmoving. "I am here to teach myself."

The Earth Mother's actions seemed masochistic to Bermuda, but she was not one to judge. The quartermaster, too, punished herself for a long, long time. Forgiveness came slow to the woman, but with Umbriel's help, she managed to seize a tangible amount of clemency. It felt much better than writhing in self-pity. When the short-lived light of the sun finished stabbing her eyes, Bermuda lowered her hand.

Umbriel's shoulders forced themselves back. The grip she had on her wrist tightened. Her pulse hastened, but her voice remained composed. "They're here."

Bermuda squinted her eyes, her brows knitting together as she searched for a sign of Umbriel's announcement. She did not have to look long.

A burst of fire rose upward in the far distance. It sprang twenty feet into the sky before it fanned out, circling the town. Within a minute, the ring of flames spread across the entire city, until it met back at its source, burning unnaturally, with no evidence of an accelerant.

Like the ocean, the ginger inferno ate the horizon, spawning suffocating amounts of black smoke that destroyed any glimmer of the natural sky. Shrieks of the townsfolk rose up with it, swirling in the abyss of toxic smog. Bermuda gasped, her hold on the post increasing as she frantically searched for physical signs of manifesting gods.

"They're sealing us in," Umbriel informed her, her heart beating faster as she tried to maintain her poise. "Nobody escapes."

A low rumble of thunder sounded on all sides. It almost felt as though it shook the ground. Without warning, a flash of lightning cut the sky in two. The screams grew louder, more panicked. People scattered throughout the streets, digging their heels into the cobblestone as gods appeared before them out of thin air.

Mothers reached for their children. Husbands reached for their wives. Some fell immediately to the influence of the gods, who fed heartily on the newfound fear. Another growl of thunder rattled through Umbriel's bones as more and more gods appeared below.

"Shit." Bermuda leaned forward, straining her eyes to see through the rising smoke. "I thought there were only eight of them—seven with Madros slain."

"They secured the God of Fire," Umbriel breathed, turning a full circle to take in the entire sight of the blaze that fenced them in. The Earth Mother felt the poison of an adrenaline dump flow through her, something she thought she mastered the ability to control. "And the God of Thunder ..."

The news was unwelcome. The elemental gods were a different breed from most. Able to manipulate the environment without running the technical risk of altering mankind's free will, the people were at the mercy of their destruction. "Bermuda ..." Umbriel turned to her, unable to hide the dread in her eyes. "They amassed an army."

CHAPTER THIRTY-ONE

"Brack, Bermuda, Granite, you're at the forefront! Possessed mortals are on you. I'll handle the gods."

Kazuaki's orders sliced through the entrance hall into Bartholomew's home, their potency commanding the room's entirety. The captain's eye blasted to Penn, who knelt beside the beast, his arms around the tugging animal's neck. The dog whimpered, its nails clicking on the tile as it tried to reach Granite. "Penn. Gods help you if you do not keep that dog in check. I need Granite at full concentration."

Penn nodded, reeling the beast back against him and pulling the wriggling animal into his chest. The captain's words were harsh, but he understood the sentiment behind them. They only had three crew members as it was, along with Rennington and the footmen of Southern who remained lucid enough to do combat. If anything happened to the beast ... if Granite could not do battle ... the odds were not in their favor. His value as a fighter was unmatched. "Yes, Captain."

"Good man." Kazuaki turned to his crew. "Fall out."

They exited Bartholomew's home, donned with whatever useful components they managed to take from his armory. Kazuaki stared ahead, watching as pandemonium lit in the eyes of every citizen who continued to clutch their good mental standing. The picture before him was painted by chaos and nothing more.

From a short distance, he saw Rennington standing at the head of a large group of Southern footmen. Kazuaki could not tell what he said to the men, but judging by the fierceness that spilled from his face and the way he valiantly raised his falchion to the sky, the captain surmised it was motivational. The footmen howled and dispersed into the crowd, organized and undeterred.

"Gods-speed, comrades." Kazuaki's black hair whipped around his shoulders as he turned to his small band of societal rejects. "See you at the end."

Brack raised twin battle axes to the sky, howling as he charged after the footmen into the bedlam. Granite's approach was steadier, more intimidating, as he hauled a mercilessly outsized, spiked mace over his shoulder.

"Well," Bermuda breathed, her hands at her hips, ready to reach for her weapons. She glanced at the captain, her adrenaline pumping. "Once more into the fray."

Kazuaki's heart pounded from the cage that was his ribs. He stole a final glimpse of her. The picture of faultlessness. As a surge of chemicals filled his veins, he scooped her up in his arms and placed her back against the exterior wall of Bartholomew's home. His hands slid under her thighs. Her legs wrapped around his waist once more. The kiss they shared was short, but what it lacked in timing it made up for in unrestrained passion.

He knew he couldn't taste her forever. Kazuaki pulled away, barely, his forehead against hers as he spoke against her lips. "Don't die."

The quartermaster slid her arms around his neck, arching her back as she savored one final sensation of his mouth on hers. Her fingernails curled into the back of his scalp as she smirked, confident. "Nothing's killed me yet."

It took everything he had in him to release her. In one moment he had all of her, and in the next he had none. The two lovers parted ways, jolting full force into the disorder that awaited them.

Brack drove his axe into the stomach of a man wielding a sharpened piece of rubble. He did not linger to see if he perished. There were too many. As more lesser gods and goddesses drizzled into the streets, countless more humans fell to their demands. If he wanted to ensure the safety of Southern's unpossessed mortals, he had no time to waste.

Shrieking citizens of all ages and backgrounds sought refuge where they could find it. Hiding spots were limited. There were too many who required them. Granite stomped over to a cowering family, their arms around one another as a stampede of depraved mortals approached them, salivating. With a forceful grunt and a single sweep of his mace, he gutted an entire line.

Their bodies fell back like weightless pins. The holes in their flesh leaked their insides. But for each one he destroyed, several more appeared in their place. The power that the gods had amassed in their short sovereignty of fright throughout Panagea, had earned them enough raw supremacy to command the minds of many.

Kazuaki cut his way through the crowd, shoving both manipulated and terrified men and women aside. There was no time to disassociate. Not if he wanted to spare their lives. His eye captured a lesser god he did not recognize, standing before a collection of screeching souls. Chanted nonsense spilled from his throat. He tried to turn those before him. His attempt was unsuccessful.

Before the lesser god commanded a single, scared spirit, the twin blades of Kazuaki's katars ran him through. He uttered a grating sound that matched the death of Madros. The group before him screamed and disbanded.

A trickle of blood seeped from his open jaw. Kazuaki twisted the blades. The lesser god's hands wrapped around each pointed piece of steel and he scowled. Though the captain was to his back, he knew exactly who he was. "Kazuaki Hidataka ..." he muttered, choking on rising, viscous fluid in his throat. "You're here ..."

Before he died, Madros had warned the others of Mimir's betrayal. Of the captain's possession over the enchanted weapons. But of all the places in all of Panagea ... they did not think they'd find him here. "Where—is Mimir?" the deity gurgled, trying and failing to face the immortal.

Kazuaki frowned. "That hardly seems like anything you should concern yourself with." In one swift effort, he pulled the metal from the monster's body and helped him to the ground with a sturdy kick from his boot.

The captain knew he was dead. He saw the edges of the lesser god's body turn to smoke. A low wind carried the fragments away on the breeze, heated by the intensity of the burning fires. One down. Gods only knew how many more to go.

Umbriel lowered her body out a window from Bartholomew's home. Her bare feet graced the stone ground as she moved through the madness, ethereal and fixated. Bodies fell all around her. Though her heart bled for the deceased, she tried not to pay them much mind. She needed all of her wits.

"Mother!" she called to the glowing apricot sky, the clouds that absorbed the color of the flames. "Appear before me, that I might plead once more for you to stop!"

Her voice was lost in the rising discord, but she knew the lesser goddess heard her. She always did. Whether she appeared or not was more unpredictable. A shapely profile formed before her, silhouetted by the inferno in the background. Umbriel lifted an arm to shield her eyes, squinting through the blinding light. "Please, mother. End this madness. Remember how much you loved humans!"

The shapely hips belonging to the body that appeared before her moved. One long, perfect leg stretched out before the other. Umbriel withdrew, taking a step back when she realized it was not Naphine who stood before her.

Havidite grinned. "I did love them. With all my heart." She inclined her chin, looking down at Umbriel with poison in her eyes. "I wanted them to thrive. You, Earth Mother ... you and your half-blooded kind took that love away from me."

Umbriel pulled back on the wild racing of her pulse, holding her ground. "Love is a boundless thing, Havidite. There was always enough for us both."

The goddess held out her arm. Out of the ether, a wooden bow appeared in her hand. A matching quiver dusted onto her perfect, carved shoulders. "It was never enough." Her face looked beautiful even as she withdrew an arrow from behind her, fluid in her movements as she lined it up. "Not after you."

Umbriel's eyes widened as she drew the arrow back. There was no convincing her. Havidite had marinated in her hatred far too long. The Earth Mother dodged the first assault, disappearing into a mob of raging men and women, both belonging to the gods and not. She thought she could lose her. If she kept a good pace, she could outrun Havidite's rage.

One of Kazuaki's katars decapitated a goddess. Her head severed from the spine and collapsed onto the blood-painted stone. Satisfied upon seeing the fingers of her body turn to ash, he turned. Before him, a familiar face stared, unsympathetic.

"We meet again, Mr. Hidataka."

Kazuaki cracked his neck and positioned his katars before him. Olnos looked much healthier than the last time the captain laid eyes on him. No longer a withered, fragile being, the God of Metal stood before him in grandeur, looking the part of the warrior Kazuaki surmised he had been in his prime. Surrounded by steel both defensively and offensively, the lesser god represented the picture of a classic, ancient combatant.

The immortal scowled. Though slippery blood threatened to loosen his grip on the katars, he maintained a firm hold. "Do not beg," he muttered, his eye on Olnos. "I still won't speak your name."

He didn't need him to. Enough already had. Olnos raised his hands, summoning his vast gathering of turned humans toward him. "Then you will scream it." With one gesture, he sent a small portion of his army to Kazuaki and the rest to the crew.

Kazuaki tried to bring his katar across and into the ribs of a turned mortal, but the steel bounced off the flesh, leaving no trace of damage. Reverberations from the force of the metal hitting human skin traveled up the blade and into his arms, forcing Kazuaki to curse. Of course. The weapon forged by the gods could not harm men.

With swiftness, the captain sheathed one of the katars into the custom-built scabbard on his back. He removed one of his most trusted pistols and fired as much as it allowed. It was not enough.

A rusted piece of pipe plunged into his stomach. Kazuaki grunted, tossing his empty gun. He ripped the pipe from his aggressor's hands and his guts at the same time, before he struck the man over his skull.

The blow brought the mortal to his knees. Kazuaki rammed the hollow tube into the eye socket of a maddened woman who tried to impale him with an iron fence post. For as many as Olnos sent his way, he knew he sent more to his crew.

The horde the God of Metal unleashed on him served a purpose: to hinder his movements. Olnos knew they could not bring death to the captain. He only wanted them to slow him down. The real threat was in the mass he unleashed on his comrades. Kazuaki brought another body down with a cutlass he tore from his hip. He stepped on the rising collection of corpses, trying to see above the lawlessness. Trying to find the crew. Trying to be sure they clung to life.

The first thing Nicholai saw as he thundered down the stone streets on Rhirvin's cycle was the smoke. Like a colossal, leaden wall that cauterized into the clouds themselves, it was impossible to see through. It stretched as far as his eyes could see from his vantage point on the ground, consuming everything it touched in its blanket of suffocation.

Numerous buildings crumbled before him. Seeing through the shattered remnants of the town outside Bartholomew's bordered on impossible. It wasn't until he guided the cycle around a corner that he saw the soaring flames that birthed the wall of smoke.

"Dammit, dammit, dammit—" Nicholai's eyes widened as he tried to brake, having come upon the fire too unexpectedly to react. But the cycle was too fast. It divided through the ring of fire with little reduction in speed, blowing out the other side of the blazing barricade.

The Time Father coughed, his lungs shriveling in his chest as a trail of smoke followed him. Then he saw the actual wall. The one made of bricks, not flames. "Come on, come on!" he choked, all his pressure applied on braking the metal bullet on which he rode. He tried to turn.

The bike responded, but the act of braking coupled with a jerky turn threatened the mechanism's balance. Nicholai thrust his foot out, digging the heel of his once refined boot into Southern ground. His heart pumped with a violent unruliness until he realized the cycle decelerated to a complete stop, and he managed to avoid destroying it.

That victory was second to the fact he also managed to not break any bones, though his ribs still throttled with the sting of their previous injuries.

Nicholai patted at his clothing to be sure he didn't catch fire upon entering the town. Save for a few singed areas, he was no worse for wear. The Time Father dismounted the cycle and pushed it into an alley before he ran out to assess the goings-on.

It was as if the Underworld opened its mouth up to swallow the living. Somewhere, the dividing line between realms gave way, inviting the grotesque abyss of perdition to mingle with the mortal world. He swept both hands through his hair, his eyes darting about, trying to find those he knew. Those he loved.

It was easy to spot the captain. Chaos followed that man wherever he went. It appeared as though he was fighting his way to something. When Nicholai followed the direction the captain tried to carve through the crowd, he spotted Brack, Bermuda, and Granite, as well as Rennington and the footmen. They struggled but held their own against the monsoon of wild men and women. They were so far away. It would take Kazuaki forever to penetrate the crowd and reach them.

A flash of silver caught his attention. Through the sea of bodies, Nicholai caught sight of Umbriel, her movements agile, yet frantic, as she climbed through her environment. A commanding woman followed her every move, wielding a bow and arrow. The Time Father's stomach squeezed when he saw the goddess draw back her shaft and fire.

The arrow pierced Umbriel's shoulder through the back. The Earth Mother seethed as she stumbled, catching herself before she fell to her knees. She reached back, trying to grab it and rip it out to allow herself to heal the tissue. But Havidite was fast. Umbriel spun around to face her, striking a defensive position.

Havidite smirked, another arrow lined up.

"Naphine will kill you," Umbriel uttered, the soles of her feet sliding in a pool of spilled blood. Though her mother lived on opposite sides of Umbriel's ethics, the goddess still loved her daughter. Of that, Umbriel was certain.

Havidite laughed. The sound was cold. Her body barely moved, as she did not want to disrupt her aim. "It's a risk I'm willing to take." Her arrow released, but not before her perfect aim was disturbed by the chain wrapping around her throat.

The arrow vanished somewhere into the crowd, bouncing off a mortal's shoulder before it clattered to the floor. Havidite dropped her bow, freeing her fingers to claw at the chain around her neck. She gasped for air, bucking as vessels burst in her crazed eyes.

Umbriel gasped, glancing at Nicholai as he gripped his Chronometer and chain. He held it tight around the goddess's throat. The metal of the god-forged gift dug into her flesh, leaving marks in the shape of the links. He tore his eyes away from Havidite long enough to find Umbriel. "Run!"

The Earth Mother bolted, knowing Havidite could issue Nicholai no harm. She ripped out the shaft in her shoulder with a wince, returning life to the damaged muscle and flesh.

When he could no longer locate Umbriel in the crowd, Nicholai released his grip. He fell away from Havidite's wings as he clutched his Chronometer in his hand. He only wished to save Umbriel; he did not wish to destroy anybody.

Havidite gulped for air, her hands around her throat as she scorned the Time Father with bloodshot eyes. A temporary confusion danced in her pupils, but when she saw the Chronometer, she knew. With a huff, the Goddess of the Harvest disappeared, wishing to distance herself from the man who could harm her, but she could not hurt.

Bermuda tripped as she backed up into a cadaver. She utilized her unexpected position to her advantage. Several quick jabs into the thighs of those who towered over her brought some to their knees. Others needed more convincing.

The quartermaster no longer looked human. She appeared to be more of a figurine, carved from scarlet wax. The fluids of no less than a dozen men and women showered over her, seeping into the crevices of each fold of skin and corner of armor. But the blood did not belong solely to them. Many lucky hits coaxed her insides out of the skin suit that encased her. She was not alone.

Granite dripped from his brows to his boots as he whittled his way through a horde.

Brack appeared much the same, but worse. One of his arms dangled from his shoulder, limp and severed from the socket. An advancing group of civilians surrounded him. Some wielded falchions stolen from the corpses of dead footmen. Others were content to fashion weapons out of found rubbish.

With his back pressed up against the walls of one of the few buildings that remained standing, he stared at the seven approaching bodies. One-armed and enduring a crippling blood loss, he knew the odds were not in his favor. "Right." He inhaled, savoring the small bits of freshness that lingered in the burnt oxygen around him. His axe settled into his only functioning hand. He would go out in the blaze of glory. There was no other way for Brack Joney to exit the world. "Here we go."

Gunfire dominated the screams of panicked people. One by one, the bodies before Brack fell. Boom. Fall. Boom. Fall. Seven times their heads exploded from shotgun shells. He watched, shocked, as they crumpled to the floor.

The man gazed about, trying to find the location of his savior, but the environment remained too frenzied to pinpoint the source. "Thanks," he uttered to the ether, knowing wisdom remained in paying respects, whether one knew where fortune stemmed from or not. He dashed off into the crowd, not wanting to find himself backed against that wall again.

Smoke wafted from the barrel of Bartholomew's shotgun as he stared out the window of his home. His eye remained fixed in the weapon's sight. A single tear ran down his jaw as he watched the lives of the people he shot, his people, drain away into the earth.

Olnos grunted, unable to disguise his frustration at the rate in which his influenced army fell. Though a large number of Southern civilians remained, cowering in corners across the town, they were running out of mortals to possess. The God of Metal knew they could not seize control of everyone. Corruption was their goal; decimating mankind and waving their retribution like a victorious banner. But they could not turn everyone. Whether the gods wished to admit it or not, they needed mankind more than mankind needed them.

"Havidite," Olnos growled, stepping back beside her. "We need to fall back."

"Never!" She turned to him with acid on her tongue. "We have only whispered our anger to these people. We cannot leave until we scream it! For us, Olnos. For Panagea!"

"We can torch the city until it is reduced to ash. We have. But if we kill every human, there will be none left to feed us their prayer." Olnos narrowed his eyes. "You must think wisely, Havidite. We cannot help Panagea if we are dead. We shall continue this. But not here." He turned to Kazuaki, scowling at the immortal as he watched him obliterate another lesser god. "Not with him."

Havidite followed Olnos' gaze to the immortal captain. They had no recourse against him. Their armies could not destroy him. He was the only wrench in their grand design. The air clogged with ashes of dead gods and goddesses all around his person. She knew Olnos was right. These people would fight until there was nothing left. She couldn't let her ego destroy their chance of success.

They needed to regroup and restart. Panagea was vast. They could resurrect their efforts elsewhere with more success. Somewhere far from the reaches of Kazuaki Hidataka. "Fine."

Channeling a message to the other lesser gods and goddesses across the mental network that connected them, Havidite vanished in a whirlwind of feathers that swirled from her wings. All that remained were two tattered, dappled feathers, which floated down until they settled on the blood-stained cobblestone.

Cowering citizens looked on. One by one, the omnipotent beings sent the people final chastising looks. Then they faded into the atmosphere. After several short minutes, all that remained of the lesser gods was the aftermath they created.

A river of red flowed through the cracks of every imperfection in Seacaster's stone streets. The fountain in the town center, once a pristine gush of clear water, was tainted pink with diluted fluids of the bodies that fell inside it. The fire raged around them, threatening to finish what the lesser gods started. Surviving footmen put the last of the turned humans down, as mercifully as they were able to.

Umbriel panted, leaning with one hand against the wall of a standing building. She gazed at the inferno that surrounded them, the blaze reflecting in her eyes.

The Earth Mother jumped at the touch of a gentle hand settling onto her shoulder. She spun, taking in the sight of the being who stood behind her. "Dimjir ..."

The God of Mercy gave one small nod. He looked out over the ravaged battlefield, across the countless souls who summoned him. "I am sorry, Umbriel. Please, remember, we are not all as unforgiving." He lifted his eyes to the heavens and closed them. "Fear not. Help is on the way."

She followed his eyes to the sky, confused. When she moved to direct her gaze back to his face, he was gone.

A drop of water hit the bridge of her nose. Umbriel lifted her hand, touching the liquid with the tip of her finger. It was clear. Her attention shifted once more, back to the sky where Dimjir had looked. Soon, the sparse droplets turned to more.

The thin material that made up her clothing clung to her body as a monsoon fell from above. Diluted, the once scarlet liquid swirled around her bare feet. The rain's elixir washed away the blood on the streets and doused the fires. Umbriel closed her eyes. The heavy nectar from the skies streaked down her skin. She silently thanked the Goddess of Rain, who Dimjir undoubtedly summoned.

Kazuaki gazed on at the ground, his shoulders rising and falling with each tortured breath. Despite the help from the rainwater, he still looked like a demon, covered in chaos. Though he felt the gaping hole in his internal organs close, as all his would-be fatal injuries did, the entry wound remained. That was no surprise. What came as a shock was that it still burned, unlike any other injury he had experienced before. He'd deal with it later. His interests rested more in those who managed to survive.

He spotted Bermuda first. Even across a large distance, she found his eye like a lighthouse at sea, piercing through the fog of the hell that surrounded them. Brack and Granite stood beside her. And Umbriel. He frowned, unsure when she entered the fray. At least she looked unharmed.

Survivors crept from their hiding places with terrified optimism. Mothers and fathers clung to their children's small hands, poking their heads out to peer at the Southern footmen left standing. To the crew. To the strange, black-haired man who somehow succeeded in slaughtering omnipotent creatures.

With the fire doused by the strong rains, all fell silent. Only the splattering of raindrops on the earth sounded. But over the noise of the falling water, a single set of clapping hands met the captain's ears. He turned, squinting. Two familiar figures lumbered toward him.

Mimir, the source of the clapping, approached with a huge grin as rainwater vanished into the shadows of his body. Jernal, following at the lesser god's heels, held an immovable look of caution on his face.

"Well done, Captain." Mimir gazed to the sky, where the ashes of dead gods and goddesses were brought down to the earth by the heavy rain. "You killed many. But when compared to the number of lives you saved, my gods ... it's incredible."

"Mimir." Kazuaki's eye narrowed as he straightened his posture, though the wound in his stomach prevented him from righting himself fully. "I thought you were in Southeastern."

"Oh, I couldn't miss this." The lesser god stood before him, an arm's reach away. "Your most glorious moment. Captain Kazuaki Hidataka, the savior of mankind. A monumental deed deserves a monumental reward." His glowing eyes flicked to the wound in his gut. "And it appears you got one. You look good. Some might even say you look ..." He paused, shooting his focus to the captain's eye before his face split into a mad grin. " ...cleansed."

At that moment, each truth fell into place. Kazuaki knew everything. The reason Mimir risked his life to pluck the katars from the god's realm. The reason he shed light on the location of the god's war. The reason for it all. He touched the hole in his stomach, knowing now why it did not feel as all his injuries past did.

The subtle grip of immortality faded from him. A single, heroic, good deed. Saving the lives of many, to make up for the life he took out of greed long ago.

The mermaid's curse was gone.

Kazuaki's eye grew dark as he stared at Mimir. "This may have cleansed my soul," he uttered, rain slithering into the facial hair on his jaw, "but I am not dead yet."

"No." Mimir nodded in agreement. "Not yet." He reached over, pulling Jernal's falchion out of its scabbard and handing it to the soldier. He knew, as a lesser god, he could not harm Kazuaki. "The time has come to repay your debt, Commander. What a stroke of luck that he is weakened from battle. Kill him."

Kazuaki flashed cold eyes at Jernal, breathing heavily. The soldier took the handle of his falchion. He did not move. He stared at the newly mortal legend before him, thinking back to every shared moment. Every attempted good deed they tried to perform in Northwestern. Every time the captain and his crew showed a thorough, honest interest in the survival of one another. Every life the captain saved in Southern today when he slew the gods who doomed them.

Panagea needed Kazuaki Hidataka.

Jernal looked at Mimir. He wanted nothing more than his freedom. But the cost was too high. He threw his falchion to the wet stone on which he stood and squared his shoulders. "No."

From the expanse, Bermuda stood on the tips of her toes, trying to make sense of why Mimir stood on the battlefield with Kazuaki. When she saw the lesser god hand Jernal his falchion, her heart sank. In a single moment of understanding, the hair on her arms stood on end. "No." She broke out into a run.

"No?" Mimir turned to Jernal, a look of offense painted on his face. "If you do not honor your commitment, Commander, you will be forever indebted to me until the day you die and beyond."

Jernal nodded, his posture grave. In his head, he whispered his farewells to his wife and children. "I know."

"I see." Mimir frowned. He turned away from the disappointment that was Jernal and looked at Kazuaki. "Well, dead or alive, Captain, it matters not to me. You will find your death eventually. But you still made the deal. You *belong* to me."

Bermuda's heart thundered as she shoved her way through the people who slinked out of their hiding places. Her boots splashed through the collected pools of rainwater and blood as she forced her way to Kazuaki.

The captain turned to face her. The look in her eyes as she ran to him. The panic. The pain. He remembered them. It matched the expression of the false Bermuda from his time spent in the in-between. He looked to Mimir. Under his contract, he could not destroy him. But Bermuda could.

With all the strength he was able to muster with his wounded stomach, Kazuaki hurled a single katar toward her. The blade eviscerated the ground, the tip driving into exposed dirt left beneath the upturned stone.

As she ran, her hands seized it. Her fingers anchored around the handle. Mimir stood only ten feet away. Bermuda released a war cry as she swung, her target Mimir's neck. But the steel met nothing. The lesser god disappeared, taking both human pieces of his property with him.

She died inside when she felt no touch of flesh on her blade. Bermuda spun in a circle, searching everywhere, the eyes of countless citizens, footmen, and the crew upon her. Her chest rose and fell with each panicked breath. Rage and loss boiled in her gut.

He was gone. Mimir did it. He got everything he wanted. Everything he had his eyes on from the start.

The quartermaster drew her head back as a wretched, anguished scream flew from her throat and disemboweled the sky. It echoed through the broken city, joining the smoke and the ashes of the lesser gods Kazuaki destroyed.

The consequences of his bargain came full circle. He gained his mortality. All he ever wanted. Bermuda's arms shook. The price was too high. She dug the blade back into the ground and leaned on it for support as she hung her head, water dripping from the strands of hair that dangled past her jaw.

After hundreds of years of walking Panagea and traversing her seas, the legendary Captain Kazuaki Hidataka was gone.

CHAPTER THIRTY-TWO

Navigating through the various towns of Eastern brought about an illuminating experience. The varying degrees of health Elowyn spied along the way, only served to showcase the unpredictability of her division's state.

It was mostly the cities that were reduced to ash, but some residents were too stubborn to abandon the places in which they grew up. Other towns looked scarcely affected at all, most of their structures still in good standing, having avoided the raw power of Panagea's historical disasters as well as the lesser gods' wrath. Most villages lived somewhere in the middle of 'adequate' and 'extinction'.

That was where Brendale fell on the scale.

The people who remained on the streets did not hide their avoidance toward Elowyn. They moved out of her way without a word, some even going so far as to cross the street to elude her. She did not blame them. No one knew that beneath the horrifying visage of armor plates and threatening blades, a small woman stood. The only thing the citizens saw, when she barreled down the cobblestone, was a warrior. And though that warrior wore the attire of an Eastern footman, the public still could not surmise whether the armored individual was friend or foe.

Elowyn tried to remember the directions written on the sheet of paper Mairyn gave her. She remained certain she followed them correctly, but as she stood in the corner of an alley flanked on both sides by industrial plants, her confidence dwindled. *Through the sewage pipe …* she thought to herself, wrinkling her nose behind her helmet at the unpleasant reality that awaited her.

Then, she spotted it. A circular opening jutting out of a brick wall. It looked unassuming. Larger than most traditional sewage pipes, and out of place in the fact that it did not appear to run below ground. With little other options, Elowyn approached it. She placed her armored hand on the lip of the pipe, as she ducked her head down to peer in.

She saw nothing but blackness. Blackness accompanied by the smell of human shit.

While it didn't appear to operate as a customary sewage pipe, citizens seemed to have had no qualms emptying their piss pots into the hole. As Elowyn lowered her legs into the opening, she tried to remind herself that this wasn't the first time she'd been covered in bodily fluids. It came hand in hand with being a medic. It was that mantra alone that kept her from gagging as she slid her iron-encased body down the narrow opening.

Though she couldn't see an inch in front of her face, she felt the pipe slant downward. The air around her cooled the farther she descended. Before long, a dim light appeared at the bottom of the tunnel. Her greaves touched the ground and she slid herself out of the claustrophobic tube, happy to leave the intensified scent of feces behind her.

Elowyn's travels brought her to an unfamiliar place. Stretching out before the slits in her helm, a cavernous environment met her partially obscured vision. Dancing torchlight flickered off the fragile sides of countless tents, kept alive by basins of oil. The movement of shadows in the distance, which Elowyn identified as people, carried on without noticing her. Flattened surfaces, carved away by the hands of men, stretched out beneath her feet. While some surfaces boasted a finished appearance, others were in a clear state of incompleteness, as if the efforts were abandoned.

She did not receive much time to soak in the rest of her environment before the blade of a halberd touched the armor around her throat. Elowyn did not move, choosing to avoid escalating any unnecessary confrontations.

"Who are you?" a voice questioned, authoritative and demanding.

Without turning, Elowyn offered an answer. "I was sent here by Mairyn Catteral."

The man assessed the suit of metal worn by the new arrival. Authentic, Eastern-issued materials. The individual's presence seemed legitimate. Though he withdrew the halberd, he remained skeptical. "Did Mairyn also tell you to barrel in without warning? You're either very brave or very stupid, soldier."

Elowyn still refused to move, but she took some relief in the man's removal of his weapon. When she turned, she realized he offered a hand to help her to her feet. She reached out her iron glove and accepted, coming to a stand. "Catty didn't tell me much," she said. "Just that you could use my help." Elowyn gazed at the hollow space, unsure how a dwelling like this existed in Eastern without her knowledge. "What is this place?"

The man looked out to those who lived farther in the camp. A few soldiers were present, wearing the appropriate ensembles that dictated their ranks. Even more civilians subsisted in the distance. Women and children, hovering over cauldrons sitting in beds of fire. Various scents of primitive stews greeted Elowyn's nose, and she was grateful for a reprieve from the ever-present stench of human waste.

"An unfinished project of Avital York," the unidentified man stated, gesturing around them both. "When he ran out of space above ground, he thought he could utilize the space below ground, as well, effectively doubling his industrial efforts. This was the first underground test city he commissioned, but it only got as far as this before it was deemed too dangerous to continue." The man shook his head. "The integrity of the ground was too brittle. The project was decommissioned shortly after. This is all that remains. We thought we'd make the most of it."

Elowyn soaked in the sight of it all, an incomplete underground world built on greed. She clenched her teeth, finally turning to steal a glimpse of the man who nearly slit her throat. A classic soldier, a symbol of Eastern through and through. Short hair, square jaw, broad shoulders. A copy of almost every footman she ever came across. "I take it you don't get many visitors," she muttered.

"We prefer it that way." The man rested the pole of his halberd against his shoulder. "It's hard to know who to trust since the lesser gods invaded. We do not have many supplies, so we keep our numbers small. These are the friends and family of Eastern soldiers, and not a soul more."

Elowyn nodded. She seized the medallion given to her by Mairyn Catteral and held it out to the man as if that would validate her presence. "Seems like a wise way to keep resources attainable."

He glanced down at the medal and nodded, recognizing it for its worth. "They are hard to come by. We do not make many surface trips, to limit the chances of discovery." He cast a scrutinizing look toward her. Though she could not see it well, she felt it, even in the darkness. "What do you have to offer us, soldier?"

Elowyn assessed him, as well. She was not one to feed her plan to useless individuals. He appeared fit, lucid, capable: the clear leader of this band of underground dwellers, who did not shy away from protecting them from uninvited guests. He'd have to do. "I believe I can stop the lesser gods from affecting the minds of men. But I need help breaking into the new medical facility. I know supplies are few, but I'll need them if I'm to make any achievements."

The man spat, disgusted. "A waste of money from the division leader who abandoned us. It'll be of no help." His arms crossed over his chest and his level of scorn returned. "And that's an awfully big claim to boot."

"I have a background in pharmaceutical sciences," Elowyn shot back, her voice firm and unyielding. "I know I can utilize that to our advantage. Let's just leave it at that for now. No use explaining it if I can't get the goods."

The soldier scowled. He shook his head. "Our 'insightful leader' Elowyn Saveign has turned Eastern into a division full of medical professionals," he muttered, his loathing evident as the words rolled off his tongue. "What makes you so sure you can do what countless others haven't?"

"Because," she interjected, her expression flat behind her helm. "I'm better than they are."

Against everything, the soldier emitted a haughty laugh. "Arrogant or confident, I cannot say." His amusement faded, replaced once more by a dose of injected caution. "What's a warrior need a background in medicine for?"

Without missing a beat, Elowyn muttered, "You want a feckin' novice sewing your gods-damn arm back on when it gets ripped off in battle?"

Silence followed. Then a grin. The man lowered an accepting hand onto the hard metal of her pauldron. "All right, soldier. Let's talk. Maybe we *can* help each other. Besides, any friend of Mairyn's is a friend of ours." The commanding presence in his voice slipped for a moment. "Edgar Catteral was a good man." A brief moment of quiet passed between them before he returned his gaze to her. "My name is Wulfgang Hion."

Elowyn smirked. "Of course it is."

Wulfgang arched a brow, confused, but shook it off. "What did you say your name was again?"

The Time Mother wavered. She remembered the words of Mairyn Catteral as she stared at Wulfgang's face. She needed to maintain the illusion that she was a soldier. A man. From behind the armor of Mairyn Catteral's deceased husband, she said, "Friends just call me E.P."

Wulfgang nodded, extending his hand to shake. "Well, then, E ... welcome to the Underground."

* * *

Avigail thought she'd feel the efforts of her travels in her legs more than she did. It must have been adrenaline that kept tired muscles at bay as she trekked to Striburn. Her arms should have ached from carrying her pack of supplies, despite how limited they were.

Her throat cracked with dryness—but at least the residual smoke that still lived in the Northwestern skies did not burn her eyes. She impressed herself. The miles she covered were unprecedented. The soles of her feet throbbed with a rawness the first time she had tried escaping from Edephat's Home for Girls, but now, she felt nothing.

The lingering smoke failed to singe the walls of her nostrils, but she still smelled it in the air. She found herself grateful it continued to hover in the atmosphere. It helped cover the scent of the rotting dead. The flames spared her the horror of humanizing the corpses; most of what made them men and women had melted away, but Avigail knew what the charred lumps of darkened tumors on the ground used to be.

She wondered if any of them used to be her father.

The airship was nowhere in sight. It was a bulky thing, hard to hide, particularly when most of the landscape was leveled by mass destruction. Avigail ran her tongue across the splitting skin on her lips, hoping the small amount of moisture would bring her chapped mouth reprieve. She walked more, farther into the open arms of the desolate Northwestern town.

Nobody remained to question. The place existed solely as a ghost town. As Avigail spun in a complete circle to take everything in, she doubted even spirits would choose to linger in this place.

Her eyes fell to the ground and her face scrunched together. Avigail slid her pack off her shoulder as she knelt to the earth, reaching out to place a gentle hand on the disturbed layer of ash. Wilted red petals from a sea of dying anemone flowers hid the ground. She brushed them away. Pressed down into the half-inch thick sheet of dust that coated Northwestern, was the unmistakable shape of a dog's paw print.

Granite's beast.

She followed the tracks with her eyes, some easier to find than others. The animal had no clear path. It was a wild and unpredictable thing. After some effort, she trailed it to a perfect, vertical line. The place where the ramp of the airship came to rest, she guessed. Avigail verified this when she saw the unmistakable pattern of tire tracks, large and almost certainly belonging to the airship's landing gear.

They were here.

But they weren't here anymore.

Whether that was because they moved on to another town or because they perished, the young Houton daughter had no educated guess. Avigail thought, perhaps, the absence of the airship indicated they moved on. But as she took in the condition of the buildings and structures made from materials that matched or surpassed the airship in durability, she wasn't sure. If the fire possessed enough strength to decimate a civilization, she ventured that it wouldn't be beyond comprehension that it could swallow all evidence of an airship, too.

Avigail depended on her father still being in Vadim's home town when she left. She cursed herself for not thinking it through. Rash, impetuous decisions put her in precarious situations before, but nothing that matched this. The last thing she knew was Revi Houton would be here. But he was not. She had no other leads.

Desperation grew inside her. It started out small, a seed, but it split and flourished until it filled the interior of her body. It was the kind of desperation that reminded her of all the people she had encountered along the way. The people on the steam train in Southeastern and Southern. The people she saw wandering through the ravaged lands of Northwestern. The people who ranted and raved about gods and goddesses, and everything that came along with them.

Avigail pressed her lips together. The sound of complete nothingness touched her ears. It was the kind of silence that felt so unnatural, her brain tricked her into thinking she heard a distant, high-pitched noise just to ease the burden of being walled in by oblivion. She thought again of the people. Of their stories. Despairing times called for risky actions.

People were not all bad. Avigail thought she had Revi pegged. That he was nothing more than a coward absent of redeemable qualities. But what she'd discerned from Everly and Thom ... what she learned now, staring at the peril he willingly threw himself into for the sake of others ... she couldn't fully believe that anymore.

If the lesser gods were born of men, as some of the people she encountered claimed, then surely not *all* lesser gods were bad. They were born to answer prayers, weren't they? And even if they weren't ... even if her dicey gamble did not pan out ... she learned in her travels that lesser gods could not physically harm humans.

As her eyes scanned the destruction that stood before her, she doubted that last thought very much. But without any ideas as to where Revi could have gone, or whether or not he was still alive, she couldn't see beyond the necessity of the risk. Avigail tried to swallow, but her lack of saliva left her throat empty. Her chest felt empty as she lifted her eyes to the dead sky.

"I don't know what I'm doing. I don't know who I'm talking to, or if I'm even talking to anybody." Her voice lost itself in the endless expanse, but Avigail straightened her posture and continued. "But I need some help. I need to find someone. If the gods are as omnipotent as everyone is saying ... please, send one down to help me."

Her plea was met with a weak gust of wind. She dug her fingers into the bottom edges of her shirt. Avigail stood for what felt like several long minutes, allowing her legs an opportunity to rest, though it didn't feel like they needed it.

Optimism dipped. Her jaw clenched and her eyes fell to her feet.

She was on her own. No surprise there. It was a stupid idea, anyway. She didn't need them. She answered her own prayers since she was a kid, absent of help from anyone else. And that was okay. She was used to it, and she was good at it.

Avigail drew in as deep a breath as she could, though her lungs felt unfulfilled. She walked, unsure where to go. Back to Southeastern, perhaps? The idea of waiting for Revi Houton to return was revolting. She spent her whole life waiting for that man and had no intention of doing it again. But where else was there to go?

With no direction, Avigail tread, content to leave the scattered remnants of this town to rest. She would continue to search Northwestern. Perhaps someone, somewhere, saw him.

She did not get far before she felt the distinctive swirl of uneasiness. The weight of watchful eyes. Avigail stopped. With a slow twist of her neck, she glanced over her shoulder.

The figure looked approachable, unintimidating, though he towered over her at six feet and some odd inches high. Thin strands of luxurious golden hair wafted in an unfelt breeze. Save for the large gray wings that split out from the bones of his spine and shoulder blades, he appeared human. And yet, an indisputable absence of human essence enveloped him. He was nothing if he wasn't otherworldly.

"Hello, young lady," he said, his speech all velvet and grace. "I understand you need some help."

* * *

Edvard's trips to the psychiatric facility housing Esther Hiddle became something more than an obligation. What started as a begrudging course of action to glean insight into why the lesser gods had so much success corrupting minds, turned into a surprising event he began to look forward to. Though Esther remained trapped in a madness of the lesser gods' design, she existed as a unique insight into not only the deities' thoughts but the thoughts of the working poor.

The Western Time Father readjusted the tie that ran down his chest as he climbed the facility's steps. A small shiver of excitement slithered through him when he made it to the top. Many years had passed since Edvard Addihein felt he brought anything, other than minimum expectations, to the Western division. With Esther's help, whether she realized it or not, he felt he could initiate a positive change amongst his people. To eliminate, or at least lessen, the obvious gap between those who were most vulnerable to the gods, and those who operated in the small minority of people who had no fear.

It wouldn't be a stretch to say the last month or so Edvard spent in Esther's company crafted a strange fondness for the woman in his heart. He smothered a majority of it; the inappropriateness of such feelings was obvious. They hovered in a state of platonic respect and he did not wish to see them leave that place. But Esther's palpable intelligence shined through her ravings about the gods. Edvard caught glimmers of recognition in her when she spoke of the disparaging differences between the classes. A part of him wondered if she knew how much she helped her social circle by informing him of the agonies they endured. If she knew how her madness might change the way things were done ...

He pulled the door open and entered, having grown accustomed to the stark whiteness of the walls. They seemed like less of a sterile, unwelcomed setting now, and more of a lighted place. A place that, with any luck, would eventually discover the cure to Esther's psychosis. Edvard approached the front desk and set his hands down on the table.

"Welcome back, Mr. Addihein."

Edvard frowned. A sadness lingered in his greeter's tone of voice. "Thank you," he replied with lingering skepticism. "I'm here to see Esther Hiddle. Patient 245."

"Yes." The individual sighed, folding his hands together in front of him. "About Miss Hiddle ..."

The whiteness of the lab coat blended into the white walls behind the operative. Both blurred into nothingness, regaining the off-putting sensation they held when Edvard first entered the doors to meet Esther in the beginning. He almost couldn't process the words spilling out of the employee's mouth. They melted together, almost inaudible, but while the Western Time Father's ears refused to accept the noise as discernable sound, he understood the message.

Esther Hiddle took her own life in the middle of the night.

The operative went on to explain further, detailing that he was surprised it happened. They were careful to remove any objects that might be considered harmful to their patients. In the end, it was the shackles they put around her wrists that were her undoing. Somehow, she managed to break her own arm, which allowed her to twist her body in such a way that permitted the chains to wrap over her neck. She strangled herself long before the morning crew arrived to administer breakfast and the first round of psychotherapy.

"I see ..." Edvard swallowed, staring beyond the employee. His focus dwindled into the endless sea of white that made this place. "Would it be all right if I visited her compartment anyway?" he asked, his voice distant. "To say goodbye, I suppose."

A small frown fell over the staff member's face. He hesitated. "I ... suppose that would be all right. But please, Mr. Addihein, I request you make it quick. We already have another individual coming in to occupy her room."

Edvard nodded, slipping past the white-coated man to walk down the white, painted walls on the white, tiled floor. He did not know why he felt compelled to visit the place where Esther drew her last breath. He only knew that each footstep took him closer until he found himself standing before it.

A hand rose up and touched the cold metal that encased the room. It was strange. He sat in this space countless times upon visiting Esther. It did not seem as cruel then as it did now. As Edvard peered into the empty space, the conditions felt much more punishing.

A thin mattress. No blankets. Limp shackles where her wrists used to be. An uninviting metal bowl, absent of any privacy, for defecating. It was no wonder she did not get better. This place was as dehumanizing as anything he'd ever seen.

Edvard hung his head. He rested the top of his skull against the iron bars and stared at his polished footwear, wrapping his fingers tighter around the grates. It was odd to miss a woman who he never truly knew. Esther was as much the lesser gods as she was herself, and separating the two became impossible. But there was something about her he couldn't get out of his head. Perhaps it was what she represented. The first step in a shift for Western. The answer to the plague the lesser gods brought.

Something cold touched his hand. The Western Time Father's head shot up. Standing in the cell that sat empty not seconds ago, a familiar face stared back at him. The soft, brown skin. The tender eyes. The full, unblemished lips. Though the woman standing before him was a far more withered version than the one he remembered staring at over thirty years ago, he recognized her instantly.

"Hello, Edvard," she said, her dress blowing at her ankles though no wind touched her. She folded her tattered wings behind her, giving him a moment to absorb her presence.

His heart leaped at her touch. The guilt that flooded him was immediate and unforgiving. Despite the countless that years passed since Edvard last saw her, hers was a face that remained scalded into his memory, and forever would. The hair standing on his arms betrayed his emotions, as he met her eyes and tried to convince his tongue to speak. He only managed to utter two words. "Hello, Epifet ..."

* * *

Southeastern had no clue what horrors awaited it. Umbriel stared out the window of Nicholai Addihein's home. She had finally returned from her long stint in Seacaster, healing the injuries of the survivors. The woman observed Nenada's people through the clear glass as they carried on with their lives.

Paranoia subsisted in their movements. The Earth Mother noticed they second-guessed everything they did. Even the smallest decisions were met with apprehension as word spread that Kazuaki Hidataka, the savior of Southern, met his doom at the hands of Mimir.

The only man alive who ever slew a god. The only short-lived hope the people of Panagea had against the lessers that invaded them. Gone.

Nicholai watched her from the open door to his bedroom, encompassed by grief, not just for Umbriel's state, but Kazuaki's fate. He and the captain did not always see eye to eye, but Kazuaki Hidataka was as much a friend to the Time Father as he was a legend to Panagea. He missed him terribly.

Not wishing to allow Umbriel the discomfort of wallowing in sadness any longer than necessary, Nicholai crossed the distance and stood at her side. He tilted his head, joining her in the act of gazing out the window. "See anything interesting?"

"No." The tension in her shoulders reinforced at his arrival, as if she lived in so much shame, it overflowed into every muscle and bone. Even in her dishonor, she still projected a grace. "Not yet."

Nicholai cleared his throat and pulled his Chronometer from his shirt. He wound the crown, careful to be sure he turned it the perfect amount before he returned it to the safety of his vest. "It's not your fault, you know ... for what happened to Kazuaki."

"No. Not Kazuaki." Umbriel's heart fell for the captain. For Bermuda. For the crew. She missed him. She missed the others. Bermuda did not return to Southeastern, and the Earth Mother knew by the aura that stemmed from her before they left, the quartermaster had no intention of returning at all. Her anger would take her on a much different path than the town of Nenada. "His fate was sealed before my intervention. But I invited the gods back into Panagea, Nicholai." She turned away from the window to face him. "They will only repeat what they attempted in Southern elsewhere. It will be less poetic to spread chaos in a town that doesn't mean as much to Darjal, and perhaps a little harder to infiltrate the minds of people who are not conditioned to be so blindly religious, but they do not care for such things. They will not stop. Soon, the world will exist solely for them. I invited them back to save Panagea ... and I fear I have doomed it."

The pain in her eyes was hard to look at, but Nicholai held his gaze steady. Her words sheltered an undeniable weight. He wished to ease her suffering. "You know," the man shrugged, his tone lightening, "*I* doomed Panagea once, so ... you know ... thanks for trying to steal my thunder."

She smiled. It was small. But it felt like a victory.

"We'll figure something out, Umbriel." Nicholai met her tiny smile with a brighter one of his own. He turned to look out the window once more, watching the cautious citizens as they carried on with their lives. "People are more resilient than the gods give them credit for."

Umbriel wanted to believe him. She saw the untainted belief that thrived in his face when he surveyed his residents. It was so pure. People like Nicholai Addihein were a dying breed. The corners of her smile grew wider, more sincere, as she studied him. "I never thanked you for saving my life. Havidite has never been an admirer of mine. I can't imagine it was easy to restrain her."

"Gods, no," Nicholai shook his head. "She has the strength of a thousand men."

Umbriel chuckled once, heartfelt in her amusement. She followed his gaze back outside, her hands behind her back.

"Umbriel ..." Nicholai kept his focus beyond the room in which they stood, the only way he knew to separate any liability from what he was about to say. "The strength of a thousand men or no ... I'd always come for you."

Her smile found a permanent place on her lips. She nodded. "And I for you."

The man held her gaze. It made her heart accelerate, the way he looked at her. "I must confess ... I ..."

He paused. Her heart leaped in her chest at what he might say. What she hoped he'd say.

" ...I'm terrified Malcolm might shoot me down if I didn't."

A playful anecdote. Her heart fell, but her face showed no evidence of it. She forced a small laugh and turned back to the window.

The pair stood in the company of the ticking clocks. They did not bother Nicholai as much anymore. Enough time passed to remove the discomfort of his interval spent in the realm between realms. He counted sixty-five ticks before his curiosity bested him. "So ... what do we do now?"

The Earth Mother closed her eyes. She filled her lungs with a deep breath. A lone shoulder lifted. "I do not know."

* * *

The heavy aura seeping out of the cracks in the doors to Bartholomew's study would have deterred any being from entering. But Brack 'The Rabbit' Joney did not shy away from discomfort. On the contrary, he was often the source of it.

Still. A momentary lapse in self-assuredness kept him outside the door a little longer than it normally would have. He knew what awaited him on the other side, and it was nothing he felt an eagerness to see.

He stepped up to the door and looked down, his eyes on the brass handles. He raised a bandaged hand to it, the other arm bound to a sling after having been ripped from its socket in the skirmish. A small amount of blood soaked through the dressing as he pushed down on the handle to open the door.

Well-oiled and maintained, the door opened absent of any noise. Brack's eyes traveled across the filigree carpet and over to the chair where Bermuda sat. Her body slumped deep into the last piece of furniture Captain Kazuaki Hidataka had ever used. Though the door made no noise, and the soft runner of carpet absorbed the impact of his boots, he knew she was aware of his presence. Not much slipped passed the quartermaster.

When he stood at an arm's distance from her, the Rabbit glanced down at the empty glass she held. The last thing touched by Kazuaki's lips, except for Bermuda, herself. She flexed her wrist inward and outward, listening to the sounds of the glass as it crawled across the carved marble arms of the chair. The katar sat across her lap, unclean, still wearing the crimson stains of its many victims. Her free hand sat atop it, possessive and inert.

Brack scratched at the sideburns growing from the sides of his jaw, his voice easy. "Ship's all loaded up as you wanted, love. The others are waiting."

Bermuda stopped moving the glass. She did not look at him. "Good. I'll be right out."

The Rabbit offered a small nod.

She knew he was worried. Brack never wore disquiet on his face, but she sensed it in his behavioral shift. Bermuda ventured a guess that it had something to do with her poor history of handling deaths. She could hardly blame Brack for his concern. The way she reacted after things ended with Ty was reprehensible, weak, and pathetic. But this was different.

There was no self-pity. No feelings of responsibility surrounding Kazuaki's fate. Just pure and complete hatred, for Mimir, who stole him, and for Nordjan, who invited the lesser god back into Panagea. Her animosity was accompanied by an unquenchable thirst for retribution. When she noticed Brack made no motion to leave, her eyes shot to his face for the first time since he arrived. "I just want to sit here for a moment longer."

Her comrade flickered an eyelid, his body still reacting in unexpected ways after the battle ended. He glanced down at Bermuda while he rubbed at his eye. "You know, Bart offered for us to stay as long as we need to. There's no reason to head out so quick."

Bermuda did not falter. "I'll be out in twenty minutes."

The man's head cocked to the side. The sensation of scarcely contained venom that emanated off her was palpable. When he could no longer stand it, Brack knelt beside her. "Look ... there's no shame in takin' a break, mate. Cap's gone. It feckin' rips my heart from my chest to say it. But no matter how much it hurts, charging out there, katar drawn, slaughtering a sea of gods and goddesses ..." He shook his head. "It ain't gonna change nothin'."

"I don't need a sea of them," she muttered, the beds of her nails turning white as her grip on the glass increased. "I only need one. But if it takes a sea of them to find him, so be it."

"Mimir's covered his bases, love." Once Brack controlled the twitching in his eye, he rested his gaze on the weapon in her lap. "He said he couldn't be killed by those katars."

"Yes," she said, her metal hand gliding over the smooth steel as she stared ahead. "Kazuaki agreed not to kill him with the katars." Bermuda tore her focus from the wall that occupied it before. She locked onto Brack's pupils, her gaze unwavering. Direct. Terrifying. She leaned forward, her words leaving her in a whisper. "But *I* made no such bargain."

* * *

Home meant different things to different people. Even amid the chaos that rained down on Panagea, Rennington felt luckier than most. He had two homes. With all the residences that burned to the ground throughout all the divisions, that was certainly more than many.

The memories of being born and raised in Southern territory surfaced more frequently than they had at any moment prior. He remembered growing up, admiring the footmen of his hometown. He remembered climbing onto the rooftops of the small houses that lined the streets to get a better view of them as they marched in parades, or led Darjal Wessex' sedan chair to the churches for public appearances. Or how their camaraderie was highlighted in the event they needed to take down a thief or a convict. They weaved through the crowds with a commanding majesty. Though most maintained a steadfast appearance, the occasional footman broke the military's rigid expectations and issued a small wave to excited children who stood nearby.

Those soldiers were the picture of honor. In a little boy's eyes, honor meant everything.

Those footmen were the reason he signed on to be a soldier to Southern, back when Darjal Wessex reigned. But the late leader took his vision of integrity and partisanship and turned him into a deserter. Darjal sucked out the nobility of being a soldier when he ordered Rennington and his comrades to assassinate the children of those protesters years ago. To Darjal Wessex, they were better off dead than alive. Orphaned children were a burden on tax dollars, and he wanted all he had to go to the churches that painted him as a god. He destroyed the fantasy of the principle that Rennington built. He hated him for that.

Rennington glanced down at the Southern uniform he wore. Pride weaved through him when he slipped into each part, down to the boots he pulled on his feet. After Darjal's death, he was happy to see Bartholomew Gray turn Southern around in an incredible way. It was almost hard to remember the time when he despised the attire and what it stood for. Returning to his duty in Southern felt right. It felt good to be a soldier again. To fight for something, and someone, worth fighting for.

Southern remained his first home. It ran through his veins. But his other home called to him. The place that scooped him up when Panagea detested his desertion. The place that sustained him when he had nowhere to go. If Southern was his blood, Kazuaki and the crew were his bones.

It was a call he couldn't ignore.

"I know I'm duty-bound to Southern," he said with a sigh. "I know I said I'd never leave again. That I'd commit to changing this place for the better. But with the captain gone ... with everything falling to shit ..." He shook his head. "Bermuda's got herself in some dire straits. That woman is bent on revenge. Avenging the captain, and all that."

Rennington paced, his feet shuffling across the ground. It was visible to anyone who gazed upon him he writhed in discomfort at having to leave. It was hard enough tearing himself away from Southern when he had accompanied Kal Rovanas to Northwestern. "I'm sorry. I know it's not easy to hear. I know you want me here, but ..."

The man lifted his hands to his head. His fingers crawled under his cap and into his hair as he closed his eyes. "I can't leave her to this fate. And the captain ... I owe my life countless times over to that man. I know I promised my life to Southern, but ... Bermuda's about to raise a shit storm in his name. I can't abandon her while she fights for what he stood for. If the situation was reversed, they'd do it for me."

Rennington closed his eyes. "I took all the right steps. My leave has been approved. I … I'm leaving tomorrow." His jaw tightened. He clenched his teeth, hard. "I know it's soon, but … she's already pretty restless, you know. There's no time to waste."

Polished boots carried him several paces forward. Rennington stood straighter. "Yes, it will be dangerous. Fighting lesser gods sounds impossible, doesn't it? I'm sure she'll handle that part, with that feckin' godly katar of hers. At the very least, I can keep any manipulated men off her and the others' asses while she slays her way to some shitty version of whatever peace she can find at the end of all this."

He sighed again. A gentle breeze touched his face. Rennington adjusted the cap he wore on his head. "That's one of the reasons I'm here, actually," he admitted. "I have a favor to ask you. If something terrible should happen … if I should die off Southern ground … I need you to come find me. Take me back here. This is where I belong."

The man cleared his throat. It tightened inside his neck and brought him discomfort. "I don't know how long I'll be gone. It could be weeks, months, years …"

Rennington stooped to sit. He rested his back against Iani's tombstone. A simple, stone monument with his brother's name etched on it, along with the years of his birth and death. "So if it's okay with you, I'd like to sit here a while. In case I don't get the chance to do it again anytime soon."

He sat in the quiet until it ate him. Unable to stand the silence any longer, Rennington pulled out his harmonica and made it sing a few soft notes. It didn't feel the same without an accompaniment. Without Iani telling a ridiculous tale to go along with it. Without Elowyn joining in on her instrument, or with her voice. He lowered it from his lips and gripped it in his palm.

Smoke billowed off the horizon. From what, he did not know. It was almost a common thing these days. Rennington guessed it would only grow more common, as Panagea faded further into a new breed of decay.

That smoke was a symbol. Once a positive one that used to signify Panagea's growing industry. It crawled out of each factory's tower with a purpose, created by the hard-working hands of those who rose to attend their jobs each day. It was a different kind of smoke now. An emblem of smoldering carnage. The symbol of mankind's fall.

A dim smirk crawled across the soldier's face. He reached forward and plucked a rare blade of grass from the earth, twisting it between his thumb and middle finger. He beckoned a deep breath to enter his lungs as he pushed himself harder into the cold stone behind him. It helped him feel the proximity of Iani's spirit. "If you don't find me, I'll come find you," he said, flicking the grass from his fingers. "And I will haunt your ass like a mother fecker ..."

A Note from the Author

From the bottom of my strange heart, thank you for picking up this book and giving your time to read it. I hope the characters crawled into your minds and live with you as they live with me. I would love to hear your thoughts if you wished to leave an honest review of your experience on Amazon.

Would you like to be among the first to know when McKenzie Austin's next book will drop? Follow her on Goodreads, Amazon, and Bookbub for notifications of new releases!

Other Books by McKenzie Austin:

The Panagea Tales series:
The Tree That Grew Through Iron: Book One of the Panagea Tales

The Gods Who Harvested Men: Book Two of the Panagea Tales

The Serpent That Swallowed Its Tail: Book Three of the Panagea Tales

The Canary That Sang to the World

The Incineration Saga series:
Followed by Fire: Book One of the Incineration Saga

Embraced by Embers: Book Two of the Incineration Saga

Made in the USA
Columbia, SC
06 December 2020